THE
BAKER
OF
LOST
MEMORIES

ALSO BY SHIRLEY RUSSAK WACHTEL

A Castle in Brooklyn

THE
BAKER
OF
LOST
MEMORIES

A novel

SHIRLEY RUSSAK
WACHTEL

Published by Little A, New York

www.apub.com

Amazon, the Amazon logo, and Little A are trademarks of Amazon.com, Inc., or its affiliates.

ISBN-13: 9781662525674 (hardcover)
ISBN-13: 9781662527609 (paperback)
ISBN-13: 9781662525681 (digital)

Cover design by Kathleen Lynch/Black Kat Design
Cover image: © esemelwe / Getty; © Rekha Arcangel

Printed in the United States of America

First edition

For my parents, Charlie and Betty Russak, who survived so that their children could live.

THE BUNGALOWS

1961

It was all Lena's idea. Not her parents' or even Pearl's, who was usually the one responsible for leading Lena down the wrong track. So, if anyone was to blame, she need look no further than the face she saw in the mirror that morning and all the mornings to come. The guilt was just something she would have to live with—probably for as long as she existed—and since she was only nine years old, that would be many, many more years of guilt. And sadness, of course. There was that too.

It didn't start out that way, though. It started out as just another day, the sky ablaze with orange August heat so that the families living in the bungalows went about their activities in slow motion, the mothers hanging shirts still heavy with moisture on their clotheslines and stopping to wipe their brows before bending low to grasp a pair of boxer shorts as they cast watchful eyes on babies still asleep in their carriages situated under leafy oak trees. Even the children who ran off to play kickball abandoned the game after a few minutes, hot and exhausted. Some of the boys gathered a few fallen twigs and used the sticks to dig tunnels in the brown earth, then watched intently as the ants emerged from their leisure and made their escape up the stick or, for the luckier ones, out and into the tepid air. The girls, who preferred a somewhat calmer environment, eyed the boys with disdain, and a few ran into their bungalows to grab a Nancy Drew mystery or another story by

Beverly Cleary and returned with a heavy blanket that they laid out under the thin shade of one of the many trees in the immense woods behind the homes.

A few of the girls came out with diaries that had gold locks that they tightly fastened with a special key. These girls walked off to a corner behind the bungalows and, trying to make themselves as small as possible, removed ballpoints from the pockets of their short shorts so they could begin writing their deepest, darkest secrets. Then there were those like Lena and Pearl, who were best friends and were happy just to spend time together doing nothing. Since they were so close, there was always something to talk about, whether it was a shared memory, a question, or even their dreams.

It was during one of these times right after a swim in the lake, when the heat pressed stubbornly against the world, that the idea came to Lena like a cool, refreshing summer breeze.

"Don't you think it would be fun to camp out tonight?"

Pearl cast a skeptical eye at her friend but said nothing.

"All the older kids go out with their sleeping bags. We could make some Jiffy Pop on the stove and eat it outside. And maybe we could sneak some Oreo cookies, a few slices of my mom's challah, maybe some other goodies. I'll bring my *Archie* comic books, and then we could look up at the stars and see all the shapes in the galaxy. It'll be much cooler outside too. So what do you think?"

Lena gazed intently at her friend and watched as a smile slowly took form on Pearl's pale-white face. Her blond curls bounced as she nodded in agreement.

That evening Lena approached her mother cautiously about her plan, emphasizing that she would be only feet away from the bungalow and there would most likely be others doing the same thing, as several of the older kids would be seeking escape from the interminable heat. After Lena reassured her mother of her safety, Anya eventually relented, much to the child's great delight. As usual, she hadn't bothered to ask permission of her father, who was just like all the other fathers in the bungalow colony, their weekdays spent in one of New York's five boroughs, where they worked as accountants, tailors, and jewelers—and at a variety of other businesses that required their presence. They returned to the "country," as they called that area of the Catskills in Upstate New York, in station wagons, still wearing their jackets and button-down shirts, arriving just in time to spend the Sabbath with their wives and children. They would remain there just until the faintest glimmer of moonlight appeared in the Sunday-evening sky, when they would again kiss their wives, tousle their sons' hair, and twirl their daughters like ballerinas before disappearing down the road in a caravan of cars on the way back to the city.

The evening Lena and Pearl anticipated had finally arrived, and despite a weather forecast that threatened rain, Lena's mother reluctantly allowed her one daughter to spend the night outdoors in their next-door neighbor's sleeping bag, so long as she remained within sight of the family's bungalow. Lena was relieved that with a houseful of children to care for, Pearl's young mother was more than happy to also let her daughter escape for the night.

As the girls settled their legs into the sleeping bag, which was well suited for one large adult male, but could also easily accommodate two young skinny girls, Lena looked up at the sky. The sun had begun to slowly dim in the west, and only the traces of stars could be seen beyond the treetops. *No sign of rain,* she thought, almost as if the universe and all its elements had conspired to make this the perfect night.

Lena glanced over at Pearl, who was wearing purple checked pajamas that matched hers exactly. Pearl's head was tilted toward the sky, just as Lena's was, watching the light seep slowly from the landscape above. Lena examined that face, as she often did. Pearl was so beautiful, and her cheeks looked like the side of a snowy mountain, so smooth and white. She had a pink bow tie of a mouth and soft blue eyes that seemed forever to be dancing. Even her brow reflected a clarity that was untroubled by worry. Looking at her friend's face now, Lena couldn't understand why they were even friends at all.

Where Pearl was tiny and compact, Lena possessed a body that was tall, gangly, awkward. And while Pearl's face was nearly angelic, Lena's cheeks were ruddy, splattered with ugly brown freckles. Her nose, while not aquiline, was the tiniest bit longer than Pearl's at the tip, and her hair was a sad mousy brown with a frizz that became only worse, as Lena had a habit of peeling the strands of split ends whenever she was nervous. So why did Pearl bother with her at all?

Of course, Lena could only guess the answer. Because despite their physical differences, even though Pearl was everything Lena wanted to be but never could become, Pearl and Lena were very much alike. Often when Mrs. Cannon would conduct multiplication drills at the blackboard, just as the answer was on Lena's tongue, Pearl would blurt it out. Or sometimes during one of their class spelling bees, just as each letter would hit the air, Lena could see Pearl out of the corner of her eye, standing off to the side mouthing the answer. Symbiotic. Lena hadn't learned the definitions of the word yet since she had only just completed the fourth grade, but when she came across it in a biology class years later, she realized that it perfectly described their friendship. Lena and Pearl had a friendship that was perfectly symbiotic.

But if Lena considered the relationship in her quietest, most alone moments, she realized it was much more than that. For some reason Lena could never quite fathom, Pearl was the only one in her life who actually listened. Often, her mother had no patience, like when Lena complained that one of the boys in the class had called her Dumbo the Elephant the day she had pulled her hair into a long ponytail behind her ears and her mother simply told her to forget about the stupid boy, finish her milk, and go outside and play. And her mother certainly had not listened when Lena woke up one night feverish with tears still clinging to her eyelashes, her voice choked by sobs and coughing, and had asked her why, oh why, everyone had to die. Anya had sat at the edge of her daughter's bed and sighed heavily before pouring a spoonful of purple medicine down the child's throat and telling her to go back to sleep. And on those occasions when Lena was younger and would timidly broach the subject of the Old Country, asking what her aunts and uncles, her grandparents, and the sister she had never known were really like, her mother's cheeks would flush red as the tears sprang to her eyes. She had tried to speak, to answer Lena's questions, but the only sound that emerged was a ghastly noise, a cross between a croak and a sob. But little by little the stories came out, so frightening that Lena was always afraid to bring up the subject.

Lena never even felt heard by her father, who was often too exhausted to respond to even the mildest of questions, like could she stay up past *The Ed Sullivan Show*, or would he reach the top shelf of the refrigerator for that pitcher of Kool-Aid? Instead, he would stare at his daughter blankly, give her another Hershey's bar, and tell her to go read a book. Lena thought he secretly wished she had been a boy.

~

Lena wiggled her toes beneath the cool comfort of the large sleeping bag, her eyes now riveted above, but there were only a few thin clouds slowly making their way across the black face of the sky, a few traces of stars, none of any consequence, to be found. Then she remembered the small package of Oreos she had brought outside and reached over to the bag, opened it, and plucked out two slim cookies, each packed with a dollop of sweet vanilla cream between the wafers. She offered one to Pearl, who took it gratefully from her hand, flashing a satisfied smile, as was her way. Neither of the girls bothered with the transistor radio or the pocket-size books in the canvas bag on the ground next to them. The girls much preferred to meditate on the story of the vast night stretching before their eyes, rather than the yellowed pages of books they had read numerous times before. And, instead of the insistent beat of the pop songs by Elvis or even Bobby Vinton, who was a much more romantic vocalist, the radio fell silent as the children strained to hear the chirping of night birds and the scratch of the chipmunks and squirrels as they scampered up the branches of the multitude of trees in the nearby woods.

After a while, the girls turned away and settled into easy conversation. They chatted about a variety of subjects, surmising what fifth grade would be like and whether Jeffrey Stoller, the cutest boy in the grade, would be in their class; the colors of their plaid pleated skirts, which came above their kneecaps; and how cool it would be to have one of those new color TV sets in their living rooms. The conversation had little serious merit yet was of major significance to nine-year-old girls for whom ten could not come fast enough. Their discussion abruptly ended as Pearl happened to glance at the sky again and pointed a slender finger.

Lena, who usually did most of the talking and asked most of the questions, had been describing her new kaleidoscope and its prism of colors when you peeked inside, one of several items she had left in her dresser back in the Brooklyn apartment, when she stopped midsentence.

The girls could do nothing but stare at the sight. A veil of light had been lifted, and in its place was a beautiful orb of gold shining within the jet-black darkness of the night's splendor. Stars bigger than Lena's freckles sparkled peacefully above. The skyscape filled the friends with a sense of euphoria, and for many minutes neither spoke, fearful to disturb the moment. Finally, Lena, still gazing up at the radiant orb overhead, asked the question that had been swirling within her mind.

"Pearl, what do you think is up there? I mean, up in space beyond the moon?"

Pearl's face assumed a dreamlike mask, and her eyelids trembled before she gave her answer. Lena held her breath, knowing that whatever her friend said, her query would not be dismissed, and that whatever Pearl's answer would be, it would be the right one.

"I think," Pearl began, her eyes still directed upward, the voice barely above a whisper, "I think it is whatever you want it to be."

Lena turned away and considered her friend's answer as she felt her loneliness, nearly a constant companion, slowly drain from her body, replaced by a blissful sense of perfect peace.

But her attention was soon diverted by a rattling sound off to the side of a nearby bungalow.

A rattling to her left where a row of metal garbage cans stood side by side, hugging the wooden walls of the home. The shower of light emanating from the moon reflected the silver of the cans so that at first the girls couldn't quite see it. But then, emerging from the shadows, the mass took form, the body taking definition, a velvety sheen. It was a bear. A cub, to be exact, making its way along the row of pails, the snout extended, sniffing the evening air as it pushed against the lid of one of the cans.

Pearl looked at Lena and then shifted her eyes to the creature, which was now only feet away from where they lay in their sleeping bag. Lena found her friend's hand beneath the cover and squeezed it. The two sat still as stone, already having forgotten the majestic moon and the glittering stars that had mesmerized them only moments earlier.

Eyes ghostlike, still on the animal, a smile slowly appeared on Pearl's pink lips, her irises sparkling with a hint of awe.

"Isn't it beautiful, Lena?" she whispered. "Just like the giant stuffed bear you have in your bedroom at home. Do you know what I'm thinking now? I'm thinking I am going to give it an Oreo. It's hungry and it's just a baby. What do you think?"

Lena paused before answering as she held the bear in her gaze. In her heart she, too, wished to approach the cub, maybe stroke its smooth black fur, offer it a creamy cookie. Yet her head told her it would be the wrong thing to do—foolhardy, *dangerous*. But before she could utter a warning, Pearl had already slipped out of the sleeping bag, an Oreo firmly in her hand as she stealthily approached the creature.

Even though Lena was awake, she felt as if she were in the middle of a nightmare. She leaned back, her legs buried within the sleeping bag. Then suddenly what looked like a giant rock emerged, as if from a dream, from the shadows. Swiping its massive paw at Pearl, it swiftly sank its teeth into her slender white neck. Pearl didn't cry out, didn't utter a sound, and neither could Lena, as, wide-eyed, she watched the mama bear carry her best friend away and into the dark heart of the woods that stretched beneath the silvery moon.

PART I

FLOUR & HONEY

1

Anya

Ever since she was a teenager, she had wanted a little girl. And in her most private moments, those minutes that were hers and hers alone, just before sleep would steal upon her, Anya would dream of that perfect daughter. It seemed as if it had always been so, even before she had exchanged sacred vows under the chuppah, even before she had felt the first quiver of life deep within her womb. In Anya's mind, her daughter would be naturally pretty, with an innate curiosity that would impress all those who came into her presence even more than her beauty. Most important, the daughter who was little more than an apparition, a wish, would most certainly be her best friend. And there was nothing in all of Lodz, nothing in the entire universe, that would ever sever that bond. So that by the time Anya was married to the man who was her destiny, a boy who had teased her on the streets when she was no more than ten, and her body swelled with the child months later, it was a foregone conclusion that a daughter, as brilliant as she was beautiful, would be born. And that was just how it happened.

The child they named Ruby, a name of English origin after an aunt who had lived to be a hundred, was all the things Anya had wished for. Her eyes were deep, like round black coals, her hair a feathery yellow, and though she was slow to smile, when she did, it was like the sky opening to a new day. As soon as she turned two and was able to speak, Ruby began to ask questions, so many, in fact, that Anya could hardly keep up with her. And if her mind couldn't hold the answers to the multitude of questions her daughter posed, surely Josef, who was much more knowledgeable about money matters or geography than his bride, would supply the answers to satisfy their inquisitive child. As she grew, Ruby became a fast learner, so that by the time she was eight, she was already helping her mother in the small bakery, taking the few coins from the regular customers, and expertly packing the stollen into crisp white cardboard boxes that she would tie tightly with long red string in a serviceable sailor's knot. She was an asset to the shop, which Anya's parents had owned for nearly twenty years. Anya's mother, who had run the business with precision and ease for most of that time, had finally succumbed to the mental illness that had plagued her for nearly her whole life before she died of a sudden heart attack. Her death was soon followed by that of Anya's father, who was so distressed by his wife's demise that he was felled by a fatal stroke mere weeks later, leaving the bakery to Anya and her new accountant husband. Both of Anya's parents had been barely into their fifties when Anya and Josef, an orphan, found themselves all alone in the world.

It was fortunate that Anya had learned the trade at such a young age, so young that she could barely hold a spoon. By the time she was old enough to attend school, most days she would forgo her studies to stand behind the counter and converse with the customers, and most nights she would knead the dough for the glossy Sabbath challah or cut the apples for the sweet rows of strudel as her mama lay in bed, sleeping or confused, too sick to even comprehend the stresses she laid upon her daughter. Anya didn't mind, though, as she enjoyed having a hand in such sweet treats and felt an incomprehensible joy as she stood behind the counter in the midst of an aromatic cloud of cinnamon and sugar. And now as she watched the smiles on the faces of the young housewives, the elderly rabbis with their knotty gray beards, or the teenage boys with their tzitzit hanging out of their starched white shirts as they took their packages from her daughter, a sense of pride filled Anya, who could tell that Ruby loved the business perhaps more than she did. In fact, Josef, who knew the finances down to the penny, swore that Ruby's participation had increased their profits since she had begun working, and Anya had to agree. Perhaps it was the way she shaped the rugalach, which always sold out regardless of how many they baked, or the extra bits of onion that she mixed into the pletzl, the flat spicy bread, that endeared her to the customers. Or maybe it was her laughter that spilled forth at some joke, like a sudden spring rain, but whatever it was, it became clear to the couple that Ruby was most assuredly good for business.

After their day of work was done at the bakery, when the little family of three walked the five blocks back to their tiny apartment on Dunkle Gasse under the illumination of the streetlamps, Anya most appreciated her precocious young daughter. As the two locked arms, moving slowly two steps behind the faster Josef, mother and daughter would meet heads and whisper secrets between the pair, the mother pausing only to clear Ruby's forehead of an errant curl or draw her closer to protect her from the swirling wind. It was in these moments that Anya knew that she finally had the daughter she had always dreamed of—her one true friend.

And nights after their plates of hearty cholent, a steaming mixture of beef, potatoes, carrots, and lima beans—a dish taught to Anya by her devoted *bubbe*—had been cleared and cleaned, and after the child was given a hot bath, Anya would sit at Ruby's bedside and begin the nightly ritual. Josef stepped into the room, his eyes already drowsy with sleep, and with a smile planted a kiss on the child's forehead, his little bubala.

Anya sat next to her daughter and began the Yiddish *leedels*, the old songs that her mama sang to her in the years before illness besieged her mind. Ruby, fresh from the bath, laid her head on Anya's shoulder. She inhaled the scents of flour and salt as she gazed up at her mother, content as only a child of eight can be, and listened and nodded to the old melodies until finally sleep seeped into the corners of her brown eyes. Finishing the last tune, Anya coaxed her drowsy daughter onto the mattress as she raised the heavy quilt to tuck her in for the night. It was only then as the child eased her legs beneath the cover that Anya remembered that her one daughter, the child that she had always dreamed of, her brilliant, beautiful little girl, was not quite as perfect as she had hoped.

2

Within minutes of the birth, she knew something was wrong. Even though Anya was not yet twenty, she knew enough to count fingers and toes. The lambskin fingers twisted around her own, five on each hand. Very good. But when she got to the toes, the new mother could see that something was very wrong. To be sure, there were ten toes in all. But the left foot was different somehow. Mangled, as if the foot had been squashed, and the toes folded in, posed toward the body at an odd angle. Anya's eyes remained fixed on the baby's foot. She didn't gasp or cry out, but instead caressed the aberrant limb in both of her hands, bringing it to her lips for a tender kiss. She was already enamored of the child, her cheeks slowly blossoming pink, the pale-yellow tuft of hair that sat atop her head, the eyes that blinked up at her own, even now filled with questions. She loved all of her. And, as she put the babe to her breast, Anya knew that if Josef—if anyone, in fact—objected to the affliction, well, they would all have to answer to her. Every single one of them.

As it turned out, after a moment of astonishment, and after the doctors had fully explained the issue, Josef sighed and, seeing the problem as a sign of "God's will," picked up the infant to inhale her powdery scent. He loved her nearly as much as Anya did.

Their little Ruby had a clubfoot, a condition of unknown causes, whereby the foot is curved inward and the tendons are shorter than normal, a problem seen mostly in males. Ruby was the exception. Some research was being done to correct the problem, according to the doctor who delivered the baby, but treatment was as yet a long and arduous process, perhaps not worth the pain the child would endure. Besides, Ruby was a girl and not destined to enter the army or a career that would involve heavy labor. Now, if she wished to become a ballerina or work on a farm, well, that was another matter.

Anya and Josef agreed that the pain of a cure would most likely be worse than living with the deformity and, besides, they could always deal with the issue when time passed and new, perhaps kinder, medical procedures would be on the horizon.

As a result, Ruby lived with the foot, which was as much a part of her as her dark, bright eyes and glorious smile.

~

Almost ten years had passed since Ruby's birth, and during that time there had been many changes, especially in the government. Anya and Josef were not the kind of people who had much use for politics. There was gossip among the customers in the store, ominous rumblings, though the couple didn't pay too much attention to it.

But one evening, Anya gave one last kiss to her sleeping child, before quietly shutting the bedroom door, then sat down at the kitchen table opposite her husband, her mind heavy with worry.

"Josef, the customers are talking again. And, well, I can't help it. I am beginning to get worried."

Josef placed his hand atop that of his young wife, which lay flat against the wooden table. The Sabbath candles still flickered, illuminating the shadows and, along with them, Anya's face. The surreal light sharpened the lines on her forehead, the dark pillows beneath her eyes. Josef understood all too well the burdens carried by his wife, whose endless hours rolling dough, pushing the long loaves of bread into hot ovens, had indeed taken their toll. And a part of him, if he allowed himself to consider it, felt helpless, working in a shop that was rightfully his wife's, allowing her to shoulder the brunt of the labor. But Josef did not indulge in such masculine fantasies, as he was a practical man. Dollars and cents were his forte, and he handled that end of the business with aplomb. While it was true that the labor had aged Anya, the work that hardened the angles of her face also bestowed it with a kind of nobility, a regal beauty.

"Don't bother yourself with those chatterboxes. Everybody always has something to say."

Anya moved uneasily in her seat and slipped her fingers from beneath Josef's.

"It's not just the natural gossip of women who have nothing better to do with their time. Their talk, talk of the world, of the Germans moving into town after town, is making me worried, for our bakery, for all of us. Josef, don't tell me you haven't heard it too?"

Josef got up from his chair to tend to the insistent whistle of the kettle on the stove. He poured the boiling water into two china cups, dropped a few black tea leaves in each, along with a sugar cube for himself, and placed them on the table. He took a long, slow sip of the tea before answering. He knew that he could no longer avoid the subject.

"Yes, my sweet, I've heard all about the Germans getting closer, perhaps doing to Lodz what they have done in other towns where those like us live. Even imprisoning us. But I am sure that our business will come to no harm. After all, we have done nothing illegal, nothing to intimidate Hitler and his minions. We are honest, hardworking people trying to make a living for our families. Everyone here knows us, respects us. We are liked.

"There is nothing for people like us to worry about, Anya," he lied, "nothing for us to fear."

Anya looked down and blew on her still-steaming tea.

"Does that matter, Josef? How much we are respected? How much we are liked? In the end, we are Jews."

Josef took another long sip of the tea, letting it burn his tongue. He wanted to help erase these thoughts from his wife's mind, tell her

Shirley Russak Wachtel

that what had happened in other places would not, could not, happen in Lodz. Tell her that all she had heard were exaggerations, rumors, and nothing more. Sure, the Nazis hated the Jews, wanted even to take their money, but to confiscate their businesses, steal the food out of their mouths, separate them from their families, or worse? No, this was not to be believed. Impossible. He wanted to calm her mind, arrest her fears, see her smile. He wanted to be a man.

Instead, Josef said nothing and could only watch Anya's hand quiver as she again raised the delicate cup to her lips. When she began to speak, he looked not at her but at the ebbing flames of the three Shabbat candles, one for each member of their family, their blue smoke rising in the air.

"Do you want to know what scares me most, Josef? It is not the name-calling by the strangers who don't really know us, or that our neighbors, even our customers, might turn against us. I am not even afraid that they will take away our business or make us eat the dirt from off the street, God forbid. No, when it comes down to it, I am not afraid of any of that. What consumes me are the children. I have heard, oh, and I pray it is not so, that the Germans are separating those like us from our children, sending them to schools or to camps. They put even children to work, too, some as young as three. And for people who cannot work, have not the strength because they are elderly, too young, or infirm, they take them away, and Josef"—Anya buried her face in her hands, covering her eyes as a torrent of tears emerged—"I am too scared to think of what will become of our Ruby!"

Josef took a deep breath as he felt the tea turn sour in his belly.

"Even if it should come to that, my dear wife, we will have nothing to fear. Our Ruby is nearly ten, tall for her age and smart too. We both know that she even can run the bakery single-handedly if she has to. She will prove herself a good worker, a capable worker, if it comes to that."

But, instead of alleviating his wife's fears, Josef watched as her watery eyes rose to the ceiling to an invisible God. As she let the tears flow freely now, gulping and sobbing, Anya could no longer help

18

herself. The one fear that had begun to creep into her mind had now overtaken it, something she could not hide. She no longer felt like a young woman, full of life and hope for the future, but an elderly woman, battered, beaten down, and hopeless.

"Oh, Josef, you don't understand," she said, when she finally had the breath to speak. "Ruby is all that you have said, all those things and more. But you have forgotten something too. What will happen to her when they see her foot? Oh, dear God, what will happen to our Ruby then?"

As the young couple sat in the kitchen, their faces showered by the light of the burning candles, all else covered in blackness, as they finally acknowledged their fears, they could not begin to know all that awaited them.

They were yet unaware that as they spoke in silent whispers amid a frightened gush of tears, next door Ruby lay awake, her dark eyes open as she muffled her cries into the pillow.

3

How had it come to this? That question plagued Anya in the morning as she sat at the edge of Ruby's bed and brushed her unruly hair, securing the curls with a barrette before sending her off to school. Or when she tried to stretch one skinny chicken leg into a meal to fill three bellies. Or as she trekked downstairs to relieve herself in a corner sewer down the street. How had it come to this?

It had been over a year now since the Germans had occupied Lodz, establishing it as their first ghetto, not a haven that offered them safety and sustenance, as was promised, but very much the opposite. And still Anya had no answers.

"Mama, I am quite sure that I will get all my algebra questions correct on our quiz today. You will see a perfect grade on my paper when I get home!" A wide smile overtook Ruby's dimpled face as she spoke.

Anya unsuccessfully tried to mimic that smile, knowing that all her daughter's actions, her gestures, were nothing more than attempts to cheer her parents during the hard times.

"I never doubted it," she said, placing half a biscuit and a glass of weak tea in front of Ruby. She preferred milk for the growing child, but as of last week there was no more to be had.

"After all," Anya continued, "you were up till late last night studying your numbers." She had the secret hope that once the family emerged from the darkness, Ruby would have a better future than that of a baker laboring all day. She would be something even more worthy. Maybe a teacher.

"Besides," she added, "you have had plenty of experience adding up bills in the shop, making change for the—" Anya stopped. She did not want to think any more about their beloved bakery, which was now no longer theirs. Within days of the occupation, two soldiers in heavy coats had walked in, helped themselves to a few Linzer tarts, and, before they had even wiped the crumbs off their ruddy cheeks, ordered the couple to close the shop in compliance with the mandates of the Nazi regime now in control. Josef and Anya knew better than to complain or resist in any way. By that time, they had heard what had happened to their young Jewish neighbor, pregnant and already a mother of three. She had questioned the snickering boys in uniform when they had eyed her lasciviously, one stopping the other just as he approached, running stubby fingers against her round belly. The young woman knew she was lucky to escape with both her honor and her life intact. Her tailor shop was locked the next morning. Those who wished to retrieve garments knew where to find her.

There was also a sign up on Moshe Weiss's cobbler shop, a mainstay in Lodz for the past thirty years. Everyone who ever had a hole in a shoe or a loose heel knew where to go, and old Mr. Weiss's tiny establishment on the corner was often filled with customers who needed some kind of repair. But when the elderly man with the long steel-colored beard had dared to query the offenders, they had abruptly knocked the yarmulke off his head, grabbed the boot he was fixing out of his hand, and hurled it at the cowering shopkeeper. By evening's end he, too, had closed up, no further questions asked. And if anyone did run into him as he picked coins off the street, they needed only look at the dark bruises on his scalp to quiet their curiosity. So Josef and Anya had simply nodded in silent acquiescence when the soldiers walked in that day, smirking and shouting before abruptly slamming the glass door behind them. The jingling of the bell still rang in their ears. Anya had been grateful that Ruby had gone to visit a friend that afternoon and was not there to witness the abomination.

Ruby sensed her mother's hesitation when bringing up the bakery. She was old enough to understand the atrocities committed by their torturers, but she also felt a pit deep in the hollow of her stomach whenever she recalled her easy banter with some of the customers, the way the dough felt, soft and pliable as clay beneath her hands as she molded it into kuchen; the warm embracing scents of apple and cinnamon as she slid the turnovers out of the oven. Of course, she never mentioned these sweet memories to either of her parents, so as not to increase their sorrows. Instead, she replied with a laugh, "Algebra, Mama, is not simple arithmetic, but letters and signs, nothing like my calculations at the bakery."

Anya smiled benevolently.

"Oh, well, what do I know of such things, anyway? I just know you are a smart student, and you will do well on any test they give you."

Ruby nodded as she finished the last bite of the biscuit and brushed the crumbs off her blouse.

"Well, off to another day at school," she announced as she took up the book bag filled with only some notepaper and pencils, and gave one last kiss to her mother, who was smiling broadly now, glad to see her daughter so eager to return to class.

As she headed out the door, Ruby didn't dare tell her mama that the reason she loved going to school so much was not that she excelled in her studies, or her attentive teachers, or even the companionship she held with a couple of the girls. It was the pathetic bowl of potato soup they served for lunch, the one thing that could satisfy her growling belly.

4

Sometimes Anya wouldn't see Josef for days. During that period, Anya would walk the streets with her head down, a green cotton kerchief wound tightly over her hair. She tried to make herself as small and inconspicuous as possible when meeting her daughter at the corner as she was on her way home from school, or when she picked up the family's rations for the week. Only Josef's aunt, an elderly woman who lived quietly down the street, and their closest neighbors knew where Josef went on these sojourns. Still, fear remained Anya's constant companion because of her husband's whereabouts. This was compounded with the daily apprehensions that one of the Nazi officers patrolling the street might cast an eye her way, his gaze lingering too long as, like a ghost, she crossed the street or emerged stealthily from the door of her apartment building.

Josef worked in the black market, securing food, sometimes cigarettes or medicine from nearby towns to which he traversed on foot or rail, with hidden bags of jewels and coins, all worthless now to their owners, to exchange for the things that were deemed more necessary than a ration card, which would buy you scant provisions, six hundred calories per day, only enough to keep your heart beating, if one was lucky. And sometimes even that was not enough. Often, when a father did not have the means to offer a trade, Josef would provide an extra portion of bread or a potato. He never accepted payment for the risks he took, as some of the others did. What good would a gold bracelet do him anyway? Instead, he would take the slimmest portion to supplement the meager rations for his own family, and in the black of night, as he skirted between the shadows of Dubrow Street, exhausted and starving, he would quietly knock on a door that would slowly open before Josef wordlessly placed a package at its entrance.

One day, in ten or fifteen years, Josef would be considered a hero for his actions and for the few lives he managed to save, but, then, in 1941, as he slipped past alleys and clung to the caboose of a train, as he watched the others, the young orphan boys of eight or nine years, hiding and scavenging alongside him, as he saw their eyes, frightened yet determined, yellow stars sewn on their threadbare coats when their mothers were still alive, flashing in the moonlight, Josef did not think himself a hero at all. A survivor, maybe. But not a hero.

Ruby knew little of her papa's activities. She knew only that they were illegal and could place his life, along with hers and her mama's, in jeopardy. She never asked questions, though, had no desire to learn any details; she was too afraid.

In the beginning, when the Germans first occupied Lodz and when they brusquely shut down the bakery, Anya had tried to remain busy by baking dozens of lebkuchen, the simple thin biscuits, spiced cookies, and sometimes some loaves of her favorite honey cake, mandelbrot, or even a challah for those who still attempted, in secret, of course, to observe the Sabbath. She used the flour and other ingredients she and Josef had smuggled from the store, along with a few dozen eggs she kept in her pantry at home, just in case the bakery should run short. But in months the ingredients dwindled, some of it supplanted by the items Josef brought home. Nevertheless, Josef gave much of his store away—to a neighbor with a sick child, to his aunt who told him one day how she could die happy if only she were to have something sweet on her tongue one last time. In the beginning, when rations were not so severe, Anya would grimace as she looked at a hardened round challah on the shelf, already half-stale. How much she would give for one bite of that challah now!

As Anya walked to the corner to await her daughter's return from the two-story building that now functioned as a school on Dworska Street, she amused herself by running through the alphabet, attaching a name to each of the letters, each name a special memory.

A was for Anya Ruchel, of course, her papa's bubbe for whom she was named. She had never met Anya Ruchel, as the Ashkenazis took their names only from the dead. Yet Anya felt she knew her namesake well, having heard the story of how she had raised five children single-handedly after her husband, a diabetic, had suffered a premature death. The woman took in sewing from the townspeople and began cleaning houses once the youngest had gone off to school. Anya Ruchel was a strong woman, to be sure, who read to her children every night, and made certain their faces had been scrubbed clean before she sent them off to school in the morning. Anya the younger was proud and grateful that she had been named after such a woman.

B stood for Bella, the name of her grandfather's old Persian cat. Her grandfather, her *zayde*, had brought the cat along when he moved into her family's apartment soon after Bubbe Sarah, Surala, had passed. She recalled rushing down the halls, trying to pet the soft white fur, but the cat was always faster. Anya couldn't remember a time when Zayde Lasar was without that cat, but even those memories were dim, since she was only six when he died.

Within minutes, she came to *E*, for *epl*. Anya's mama taught her to choose only the reddest, shiniest apples for the strudels, cutting away the brown spots, leaving the tender sweetness for the luscious desserts. How happy she would be to taste one of the slender peels now, the peels that she had once so thoughtlessly cast into the garbage.

By the time Anya got to the *G*s, only one word came to mind. *Gesund. Health* was the word that had stuck in her mind from the first moment Anya realized that she was with child. "Zei gesund" was what the neighbors, all the neighbors, called out to her as she passed them on the streets, adding that she and Josef should have only *mazel*, luck, when that pivotal time would come. This wish for good health, *gesund*, was what Anya wished for herself, for Josef, for their newborn. Although she was not a particularly religious woman, it was what she had asked for each night as she rested her head on the pillow, what she had cried for as the pains of labor came upon her that Sunday morning in September. *Zei gesund*, she prayed.

And Ruby was healthy. Except for the minor problem that none of them spoke of, Ruby was gesund. The cherries in her cheeks, her liquid brown eyes, all signaled that she was more than any of them could have hoped. And yet as she watched Ruby approach now, walking with another girl, smaller and thin, Anya could see only her daughter's sunken cheeks, her arms and legs bony and stiff as she pulled the stubborn foot behind her. Once more the sorrows had intruded, tainting Anya's happy little word game until her heart felt heavy within her chest.

Again, she thought, how had it come to this? Homes and businesses confiscated. Foods rationed, leaving only enough to feed a bird. Electricity and plumbing cut off so that they were forced to grope around in the dark of night, toss their feces into the street, send their children out to beg with copper pots like paupers. Two hundred thousand people in all. And just because they were Jews. Even the name of their town, now owned by the Germans, had been changed. There was no more Lodz, but Litzmannstadt, a place, a name, that Anya would not, could not, ever accept.

Ruby greeted her mother with a weak smile, not quite as genuine as the smiles she had given her before the occupation, but a smile nonetheless.

"Mama, this is my friend from school," she said, motioning to the tiny girl, barely a wisp of a thing, who stood shyly shuffling her feet by Ruby's side.

The child that stood before Anya was perhaps three or four years younger than her own daughter, now thirteen, which didn't surprise her, as due to a lack of teachers, the children were often grouped together years apart, with little regard to their age or ability. Nor was her skeletal frame a source of shock, for, sadly, most of the children walking about in the town were emaciated, shadows of their former selves. The few who weren't were most likely victims of disease, their bodies swelling to a doughy purple shade.

If there was one aspect of the girl that did surprise Anya, it was her eyes. They were large, almost too large, for her face, and the blue was suggestive of a dark, endless ocean whose waves held secrets Anya could only imagine. They were the saddest eyes she had ever seen.

"Would it be all right if she came back to the apartment with us?" asked Ruby, pleading. "It won't be for very long." And although Anya knew that it was probably unwise to take such a risk, that people might ask questions about the strange child, or that even the girl herself might in some way, though unintentionally, betray them, she nonetheless nodded her assent. Her daughter had so few friends, so few pleasures in her miserable life, how could she deny her this one request?

The three ascended the stairs of the building to the apartment, third floor at the end of the hall. Thankfully, Anya noticed, no one lingered about. She lagged behind the girls and, as customary, paid particular attention to Ruby's climbing, nervously watching that the faulty foot would not, in some way, betray her. But her daughter had grown adept at maneuvering the limb, and within minutes was first at the door of the apartment.

Without hesitation, Ruby invited her guest to her bedroom, where she could show off her meager though sentimental belongings—an ivory chess set that had once belonged to her zayde, Josef's father; several books, including a first edition of *Black Beauty*; a delicate gold necklace with a small Star of David at its center, which Anya and Josef had purchased upon her birth. But it soon became apparent that the invitation was extended not to display a collection of items but to offer the child something more desired, more precious. The two walked into the kitchen, and Ruby, leading the way, made her request known.

"Mama, do you think it would be all right if I gave my friend just a slice of—"

Anya moved to the cupboard before Ruby could finish her question. Anya removed a whole loaf of black bread, only five days old, procured on Josef's latest excursion, and sliced off a thick wedge for the girl. The child reached for it hungrily, but instead of stuffing the bread into her mouth, she placed it into the deep pocket of her oversize coat and uttered the only words Anya would hear her say until months later.

"Thank you."

Simultaneously, her lips stretched into a wide smile of gratitude. Anya stared at the tiny moppet. The way her hair, a mass of silvery ringlets, fell into her face, the mysterious blue eyes. *How pretty she is,* Anya thought. *How very pretty.*

Before Anya could accept her gratitude, though, Ruby had turned to the icebox and pulled out the last of the *mun,* or poppy seed muffins, that Anya had baked nearly a year earlier. Now covered with a thick layer of snow, for it had been saved for a special occasion, it was presented to the girl, who grabbed it eagerly before plunging the muffin, too, inside her pocket.

And although Ruby had never asked her mother's approval, Anya stood by silently with no attempt to stop her. She knew that ultimately the muffins were Ruby's to give, as they were always intended for her daughter. She realized, too, that Ruby gained more pleasure from the donation than she ever would have felt if she had sunk her own teeth into the sweet treat. Shortly after that, the small girl vanished from the apartment and down the stairs into the noisy street below. And within minutes after she left, Anya was apprised of the reasons for Ruby's generosity.

It had all come out slowly as the two sat at their desks, waiting for the day's lessons to begin, or sat shoulder to shoulder, sipping the meager remains of the dull potato soup served at school. Once, like Ruby, the girl had had a promising life, with parents who loved her, professors who created a home that was sparse and simple, but nonetheless warm and loving. And, like Ruby, too, she was an only child, pretty enough to warrant a second glance from passersby, yet perceptive enough to glean that her security was a temporary thing, that looming dangers awaited at each turn. As Jews, the family's future in the ghetto had been predetermined, but what placed them in greater danger was the fact that the father, like Josef, had a second job, one that was far riskier than that of a professor of philosophy at the local college. The man, an adroit speaker, wrote articles and gave speeches decrying the activities of their captors, whom he boldly labeled "filthy swine," the same name that they had thrust upon the Jews. He called his brethren to rise up in whatever way they could against their oppressors.

But he did not know that there was an informer within the small group of listeners who had egged him on, who had passed on the information so that the Gestapo showed up at their front door one afternoon, putting bullets in the heads of the girl's mama and papa just as their daughter was coming up the stairs. The murderers smirked at her but left the child alone to discover the tragedy seconds later. Except for an elderly grandfather who lived two flights down, the child now lived alone, and preferred to keep it that way for as long as she could.

The story terrified Anya, who understood Ruby's compassion for the girl. And for the first time since the walls of Lodz had been sealed, their happy lives curtailed, Anya came to the stark realization that tomorrow was not a given. Tomorrow they might end up just like the parents of Ruby's sad friend, or worse. What Anya didn't know then was that her darkest fears would be realized sooner than she thought.

5

Tante was dead. Near the end of 1941, she was found still in her bed wrapped in the cocoon of a mohair blanket, eyes still open, staring forever now at the cracks in the ceiling. Josef found her there one early Monday morning as he went downstairs to check on her on his way for another exchange. He rapped on the door, but when he received no response, he returned with a crowbar to pry the door open.

"She died peacefully, a natural death," he reported on his return to the apartment. "She was eighty-three, a good run under the circumstances." But as Anya watched her husband silently recite the yizkor prayer, the customary prayer for the dead, she couldn't help but wonder how natural, how peaceful, Tante's death had really been. While Tante was lucky to have lived by herself, unimpeded by the constant watch of their captors, Anya knew that her demise had not been as natural as some said. As with others, many much younger, Tante Gittel had perished from the forces that assaulted them daily—hunger, cold, stress, all combined to eat away at what remained of their bodies. And it showed no signs of letting up. Tante had been spared an even grimmer future.

And as Anya sat at the window later that day and watched as the soldiers carried Tante's body away, still clothed in a flimsy nightgown, out into the streets for all to see like a cow after the slaughter, only one thought crossed her mind: *Maybe Tante was lucky, after all.*

Days later, just before the moon rose over a blackened city, Anya came to a decision to take a chance. It was Shabbat, and she took the opportunity to do something special for her child. And so she went into the bedroom and rummaged through Josef's sock-and-underwear drawer until she found the small silver candelabra. As she cut three of their small supply of remaining white candles, her heart had a lightness it had not felt in months. That evening they would have a real Shabbat.

When Josef walked in the door, looking tired and dejected, an appearance not uncommon of late, he was surprised to see his mother's old candelabra polished to a sheen on top of a round metal platter, with three white candle stubs waiting to be lit. He didn't question Anya's decision but merely nodded, understanding the need, especially at this time, to cling to what dwindling faith the family had left. He glanced around the room at the bedsheets secured over the windows, to hide all that was happening inside. He hoped it would be enough.

When Anya called Ruby, who had been rereading an old translation of *Pride and Prejudice*, from the bedroom, the girl raised her eyebrows at all that her mother had prepared. She looked at her curiously.

"Why have you taken out the candles?" Ruby asked.

"Well, it is Shabbat, a holy day," said Anya, trying to suppress a laugh, "and since we have not celebrated in so long, I thought it was time we did."

Ruby nodded as Josef had, even as she took in the protective bedsheets at each window. Then she moved toward the setting and slid her hand across the smooth surface of the candelabra, as if to make sure it was real. She looked up at her parents' faces again, her expression one of gratitude. Then, impulsively, she threw her arms around them both. The light that now appeared, however briefly, in her daughter's face could only confirm that Anya had made the right decision.

As they ate their meager rations of chicken legs and a potato, instead of the silence weighing on their hearts like a heavy stone, the family engaged in a lively conversation. Ruby described how she read one of her short stories to the class, and although it was only about a girl taking a walk on the first day of spring, and the way the crocuses were blossoming and the green grass was waving in the breeze, the teacher had praised it, perhaps too much.

"I am sure the praise was well deserved. You are a good writer, after all!" exclaimed Josef.

"Ruby is good at everything she does," added Anya before her child could protest.

Then Josef, who was truly smiling now, decided to add a story of his own, even if it wasn't entirely truthful.

"I have a secret to tell you both. Tonight we will have a special dessert! Do you recall Frau Zobler, the widow who lives on the next block? Merely by chance I ran into her today, and she summoned me to her apartment, where she gave me a gift of farmers' cheese, telling me she had more than enough for one person, and since I have a family, well, she thought I should have whatever was left. Is that not lucky?"

Ruby clapped her hands at the news, her mouth already watering at the prospect of cheese, a delicacy she had not had in a very long time. Anya smiled and exchanged knowing glances with Josef, whose story she knew was somewhat fabricated. There was cheese in the cupboard, to be sure, but it had been there for at least a week, the object of an exchange on one of his secret excursions.

Anya, knowing it was her turn to contribute something to the conversation, sat up straighter.

"And I, too, have some happy news!" she announced, "but first I will show you." She stood up, then went to the closet in the hall. After a minute or so, Anya returned, holding a small object in the palm of her hand. Opening her fingers, she revealed what it was.

"It's a coin!" exclaimed Ruby, removing the object from her mother's hand and taking it in her own.

Josef looked over his daughter's shoulder at the coin, flashing a brownish gold.

"A German coin, of not much worth, I'm afraid. And certainly none to us."

Anya shook her head.

"I was just about to step into our building when I noticed it, right in the middle of the sidewalk, waiting to be picked up. So I tossed it in my pocket. I'm sorry that it is of little use."

"Oh, but it is of use, Mama!" said Ruby, unable to take her eyes off the coin. "Don't you see, it is a good-luck symbol? It means something good will happen to us, and very soon!"

Anya sighed. "Well, you may keep it, then," she said, happy that at least Ruby had something to hope for.

After the family had finished their meal and each had a spoonful of Josef's lucky farmers' cheese, Anya threw one of her cotton scarves over her head, and Ruby did the same. Then she removed a match from a kitchen drawer and, as the two recited the traditional prayer, Anya lit the candles. As she looked at Ruby's face, illuminated by the soft light, she saw a mixture of contentment and hope, and knew that she had made the right decision.

Later, as Ruby crawled into her bed for the night, Anya decided to revive another tradition. She had found the family's well-worn Bible on an upper shelf in the closet. Now sitting at her daughter's bedside, Anya turned the pages until she reached the verses in Exodus. And then, just as she had done from the time Ruby was two and had not yet learned to read, Anya began to recite the words. All about how God had saved them from their brutal taskmasters, from slavery to freedom. Even though Ruby's eyes were closed, Anya knew that she understood the meaning of the words, which now were more important than ever. When she was done, she looked at the child's face, so angelic and innocent despite the hardships the family had endured. She was glad that she had but one child. And she was glad that it was Ruby.

6

Less than half a bowl and a quarter of a potato. Ruby's eyes watered at the pitiful sight just as her mouth watered for the first taste of the daily ration that was called lunch. She looked down at her companion sitting next to her on the bench. It seemed that in the last few months, as the rations became smaller, the teachers became less animated, and students who had boasted 100 percent attendance went missing because of illness or worse. Her friend, already so small, now appeared withered, her skin taking on a ghoulish gray hue as her blue eyes, so enlarged, seemed to capture their plight in their pupils.

"Would you like some of mine?" Ruby offered as she watched the girl gulp down a few spoons even before she herself had begun to eat.

"Take some, I'm quite full already. Besides," Ruby lied, "my stomach does not feel so right today. Perhaps it was the turnips Mama cooked yesterday for dinner."

Still slurping her soup, the child cast a questioning glance at Ruby, and then with a sudden twinkle in her eye, moved Ruby's bowl in front of her and quickly devoured that too.

Ruby's stomach clenched as she watched her bring each spoonful to her mouth. She swallowed a thick wad of her own saliva just to feel the comfort of something going down her throat. A deep pain seared through her belly. Still, she reasoned, the pain of hunger was far better to endure than the pain of one's conscience. After all, the girl had no mama, no papa.

After lunch the few remaining children at the school lined up to go back into the classroom. As Ruby stood behind her friend, she was pleased to see the barrette, fashioned in silver with rhinestones in the shape of stars, clasping the ringlets of hair. Perhaps Mama knew that she had made a gift of the adornment, the very one given to Ruby upon her birth. But, if she did, Anya hadn't said a thing, and Ruby was glad for the momentary pleasure it gave the young girl.

They were in music class singing an old song about everlasting love when suddenly the voices fell away as their teacher stared dumbfounded at the front door of the classroom, where a frost seemed to grip the air.

When Ruby dared turn her head, she wasn't surprised to see not one, but two, Nazi soldiers standing in their heavy gray coats, truncheons in hand. This time neither of them was smiling.

After surveying the room, one of the officers, a balding man in a woolen coat straining the gold buttons over his rotund belly, leaned close to the teacher. She was a spindly charcoal-haired woman with lines down her cheeks that sharpened as he whispered in her ear. She nodded, then asked the students to stand as the husky officer and his partner, a fair-haired boy who looked as if he was barely out of school, strolled down the aisles, methodically eyeing each student. Suddenly the older officer placed his large paw of a hand around the neck of one emaciated ten-year-old, plucked him out of the line as if he were selecting a chicken off the butcher's block, and flung him toward the front of the room, sending the poor child careening into the blackboard. Their teacher, who was trembling like a leaf on a windy day, stood frozen in place and averted her eyes.

Next, a girl Ruby's own age, one whom she had played marbles with after school one day only months earlier, before fear had taken over the town, was singled out. The girl had had a headful of thick, dark hair and was once the envy of her peers, but in the intervening months she had been robbed of her luxurious strands, no doubt by another unknown illness that had swept through Lodz. The girl, whose name was Dvora, now looked like a shaved cat. She cried out once as the tyrant grabbed her arm and threw her forward directly into the boy, who crumpled to the floor before immediately righting himself.

The monster proceeded to the next row, passing some of the students, those who appeared only somewhat healthier, until something, a chirping sound, caught his attention. He turned back, and Ruby noticed that his focus was now on another boy, Shlomo, nearly fourteen. Just weeks ago he had informed Ruby that his birthday had already passed, and with it the induction as a bar mitzvah, an event he had been looking forward to since he was four, even before he could read. He had told her all this with a shrug of resignation. Like so many other things, after living under the thumb of the Nazis, what had once seemed so important now appeared insignificant. The Nazi, his putrid breath coming in cloudy vapors, fixed a cold eye on Shlomo and, looking as if he were bored by the whole thing, took the culprit by the arm and flung him against the others. Ruby's heart broke as she watched the boy stand up like an old man, the stain of urine spreading slowly down his pant leg. And his only crime, she thought, was having the hiccups.

Ruby felt her heart beat faster as the Nazi began to walk down the aisle where she stood in front of her small friend. She moved slightly to obscure his vision. When he had turned down the next row, she began even to feel the tingle of a smile on her lips. But, as before, a new sound drew attention. This one unmistakable. The girl was crying. Never had Ruby seen her cry before, not even when she told her the story of all that had happened, the terrible slaughter of her dear mama and papa. Even when she would walk down the street to her empty apartment, the child, starving and ill, had covered her terror with a silent stoicism. And now, in the direct glare of the Devil himself, she was crying.

The soldier moved with surprisingly quick steps, reaching past Ruby to pick up the child, who could not have weighed more than a sack of laundry, flinging her toward the others with such ferocity that it startled his partner, who had begun to herd the group toward the door. Ruby heard someone scream and was surprised when she realized it was her own voice howling, piercing the silence.

"No! You cannot take her! She has no one!"

Without thinking, she found herself moving toward the little girl standing in the middle of the condemned group. But she was too late. He had seen her. The officer stared at the foot for seconds before giving her a mighty push against the blackboard. Ruby cried out in pain as the foot twisted monstrously beneath her, and she fell hard onto the concrete floor. Even as she found herself falling, her heart felt light with one consolation. She caught the glint of the rhinestone barrette as the child ran quicker than she ever thought possible, flew past the stunned young officer, and escaped down the hall.

7

They would come for the rest the next day. By then most had gone into hiding, a futile, short-lived sense of security, for their foes were as persistent as miners, discovering and sweeping up the children, even the healthiest among them, in sewers, tucked within soot-filled chimneys, even behind their mothers' skirts. Within days, they had captured them all—almost all, that is. They hadn't taken the one Ruby had risked her life to save.

The child didn't return home that day but ran straight to Ruby's apartment, the one place where the Gestapo had no interest in looking. All would later be confirmed in the scrupulous records they kept of each household. Family after family would receive the grim news that their child had already been transferred, and the ones who had given them life, had nurtured them from infancy, would now know that their loved one had met an ignominious end along with all the others who were weak, sick, disabled—useless.

The young girl, sweaty and panting, fairly flew into Anya's arms, her face ablaze with terror. Fright had seized her throat, and it was some minutes before she could speak. Anya grabbed a clean towel near the nonfunctional sink, spit into it, and dabbed at the child's hot cheeks, pushing aside the silvery white curls from her forehead. As she did, she noticed Ruby's barrette, the stars of silver and rhinestones embedded in her friend's hair, but said nothing. Within minutes the young girl swept Anya's hand aside and fastened her large tear-filled eyes on her friend's mother. Breathlessly she began to speak, spilling forth the details of all that had happened only minutes earlier at school—how the Nazis had appeared suddenly at the school door, how their teacher's tongue had turned to ice as she allowed the devils to select the children, to take them away. And how Ruby, dear Ruby, had tried to protect her, until the foot had been spotted, so that in the end she herself could do nothing but run. Run to Ruby's apartment, where she knew her mother would be getting ready to meet her only daughter as she walked home from school. After telling the tale, the child averted her eyes and collapsed to the floor in a puddle of tears.

Anya stood motionless, her face impassive as she looked down at the girl as if she were staring at only a puddle of spilled milk. But then she, too, was seized by movement as she let her legs propel her toward the door and out into the streets.

Once outside, wearing only a simple cotton housedress, she stopped as her eyes searched up and down the street, not quite sure of her next move, or even where she was for that matter. And then, as the icy wind smacked her cheeks, assaulted her bony arms, her quivering legs, Anya stood rooted in the middle of a block in Lodz and screamed. She called Ruby's name again and again. Loud, strident screams so that even God Himself would be roused. But, sadly, the people, whose fear was greater than their mercy, would only ignore her. The Nazi officer on the corner smiled to himself, no doubt at the folly of it all. The rest hurried back to the solace of their apartments, consoled by the fact that it was someone else who had sunk into delirium this time. This time it wasn't them.

How long Anya stood on that street, screaming, she didn't know. Time, just like the hearts of their enemies, had frozen. With no future ahead, not even the past had meaning. When Anya's throat began to hurt, as her swift breaths subsided, as her tears dried in streaks upon her face, she turned back to the apartment building. And, as before, her legs led her home.

After she climbed the three flights, she did not notice that the door was ajar. She walked into the apartment and barely blinked when she realized the child was gone.

~

Now they had only each other to live for. Once, long ago, before Anya had witnessed her mother's mind turn to cinder, the woman had explained to her daughter how one lived when the world became too much. *You can only pull the string so far before it breaks,* she had explained as her daughter cried bitter tears over the loss of their beloved ten-year-old Persian cat. *And after you have broken that string, well, what will you have then?* How many times had Anya recalled those words as she learned to calm her emotions, too afraid that she would lose herself in the process? And how many times had she wished that her mother had followed her own advice?

So now, as she and Josef sat alone in the small apartment, eating their rations bit by bit as if they were putting coins into a piggy bank, rising with each ray of morning sun, slipping beneath a slim blanket as a gray mist coated the night sky, each feared pulling the string too tightly, just as they feared looking into each other's faces lest they sever the string.

After she told Josef all that had happened so that he understood the words once he had distilled them from the hysterics—the tears that came in a gush, the screams that echoed like thunder—after he understood it all, he, too, ran yelling into the streets, which were now deathly silent. And then he left, only to return to the apartment ten days later to a wife who was more shadow than flesh, to his dear Ruby's room with its bed still neatly made, to the books left unread, to the windows waiting to be opened. All waiting for Ruby to come home.

The two asked many questions that first month yet received no answers. Only a stern warning from their local gestapo or a sad shake of the head from frightened neighbors. Nobody knew where they had taken Ruby or her little friend, and, if they did, they weren't saying. Until, finally, the couple stopped asking altogether. They no longer wished to pull the string.

~

The days, the months, blended into each other so that the Jews who remained within the town knew only that it must be winter by the chill that settled into their bones, and summer by the number of beads of sweat that appeared on their foreheads. Josef had finally ended his work with the black market, for with the Nazis nearly outnumbering the townspeople, it was deemed too dangerous. Besides, he no longer had the energy or the desire for it. In fact, he no longer had the desire for anything in life, except Anya. Anya, the force that kept the hot blood streaming through the vessels in his body. Anya, who was everything. And, like the man whose eyes she saw open at dawn's first light and close slowly as the sun descended beneath the sad gray buildings, she lived for him too. It was Josef's face she saw when she dared dream about her future. And so, if the young couple had any taste of pleasure left in the world, it was with each other. Soon they began to live for their nights together when their legs entwined under the grim moon, pouring all the love that remained in their skeletal bodies into each other, devouring each other as if each were the finest cake in their beloved bakery.

Neither knew exactly when they first heard about the child. Perhaps it was in whispers from one of the hausfraus they passed along the streets, or maybe in the wails of parents who had discovered that none of the children of Lodz had survived. But in the end, it mattered not. In the end, the young girl whose short life had been only a series of tragedies was confirmed gone like all the others. Killed, no doubt, in Chelmno. Harangued and tortured only to be suffocated in a hermetically sealed compartment. Killed like their sweet Ruby—in a gas chamber.

~

Although few doubted that the vast Nazi killing machine would outlast the lives of the eleven thousand who remained in what was once called Lodz, the day arrived when a decision came down from the highest ranks of the Reich. Seeing no further need for the ghetto itself—not when the camps were functioning so marvelously—it was determined that those still huddled starving in their tiny apartments would be dispersed. So in the summer of 1944, more than two years after Ruby's disappearance, Anya and Josef found themselves on the last transport they believed they would ever take, the one to Auschwitz.

The two were only a little surprised when they were brusquely put into a stifling cattle car filled with far too many others—sobbing children, despondent parents, the sick, the tired, all with one thing in common—they wanted to live. All exploded onto the railway platform, which was also fraught with chaos—guards with truncheons in hand, snarling German shepherds. Suitcases of the Jews' remaining paltry possessions, which they had so meticulously packed, were ripped from their hands and thrown into piles. Worst of all, selections were made, separating the elderly, the sick, from those who still showed signs of health. This was the bewilderment, the terror, that was Auschwitz. More surprising to the travelers was that they had outlasted the ghetto. That they were alive at all.

The most terrifying part of the long day spent stuffed into the cattle cars, a hundred people at a time, was not the moaning even of the strongest among them, nor was it the odor of vomit and urine mingled with the stench of fear. It wasn't even the realization that upon arrival they had been separated from their luggage, the slim gold wedding band hastily torn off Anya's finger. It was none of those things. Only when she found herself separated from Josef, men to the left, women taken to the right, did she stifle a scream. She was incapable of shedding even a tear by then, and only as Anya walked with the other doomed women did she realize that for the first time in her life, she was utterly alone.

~

Ten months. How long is ten months in this eternal world? Anya surmised that it was long enough to read Homer's *Iliad*, Shakespeare's *Hamlet*, and all the comedies; to dig a dozen graves; to bring new life into the world and to fall in love again. But for her they were months filled with drudgery, aching, muscles stretched beyond their limits, but also a time that was, ironically, even miraculously, peaceful. Peaceful because her hands were always busy, so busy that she had no time to think, no time to mourn a daughter who had not yet reached womanhood when she died. So busy that she had little room in her mind for hope, for the slim chance that her Josef might still be alive.

Anya had been one of the lucky ones, if such an expression may be used, for the captors had uncovered that she was a baker. Her days were spent on kitchen duty, her hands no longer working the dough, no longer kneading delicious honey cakes, but employed in setting up the rations for the day: a bitter liquid that resembled coffee only in its color for breakfast; a sour, now impossibly thin soup made from rotten vegetables, including some pieces of potato, rutabaga, some groats, and rye flour at midday; and for dinner only a meager wedge of black bread with some sausage or margarine, or perhaps some cheese or marmalade. While the prisoners could save the bread as a supplement to the coffee the next morning, most were so famished that they downed their portions immediately. And while Anya worked the kitchens, preparing the food and doling helpings out to each of the prisoners as they watched, their eyes as large as clocks, she counted herself among the lucky ones. While she stood on her feet nearly eleven hours a day, her hands forming calluses, the purple veins in her legs bulging beneath the skin, it was still better than lifting heavy bricks or, even worse, standing at the doors of the blazing-hot crematorium, a task that often meant certain death. And it was better than having to haul the corpses from the area where they had labored, those who had become no more than a bag of skeletons, those saved by God as they worked for a better fate. She was better off, too, than some of the others, more it seemed each day, who walked like ghosts, cheeks sunken, eyes wide, suffering from the starvation sickness. These were the Musselmen, quickly identified and quickly selected for the gas chambers.

When Anya's stomach would clench with hunger, she would manage to break off a piece of the dough of the cold hard bread and pop it quickly into her mouth as she worked. Never did anyone witness or report the crime. And if she was seen in the criminal act, it was all the same to her. She was beyond caring.

Day's end offered no respite for, as with her companions, she was overwhelmed by exhaustion and looked forward only to placing her head on the rough straw mattress in the lower bunk as she prayed for a dreamless sleep. As for the few women who pushed her to chat, to share a memory from home, or a dream for the days when life might miraculously resume, Anya paid them no heed. It was as if her mouth had been sewn with thick cord, shutting it to the past, to the future. She, and many like her, knew only the present, their single wish to make it to the next day.

She didn't know it then, but the day Anya got sick turned out to be the best day of her life. She had been on her feet for nearly eight hours, carrying the vats, opening the giant freezers, scooping up the soup, trying not to think of the souls shoved into the crematoria, all consumed and transformed into ashes. Lately, though, the vast killing machine had ground to a halt. Days, weeks earlier, as the Soviet forces neared, the Nazis had begun to destroy the evidence of their barbarism, so the gas chambers, as well as the unlucky few who manned them, were gone. It wouldn't be long before the kitchens themselves would be destroyed, the Nazis abandoning even this bit of mercy, as they deemed it, and along with it, Anya and the other workers who went about their tedious routines.

But as she stood there, Anya sensed a sudden whirlwind in her belly, and then before she knew it, a violent eruption exploded from her mouth, resulting in an amorphous heap of vomit on the pristine floor. She gazed at it, as stunned as anyone else to view the bits of bread mixed with mucus, all tainted with a stream of blood. A thought flickered through her mind that she had perhaps lost a portion of her stomach, an entire organ! But before she could consider the possibility further, she felt the rough hand of the overseer pulling her forward, out the heavy doors. When, many years later, she would recall that day, only one memory would emerge as clear as sunrise—a wish. If only she could die.

But it wasn't to be, for weeks later the Nazi scoundrels had evacuated, after they departed on their death marches with more than fifty-six thousand prisoners, leaving only those too sick to make that final journey, so sick they could be ignored. Anya was among them.

8

The chocolate tasted surprisingly sweet as she held the square in her mouth for as long as she could. The Red Cross had distributed the delicacies among the human skeletons as they removed them from hell and into the daylight. Anya would later remember only kissing the hand of the soldier who beckoned her outdoors, a fleshy hand with dark hairs sprouting across its surface. Within minutes she was led off with the others. And now she was eating chocolate. Unlike so many of the other survivors—no longer victims—survivors—Anya did not feel her stomach lurch in protest, a death grip that could send her back to the hospital, or worse. Instead, the sweet settled warmly inside her, reminding Anya of a childhood she forgot had ever existed.

The ensuing days and nights in the displaced persons camp flew by like a dream. Anya lived for each day, no longer worried about what the future held, no longer wanting to die. She tried not to think about the past, either, for it was still married to the grief she held, would forever hold now. But, in fact, mere days later a new, darker fear stealthily crept into Anya's mind and within minutes, it seemed, had conquered it. She could think of nothing else. Where was Josef? Was he even alive?

She soon had her answer. One morning, lying on her mattress, still encumbered in a forgetfulness only sleep can bring, she opened her eyes to two green orbs staring at her. They were already filled with tears.

"Anya, my darling! Is it really you? Baruch Hashem! Oh, Anya, can you believe it?"

~

They were together, it was true, and yet they were all alone in the world. Still, they checked the records just to be sure. When they found out for a certainty that their one child was indeed gone, the couple resigned themselves to the loss—at least as much as any parent could. For a time, after they had taken a small, albeit temporary apartment in Munich, they resumed a futile search for the other girl, Ruby's little friend, hoping she might fill in the gaps of their daughter's last moments. Alas, they received official word that all those who were in attendance at the school had succumbed in the fumes of Chelmno. It was the best they could do without even knowing her name.

~

As they settled into their new apartment, the two dared dream about their future, dared acknowledge that they *had* a future, that they were both indeed alive, and had countless years before them. At first the comfort of this knowledge was enough. Eating three real meals a day and not old, watery soup or the leaves falling off autumn trees gave them a sense of pleasure. And soon, once again, they were ravenous for one another. Knowing that they could wake in the mornings, gaze into each other's eyes, and hear the voice of their loved one, that they could lie entwined as night swept across the horizon, skin to skin, their bodies one, was enough. It was more than they could ever have hoped, when only months earlier even taking the next breath was an uncertainty.

Josef now recalled the stories of his great-uncle Fredric Kozinski, who had gone to seek his fortune years before Hitler had risen to power, before his poison had seeped across the land. Josef had a premonition that Fredric would change his life. When Fredric was a young boy, he had dreams bigger than he was entitled to have, considering his station in life, considering that he was the only son of parents who perpetually suffered from one disease after another and relied on Fredric to sustain them by selling newspapers, stacking boxes, even collecting coins off the street, whatever it took.

Nevertheless, the dreams laid hold of the young boy and refused to subside. And so, one day after Fredric had grown to manhood, after his elderly parents had finally succumbed to the illnesses that plagued them, he ultimately made good on his goals. Though it was not to be in Poland, where the dreams of many with similar aspirations had already turned to ashes, but in a land where the dreams of young boys were still possible. Eventually Fredric found himself surveying the ocean from the deck of a steamer headed for America. Whether he was a paying passenger or a stowaway, no one knew. The stories Josef heard only told that he had arrived, catching sight of that miraculous torch rising above the seas, and soon afterward started selling silverware, finally establishing himself as a business owner. Fredric was a verifiable success.

And so now that Josef recalled that name and a glimmer of the hope it conjured, he committed himself to do the research. Was it possible that he could find his great-uncle Fredric and appeal to this one relative to sponsor them both, the poor nephew and his wife, who were seeking a new start?

At first the search seemed hopeless, for no one had recent news of the great-uncle, of his monumental dreams, the success he had found with his thriving business. No one had heard from him at all in a long time. And Josef began to wonder if Fredric was even alive. The fact was, the poor uncle was not alive, had died mere years after establishing himself. But Josef was soon to find out that Fredric had a son. A son who had inherited all his father's wealth. Although Josef and Anya had not even known of their cousin Carl Shmuel's existence, he found out about them through an old classmate of Josef's who had secured a journey abroad. It would be nearly six years later that they received a letter. It was from New York. Carl Shmuel had decided to sponsor them, as they were family, saying it was the very least he could do. They were going to America.

~

And now Josef dared dream of the future, a new start on a continent where every street, every face, did not hold sad memories. Of course, it was folly to believe, for no matter how wide an ocean could distance them from the past, those faces long gone would sneak into their dreams, the terrors of the camps causing Anya's hand to tremble as she held her glass of tea each morning. The past followed them like an obedient pup. How naive they had been! Still, they hoped.

~

Josef and Anya leaned over the shiny wooden rail and waved to no one in particular. Truly, they had never seen such joy in their lives, never even imagined the world would be capable of it again. The laughter, the beaming faces, the cork popping and slaps on the back, and they were right in the middle of it! Anya thought it all seemed like it was from the pages in a fantasy book, like the kind she would read on her own mama's knee as a child. When the couple finally turned their backs on Hamburg, the harbor that was their exit and their entrance into the future, they knew that they would never set eyes on it, or Lodz, ever again.

~

They had been at sea for only two days when Anya knew something was wrong. She had heard stories of people who had traveled across the ocean and fallen ill to the motion of the swirling waters, their stomachs churning, their faces turning a ghastly shade of green as their insides revolted, as they leaned over railings for hours on end. Oceans no doubt were filled with the muck of their illness.

Josef had suggested they come outside to alleviate her malaise. A rest on the ship's deck, a few relieving breaths of the ocean air, would do her good. Yet Anya couldn't put her finger on exactly what told her that her problem would not be so easily solved. She did not think that the queasy feeling she was experiencing was a return of the old illness that had felled her in the camp. She felt instead that her unsettled belly was the result of something that could be much worse. A condition that would stay with her—perhaps forever.

Anya's eyes drifted slowly up to the white moon suspended now like a new coin floating behind a stream of clouds in the dark sky. As she stood watching, absorbing the tranquility of the moment, her eyes followed a thin ray of light that was illuminating Josef's face as he slept reclined on one of the deck chairs. She allowed her eyes to linger there for what seemed like minutes. *How content,* she thought. *How at peace he seems!* And in that moment the realization came upon her. She averted her vision, and when she gazed up at the sky again, the moon that had seemed so full of promise mere minutes ago was in full view— orange, bold, and angry. It was then that Anya knew for a certainty that she was not ill, nor did she have motion sickness. She was with child. Another child, a child who was not Ruby, one who could never take her place. And she realized that no matter how many breaths she took, her life—her true life—was over.

9

LENA

1961

No one ever spoke of Pearl. Strange, Lena thought, especially after she had run back into the bungalow, screaming and crying in near hysterics. Her parents had jumped out of bed, bewildered until they finally were able to make sense of her words. As Lena pulled on her mother's nightgown, her father grabbed the closest weapon he could find—a large meat cleaver from the utility drawer in the kitchen. At the time, Lena didn't see the absurdity of it all, going after a huge black bear with a meat knife. Jews didn't own rifles.

Her father made her stay inside, huddling next to her mother, as he tiptoed out to where the sleeping bag the girls had shared lay open, the books and transistor radio, its antenna fully extended, resting alongside. Lena's heart beat rapidly as she saw the knife blade flash in the dark. When her father returned only minutes later, she could no longer contain her movements. She released herself from her mother's arms and ran to him as he shook his head in frustration.

"Pearl! Where's Pearl? It took her. The bear carried her into the woods, and you have to go back. Daddy, please, you have to find her!"

Her father remained silent, frozen in place, as her mother went to her, scooped her up, and held her tightly in her arms.

"It will be all right, bubala. I promise you we will find your Pearl."

"It will be all right," she repeated. But there were tears in her eyes.

Lena tried to slow her breaths as she melted into her mother's arms. It had been a long time since the child had found herself ensconced in her mother's embrace. Anya was a stoic woman, reluctant to show overt signs of affection, even to her only daughter. Lena now allowed her mother to soothe her, to put her to bed, to sit beside her until daylight crept into the sky, until she fell asleep.

When she woke in the morning, Lena was gripped anew by the fear that she would never see her best friend again. But a lump sat in her throat, preventing her from approaching her parents. There would be no more campouts that summer, and, two weeks later, her family, along with all their neighbors, packed up the clothes and whatever perishables were left and drove back to the city. As she climbed into the back seat of the station wagon, crammed in next to the tightly taped boxes and bulging suitcases, as she took one last look at the now-deserted graying bungalows filled with only the secrets held in cobwebs and a sense of withered anticipation, Lena realized that no one at all had answered her questions about her best friend. In fact, no one ever spoke of Pearl again.

~

The air was crisp as the sun scattered patches of light against the sidewalks. Lena was wearing her brand-new red-and-navy plaid pleated skirt with a white cotton man-tailored shirt, along with matching red knee-highs and new penny loafers as she walked the eight blocks to school. She was happy that it wasn't as brutally hot as it had been during the waning days of summer, when all the family had to keep them cool were two noisy standing fans, one spinning in the middle of the living room, the other in the corner of her parents' bedroom. She was glad, too, that the rain that had splattered against the windows at dawn, drenching the square of grass at the curb, had stayed away as well. And so even though she walked alone that first day of school, and even though she still missed her best friend, whose family had moved to another state shortly after their return from the Catskills, Lena's heart was light. She was determined that fifth grade would be a new start for her. She would study harder, try to improve her grades, especially when it came to math, talk to the person sitting in the row next to hers and not ignore them.

Lena merged with the stream of students all heading toward the school. Each boy's hair was neatly combed with a strict part at the side, the girls' ponytails were sprayed and sparkling, tied with a large red velvet bow or, as in Lena's case, their hair was meticulously braided and sat high atop their heads. The children's new shoes caught the light as they stepped right foot forward into the old brick building, where they were quickly directed to their classrooms, teachers leading the way. Lena was glad to be leaving the nervous chatter in the lobby of the school building, and especially happy to be out of hearing distance of the wailing kindergartners, whose screams as they were separated from their mothers brought back memories she would rather forget. She kept her eyes straight ahead. She soon found out that, like herself, and all the rest in the class, her teacher was new to the fifth grade, and to her surprise, it was a man. Her first "man" teacher ever. The notion made her feel a little afraid, but she tried not to show it.

But when he called the roll once the students were seated, Lena stumbled over her own last name, saying, "Sakloff—uh—Sokoloff"— her own name! But Mr. Kalish ignored the nervous error and said simply, "Lena! What a pretty name!" and went on to the next person. Lena's apprehensions disappeared, and that was the moment she decided she was going to like her new teacher.

During the first few months back at school, Lena had a peculiar feeling, as if she were playing the part of someone else, just like an actress. And if not an actress, she had the acute sense that she was masquerading as someone else. As long as she was in the role, she could be confident and glamorous. Just like Audrey Hepburn in *Breakfast at Tiffany's*.

What gave Lena this newfound confidence began with Mr. Kalish, to be sure, that first day when he saw her struggling at her desk with a problem in long division, and he calmly walked over to her as the others in the class worked silently.

"That's a tough one, isn't it, Lena?" he asked quietly, bending his lanky frame low so that he could view her paper. He smelled of Canoe, the same cologne her father used. Lena blinked away the tears of embarrassment that were in her eyes and nodded. Her voice had gone numb.

Mr. Kalish placed his index finger on the page in her workbook.

"See the first number? Five can't go into two, so you carry it over to the next digit, twenty-four. Five goes into twenty four times, then carry the four. Now five into forty-nine, that's nine. So your answer is forty-nine with a remainder of four. Do you see?"

She nodded again, but her eyes never left Mr. Kalish as he continued walking down her row, leaving a strong scent of Canoe in his wake. She knew then that this was different from the way she felt about all the lady teachers she'd had, who were nice enough but brusque and somewhat impatient. She actually *wanted* to please Mr. Kalish and determined to work a little harder in his class, study a little more. Lena didn't realize it then, but she had begun to have a crush on her fifth-grade teacher. That just added to her determination.

But it wasn't only Mr. Kalish who changed Lena's attitude about school, about life in general. Sometime in the week before school began, she had come to the realization that without her close friend, she was all alone, that she had no one by her side to help her if she stumbled over a line as she read out loud in class, no one to confess to when she liked a boy, to complain to when the snobby girls in the lunchroom ignored her, when neither of her parents showed up for back-to-school night. That was when Lena determined that she would be her own champion, her own best friend. She would assume an air of confidence, be the first to raise her hand when a question was asked, find a quiet girl, one like herself, and approach her in the playground at school. Sharing a Spalding, they would play "A, my name is Alice" together. Maybe she would even run for GO office, the school's general organization. Not the president, but a secretary for now. She would be so confident, so cool, that no one would even know she was faking.

By November, Lena had made a few friends. None was as special as the one she had before, but all were fun to be with. She had even been to their homes on a few occasions to do homework, browse through the teen magazines, or watch the afternoon soap operas on TV. Once, they had put together a scene from *West Side Story*, the new film that everyone was talking about. Each of the others wanted to take the part of Maria, but not Lena. She opted for Riff, the no-holds-barred leader of the Jets. One lazy Friday afternoon, as some of the younger kids played jacks in the street, as a few of the mothers were hurrying home with their Sabbath chickens, as the rumble of the subway cars could be heard from down below, the four friends twirled their skirts or, in Lena's case, swished her bell-bottoms, dancing and leaping in the streets, singing at the top of their lungs, "Tonight! Tonight won't be just any night!" It was the best time.

Sometimes when the friends gathered at Cindy's or Barbra's house, one of them would suggest going to Lena's apartment on Ocean Avenue. That was when Lena would shake her head sadly and say that her mother was sick with a head cold or someone was coming to wash the carpets. And while Lena would silently congratulate herself for being such a good actress, she knew that she was rapidly running out of excuses.

It wasn't as if her apartment was messy or in a bad neighborhood; it wasn't that at all. If she really thought about it when she was alone in bed at night with the bedroom door opened just a smidgen and the night-light in the hall illuminating the stuffed bear at the foot of the bed, she had to admit to herself that she was, in fact, ashamed. And while it hurt Lena to think so, she knew that Anya could never measure up to her friends' all-American perfectly dressed, friendly, and generous mothers. For one thing, Anya had never taken the time to learn how to speak English correctly, referring to a tuna casserole as a "cassera" and constantly addressing Lena's friend Barbra as "Barbury." She would have been absolutely mortified had any of her friends heard those faux pas.

Her mother didn't dress in the latest styles, scoop shirts or capri pants, and adorn her face with bright-red lipstick. Instead, when she wasn't working at the five-and-dime, as she did most mornings when Lena went off to school, Anya usually wore a plain checkered housedress and hurriedly would twist a rubber band around her unruly hair. If a clip were to come off her bra, she didn't rush out to buy a new one, but would sew the clip back on with thick thread. She didn't keep rollers in her hair at night so that she would have fluffy curls in the morning. She didn't even wear pearls. All those things her mother considered *nareshkeit*, nonsense. According to Lena's parents, as long as they all were healthy and had food in their bellies, and warm beds to sleep in at night, they were fine. Who needed anything else?

Before falling asleep, as Lena turned her face to the wall, she felt like the most ungrateful daughter in the world. She had been born with an understanding of her parents' trials, all the losses they had endured back in the Old Country. It was as if everything that had occurred before Lena's existence had been wiped away with one of the broad erasers Mr. Kalish kept in his room. While her parents told her endless stories of those days, Lena craved more details. But she knew enough to never want to press them for further information. To do so would be rubbing salt in the wound.

Without warning, tears filled the young girl's eyes, for she told herself that her parents were good, kind people. They never yelled at her and surely never lifted a hand against her, even though her daddy had pointed to his wide black leather belt on more than one occasion. Nor was she denied anything that she wanted: the new saddle shoes that were so popular among the kids at school, the Chatty Cathy doll, or the blond Barbie with the poufy hair Lena had coveted when she was younger. She tried to convince herself of all the reasons she should be proud to have such parents. And yet, as the moon came slowly through the slats of the venetian blinds, shedding light on the crumpled pillows, the moist stain of her tears, she just couldn't convince herself. Because Lena *was* ashamed. So very ashamed.

~

When Lena came home from school one rainy November afternoon, she was pleasantly surprised to see Anya sliding one of her sponge cakes into the oven. Placing her books on the kitchen counter, Lena could almost taste the sugary sweetness on her tongue. She walked over to her mother, put a hand on her shoulder and, because she was already half an inch taller than Anya, bent low to lean in.

"It's looking good, Mommy! But what's the special occasion? You haven't baked since Rosh Hashanah."

Anya smiled warmly and patted her daughter's hand. Lena was surprised to hear her respond in English, Lena's first language.

"The Thanksgiving is coming, just two weeks, so I freeze," she answered in broken English. The rain pelted against the kitchen window as Lena turned and retrieved a bottle of chocolate milk from the refrigerator.

"Don't spoil the appetite," Anya warned. She added, "Tonight we have flanken, some potato, and Mott's. Your daddy likes."

Lena made a face as she poured the chocolate beverage into a *Flintstones* jelly glass. Meat and potatoes, or chicken and potatoes, maybe fried fish, a bowl of chicken soup for the Sabbath, and of course a small dish of Mott's applesauce to top it all off. Maybe she could persuade her mother to open a can of purple plums instead. At least there would be sponge cake in a couple of weeks.

Josef was late coming home, so mother and daughter had to share dinner that evening as an angry rain-dappled wind banged against the windowpanes.

"Daddy has not even an umbrella," Anya lamented as she placed another piece of the flanken on Lena's plate. Her daughter ignored the remark and launched into a description of the report she had presented at school on the Reconstruction period. But when her mother responded with only a simple "That's nice," she abandoned the narrative, instead focusing on the meal.

"You like?" Anya asked as she continued eating, looking at Lena out of the corner of her eye.

"Mm-hmm . . . ," Lena muttered, dipping a stringy slice of meat into her small dish of applesauce. Sometimes she wondered why she even tried having a conversation with her mother. In their family of three, eating was a business to be focused on with every cell of one's brain. It was the business of staying alive. Everything else, just like her oral report, the one she had received an A on, was nareshkeit.

Later that evening, Daddy would come home drenched in a gray tweed suit, large drops of water falling off his black fedora. As Anya began warming his dinner on the stove, he reached into the pocket of his trousers to retrieve a large Hershey's bar, which was still cold and dry, and without a word, he handed it to his daughter.

"You had to stop for the candy in this weather?" Anya scolded, but nonetheless cast him a warm smile.

"Thanks, Daddy," Lena said, grasping the bar tightly, her one reward for enduring her mother's tasteless, uninspired dinner. She gave her father a quick peck on the cheek and watched as he removed his hat and, even before changing his clothes, sat down to his meal, which was always twice the amount that Anya and Lena ate. He was the man of the family, the breadwinner, after all.

As her mother poured herself a glass of Lipton tea, slicing a wedge of apple into it before sitting down opposite her husband, Lena knew it was her cue to leave the room. She knew also that there would be little conversation between her parents until her father had cleaned his plate, sometimes not till after he had seconds. Nothing pleased Anya more than watching her husband eat her cooking.

After Lena had changed into pajamas and brushed her teeth, she settled into bed with her latest Nancy Drew book, *The Bungalow Mystery*. Just a coincidence that the story took place at a bungalow colony, she told herself, as she checked the back page of the book, and the date on the card that was inserted in the envelope. She was the fifth person to borrow the book from the library, which meant that most of her friends hadn't read it yet. Lena had eight more days to complete the mystery.

As the rain subsided, she had finished the first two pages but found that she could no longer concentrate, as the sounds of her parents talking down the hall caught her attention. As usual, they conversed in Yiddish, throwing in a word or two in Polish.

Lena leaned over and shut off the light on her pink Cinderella lamp, a relic from when she was a toddler. But she couldn't sleep. Instead, her senses were heightened as she struggled to hear her parents' conversation. In her heart she knew that even if she could hear what they were saying, she would never truly understand them, just as they couldn't understand her school, her friends, anything that mattered.

~

The following Monday, instead of visiting one of her friends, Lena went straight home. She ran most of the way as she approached the fifth-floor apartment, thrust a hand down her white button-down shirt, and retrieved the single key dangling from a lanyard around her neck. The lock clicked open immediately, and she tiptoed in as if she were entering a stranger's apartment, not her own.

"Ma?"

The only response was the ticktock of the large Kit-Cat clock on the kitchen wall. Lena breathed a long sigh of relief before entering the bedroom. Her bed was still unmade, pajamas lying on the floor at the side. It wasn't as if she had expected to find her mother home, as Anya had informed her days earlier that she was needed to cover for someone who was having a dental procedure. She would be at work till seven, the one day the five-and-dime was open for late-night customers. And, Anya had emphasized, dinner was already in the fridge. All Lena had to do was warm up the chicken soup and meatballs once her father walked in the door.

Lena felt a surge of excitement as she pulled off her shirt and pleated skirt, rolled down her socks, and grabbed her large gray sweat-shirt with the big green letters JETS across the front. She found a pair of stovepipe jeans in the bottom drawer and, still in bare feet, trotted back into the kitchen. She didn't stop to think about the first time she had taken matters in hand, the day Anya had scolded her for using the oven without permission, for messing up the kitchen counter with the flour she'd poured for her chocolate chip cookies. She had stayed in bed, crying silently for hours after that. And the cookies hadn't turned out very good anyway.

She washed her hands vigorously in the kitchen sink, then moved toward the pantry, where the ingredients were waiting for her on a shelf all the way in the back. It was an easy reach for the mixing bowl and metal loaf pan—no need for the step stool her parents kept in the coat closet. When she had arranged the flour, baking powder, salt, raisins, honey, and oil on the counter, she opened the refrigerator door and picked out two white eggs, which she added to the other items. She set the oven to 350 degrees and, with a broad smile on her face, Lena set to work.

After she had placed the cake in the oven, Lena replaced what was left of the dry ingredients in the pantry. Afterward, she scrubbed the large mixing spoon and bowl with a Brillo pad, dried everything with the red terry cloth towel that hung from the stove handle, and returned the utensils back into place. And then she waited.

It wasn't easy, though. She brought in her math workbook and made a vain attempt to work on the problems for homework. But she simply couldn't concentrate, listening to the steady hum of the oven as it did its work, imagining the sweet scents that would soon sneak into her nasal passages. She closed the book and began to pace. The linoleum felt cold beneath the soles of her feet, and she found herself finally giving in to her own curiosity. Lena's heart sank as she felt a blast of hot air when she opened the oven door. The mixture looked like a lump of dough, just as it had when she had placed it there. She peered up at the Kit-Cat clock on the wall, its tail swishing rhythmically back and forth, and was relieved to note that only ten minutes had passed. She continued pacing. It was only after a few minutes that she began to regret what she had done. Mama had never encouraged her baking, told her that she was too young for that, that using the oven was too dangerous, and that she should concentrate on school instead. She didn't even like it when Lena watched her as she stirred the batter or, worse, asked to taste one of her unbaked chocolate chip cookies. Lena wasn't sure why her mama was so adamant, and guessed that sharing this activity brought back sad memories from the Old Country. Or maybe she just didn't think Lena was good enough. Nevertheless, she was determined to prove her wrong.

Sometimes Lena thought she heard footsteps, the turning of the lock at the front door, but after holding her breath for a few seconds, she realized it was only her imagination. It would be hours before Mommy returned home.

Finally, like the breath of an angel, a glorious scent began to fill the air. She ran to the oven and peered inside. The mass had begun to swell and had assumed a golden-bronze tint. Little black raisins that resembled eyes peeked out at her. It wouldn't be long before she would have her first delicious honey cake. Just as good as her mommy used to bake before she was born—maybe better.

Anya was late. By the time she returned, both Lena and Josef had finished their dinner of leftover chicken soup and meatballs. Lena had even taken the liberty of opening a new can of purple plums for dessert. But throughout the meal, her eye kept wandering over to the counter where the tin pan filled with the sticky honey cake was left cooling on a kitchen towel. Josef had noticed it as soon as he had walked in the door. He had raised one inquisitive eyebrow.

"What's this, Mommy baking again?"

"No, Daddy. That was me. I did that all myself," she said, trying not to puff out her chest too much.

"That so?" he said, hanging up his dry raincoat, the one he forgot to bring on that rainy day a week earlier.

Josef winked at his daughter, then hesitated before sitting down at the table.

"And what's Mommy going to say to that?"

Lena felt her heart skip a beat. What if her mother didn't like the fact that Lena had presumptuously used the ingredients, taken out the pots and pans, turned on the oven? But before she could respond, her father's voice invaded her thoughts.

"Look at you," he gushed. "You're getting to be quite the big girl. Setting dinner for your father. And, well, I cannot wait to taste that delicious-looking honey cake."

But it was already too late for Lena to absorb her father's words. He had planted the seed of doubt, and there was no way to redeem it.

By the time Anya walked in the door, Josef was already nestled in the familiar leather recliner, mouthing the words of an article, practicing his English as he read about the building of the Berlin Wall. But Lena remained fixed in the metal chair in the kitchen, her barely eaten meatballs still on the plate as she stared at the evil loaf of honey cake. She was trying to decide whether she should hide it in one of the drawers in her dresser or even wrap it up tightly in aluminum foil and quickly push it into the back of the small freezer when Anya, sniffing the air, set her eyes on the pan.

"I thought I smelled my honey cake," she said, walking over to the loaf and giving it a poke with her finger, then suddenly turning toward her daughter.

"Lena, was this you? You did this?"

Lena felt a heat rise throughout her face. Unable to speak, all she could do was nod. She watched as her mother poked the loaf with her index finger and picked off one of the raisin eyes before looking over at Lena again.

"You make this?" she repeated.

"Yes, Ma, I made the honey cake."

"How you know to make?"

Lena felt as if she were being grilled like one of those criminals she had seen on a police show she watched on TV.

"How you know to make such a cake?"

Lena shrugged, her gaze unwavering.

"From you. I learned how to bake by watching you."

An air of confusion floated across Anya's face, and it seemed as if she had removed a mask as she gave a little shudder, as if she were remembering something. She took off her trench coat and went into the living room to join Josef. Before long, Lena heard the two speaking their mixture of Yiddish and Polish in hushed tones. She remained immobile in her seat, ignoring the unwashed dishes, even the honey cake she had worked so hard on, which had looked so festive only a couple of hours earlier, and now appeared somewhat sad and pathetic. She thought of going into the living room, interrupting their conversation. But, instead, she got up, brushed off the thin coating of flour dust that still clung to her hands, and walked over to the counter where the cake sagged in the pan, eyes still looking up at her. No longer needing the towel, she picked up the metal pan with her bare hand. Then, standing over the garbage pail in the corner of the kitchen, Lena shook the tin and watched as the sides of the cake slowly separated from the metal and broke into pieces as it descended to the bottom.

~

Lena let the water run until it was just hot enough. Then she delicately placed her right foot into the tub, followed by the left, before lowering her body into a sitting position. Eventually she could feel her flesh turning pink, so warm, as if she herself had been gently inserted into an oven. She raised one finger and watched as one of the hundred white bubbles that surrounded her popped softly. And when she breathed in their dreamy scent of lavender, Lena wondered whether this was what it felt like to be in heaven.

She leaned back, wishing she had her own pillow against her shoulders. Each time she placed her palm against the delicate bubbles, they would burst, forming rivulets that drifted lazily toward the edge. She tried to make her mind go blank, all her thoughts sailing away like the little streams that caressed her skin, so calm, so peaceful. And yet something she couldn't exactly put a name on held her back. She knew she shouldn't have such concerns, that she was too young, too innocent, to be besieged by problems. Whenever she would worry about a math exam or that she would be late for school, Mommy would turn to her with a sour face.

"Lena, you worry. You are too young for this. Your daddy and I have worry, have always had worry. But you, Lena, you are the luckiest girl in the world."

Lena closed her eyes, tried to take in the truth of her mother's words. She was only ten; she had her whole life ahead of her. Full of possibilities. She lifted one hand out of the water and examined the lines in the palm. She realized then that a part of her wanted to remain, to stay in the bath forever and never leave. Because if she stayed, she could be whatever she wanted—a famous singer on the stage, the first woman in space, or a baker with her very own shop. Lena closed her eyes and listened.

She was grateful that she could no longer hear her parents' voices down the hall, only the drip of the leaky faucet. And again she wished she could stay in the safety of the bath, but already the heat vapors in the air had begun to vanish as the water cooled. But when she opened her eyes, she knew she couldn't stay, that she would have to leave the tub, the room, and go back to her hopeless life. A life where she wasn't the luckiest girl, only a girl with a dead sister who would always come first.

10

Lena thought she had her life all planned out. Her guidance counselor had suggested she might be a good candidate for a scholarship to Cornell, but not wanting to travel too far from home, she turned it down and was now in her second year at Brooklyn College. For Lena, leaving her parents' home on Ocean Avenue to go off to a school in Upstate New York seemed as absurd as flying to the moon. Besides, Brooklyn College was an excellent school—and much safer.

Deciding on her major proved to be trickier. Somewhere in her head floated the idea that she would become a lawyer. It wasn't that she had any particular interest in law, but devoting her life to the pursuit of social justice seemed like a noble calling. A career as a lawyer would mean that she could major in almost any subject in the humanities, and, after completing the required core courses, she would never have to take another algebra or geology class again. Of course, her true passion, the thing she wanted to spend her days doing, was baking. Since the honey cake fiasco years earlier, Lena had continued to keep a watchful eye on her mother whenever she baked her rugelach for the Jewish New Year or the hamantaschen when Purim came around. Between those occasions, Lena would make versions of her own baked goods, even creating a few original recipes like a chocolate layer cake with strawberries or peanut butter nougats. Sometimes, if the finished product was good enough, she would share it with her friends and even her parents. If, however, the dish lacked the right amount of flavoring or was oversalted, before anyone could see it, she would secretly toss it into the garbage with all the other failures. For their part, Anya and Josef largely ignored her efforts, deeming some of her creations "very good," holding back their praise as they cautioned her to pursue a more solid, profitable career. And even though Lena wished that baking could possibly become a full-time career, and even though when she was a girl, she had coveted the idea of owning a bakery just as her parents had prior to the war, she knew the real reason they discouraged her. There were too many memories. Memories of another daughter who had been a baker, possibly the best baker in the world. As a result, for Lena, baking remained a hobby.

As far as her social life was concerned, Lena had that planned out too. She would find a nice Jewish boy at one of the dances for singles they ran at the synagogue, marry him when she completed college, and, after pursuing that nebulous career, settle down in a suburb and begin a family. But she knew that wouldn't happen for many, many years. For now, though, she would have to figure out just how to attract a decent boy when one had hair the color of a dead mouse, had ghostly white skin, and was two inches short of being six feet tall. That was just the way Lena saw it.

Still, it was nice to have a plan for life. And *that* Lena was feeling more independent, more confident, and had a close group of friends— and yet she once did have a best friend, someone who was more than a friend, really. She thought about Pearl when she was lying in bed reading *Jane Eyre* for the first time and wanted to share how much she cried at the ending, when Jane could finally be with her Rochester. Or how nervous she felt when she attended her first dance at the neighborhood *shul*, or how thrilled she was when she spied a rabbit munching on a leaf on the quad. She wanted to share all these things—not with a classmate she studied with for tests in Spanish or a pen pal in England whom she had never even seen but a true best friend. Lena had resigned herself to never seeing Pearl again, for, after that awful day, her parents informed her that they were never returning to the Catskills. It was useless to ask why, useless to ask why Pearl and her family had not returned to Brooklyn, useless to ask if she was even still alive. Instead, she had no choice but to remain with the memories. And the hope that someday Pearl might return.

∼

She knew that plans were a wonderful thing to have. They were the fuel for our engines that kept us moving toward the goal. Plans inspired us to work hard and to keep going despite the obstacles that came in our path. Plans inspired us to keep dreaming, to make more plans.

And so it was with Lena, who woke up each morning with a smile as wide as the sun, with a sense of determination that each new day was bringing her a step closer to realizing her plans and, not inconsequentially, the dreams of her parents. Sometimes, though, the most ambitious plans could be obstructed, twisted, changed entirely, or tossed aside.

So, one early gray November morning when the skies threatened rain, as she boarded a bus for her 8:00 a.m. class in philosophy, Lena had only an inkling that things for her were bound to get better, although she didn't know quite how. She didn't yet know that this day would change all her plans for college, for marriage, for her future. Because that was the day she met Luke.

11

The black sky slowly became infused with purple before a mellow daylight spread across the darkened bedroom. But unlike all the other days when she had to get up early, plod into the bathroom, then make a half-hearted attempt to find the clothes she had laid out the night before, Lena's heart was light with anticipation. She wasn't exactly sure why as she applied shiny black eyeliner and two dabs of rose pink to her cheeks. Maybe it was because she was wearing the new royal-blue ski jacket she had purchased for the change of seasons from the money she had earned from her job at the day camp last summer. Or maybe it was the fact that Professor Robison, a hulk of a man with blond hair who resembled Paul Bunyan, with a hearty voice that could shake the desks in the room, no longer intimidated her. Not since she began speaking up in class and had earned a sparkling A on the last essay she handed in. Maybe it was a combination of those things. Or maybe it was something else.

After pouring herself a glass of orange juice and zipping up the new jacket, Lena grabbed her book bag and quietly shut the apartment door, careful not to wake her parents. She blinked a few times, trying to adjust to the new hard contact lenses, which gave her a more sophisticated look, far better than the tortoiseshell glasses she had begun to wear in junior high. Now as she slipped outside, she felt something akin to happiness, like a spark in the air signaling imminent snow. Lena puzzled over her reaction as she walked the blocks briskly toward the bus stop. Usually she hated the snow, especially the kind that slicked the sidewalks, turning them into treacherous rinks of ice. She had fallen at least once each winter season and, so far, she had been lucky, avoiding breaking a leg or worse. Always after a snowfall, there were the repugnant mounds at every curb, streaked with mud and dirt that eventually slithered down the metal sewers in streams of ugly water. But today, she thought, wouldn't it be delightful if the sky opened to a glorious avalanche of snowflakes? Wouldn't that be just grand? The bus stopped with a grunt, and she stepped up gingerly.

He didn't get on the bus until the third stop. When he slid into the seat next to her, Lena constricted her muscles so that she took up as little space as possible next to the stranger. She continued to look out the window.

"Early class?"

She lifted her eyes to meet his. His eyes were dark, the darkest she had ever seen this close. The rest of his long face was hidden by an equally dark scraggly beard. She quickly sized up his body, which was thin, almost skeletal. He wore a plaid button-down blue shirt open at the neck, a few curly hairs peeking out. And despite the season, he wore sandals that exposed long white toes. When he put his hands together, a colorful rope bracelet emerged from the cuff.

"Y-yes," she answered tentatively. "You too?"

"Shit, yeah. It's sociology, whatever that is. To tell you the truth, I forget to go half the time. I only registered at school because it was a hell of a lot better than getting my head blown off in 'Nam."

"I see," she said, lowering her face as she looked up at the dark eyes. This wasn't the usual type of person she engaged with.

"What's your deal?"

"Excuse me?"

"What's your deal? Why are you going to Brooklyn College? I know it's not to get out of the draft."

Lena laughed, despite herself. She met his eyes fully now.

"I'm not really sure either. But I guess I didn't have much of a choice. It's what my parents want."

At this, he let out such a guffaw that she was momentarily startled.

"And I suppose you live with Mommy and Daddy too?"

Lena pursed her lips, moved closer to the window. Why was she even talking to this weirdo?

"Aw, come on," he said, poking her in the arm with his elbow. "I'm just kidding. It's kind of nice you're still living with them. I got thrown out of my old man's place."

Lena tried not to look surprised, hoping that the stranger hadn't observed her eyebrows rise just a little bit. Truly she could never imagine doing something so awful that it would warrant being thrown out of her parents' home. She said nothing. But it wasn't long before she snapped back to attention. He continued talking. He explained that he was thinking of majoring in math, with the ambiguous intention of becoming an accountant. When he caught her making a face at the confession, his mouth turned up at the corners.

"Not your favorite subject, eh?"

She just shook her head, the words sticking in her throat. *He has a nice smile,* she thought.

"Well, I'm not saying it's my favorite either. It's just something that's always come easy to me. I can always figure out the numbers in my head, without paper and pencil. I guess that's my only talent." He laughed at himself, as she tried to discern what was behind those green eyes. It only made her feel a little uncomfortable. *He looks like a taller version of Davy Jones of the Monkees,* she mused.

He went on talking about himself, telling her that he lived on Avenue M with a couple of friends and had a part-time job pumping gas at the local Sunoco blocks away off Nostrand Avenue. It was boring but good money, enough to get him through on the tuition, rent, and some pizza during the week. He went on with the details of his life, telling her that he was a pacifist at heart, but not so devoted that he would take part in protests. He had two younger brothers at home, neither of whom had ever been thrown out of the house, but who knows what might happen in the future? His dad, who worked for a paper company in the city, was Jewish (in name only), and his mom, who was a housewife, was a Catholic (in name only). They fought a lot, but not all the time. He hadn't asked Lena anything about her own life, which she didn't mind at all, for she still wasn't sure the lump in her throat had dissolved.

She didn't have to think about it much, for soon the tires of the packed bus had slowed to her stop, and the students with early-morning classes had begun to exit, pushing through the aisles. The boy, suddenly aware of where he was, abruptly stopped talking, got up, and waited for her to stand up and move past him. Her legs wobbled as she descended the two broad steps. They walked the three blocks toward the college together. This time he was silent as the pregnant clouds merged, releasing silvery flakes that came to rest on the shoulders of her royal-blue ski coat and the tan sweat jacket that was open across his chest.

Just as they reached the tall gate at the entrance, he stopped, suddenly remembering something.

"Hey, what's your name, anyway?"

She startled.

"Oh, Lena. I'm Lena."

"Okay, Lena, so how about we get together sometime? Did I tell you my name? I'm such an idiot! Luke." As he spoke, he thrust a hand into his pocket and produced a black ballpoint, which he extended to her.

"You can write your number right there," he added, flashing the palm of his right hand.

Lena hesitated for a moment before grasping the slim pen. She glanced at his face, the scraggly black beard hiding all but his ever-changing eyes, then looked down at the toes that peeked out from the out-of-season scuffed sandals. She had a sense that he had been to places she had never seen, done things she had never done. He looked at her with those dreamy eyes as if she were the most interesting person in the world, the only person in the world. She found him handsome, alluring, but mostly she liked the way his mouth curled only a bit in the corner, suggesting a hidden secret, something shared between only the two of them.

She began writing her phone number, then paused as she wondered if she should give him her real number or a phony one. He wasn't the typical type of boy she would talk to at the local synagogue dances. This stranger was different, just dangerous enough to be attractive. But then she realized that he was no longer a stranger. He was Luke. Before she could think any more, she quickly jotted down her real number.

12

Floating. *Anything is possible,* Lena thought as she let her head fall back into the soapy water. She watched as the strands of hair splayed out on the surface like a magical fan. If only . . . if only she could stay here forever in the liquid warmth of its embrace. If only she were ten again, at an age when there were no choices, when life was simple and all her activities, her schedule, her very existence was dictated by her parents. But now that she was nineteen, things had become complicated. All her plans, which had appeared like a newly painted road, so clear, so distinct only months ago, were now muddied by indecision. Lena no longer knew what she wanted anymore, and when she caught her reflection in the lavender-scented bubbles, she could barely recognize herself.

She plunged her head farther into the bath so that now she was completely submerged, listening only to the soft swoosh of the water as it encircled her. If only she could stay here in the womb of the bath, where she didn't have to think about the sociology paper she had barely begun to write and that was due on Monday. Where she didn't have to think about Luke or her virginity, which wasn't lost yet but soon would be. Where she didn't have to think about the disappointment she was to her survivor parents. If only she could stay here forever . . . if only. It seemed like her entire life in the past few months was filled with "if onlys."

But Lena knew that she could not remain breathing, inhaling her desires, in the tub forever. In a few minutes, she would step out and watch as the wetness slipped off her skin, soaking the fluffy white rug beneath her feet. She would wrap herself in the jumbo towel, dry off the last of the moisture, and dress quickly in stovepipe jeans and the navy-blue Huk-A-Poo shirt with little sailboats, go downstairs, where her parents were eating lunch. Where she would tell them that she was leaving to meet a friend at the Grand Army Plaza library to work on a research paper for English class. She knew they would barely look up from their tuna salad sandwiches when she spoke. And before she left, her father would call out "Zei gesund!"—a customary admonition to be healthy, stay safe. But this time, as she closed the door behind her, Lena wasn't so sure that she would abide by the warning.

~

Luke was waiting in front of the Loew's Kings Theater on Flatbush Avenue when she arrived. In the three months since she had met him on the bus that Monday morning in November, the two had seen each other each Saturday for a hamburger lunch at Wolfie's near the college or a matinee at the movie theater for a viewing of the latest film release. Today it was *Love Story*, a highly touted film with the actors Ryan O'Neal and Ali MacGraw. Lena was particularly eager to see the movie, as she had recently read the bestseller by Erich Segal. But what she was most looking forward to was sitting next to Luke as he wound his arm around her, as he planted small kisses behind her ear, as he complimented her on the scent of her Giorgio perfume, the soft waves in her hair. And try as she did to pay attention to the action on the large screen in front of them, it was becoming increasingly difficult, even if it was a popular film like *Love Story*.

He wiped the tears from the corners of her eyes as they exited the movie theater.

"Pretty sad story," he said, pulling her close as they walked against the wind. She nodded.

"Nearly as good as the book," she observed, "but most films usually don't live up to the standards of a novel, don't you think?"

Luke murmured something that sounded like an assent. He steered her around the corner and toward the apartment on Avenue M. It wasn't the first time she would visit the second-floor walk-up, with its dull yellow kitchen and refrigerator empty, save for some beer cans and a stale container of milk for morning cereal. Luke's room was the one with the waterbed, which he purchased with savings, while his roommates, who were out that day with their own plans, shared a larger bedroom down the hall. She had been on the bed once before, and only out of curiosity. When she lay on it, though, it didn't remind her at all of the soothing feel of her warm bath at home. Rather, it was more like bobbing on a raft in the middle of an ocean. A raft that she might fall from at any moment.

She felt a quiver of excitement as she usually did when walking into the small living room with its funky patchwork-green-and-brown-quilt couch and brown-velvet tub chair that swiveled 360 degrees. A large RCA TV sat precariously on a flimsy metal stand, and in the center of it all was a round wooden table with a couple of half-filled plastic glasses on the surface that, if truth be told, needed some dusting.

Luke retrieved a can of Tab from the fridge. It was one of the appliances in the galley kitchen, which boasted a sink with a ring of an undefinable substance around it, one oil-splattered stove, and a counter the size of a small bath mat. In other words, Lena concluded, it had all the features of a typical bachelor pad.

Luke pushed the empty plastic cups aside and plopped down next to her. Lena took the cup from his hand and felt the bubbles tickle her nose as she took a long, slow sip of the soda. Then, for no apparent reason, he stared at her, and in that moment took in all of her—her face, her breasts, her hips. A quiver went up her spine. No one had ever looked at her in quite the same way that Luke did, with a desire that seemed all-consuming. Surely not the boys she had dated in high school, with neat haircuts, boys who would take her out bowling or for Chinese food on Nostrand Avenue on weekends. Luke, though, was different, more mature, and possessed an aura of worldliness that made her think he could handle any crisis that might come up. He made her feel protected, and she felt excited just to be in his orbit. Lena knew that he didn't have any other girlfriends, and he never told her about any past relationships, so she counted herself lucky. He was the only one in her life who had ever made her feel like she came first, and she liked the feeling.

"Comfortable, Lena?" he asked, getting closer as he nuzzled against her neck. She nodded, loving the way he said her name, putting the emphasis on the *e*. She took another slow sip, this time longer than the last. He walked over to the TV, and soon an old episode of *I Love Lucy* filled the screen. Lena closed her eyes for only a second, trying to squelch a sigh of relief. She had no need to worry, at least not today.

Only a few of her friends, and not the particularly close ones, had confessed to losing their virginity, reasoning they were practically engaged anyway. She had listened to their confessions with a slight shake of the head and a smile, just to show that she understood, that it was all quite natural, expected even. But the truth was, she didn't understand. How could she relent when she had been told all her life that girls like her, nice Jewish girls, waited to do the thing only after a shiny gold band was firmly placed on their finger? But that was before she met Luke. Before her heart quivered when he would lock eyes with hers, before she felt a tingle in places that she couldn't dare mention. She wasn't one of those girls, but soon she would be. Not today, though. Not on a bright Saturday afternoon when they had just seen a movie about a girl who dies too soon, not when the two were seated on a patchwork sofa drinking cans of Tab and laughing over the antics of Lucy. Not when the sun was cooling in the sky and within the hour would be swallowed by the night. Not today. Not now.

But there would come a day—or maybe a Saturday evening—when she would casually inform her parents that she was headed for a dance with her friend Wendy, at whose house she planned to spend the night. An easy fib, especially when she had the support of a trustworthy friend. And that evening, when she and Luke were together on the ugly patch-work sofa, as he offered her a blunt (which she would again decline) and some Ripple straight out of the bottle (which she would accept), she would let him kiss her deeply in a way he had never done before, touch her beneath her blouse this time. And then she would open herself as his fingers explored beneath her Levi's. She would congratulate herself for putting on the new black lace bra that morning, the bikini underwear. She would let him lift her up as he walked into the bedroom, just like a groom carries his bride on their wedding day. And this time, when she eased into the big round waterbed, it wouldn't feel like a raft at all.

But that day as dusk spread across the sky, he led her only to the door of the second-floor apartment, kissed her once, and said he would call. The lock clicked softly as she left. As Lena walked the long blocks stretching toward home, where her parents waited for her, the destination seemed farther now that she was by herself, as she tasted the mint of his peppermint Life Savers, still on her lips and tongue. She was no longer thinking about what it would be like to be with Luke. She could think only about her parents. And what they would say when they found out.

~

Lena stood in line, waiting for her turn with the clerk at the registrar's office. The papers in her hand had all been filled out and now felt as if they were soaked in oil. She held them so tightly that the skin on her thumb and forefinger had begun to turn white. The clerk, a student like herself, with long blond hair and a splash of bright pink pasted to her lips, reviewed the papers as Lena waited impatiently, trying to suspend her mind. Even now that all the decisions had been made, now that it was all in writing, Lena felt a sense of shame wash over her. She turned her head, pretending to survey the students outside as they ran past the long, narrow window, hurrying to their next class. She didn't want to look at the blond girl. She didn't want to be judged.

"You're all set," the girl said, the pink lips curving into a smile as she handed a stamped form to Lena.

"Thanks," she mumbled, and turned quickly toward the exit. The five-minute walk back to the giant gates of the campus, the ones that had looked so immense and foreboding only three years ago, now appeared endless. As she moved past the gates out into the street, it seemed as if her old life had fallen away and she had entered a new phase, a new life, if she really considered it. She joined the crowd of students mingled with professors, staff, then sanitation workers, the cops at every corner, children whose hands were securely encased in their mothers' as they headed home for lunch. It was too beautiful a day, with a round sun riding high in the sky and a wisp of lilac in the air, to get on another bus. And so she decided to walk all the way back to the apartment, hoping that the stroll would clear her head, lighten her spirit, as she tried to convince herself that she really did have what she had always wanted.

Her parents' reaction had stunned her. She had delayed telling them, though, fearing the worst. Like most other survivors, they were determined that their children would have a better life than they had. That was the reason most came to America—to establish new roots, make money, and provide their children with a college education that would open doors of opportunity in this new land. And in that way, all their suffering would be redeemed. But Lena felt certain that when they realized that their daughter was not the agent of their dreams, would not be the answer to the prayers they'd had as her father's arm had shriveled to sticks and her mother had swallowed more tears than food in the concentration camps, they would have no choice but to disown her. Instead of the angel that had come to redeem their tragic lives, she was now no better than their captors, slamming the iron door of the gas chamber as they struggled for breath.

But when she told them, everything coming out in a rush of words, that she and Luke were a couple most assuredly headed for marriage (although he had brought up the subject only once), that she would leave college, go back at a later date, maybe to work, but mostly to figure things out, their reaction was surprising. Instead of hurling harsh accusations at her, instead of her mother blinded by a mask of tears as she ran at Lena with hands shaped like claws, instead of her father shouting so loudly it would bring the roof down on their heads, the response was quite the opposite. It was, she soon realized, one of quiet resignation—not at all what she had expected.

Anya had asked her to repeat all that she said several times, perhaps because with her faulty English, she couldn't quite comprehend what her only daughter was telling her. But the real reason, more likely, was that she needed to hear it more than once so the words sank in. Lena had a boyfriend, which was good; it was their hope as they had raised her all those years, that someday their daughter could build a family of her own. But the boy was only half-Jewish, and not at all if one considers that in the Jewish faith only children born to a Jewish mother were looked upon as Jews themselves. What was more, the boy had no prospects, just a dim hope that he could be an accountant or perhaps a math teacher one day. Worse yet, he was no longer living under his parents' roof and had no one to lean on for support. Perhaps his intentions were to look to them for money, a handout. Who knew?

Despite being prepared with emotional armor to confront their reactions, Lena again found herself confused and vulnerable as her mother tightened her cheeks to hold back the tears and her father turned his back to her as he sulked quietly before the kitchen window, the sounds of children at play filtering up past the building's brick facade, taunting as it weaved through the rungs of the metal fire escape.

Finally, after what seemed like hours but was only minutes, and after inquiring about his address and phone number just in case, her parents gave their answer. Anya's face relaxed as her eyes, brimming with an ocean of tears, stared at her daughter as, simultaneously, Josef turned toward her, his own eyes warm, accepting as he chose his words.

"It is not what we had dreamed for you, my Lena, I admit this. But—"

"But if you are happy, then—" Anya hesitated as she lifted her head toward her husband. The children's chatter in the streets reached a new crescendo as Josef finished the sentence.

"Then it is what we want too," he added in a lower tone, as if to convince himself of the words. "We want only your happiness."

Lena is three years old. There is no clatter of rain that night, no blast of thunder threatening against the walls. Instead, there is only the moon, a full white moon, smiling down on a night when the birds have timidly begun to cast their melody to the sky and where the fears of sleeping children have now settled back into the dark earth where they belong. And yet here she is again, tiptoeing ever so lightly into her parents' bedroom, hoisting herself upon the mattress—and finding the smooth skin of her mother's arm, she nestles into the space just beneath. The mother's eye flickers briefly and does not betray whether she is compassionate or feels irritated at the intrusion. She only moves her body slightly to make enough room for the child, and neither hugs her tightly nor does she utter a soothing word as the father sleeps soundly next to her. The child knows only that when she awakens in the morning, she is back in her own bed, snuggled tightly beneath a red flannel blanket.

Lena felt like that little girl as she watched her parents wordlessly leave the kitchen and walk into their bedroom to have a serious discussion in Polish, no doubt, about their daughter's circumstances. She stood looking at the old, chipped radiator that her mother had leaned against only minutes ago. Lena remained like a warrior who came with weapons, dressed for battle, only to find that the enemy had left the field.

In her head, Lena replayed the monologue she had rehearsed and rehearsed again before the meeting with her parents. She had told them all, well, perhaps not everything, not the part about her seeing a doctor for birth control pills, or that it was Luke who had convinced her to drop out of college, which he saw as pointless. She had failed her sociology class in the last semester, a result that would have been earth-shattering in the years before she'd met Luke. And yet the earth hadn't fallen apart, and the more she thought about it, the more Lena was resolved to pursue those things she really wanted. Graduating from college and law school would take years. In fact, at that moment, she wasn't at all sure what it was she wanted. Except for Luke, of course.

Yet as she stood in her parents' kitchen, the sounds from below finally silenced, Lena felt a cyclone of questions whirl within her brain. Why had they done it? Giving and not giving their love all at once? And again, she was that little girl, welcomed but not embraced in her parents' bed. And awakening confused in the morning.

All Lena knew for a certainty as she stood in front of the cool white radiator was that she could no longer blame them. For that, she had only herself.

~

Just as she reached the door to Luke's apartment, even as she grasped the key that he had presented to her several months earlier, Lena had a sudden change of heart. She felt the weight of the key in her hand, dropped it into her pocket, and rushed outdoors. Lena stood under the small awning for several minutes, sucking in the air, letting it fill her lungs. But nothing seemed to help the feeling that she was choking, not on anything she had eaten, but on her own thoughts, the fears that were converging, taking up all the space in her brain, leaving her befuddled and frightened. Was this a panic attack?

She briefly considered going home as the tears, of their own volition, began to stream from her eyes. The safety of home and her childhood seemed appealing at that moment. But she knew that just as she couldn't let Luke, who might not understand, see her that way, she most assuredly could not go home, bewildered and defeated.

Instead of sorting things out in her brain, the things that had seemed so sensible, so reasoned when she had set out that day, now seemed rushed and stupid. All that was left were questions. Why, at Luke's suggestion, had she pursued a job working for a local tax lawyer just to "test the waters"? Why was it enough for her to abandon her own education so quickly? Why had she given herself to Luke, this stranger, so easily? Why had she stood up to her parents the way she had, risked hurting them again? Why did it seem as if her brain was permanently incapacitated whenever she was in Luke's presence? Why had she risked everything?

It wasn't until she saw Luke's elderly landlady pulling along a cart filled with groceries, a concerned expression on her small, wrinkled face, that Lena realized where she was. Just as the woman was about to speak, her eyes exploring Lena's face empathetically, Lena quickly brushed past her, too ashamed for an encounter. She let her legs lead her forward as she touched her cheek, felt its heat, the moisture of her tears. After walking several blocks, she now realized that she was far from the apartment, but also nowhere near her own home on Ocean Avenue. She slowed her steps and was soon relieved to find herself standing in front of a familiar place. A place where she had spent several years of her childhood, especially as a young student. The local library, except for the new posters and Easter decor on its facade, looked the same as she remembered it.

As she stood outside deciding whether to enter the building, Lena watched as a few retirees left in a group still chatting excitedly about their book club discussion, and the young mothers bent toward their preschoolers, who toted too-large books, as they exited. It wasn't until she had decided to turn, go back to the apartment, that she saw her. She was wearing a short denim skirt and matching shirt. Her pale-blond hair bouncing against her shoulders as she hurried out the doors of the library. Lena blinked, unsure at first. But when she opened her eyes, it was too late. It had been ten years, and now, once again, Pearl was gone.

13

Chocolate raisin babka. Hamantaschen pockets for Purim, oozing gooey apricot. Lemony sponge cake that melts on the tongue. Rugelach and mandelbrot and chocolate coconut macaroons. White cake with fresh apple in each morsel. All surrounded by a crown of marzipan rainbow cookies flashing yellow, red, and green.

These were the dreams Lena remembered as she wiped the crust from the corners of her eyes. But as she awakened, she was surprised to see not an array of aromatic delights, but her mother, seated next to her on the edge of the bed, a worried expression plastered to her face.

"You are awake."

Lena looked around and reached for her glasses on the night table, trying to get a better picture of her surroundings. She was not quite sure she was the one being addressed. But the two were alone in the room, *her* bedroom, with the vaporizer on her dresser saturating the air—not with a sugary scent, but the noxious odor of Vicks.

"How do you feel?"

The voice came from far away, but since there was no one else in the room, Lena guessed the question must be coming from her mother. She opened her mouth, but no sound came out. The voice continued.

"Your daddy and me, we were so afraid. *Oy, mein Gott!* We lost almost our minds!"

Lena stared into her mother's face. Yes, it was she. And yet the woman who sat placing a cool hand on Lena's forehead now was almost unrecognizable as the mother she knew. A sudden wave of exhaustion swept over Lena, like a cold wind. She desperately wanted to close her eyes, to go back to the place where luscious desserts sat primly on fancy platters, all waiting for her touch. Nonetheless, she opened her eyes wider in the hope that her ability to listen would return, and with it, understanding.

This mother did not seem like the mother she knew at all, with her puffy eyes, tear-streaked face; even the voice carried a note of hysterics.

"You are better, right? *Oy*, Lena, you were sleeping for so long. But the sleep was good, no? Better for your body, so sick you were, so scared Daddy and me were. But all is okay now, no?" The eyes pleading.

"Y-yes, I'm fine."

Lena didn't know if the words had emerged from her lips until she saw a thin smile come to her mother's face. Anya moved to embrace her daughter but hesitated, afraid to hold her too closely, as if she might break. Lena just wanted to go back to sleep.

Anya shut her eyes briefly as she took a deep breath, hoping to be cleansed of some mysterious terror.

"Your daddy, he goes to get more medicine."

She glanced at the small clock on Lena's nightstand, but not long enough to absorb the time.

"He is coming back soon."

Lena reached out instinctively to pat her mother's hand. Had it really been so bad? Still, she hadn't a clue what had happened to make her mother so distraught. Whatever it was, it was clearly her fault. But since she could neither apologize nor defend herself for the enigma, she sat quietly counting her breaths, only a part of her hoping her senses would return. She watched the tension seep from Anya's body, saw the color reclaim her face as a calmness set in.

"I'm okay," said her mother as if to reassure herself. "You are okay, so I am okay too."

She settled against the propped pillow next to Lena.

"What happened, Ma?" Lena asked, suddenly finding her voice.

Anya surveyed her child, took in her eyes, her whole face, genuinely surprised.

"You forgetting everything already?" Then again: "Everything, the running away, the sickness. You forget?" Her face flushed as she stared at Lena in disbelief.

"*Oy*, Lena, you make us so scared!"

"Ma, I was dreaming. That's all I know, I was dreaming of delicious—" she began, then thought better of it. "I can't remember anything. Was I very sick?"

Anya gazed down, brushed some lint from the red cotton comforter that still covered Lena, and began.

"You were sick. Very sick. But you are okay now, is it not so?" This time she didn't wait for reassurance but continued.

"But why you run away? We come home from the work and already the sky is black outside. We think you home now maybe studying. But no one come to the door, no one in the kitchen, in the bed, and your daddy and I think that maybe you with the boy. So we call him."

"Wait—no, you called Luke?" Fully awake now, Lena stared at her mother incredulously.

"Well, what we can do about this? It is dark already and you are not home. The boy, he says he does not know where you are. Then he says not to worry. Not worry? How can we not worry if our daughter not in the house, not with the boy, not leave a note on the Frigidaire, even? And, Daddy, he tells me the same, 'Don't worry. Maybe she is in the library, or the bus is broken.' But even when he tells me this, I see the red marks in his eyes, and he is not breathing the same, and I know he is just like me. He is worried too. Maybe more."

"Ma." Lena leaned toward her mother again as she allowed compassion to overtake the anger she felt at their contacting Luke. "You get too excited. Nothing happened to me."

Swiftly Anya pulled her arm away, as if it were struck by a match. Her cheeks flushed crimson.

"Excited? What you think, I am made of iron? I think maybe you are running across the street and a car hits you, or maybe, *oy*, how can I say this? Maybe somebody grab you up and we never see you again!"

At this, Lena gazed at her mother's face as it seemed to shatter suddenly like a frozen lake of ice, releasing a torrent of tears.

And this time it was Lena who took Anya into her arms, stroked her hair, as she murmured, "You're fine, Mommy. We both are." And again she was transported in time, to the little girl in need of her parents, the girl who was given so much and yet not enough. Instead, it was she who tried to comfort *them*. There was only one thing she knew for sure: she would do everything in her power to prevent them from going back to that other time, the time they rarely spoke of. The time that was still too much to bear.

Finally, after many minutes, Anya released herself from her daughter's embrace. She reached for a tissue on the nightstand and dabbed at her eyes. Anya scrutinized Lena's face and, recognizing the fear in it, even managed a wan smile of reassurance.

"Okay," she said, and as she found her voice, she regained control. "You're right. What do I have to cry about? So silly!"

Lena lay back against the pillow. She closed her eyes, inhaled, allowing a stream of the Vicks to clear her lungs, her throat, hoping it would cleanse her mind as well. But the effort was futile. She still couldn't remember.

Like most mothers, Anya picked up on her child's frustration, trying to fill in the blanks.

"It was two hours, maybe three, that we, me and your daddy, go to look for you. We call Wendy, Lisa, all the girls, and who else, I don't know. I think maybe they get a little scared also. So, when nobody has an answer for you, we go outside, one way for me, another way for Daddy. And we think, where can she be? Where can our Lena be in the middle of the night?" A sound, like a child's cry, emerged from Anya's throat, but this time she stopped it and continued.

"I look by the park; Daddy walks so many blocks to the library, which is closed already. I guess we are both like crazy people. And when I see a police car or hear the noise from an ambulance, *oy vey*, Lena!"

Lena instinctively reached out, grasped her mother's hand. Anya pursed her lips for only a moment with a new resolve.

"But thanks to God, Daddy finds you. He finds you and brings you home, where already I come back crazy with worry."

Lena fixed her eyes on her mother as she silently urged her to go on.

"He sees you in that place. Oh—I forget the name. Like a drugstore where sometimes the man makes you the egg cream that you love so much. You know, where Daddy and me take you when you was a little girl. Oh, what was it?"

"Doc's?"

Anya gazed at her daughter, her eyes alight. And for the first time that morning, a genuine smile appeared on her face.

"Ah! That is the one! Doc's!"

She gathered her thoughts as she remembered.

"But when he finds you there, you are sitting on a stool, half the egg cream left in the glass, with your head down on the counter. Nobody else even there. You are sleeping, he thinks. Not in your bed, but in that place. And when he touches you, you jump up, and you are scared. I think you are scared with the fever. But Daddy says you look like you are scared of *him*. Lena, how can you not know your own daddy?"

Lena blinked. It was all more than her mind could absorb.

Anya seemed not to notice Lena's lack of reaction. She was somewhere else.

"Anyway, you was a sick girl when you are back in the house. Your face, it was swelled up, the white in your eyes filled only with red. Lena, you was very sick. And we get such a shock when we see your temperature is over one hundred and four! Such a shock," she repeated.

Anya took another long breath and, after the pause, related the rest of the tale in a blister of words, afraid to hesitate, afraid that in doing so, she would release another rush of tears. She told her how the couple placed her in a cool bath to release the feverish heat that was emanating from her skin. How then she shivered so, they feared she might not stop, so they had no choice but to call the doctor even if it was after 10:00 p.m., in "the middle of the night," and how the doctor, also concerned, called the all-night pharmacy so that they could make up her medication. It all sounded like the flu, he said. And how, later, Josef had walked the nine long blocks to pick up the medicine, even if the night was blacker than ever, and with the clouds hiding the face of the moon that cool night, he had to be extra careful, afraid of the criminals who might be lurking behind parked cars, against tin cans, waiting in the alley. But he did it; Josef made it back home in less than an hour, thanks to God, driven only by the need to save his sick daughter, his only daughter. Because what choice did he have, really?

And then, after being bundled back into her bed, beneath the massive comforter, after taking spoonfuls of the doctor's medicine, and breathing in the noxious odor of the Vicks, which puffed its steam in the corner of the room and would, miracle of miracles, open her sinuses, Lena slept. She slept so long that her parents began to worry, almost as much as they had worried when Lena was gone. Yet, as they saw her expression settle peacefully as she slept, as they heard her breaths come slow and tempered, her body would wrestle the demons, ultimately exorcising them. Only then did they know in their hearts that Lena would be fine. And that this time they had saved their daughter.

By the time Anya had finished telling her all that had transpired, her shoulders slumped suddenly, tired from the effort. Neither mother nor daughter noticed as Josef entered the bedroom, stood close to the door, still in coat and hat, a white paper bag containing more of the red liquid medicine dangling from his hand. Josef, whose silence usually matched Anya's loquaciousness, listened, his eyes never leaving his daughter's face as he scanned her pupils, the outline of her body beneath the thick covers. It was not until Anya had stopped talking that the two finally became aware of his presence, and that they saw the trace of a smile appear on Josef's lips. Satisfied, finally, he walked toward his child and pressed his lips to her forehead.

"Very good," he whispered before finally peeling his eyes from her face.

It was only after they left the room, as she recaptured the moments just before her disappearance, like flakes of snow coming together in a great white collage, that Lena, alone now, felt the freedom to explore her thoughts. She saw in the corner of the bedroom the huge fluffy pink teddy bear with aqua-colored glass eyes, and she remembered. She recalled the times when she was little and had begged her parents to take her to the Bronx Zoo, just so she could meet the real thing. She remembered, too, their calm explanation that real bears did not possess pink fur and they knew none with eyes that particular shade of blue. Anya and Josef had purchased the bear soon after her birth, because it was a pretty thing they had set their eyes on in the window of a toy shop, and nothing more. After they had explained its origins, Lena never looked at the stuffed animal in the same way, but sometimes, when she had had a particularly bad day at school, or an argument with one of her girlfriends, she would find herself talking to her fake friend as if it were a trusted adviser. The bear, which bore no name, never provided any answer, of course. Nevertheless, just talking to it gave Lena a modicum of relief.

"What was I doing at Doc's?" she asked it now. The bear's only response, as always, was a stony silence. But then, as she stared at its round aqua-colored eyes that glistened in the light of early morning, she felt something inside her move until it became a sudden upheaval followed by a gush of tears. And, with that, the hours came flooding back. And she remembered.

She had seen her just outside the library. And though the years had molded her body to womanhood, etched strong contours into her face, her identity was unmistakable. It was Pearl. After all those years and the questions she dared never ask, the anguish still remained, always bubbling below the surface. If she asked about Pearl, and the bear that had carried her deep into the woods, the very real bear this time, she knew that her parents would look at each other, their eyes exchanging a secret code that Lena could never fathom, and they would tell her calmly that Pearl was safe, that she need never ask of her again.

But though she kept her anxiety, her fears, to herself, she complied with her parents' wishes even after all these years. And though they assured her that all was well, there were mornings when she would wake up, move to the window, and stare at the street below, hoping to catch sight of the girl with soft blond hair, skipping down the street. In the evenings, too, just as Lena would rest her head against the soft pillow, her ears strained as she hoped to hear the melodic voice calling up to her, asking her to come outside and play.

And now, when she was so much older, no longer a child, not even a teenager, instead of letting the memories dissipate as water drops from a spout, the need to see her old friend grew, became more entrenched in her mind, a kind of desperation, a deep cavern that needed to be filled. What was more, she knew it could not be filled by her parents, who, though loving, were people she could never take fully into her confidence for fear that she might hurt them yet again, a hurt that this time might never be repaired. Nor could she confess her worries to Luke, her boyfriend now, for even though he treated her with a warmth she had never known before, she felt certain he would not understand. No, it was only Pearl who could truly understand, who could advise, who could settle her and make her whole again.

And so that day, after the first astonishing glimpse, she would run down the crowded street, pushing against the pedestrians who got in her way, straining her eyes past the sharp light as the sun declined into darkness, hoping to see the long denim coat, the swish of the long ponytail. And when she couldn't see her, when every sighting became a false apparition and her head began to ache, her bones to shiver, her eyes fell upon the dazzling light bulbs in the dark, the old sign beckoning her to enter. She would order an egg cream, no pretzel this time, place the few coins she had left in her purse on the counter and, after a few sips, rest her head on its smooth surface. Just for a moment until she regained her strength. Because she would have to go out again to search for her and find her. She would have to see her again. After all, they were still best friends.

14

She was not one of those girls who dreamed of a fancy affair that was more extravaganza than wedding. She never wanted a grand poufy gown with bell sleeves and a veil of French lace that trailed three feet behind when she walked. Or the six-tiered strawberry-and-chocolate cake that you had to reach way over your head just to slice. She never wanted to be Cinderella.

So, when Lena finally did get married, it was a small ceremony in a corner synagogue where they didn't know any of the congregants, along with a reception (if the term could properly be used) held at Senior's Restaurant on Nostrand Avenue. Out of respect to her parents, she wore a white minidress with tiny eyelets and a matching short veil that barely covered her eyes. And though she didn't feel much like wearing white, making her feel somehow false, pretentious, as she slipped the dress over her head that day, her heart warmed at the sight of her mother's approving smile. The choice no longer troubled her.

By the time the three of them exited the cab in front of the square-shaped brick building, her father ceremoniously opening the wide front door for them, Lena's belly had stopped rumbling. When she saw Luke already there in the spacious lobby, standing in front of a giant gold Tree of Life sculpture, looking somewhat uneasy in a navy suit, white shirt, and red-and-blue paisley tie as he cupped a pink corsage for Anya in both hands, Lena felt little ripples climb up her skin, just like on the first day they met. She couldn't keep from smiling.

"Hello, husband," she said, walking up to him and impulsively planting a kiss on his cheek. He smiled back, embarrassed when she adjusted the royal-blue velvet yarmulke that resembled a beanie as it sat propped upon his head. As he shook her father's hand, gave her mother the corsage along with a quick hug, she felt her heart resume its normal rhythm.

It was only then that she acknowledged the silent fear that had gripped her these last few days, as the date grew closer, that Luke, more reticent of late, might have second thoughts. That she would arrive at the synagogue only to find a cold, empty lobby, the light from the stained glass reflecting the sheen of the huge metal Tree of Life with its tarnished leaves announcing congregants' weddings, bar mitzvahs, and other special occasions, not the joy of a young couple about to be wed. Then there would be the confused stares as the rabbi, a small round man with a neatly trimmed graying beard, glanced hurriedly at his watch, afraid that he would be late for his weekly visit with a congregant who was ill at the hospital. She braced herself for the shock. She had heard of an acquaintance who made plans for the big day, had her dress picked out, selected the venue for their honeymoon, only to have her fiancé tearfully back out in a phone call. A phone call! Lena wasn't afraid of the embarrassment, what others would think, though. She was most afraid of losing Luke. As she looked at her parents now, their eyes filling with tears, she wondered if they were thinking the same thing.

But it was not to be, because there he was, waiting for her, and then the couple, along with her mother, wearing a rose-pink suit with big brass buttons, and her father, dressed in the only suit he had—a black three-piece number with a silver-and-white-striped tie reserved for special occasions, like bar mitzvahs, funerals, and now his own daughter's wedding—were soon whisked away to the rabbi's study. With two congregants they had never met before as witnesses, they signed the ketubah, the Jewish contract proclaiming them married.

Within minutes, Lena would find herself in the sanctuary at the front of the shul, as the two waited to exchange rings—simple round bands without a break—signifying the wholeness of their union. He was still there next to her as he broke the glass and as they kissed for the first time as man and wife. He was there. But before all of that happened, her father stood behind, politely taking her lime-green spring coat as she slipped out of the sleeves, as she felt her anxiety, too, slip from her, like melted snow. And she wondered why she had been so afraid in the first place.

It would have been so easy for him to say no. To opt out of the event, calling it a sham, chastising her for believing in such foolishness in the first place. It would have been easy because, for him, it was just going through the motions. A marriage and the "whole wedding thing," as he called it, was nothing but an outdated ritual performed in service to a god he no longer believed in. Nor would he concede to the institution of family, as he no longer had a relationship with his parents, not even with his two younger brothers who, he insisted, were collaborators in a conspiracy against him. If Lena ever dared broach the subject, he would become closemouthed, shut down like a lockbox, tell her in no uncertain terms never to speak of them again. And so, if Lena had any questions about what it was that could so turn him against his own family, the parents who were there from the day of his birth, the brothers he played leapfrog with, traded baseball cards with as a child, she kept them to herself. And that was why seeing him there that Friday morning as he stood shifting nervously from one leg to the other, she knew just why he had decided to show up. It was for her. And she loved him all the more for it.

She didn't pay attention as her parents walked her down the aisle, as her father placed a soft kiss on her cheek before handing her off to Luke. Nor did she hear the words of the rabbi as he said the traditional prayers, not even when he spoke of the couple's attributes, mostly Lena's qualities that had been fed to him via her father. She didn't note the words as he extolled the responsibilities to the younger generation, *their* generation, to assume the burdens of those who came before, those present and those lost, their obligations to transform the ghosts of their dreams into bright reality. She barely looked up as they exchanged the slender gold rings that would bind them in holy matrimony. It was only when she heard the shattering of the glass as Luke's foot went down, breaking it into a thousand pieces, a symbolic ritual representing the sorrow as well as the joy of marriage, that Lena awoke. And it wasn't until that moment that she realized, amid the shouts of "Mazel tov" as he pulled her toward him in a kiss, how much she had wanted this. She was married. Finally, she was a married woman.

When she looked up at the face of her husband for the first time, Lena was surprised to see him swiftly wipe a tear from the corner of his left eye. She knew then that he had wanted this too. And in that moment, life couldn't have been more perfect.

~

She hadn't expected it. Josef handed her the crisp white envelope just as the waiter, with a flourish, set down four plates of deep-fried french toast made with wedges of challah.

"For you," her father said simply. "For you both," he added, indicating Luke, too, with a sweep of the hand.

The envelope felt warm as she took it from his fingers, realizing that it probably had been secured in the inside pocket of the black jacket since early morning. As she met his eyes, he nodded, indicating that she should open it. Her hand trembled as she slid the polished white thumbnail behind the seal and removed the folded check inside. The name, written with his characteristic tightly scrawled loops and ending with a broad upward circle that looked somewhat like the tail of a pug, said, "Mr. and Mrs. Bronfeld." But it was the number on the next line that most interested the young couple. Incredulous, their eyes held the numbers like magnets. Twenty-five thousand dollars.

Lena lifted her eyes to Luke, whose face, a mask of white, was nearly unrecognizable. And since neither could utter a word, it was Josef who spoke first, stating the obvious.

"It is a present from me and Mommy. Maybe you will use it for a down payment for a house. You know, for when you have little ones."

Luke sat mute as, finally finding her voice, the words tumbled out of Lena's mouth.

"We appreciate this. I-I can't tell you how deeply we appreciate it. But it is too much. It's your life savings, and we can't—"

It was Anya who stopped her as she placed her hand upon Lena's.

"It is not our life savings. We have more, more from the Old Country from the German restitution, and you remember the cousin, Carl Shmuel? The cousin who brings us here so many years ago? You remember he died of a stomach cancer, God forbid, who can speak of that, anyway? Cousin Carl, he was a bachelor, and he left in the will this and more. Besides, what do your daddy and me need so much for? It is for you, you and your new husband. Everything is for you."

She held her daughter's eyes in hers as a tear slid down Lena's cheek, dragging the new jet-black mascara with it. She dabbed at it with a blue cloth napkin.

Lena remained silent, all her objections now stuck in her throat.

"Thank you. Thank you both so much," said Luke as his shock finally dissipated. He pushed his plate back and walked around to the other side of the table to give Anya a hug and shake Josef's hand. As Lena stood to follow, she felt the eyelet of her white dress snag on a loose nail in her chair. She quickly untangled it, moved toward her parents. They held her tightly, so tightly that Lena had to catch her breath. She kissed their cheeks. And again the words floated. "Thank you."

But as she sat down, her hand still shaking as she poured the maple syrup over the chunks of french toast, Lena knew that it wasn't gratitude she felt. It was guilt. Guilt for not being the perfect daughter they had hoped for, for leaving school, for marrying someone who was not quite Jewish. For not being enough.

~

It had been nearly a year since the couple settled into the apartment, and Lena's life had changed considerably. She didn't read much anymore. When she thought about it, trying to figure out why many of the things she used to spend her time doing no longer gave her any pleasure, she had only one answer. For as long as she could remember, she had filled the empty spaces in her life with activities or things that laid claim to her thoughts and made her happy—well, at least for a little while.

The girl who loved to read the classics that featured tragic heroines— novels by the Brontës, Jane Austen, du Maurier, or Herman Wouk, and more recent potboilers by the likes of Jacqueline Susann—were enjoyable because they all featured women she could relate to, women who were heroines, had conquered the odds, while she had remained a captive to her own circumstances. She liked nothing more than to watch old films, musicals like *Top Hat* where suddenly she was dancing across a ballroom floor with Fred Astaire or *Casablanca*, looking through the eyes of Ingrid Bergman as she said one last goodbye to her true love. Even the antics of the Marx Brothers could provoke a smile as she sat alongside on a car ride down an old mountain road. It all made her so giddy.

Going to school, proudly showing off the 95 on an English literature exam, even acing a geometry test after struggling to comprehend sine and cosine and parabolas for nearly a week, only to hurry home at three o'clock just so she could share the results with her parents, all seemed so silly to her now. So immature. So did time spent writing parodies of Beatles tunes or changing the words of "To Sir, with Love" to "To Mike" or whoever the crush of the hour happened to be. Shopping at Abraham & Straus or Martin's department store, a weekend activity she shared with her mother, but more recently with friends, no longer gave her the rush it used to. Unwrapping the new suede tobacco-colored fringed handbag or placing a new pair of earth shoes on the floor of the closet next to the red platform shoes with a wide buckle she had purchased a week earlier could always tickle her heart—or at least it did for an hour or two. But now something held her back from the joy these activities gave her. She was a married woman, a woman with responsibilities, keeping a home for Luke, finding ways to save money for their future. She had no more time for frivolous things.

As Lena stood in front of a dryer in the launderette a block from where they lived, folding her husband's blue-and-white-striped boxer shorts, she wondered at the folly of the past years, the years before she met Luke, her obsessive need to seek fulfillment outside her own life, which when found only gave her a temporary pleasure. Because now, Luke filled in the gaps. It was Luke who made her life complete.

Lena folded the last two articles of clothing, still toasty from the dryer, placed them in the cart, and began the walk back to the apartment. The sun was warm and soothing on her shoulders, encircling her like a lover, and she was reminded of Luke. She sidestepped the dog walkers, the Jamaican nurses, their uniforms impeccably starched, as they pushed their elderly patients, excessively bundled for the season, in wheelchairs. Lena realized she hadn't taken anything out of the freezer earlier that day for dinner. Perhaps it would be another chicken to roast or some lamb chops if she could find the mint jelly. And, if she had time when she got back, she would make another batch of cookies. How Luke loved her chocolate chip cookies!

Lena walked up the stone steps, the metal cart bouncing behind, then removed a key from her rubber key purse. The lock clicked open, and she switched on the light in the living room. At once the small crystals of the ceiling chandelier crackled, filling the gray room with light. The chandelier, along with a lamp with a prim white silk shade she had taken from her parents' apartment, some kitchen towels splattered with orange beagles, and a new aqua-and-white comforter with matching drapes for the bedroom, all added a note of femininity and care to the onetime bachelor pad that now served as a home for the couple. Yet even now, as Lena carefully removed the folded items from the cart, as she ran her hand delicately over Luke's polos, which were still warm from the dryer, even now that she was settled in the apartment, she felt like an interloper. She dismissed the thought as irrational, yet she couldn't help feeling that it was still Luke's place, that she was still that young, naive college student timidly walking into a room with a menacing waterbed.

When she had finished putting the clothes away, Lena snapped the cart shut and placed it firmly into the coat closet, squeezing it between two coat-laden hangers. In the kitchen she felt somewhat more comfortable as she retrieved a round Tupperware container from the small refrigerator and removed the dough that she had formed into a ball the night before, then let it stand on the butcher block counter at room temperature. She checked the icebox and, happy to see that, yes, she had a chicken sitting snugly in its center, she removed that, too, sniffing it once before letting some hot water flow over it for a quick defrost. As she peeled a couple of bumpy Idaho potatoes, Lena became aware of the stinging odor of bleach that still saturated the air. She had scrubbed the sink, the faucet, the counters, early that morning just after Luke left for work. *That is good,* she thought. How many times had her mother reminded her that to be really clean, a house must smell clean?

Satisfied, Lena dropped each potato wedge into a square pan, adding a cup of vegetable oil before she began to prepare the thawing chicken. After bathing the fowl as carefully as if it were a newborn, she shook on the spices, the garlic and onion powder, some thyme and paprika, and set it all into the center of the pan, covering it with aluminum foil before turning the dial on the oven. Later she would add a can of corn, and one of carrots, to complete the meal.

She glanced around the small kitchen and found it all neat, in order. She was glad she had decided to make everything kosher, with two new sets of plates and silverware. It was her mother's request, for whom the observance of kashruth was a requirement. Lena didn't mind following the tradition, even though it meant being a bit more careful when food shopping. She even had a candelabra for Shabbat in one of the upper cabinets, one of the gifts presented to her by her parents when she married, though she never once thought to use it.

After taking a break to refresh her face in the bathroom, she set to work on the dough, which, after a few minutes of pounding and kneading, was now pliable, obediently molding itself as it flattened against the wood counter. This was when Lena felt most at home, mastering the dough to her will. It wasn't long before, while she popped the semisweet chocolate morsels into the mixture, she could detect new aromas as the air took on the fragrance of garlic and other spices blended with the lingering odor of the bleach. Later, as she used her flour-coated hands to shape the loaf into small balls that she placed on a cookie sheet, she barely detected the sound of the key turning in the lock of the front door, didn't even know that he was back home, not until she felt his arms encircle her waist from behind, not until she inhaled the familiar scent of his cologne as she turned her face toward him, their lips meeting in a kiss.

"My happy homemaker," he murmured into her ear, and, despite her disdain for the term, Lena couldn't help but giggle like a schoolgirl.

~

Later, the two sat cutting into their chicken and savoring the vegetables as a recording of Santana's "Black Magic Woman" crooned on the cassette player in the adjoining living room. She watched as Luke scooped up another helping of the corn niblets. As she sat opposite her husband, with each breath Lena felt a sense of unease, now verging on hysteria. Almost as if her presence in this apartment, with this man, were an anachronism, as if she didn't belong. As if she were living someone else's life. She tried to dismiss the thought, and instead scanned his face for some sign of displeasure.

"Are the carrots too cold? I added them later, and maybe—"

A smile overtook his face, making him look like a very young boy, not a man already in his twenties.

"No, it's perfect," he said, gazing at her, then quickly shifting his eyes back to the meal. "Everything is perfect."

Still, a few minutes later, as they continued to eat quietly, as she sneaked glances at the set of his jaw, his downcast eyes, she couldn't help feeling that something was amiss. He seemed preoccupied. She decided to try another question.

"How was work today?"

He was in midbite and let go of the fork. It dropped with a clang. But then, as if nothing had happened, he picked it up, stabbed at a piece of the chicken, and shoved it into his mouth.

"Work was okay," he said between bites, but when his eyes met hers again, she saw something she had never seen before, a look like he was holding something back, a deep-seated anger she hadn't thought him capable of. She dropped the subject. As they sat quietly chewing their food, though, a thought came to her. Luke never asked about *her* day. Not once. What would she say anyway? That she had cooked soup and ironed his shirts?

The couple finished their meal in silence as the driving beat of the song held its last note. It was only later when they sat on the funky plaid sofa, biting into the warm chocolate cookies, whose scent was now dissipating into the air, that he spoke again.

"It's really shitty, Lena."

"What's that? What did you say?"

"My job, Lena. It's the worst. My boss, Mr. Snead, is the biggest crook on the face of the earth. He is always trying to get me to cook the books, you know, play around with the numbers. And he told me he's cutting my hours again. Not that it makes a difference. I'll just be doing the same work, staying late, for the same amount of pay. He's always pleading poverty, which is a crock of you-know-what. Let me tell you, this guy has got plenty. He's a goddamn grocer, and people always need to eat, so he'll be riding high for years to come. *Snead*," he said, snarling the name. "Scrooge is more like it."

Lena swallowed the last crumbs of her cookie, following it with a long sip of Sanka. She suppressed a gasp as she felt the liquid burn her tongue. Lena didn't quite know what to say. She knew that Luke didn't love his job, but until now she hadn't realized to what extent. It was the third job working the payroll that he'd had since he'd made the decision to quit college. None had been ideal. But this one, the latest at the local superette, had supplied him with nearly eight hours a day; plus, since it was only blocks from the apartment on Avenue M, he was saving money on the commute.

"Well," she said finally, "maybe you can look around for something else, you know, during the time you're not working."

He shifted uneasily in his seat on the couch, brushed some cookie crumbs off his jeans.

"What's the point, Lena? It'll only be the same thing. No matter who I'm working for."

She nodded. There was little else she could do, she knew, when Luke got like this. Little she could say to persuade him when he became obstinate, even though this wasn't the plan. She felt a pang of guilt at ending her semester at school so abruptly, at not yet having a plan of her own. But he would continue working, gaining experience while going to school part-time in the evenings. Eventually he would graduate, take the CPA exam, and then their worries would be over. Or at least that was the plan.

But now she realized something that she had feared all along. Not all plans go according to schedule; not all people live up to their promise. And so there was nothing left to say.

She picked up the bowl of leftover cookies and went into the kitchen. As she placed them in the ceramic cookie jar, she silently berated herself for her response. When had she stopped voicing her opinions? When had she become merely reactive to the things around her? She loved him.

Lena didn't always take her mother's advice. But now, as she readied herself for bed, dabbing her cheeks with cold cream, just as her mother did each night, donned the red negligee he had given her as a one-month anniversary gift, a nightgown she felt awkward in, but one that he loved, she was glad that she remembered her mother's words when it came to men. "Never meet anger with anger, Lena," she had advised the night before their wedding. "Nothing good can come of it. You need to be patient. And after a while, when things are still, you can quietly tell him why he was wrong. That's when they listen." Lena had shrugged as her mother slipped quietly out of her room, not really paying attention. But now, as she gazed at her image in the mirror, somewhat unrecognizable, the words came floating back. She had remained quiet all that evening, not wanting to fuel an argument. Tomorrow or maybe the day after she would delicately bring up the subject of work again. When things were still. For now she wanted only peace. Peace and the enjoyment of their time together.

And, within minutes, she found it. The tiny kisses planted on her neck, the words whispered in her ear, the closeness that bound their bodies together. She placed the tip of her finger on a round spot sitting on his right shoulder. It was as soft as a baby's skin, a scar left from an old bicycling accident he'd had as a child. She kissed it tenderly. And when their lovemaking was over, Lena tightened her grip and caressed the smooth plane of his back. And she knew then that she was happy, really happy. Maybe for the first time in her life.

∼

They had not spoken of the matter again, not the next day, not for the next few months. And as time passed, Lena had forgotten her mother's words, and nothing was said. At first Lena didn't notice the change in her husband, how he grew more sullen each time he walked in the door, how he had become indifferent, then impatient, when the rain interrupted their walk, impatient when dinner was not exactly on time. Then, when they had been married just over a year, something happened that would change her outlook completely. It was not a total surprise.

"Lena, it's an impossible situation."

She looked up, doe-eyed, from her bowl of coffee ice cream, feigning ignorance.

"My job. An impossible situation. I had no choice."

She froze, afraid of what would come next.

"Luke—what are you saying?"

His eyes met hers, defiant.

"I quit my job."

She felt her heart quicken. A coldness fell over her, draping her body. Since they had met, she had the sense that she didn't belong here, not in this place, not with this man. She had a fleeting thought that she was becoming unrecognizable. A ghost. Lena felt the words escape her lips but couldn't yet comprehend them. From somewhere far off, though, she could hear him. He was speaking, but none of it was making any sense. Now he was the one who was calm, in control.

"Night and day, day and night, he wanted me to work. And for what? So finally I got up the courage to ask for a raise. Only two bucks an hour. Is that too much to ask? And you know how he answered me? Do you know?"

Lena shook her head, her vocal cords frozen in her throat.

"He laughed at me. Told me I should be happy with what he gave me. Told me it was more than enough for someone who hadn't even graduated college." Luke, picking at his nails, glanced at her for a response. Finding none, he continued.

"So I told him off, Lena. I told him I'm done with the work, the pay, with the old snake. Bye-bye. Sayonara. I'm gone." He wiped his jeans and, as if to accentuate the point, got up and walked into the bedroom.

Lena sat dumbfounded, staring at the empty space on the sofa Luke had just occupied. As someone who had always planned each step in her life, or at least tried to, this was all uncharted territory. She wondered, as she sat staring at the spot, as she could feel her eyes begin to water, what to expect from him and, more important, what he could expect from her.

When she finally mustered the courage to follow him into the bedroom, she was surprised to find him curled like a fetus, face down in his pillow. The water inside the bed sloshed lazily beneath his body. It occurred to her that Luke was floating away. Maybe forever.

"Luke?"

This time he didn't respond, merely shifted his head deeper into the pillow.

"Luke? Look, it's okay. I'm not mad. Really, I'm not."

He sat up, steadying himself as the waterbed shook beneath. A lone figure on a raft, she thought, and took pity on him.

"Are you sure, baby? Are you sure you're not angry?"

She sat down, the bed shaking more vigorously under her weight.

"No. Why would I be? I mean, you were unhappy, right? It wasn't like you were going to make a career working for that snake," she said, using the same derogatory term he had used to describe his now former boss. "Besides, slavery was outlawed more than a hundred years ago."

He smiled at that last comment, and seeing that smile bring new energy to his face, Lena felt better, almost believing that he had done the right thing in leaving his job. As she continued to soothe him, she became emboldened, gaining faith with each word.

"Oh, Luke, you're going to do great things, I'm certain of it. You'll get your degree, then ace the CPA exam. And meantime, there are plenty of other jobs working the books, plenty of business owners look-ing for an ambitious young man to take charge. Bosses who won't take advantage of you."

As he listened to her, he sat erect, the smile now flooding his face, his enthusiasm as he grinned so great that Lena imagined she saw sparks shooting from his black beard. He reached over and brought her close in a hug. Then, just as quickly, he was on his feet, burrowing through the drawer of his night table.

"You're right, Lena, right about everything. Except for one thing. I'm never going to work for anyone again, not if I can help it."

He recovered a yellow striped legal pad and pulled some newspaper clippings from within. He glanced through the papers, then turned his attention back to her, a self-satisfied expression on his face.

"Lena, I've been waiting for the right time to tell you this. It's something I saw in the paper, and I think it's perfect. Not just for me, for you, too, for the both of us." He placed the clippings on her lap, the smile, silly now, she thought, remaining on his face as she skimmed the ad.

"It's a bakery, Lena, just like you always wanted, right? Wasn't it your dream to have your own bakery, just like your parents had back in the Old Country? What they're selling here is an Italian bakery, but that can easily be changed to a Jewish one. I mean, they already have the ovens and the workstation. And I know it's not near where we live, but it's still in Brooklyn. Bensonhurst. Mostly Italian, I know, but they still have plenty of Jews there, right?

"Just think of it—you could be braiding challahs, mixing the dough for the honey cakes, not worried about your mom always having something to say. Just minding your own business. *Our* business. I'd take care of all the finances. All you'd have to do is bake. So what do you think?"

Lena stared at the ad, then back at her husband, and try as she might, she could not comprehend what was before her. She couldn't recall ever telling Luke that she wanted to own a bakery. Lena had toyed with the idea of going to law school, becoming a lawyer once she graduated from college, of course. But the bakery was a dream she hadn't shared with anyone, fearing that it sounded too foolish. Baking, as much as she loved it, was just a hobby, wasn't it? She tried to speak, respond to the newest of Luke's revelations, and when she did, one question, the only question, came to mind.

"Luke, how are we paying for this?" She watched as the enthusiasm he exuded slowly ebbed from his face.

"Well," he began tentatively, and his eyes, which had sought hers only moments earlier, now avoided her own.

"Well, we actually do have a down payment, don't we? We have it in the bank."

And with those words, slowly, a door in her mind opened to reveal what he really meant. Still, she sat motionless, waiting. Waiting for him to say it.

"The money your parents gave us. And once the bakery is established, once it is successful, we'll make that money back, and more. The way I see it, it's a win-win situation."

And that was it. The thing Lena had feared, that her foolhardy husband would place them both in jeopardy, had come to pass. This time she didn't wait to summon her response.

"You mean the gift my parents gave us on our wedding day? The money they had kept in the bank for all those years so we could use it as a down payment for a house, a foundation for building a family one day? Is that the money you want to risk for a ridiculous business venture? You said you checked it out, and that it would be perfect, but you forgot one thing, Luke; you forgot to let me know, to have me come with you to do the checking. Because you know that I wouldn't have agreed, that's why you never asked. And you know what? You were right. It's a dumb idea, Luke, and a risky one. I'm not going to fritter away everything my parents have given to us, all their sacrifices, for some pie-in-the-sky fantasy of yours. I won't do it. If you won't put in the work for our future, if no job is ever good enough, then that's okay. But don't ask me to gamble my parents' dreams for their only daughter on one of your fantasies. I won't do it, Luke. I won't."

Lena stepped off the bed, feeling slightly seasick. And this time she was the one who left, as Luke, now pale and trembling, stared at her in disbelief.

~

Less than a week later, Luke was back at work. It didn't take much for him to get his old job back from Mr. Snead, with only a slight raise. When he came home each night, still tired, still sullen, he never uttered a word of complaint. And while Lena was glad that he hadn't brought up the issue about their buying an old bakeshop together, there was a gnawing sense, like a buzzing in her ear, an itch under her eye, that told her things weren't quite right. She worried that their lovemaking, which remained steady, had become robotic, the passion seeping away.

Whenever they sat watching TV late at night, she would feel his eyes upon her, studying her, as if he had begun to hate her just a bit.

During the day, when the sun was full and the walls indoors were free of shadows, she tried to put these disturbing thoughts out of her mind. Instead, she would go to her job, where she worked as a law clerk in Lower Manhattan, pretending to be enthusiastic about what she was doing while planning the gourmet meal she would have ready for Luke at day's end. Maybe she would investigate completing her education, taking the LSAT, and applying to law schools. That would surely make her parents happy. Lena had all but abandoned baking cookies and cakes, afraid that the memory of their lost opportunity would plant the seeds of resentment in Luke's mind.

Once a week, on a Friday night, the Sabbath, she would have dinner with her parents in the old apartment. Of course, Luke was always welcome to join them, but inevitably he would decline, saying it would be best to give them some time alone together. Lena never objected to the gesture, and she found herself looking forward to the three of them as they once were, her mother lighting the Shabbat candles amid the aroma of the fragrant chicken soup, feeling the tender pieces of roast chicken against her teeth, seeing the dreamy look on her father's face as he sliced into the still-warm challah.

They would speak about the little things, harmless discussions about her job, or Lena's new recipe for tuna casserole. They never questioned the couple's long-range plans, never prodded about what the future would look like. Her parents had lived through too much turmoil to look ahead when things were good, to want more. And right now things were good. Soon Lena would find herself wondering again why she ever wanted to leave home in the first place.

~

Lena woke up suddenly. Too exhausted to even lift her head, so she couldn't tell what the time was flashing on the clock radio. She guessed it was sometime in the middle of the night by the shade of illumination filtering through the closed blinds, a deep charcoal gray, by the whisper of silence that enveloped every corner of the bedroom. She had turned her head, hoping to find solace in the old stuffed bear in the corner, when she realized that no, she wasn't in her childhood home, but in the apartment with Luke.

She felt herself fully awake now, yet incapable of movement, and so she took the time to look at the man next to her. Deep in sleep he lay, mouth open, breathing in short whimpering sounds. A strand of his long hair draped across one closed eye, his arms and legs akimbo, taking over most of the bed. *He is so vulnerable, like a child,* she thought. She wanted to brush aside the one strand of his dark hair but resisted the urge, fearing she might wake him. Instead, she turned and pushed her face deep into her pillow, hoping to lose herself in the oblivion of sleep.

But her mind became only more active, like a rapidly ticking clock. She hadn't given much thought to long-range plans when she lived with her parents in the apartment that always smelled of hot chicken soup and warm bread, the place she still thought of as home. But now she was forced to think about such things. And there, in the darkness, she finally acknowledged the feelings she had carried over the last month. The pinprick of doubt overtaking her, a feeling that her essence was crumbling away bit by bit, just like the chocolate chip cookies she used to bake. Lena sensed Luke's movement as he turned away from her. She pushed her head deeper into the pillow, hoping he couldn't hear her sobs.

~

On a Tuesday morning in early June, Lena, wearing her glasses, bags under her eyes from lack of sleep, strode into the Dime Savings Bank on the corner of Avenue J and Coney Island Avenue. She filled out the necessary forms, which she presented to the bank manager. After a quick review, he disappeared into the back, and within minutes he emerged and handed her a check. With interest, it came to over $25,000.

PART II

MAKE THE DOUGH

15

Lena scanned her mother's face for a sign. Silently, Anya walked past the waist-height counter, running her finger across its shiny surface for errant crumbs before entering the workstation in the back. Josef, hands clasped behind his back, followed with a blank expression as if waiting for her cue. Anya opened the massive door to the industrial refrigerator and sniffed at the jumbo vat filled with butter. She placed her hand against a plastic jug of milk, testing its coolness, then opened the lid and peered inside for bubbles. Her eyes followed the neat tubes of icing in every color of the rainbow, glanced up at the shelves at the glass jars filled to the brim with chocolate and vanilla chips, black raisins, pecans, almonds, and other delicacies. She rotated the dial on the massive professional ovens and waited as the burners sparked to life, radiating a bright yellow-orange glow. Before she returned to the front of the store, she made sure to pat the hefty sacks of sugar and flour. Anya retrieved a pair of reading glasses from her purse and inspected the certificate of kashruth that hung behind the cash register on the wall, certifying that all the goods sold, both dairy and parve, were indeed kosher.

Anya peered into the glass showcase where cakes of vanilla, chocolate, some with sliced apples and strawberries, stood in line for approval. Cookies sprinkled, frosted, or covered in melted chocolate dazzled neatly in perfect rows, and off to the side the traditional honey and sponge cakes waited patiently to be lifted and presented to the next customer craving a sweet.

"Well, Ma, what do you think?"

Instead of responding, Anya pursed her lips and looked at Josef, who was now at her side.

"This business, this bakery business, it is a very, very hard business," she said finally, adding in a lower tone, "I did not want this for you."

The silver bell above the front door tinkled.

"I'll be right back," said Lena, who set a smile on her face as she joined a mother and her young son. Once the boy pointed to a large black-and-white cookie, Lena retrieved the item, wrapped it in tissue paper, and handed it to the child, who wasted no time taking a huge bite of both the chocolate and vanilla sides at once, as the mother, a well-dressed woman with her blond hair teased to an unnatural height, gazed down at him. Looking as if she were in a hurry to get home, she placed a dollar on the counter. The bell tinkled once more as the door closed behind them.

Ever since the first day the bakery opened a week earlier, Lena had discovered how happy it made her to see the expression on the customers' faces as she handed them a cream puff or a gooey brownie. It almost made all the expense and the effort in running the bakery worth it. Almost. When she turned to face her mother again, Lena's smile quickly faded. She had a premonition that they would find fault, and that was the reason she had been reluctant to invite them earlier. Her parents remained in the same position as before the exchange.

"So you don't like the bakery? You think this was a bad idea?"

For the first time that afternoon, Anya faced her daughter directly, her eyes pinning her in place.

"I never said such a thing. Besides, it is done already. It is—it is just—I think this business is too much work."

Lena shook her head, gazed at her father for support and, finding none, countered, "We only opened, and it takes work to get the business going, but once we're established, once we settle into a routine, it'll be fine. I've already hired an assistant baker, Risa, someone who has had experience in the city, and just yesterday, Luke found a high school senior to help at the register. But forget all that, just look at this place! It's as good as—no, better than—the bakery you and Daddy owned back in Poland. We've got much more of a selection of baked goods too. Every kind of bread, traditional macaroons and French ones, even Italian cannoli!" she continued, her voice gathering momentum.

Anya sighed.

"I can see it. You have everything. Does she not, Josef?"

Lena's father was examining one of the business cards placed next to the cash register.

"Brooklyn Girl's Bake Shoppe," he read, turning over the card with pink lettering in his hand. "That's a good name. You were born in Brooklyn."

"That was Luke's idea. He liked the sound of it," mumbled Lena, barely glancing his way. She was still thinking of her mother's lukewarm response to the business venture. No matter what Lena did, no matter how many accomplishments she had, it seemed like she could do no good in her mother's eyes. It hadn't been her idea to work in a bakery, much less own one. She preferred to bake as a hobby, the occasional challah for the Sabbath or some sugar cookies as an after-dinner treat. Knowing how much effort the project would entail, how as a business owner she would rarely have a day off from work, never a quiet moment to herself to watch a movie or lean against the windowsill, feeling the sun on her neck as she sat reading a book, she was hesitant. No, in the back of her mind there would always be the bakery, pondering how much of a profit they had made during the week or worrying about running out of the month's inventory for sugar. She knew this, and yet she had agreed, taken the savings, her *parents'* savings, invested it all as a down payment, not for the home it was intended for, but for a business. A business she now knew she never really wanted.

And still she allowed it. She did it, took all the risks, even though something inside her told her that the bakery was doomed to fail. She did it. She did it all for Luke. And maybe a little for her mother too.

"You won't say it, will you?" she reacted, feeling both her voice and her blood pressure rise. Lena thrust her hand into the glass showcase.

"Mommy, try one of these." Lena pulled out a tray of chocolate rugelach and, forgetting about the tissue paper, plucked one out.

"Here," she repeated as she felt her hand trembling, "try one. I know they're your favorite."

Lena felt her mother's eyes on her as she hesitated before, with two fingers, Anya took the delicacy. A thought came to her. *She must think me a crazy person now*, and maybe, at that moment, she was.

Anya nibbled the crisp edge of the rugelach before popping it into her mouth. When she finished chewing, she licked the chocolate crumbs off her fingers.

"It's delicious," she said, but her expression remained the same. Indifferent.

"Do you see?" said Lena, conscious that her voice was higher than she'd like. "I can bake. I can bake every bit as well as you. Every bit as well." She stopped, unwilling to cross the line. But her parents already knew; she could tell by the quick glances they exchanged. She could tell by the sadness that now veiled their eyes. Josef released a mournful sigh before speaking.

"Lena, don't you know you are everything to us? Don't you know that Mommy and me, we are both very proud of you?"

Seeing the tears come to her father's eyes triggered something in Lena so strong that she had to run to the back of the bakery as she felt the sobs rise from deep within her, exploding to the surface. She hoped that her parents wouldn't follow, wouldn't tell her she was being too emotional, just an immature, stupid girl.

Once more Lena found herself yearning for Luke to tell her that she was smart, capable, even beautiful. She needed her young husband to assuage her fears, to affirm that, yes, all her dreams would come true. That she was better than all the rest.

~

Lena opened the bedroom shade and looked out at an early-Monday-morning sun. She hoped it wouldn't rain that day as predicted and looked forward to Luke and her taking a leisurely walk along Kings Highway and browsing at all the shops. But if the skies turned gray and opened to a torrent of rain, it was just as well, for she had borrowed several books from the library and was looking forward to reading at least a couple of them. And maybe giving one of her friends from college a call to catch up on the escapades of Luke and Laura on *General Hospital*. Watching the soap opera was the sole guilty pleasure she would indulge in, but only on Mondays, the one weekday when the bakery was closed. She was glad that she still maintained a friendship with some of the girls, even though it had been over a year since she had quit college. All had gone their separate ways, some to begin grad school, others starting jobs as teachers or administrative assistants. Sometimes Lena missed those days when she could have a long gabfest with a friend, chatting about a recent bestseller. She wondered if those friends didn't look down on her just a little bit for dropping out, even as they praised her ability to run her own business.

She also missed being in the classroom, the times when she would participate in English class, pointing out the imagery in a poem or short story. Whenever she tried to tell Luke about a surprise ending of a book she had just finished or how she would dream of a character who had captivated her, he would just smile and utter a useless phrase like "That's good." Luke didn't have time for reading.

But there was one thing Luke did know a great deal about. He had opened a business checking account; secured a credit card; arranged for an SBA savings account, a start-up business loan to supplement the money from her parents; established a line of credit; obtained new equipment, including the massive oven; and figured out the pricing for all the goods. He had even found a lawyer to help file their brand with the US Patent and Trademark Office. And though he kept reminding her that she was the Brooklyn Girl, the true heart of the business, Lena knew that he was responsible for it all. Why had she ever doubted him?

When she was with Luke, when he held her hand as his thumb ran across the skin while they strolled along the bustling shopping district, all her insecurities faded away. She didn't worry about her success as a baker, the need to always please her parents, that she wasn't exciting enough, pretty enough, to keep a man like Luke. Nothing mattered when she was with him.

As usual, as she peered into the window of the Joyce Leslie dress shop, admiring a polka-dotted midriff top, the conversation turned to the business.

"That new girl, the high school student I just hired for up front, how is she working out?" Luke was able to do a lot of his work, along with studying for the CPA exam, from home, so she hadn't seen much of him at the bakery after the first few weeks of its opening.

"Oh, you mean Louise? She's fine, I guess. Very sweet with the customers, especially the children that come in. Though sometimes she has to cut out early to pick up her little brother from school."

"Well," said Luke, pulling her close as someone whizzed by on a bike, "it's a good thing you're there all of the time. Most of the baking is done early in the morning and at night anyway, so you are available at the counter most afternoons."

"You're right, I suppose," she said, biting her lip. "I'm tired, though, Luke, you know? Sometimes, it's a lot."

"Yes, I get it. But you love what you do, right? Baking those cookies, the cakes, and bread. You're an outstanding baker, Lena. And when you love what you do, I guess it makes it all worth it."

She didn't answer as he guided her toward the window of a jewelry shop.

"Look at those diamonds, Lena!" he said, pointing to the rows of diamond rings set in platinum and silver. "Soon, very soon, I'm going to buy you one of these now that the business is taking off. I know I never gave you an engagement ring, and I'm sorry about that. You deserve that and more. Nothing's too good for my Brooklyn Girl baker."

Hearing the compliment, Lena felt a shiver of excitement run down her neck. She stared for a while at the glittering assortment of stones—round, emerald cut, and pear shaped, the most popular.

"I don't know, Luke. I can't really keep a ring on when my hand is in the dough. But perhaps a watch," she added, pointing to the row of Seiko watches at the bottom of the case.

Luke looked disappointed but paid attention as she indicated one of the Seikos with black roman numerals, a mother-of-pearl face set in a simple gold metal stretch band.

"It's nice enough, I guess." And then after some consideration, he added, "Let's go inside. I'll buy it for you!"

Lena shook her head, pulling her husband back. As usual, Luke was just too impetuous.

"I appreciate the gesture, baby, but that watch is over three hundred dollars! Why don't we wait a few more months until the shop begins to turn a profit?"

After some seconds, he peeled his eyes away from the bauble and took her hand as they continued their walk along the avenue.

"Okay, Lena. We'll wait until the bakery's successful," he said, giving her hand an extra squeeze, adding, "but I think that day will come sooner than you think."

~

It turned out that Luke's prediction was right—two weeks after opening, they held a grand celebration and, at Luke's suggestion, offered free oatmeal cookies to the first fifty customers. Since it was a sunny day in April, just past the Passover and Easter holidays, it seemed that all Bensonhurst and even parts of Borough Park came out for the event. Even the local city councilman, never one to miss an opportunity for publicity, attended, proudly cutting the ribbon and shaking everyone's hand. As the customers flooded into the shop, each leaving with a challah, brownie, or other treat in addition to all the single cookies, Lena worried that their supply would run out. Even Anya and Josef had come to the grand-opening party, and it wasn't long before Anya donned an apron, helping the customers choose between the apple and prune danishes. Josef watched from the side until, after an hour of the chaos, he, too, was putting on an apron to relieve Luke from duty at the register.

Lena marveled at how easily her parents slipped into their roles, how adroitly her father handled the change, how her mother smiled as she knelt into the showcase to retrieve a brownie. It seemed like no time had passed at all since those prewar days when they, too, had their business.

After the last customer left, after her parents had wiped their hands of the chocolate and crumbs, and her mother had been persuaded to take home a leftover raisin challah, Luke sat counting the money in the register.

"Eight hundred and fifty-five dollars and twenty-two cents!" he announced, his face flushed with exhilaration. "Not bad for one day."

Lena closed the new white blinds. She had carried the same smile on her face since she had greeted their first customer, a stout elderly woman whose head was covered by a green paisley kerchief. She had worn a long olive-green cotton dress that came down to her brown orthopedic shoes. As Lena had handed her the free cookie, the grateful woman, smiling, had wished them luck in broken English. Lena had guessed she was Polish, a survivor like her parents.

Each customer who came after would do the same. Lena had thanked each one, keeping the smile plastered to her face, as the crowd of customers came and went. She had the same smile on her face now as she finally took off her apron and turned to Luke, grateful that he saw only the smile and not the worries she hid behind it.

Her parents would return, mostly on Sundays, to help out at the bakery. But after a couple of months, Lena persuaded them to stop coming.

"You both work all week long, and you should be able to relax, at least for some of the time," she had told them, adding, "Besides, we can afford to hire more assistants." As she said the words, though, her parents knowing better than to offer resistance, Lena wondered if they had guessed the truth. A part of her enjoyed having Anya and Josef at the shop, knowing that there was no one who would work harder, no one she could trust more. They would continue working there, even coming in on Thursdays, when the store stayed open until 7:00 p.m.; she had only to ask. Still, Lena knew that she had no options. She had something to prove to her parents, to show them that she could do this. More important, she didn't want them around when she failed.

16

By all accounts, the Brooklyn Girl's Bake Shoppe was a success. Eight months after the grand opening, the couple had accrued enough of a profit to not only pay off the interest but make a dent in the down payment as well. At first Luke said he needed the time to study for the CPA exams, but after a few months Lena noticed that the study guides had disappeared, and in their place was an assortment of video games for his new Magnavox Odyssey. Often, when she returned home after a day's work, she would find him sitting cross-legged on the purple shag rug in front of their RCA TV, working the controllers feverishly. Each time she entered the living room, she felt as if she were entering a version of the Twilight Zone, the light streaming from the set, where a small ball raced over a net in a game of *Pong*. When she asked him why he wasn't studying, his eyes still fixed on the game, he told her that the shop was doing so well now that he no longer saw the point in it or even becoming a CPA at all. Besides, he continued blithely, he had plans for another Brooklyn Girl's Bake Shoppe, this time maybe in Flatbush or on Kings Highway. Pretty soon, he added, stopping his play just long enough to glance in her direction, they would be able to hire more bakers and cashiers, and neither of them would have to go to work at all, just oversee the business.

"Great! That way we can spend all day playing video games together."

Her words came tumbling out with no forethought. Luckily, he hadn't heard, as his fingers continued furiously working the controls. She moved into the bedroom.

Lena lay face up as the waterbed rocked beneath her. After two years, she had grown sick of its motion and worried that, after all this time, the bed might spring a leak and the water would come splashing out, flooding the carpet and the mahogany dresser, drowning them both as they slept. But, of course, she was just being silly, too anxious about everything. Wasn't Luke always calling her a "nervous Nelly," the same term her father would sometimes use when she lived at home? Nevertheless, she had asked Luke to buy a new mattress, a traditional one like a Beautyrest or a Sealy Posturepedic advertised in the Macy's catalog. He readily agreed to the idea, as he did to most things, and yet here she was, years later, still trying to fall asleep in a bed that made her nothing but seasick. She recalled now that he had promised her a watch. She had one now, only it wasn't the watch she wanted, the one with the gold metal band. She was still waiting for that too. But could she blame him for anything? It was Luke, she reasoned, as she removed her shoes and kicked them off to the side of the bed, who was responsible for finding the shop, helping set up the equipment, figuring out the financing. It was Luke who had made them a success.

~

Louise sat on a stool, chewing on her pen as she read a book. Lena wiped her hands on her apron and walked over to the young girl Luke had hired early on. The shop had been vacant for the last half hour, and the afternoon rush wasn't expected for another thirty minutes. Although the two had exchanged pleasantries and talked about what was required for the business, in the months of establishing the business, there hadn't been much time for chitchat. Lena was curious about her.

"Can I ask what you're reading?" she said, peering over the girl's shoulder.

"Oh, sure," she answered, holding up the book so Lena could see its title. "*Great Expectations*. It's by an English writer named Charles Dickens. Have you heard of him?"

Hearing the title, Lena's face lit up, as if she had just recognized an old friend.

"Of course," she said, taking the stool next to Louise. "I've read some of the others too. *David Copperfield*, *Oliver Twist*. What else are you reading in class?"

Louise shut the book and looked down at the ground. It appeared that no one had ever asked her that question before.

"Let's see," she said finally. "We just finished *Pride and Prejudice*, oh, and *Jane Eyre*. Last year it was *Catcher in the Rye* and *The Great Gatsby*."

"Oh, I loved *Jane Eyre* and *Gatsby* too," said Lena as she leaned forward again to take the book from her. She examined the back of its jacket. "Oh, and yes, I forgot about *The Tale of Two Cities*. I think I enjoyed that one best of all."

"It seems like you've read a lot of these books. More than me. Maybe you could tell me about this one so I wouldn't have to read it," Louise said, half joking. "It's kind of long and boring."

Lena laughed.

"Just stay with it. I promise it will be worth it at the end." Then she asked, "Are you taking honors English at school?"

Louise shrugged. Her long jet-black hair caught the sunlight streaming through the store window and sparkled with a youthful glow.

"You're right. I'm usually good at English, but sometimes, you know, all the work gets to be a bit too much."

The jingle of the doorbell interrupted their conversation, and Lena jumped up from her seat so that Louise could continue her reading. She hurried through the amenities, greeting another young mother who gushed about the custom chocolate layer birthday cake Lena had baked that morning for the woman's three-year-old son, complete with a muscular Superman character dressed in his customary suit with red and blue icing and ready for takeoff. Lena was glad when she finally shut the cash register and the woman carrying the precious item left. Quickly, Lena resumed her seat next to Louise. This time she didn't worry about interrupting her. As she resumed the conversation again, Lena had a peculiar feeling. It was as if something long hidden inside her heart had opened, and she let it flow readily, wave upon wave of excitement as they discussed the literature. Just as she had done only a few years earlier back in the classroom. She hadn't realized how much she missed those discussions until now.

"Are you still going to college?" asked Louise finally, tiring of the book talk.

"N-no, no, I'm not in school, but"—Lena felt the words stick in her throat—"I'd like to be." Once the words had emerged, she felt a rush of relief. She had said it, hadn't dared think it until now. She wanted to go back. She needed it.

"Louise, you mentioned that you were applying to colleges. Which ones?"

The girl put the book down and, when she began to speak, became more animated than Lena had ever seen her. When Louise brushed the strands of black hair off her forehead, Lena took note of her eyelashes, which were long and encircled the darkest eyes she had ever seen. Until that moment she hadn't realized how pretty she was, how young. They were only seven years apart in age, but to Lena it seemed like an entire generation.

"I'm thinking of a state school, my parents can't afford anything else. So it'll be City College or maybe Rutgers in New Jersey. Anything but Brooklyn. I've got two little brothers at home, and I need to get away. You know, have the experience? Maybe join a sorority or a house plan, or even cheer for the teams. I'm lucky that my parents are all for it. I'm thinking of going into elementary education since I've always been good with kids. I'm up for any college that we can afford, something not too far away, any place but Brooklyn College. It's just too close." She leaned in and turned her eyes directly at Lena. "Did you know that I will be the first in my family to go to college?"

"Really? Well, so am I!" She blurted the words out, regretting them instantly.

"Wait a minute," Louise said, opening her deep-brown eyes large. "I thought you said you didn't attend college."

"N-no, I don't"—Lena hesitated—"but I did. I mean to say that I began college, but I quit. I quit to run the business." A feeling of shame washed over her, and she couldn't quite understand why.

"Oh, so you left school to become a baker."

Lena considered this.

"Well, I didn't, not really. I've been a baker all along, and Luke found this bakeshop, and, well, the rest, as they say, is history."

"When you were in school, were you studying culinary arts? Is that even a major?"

"I suppose it may be, but that's not what I intended on majoring in."

"What were you majoring in, then? English?" asked Louise, leaning forward.

It dawned on Lena that she didn't quite have an answer, hadn't decided on the career she wanted to pursue. Not until the words came rushing out.

"Maybe. English with a minor in Spanish. I was thinking of prelaw." Not until she had said it had she realized that yes, yes, that was what she wanted to do. Once, she had wanted to become a lawyer. And she still did.

"Well," said Louise, returning to her book, "it's great that you can bake all these delicious cupcakes and stuff. Your own bakery. Pretty great," she repeated.

Lena smiled. If only Louise knew how wrong she was.

~

"The bakery can practically run itself."

Lena listened to Luke as she cut into her minute steak. She knew that he had said it as an offhand remark, yet now she wondered whether she could believe him. He was bragging about Brooklyn Girl's Bake Shoppe as usual, telling her what an extraordinary baker she was, not only for the Orthodox Jews who frequented the shop, but also for the Italians, whose numbers were growing in the community every day. He also bragged about his own skills, though indirectly, how it was genius to find the perfect store in the perfect neighborhood, how within a few short years the bakery would be theirs free and clear, and now with an assistant—one who had trained in baking breads and pastries—as well as another young girl who helped on the retail side of the business, they could take some time off, look into expansion.

Funny, Lena thought, bringing a french fry to her mouth, that he hadn't mentioned her parents. Funny because if not for their substantial contribution, they could never have afforded the bakery in the first place. She set down her fork and wiped her lips with a paper napkin. Nevertheless, Luke was mostly right. Once they had the money, he alone was responsible for their success.

That night Lena had trouble falling asleep. She tried counting the rhythmic waves of the water as it sloshed beneath her body, but it was to no avail. A full moon pierced through the blinds, and when she finally opened her eyes, she couldn't help but follow its misty light. It was a strange feeling, and she was baffled as to its meaning. Luke insisted that they were at long last successful, happy. The future lay ahead as bright as the rays that now mesmerized her. Successful and happy. Was it that? Were they really successful and happy with all they had yearned for now within their grasp?

Lena felt the moisture of a tear clinging to her eyelash. Luke had even hinted that perhaps now might be the time to start a family. She was only twenty-three. She wanted a family, always knew that she would have a child someday. But was now the time?

As she lay there, waiting for an elusive sleep to sneak beneath her eyelids, Lena recalled Luke's promises to her. A dazzling diamond ring. A watch. Were they all just empty words?

She lifted her head to look at the number that was lit up on the alarm clock on Luke's night table. But the effort was futile. Without her contact lenses or glasses, it was all a blur. Was it two a.m. or three? She had to be at the bakery by five. The moon would have dimmed by then, giving way to a gray, then stark, daylight.

Lena arose, careful not to awaken Luke and, instead of reaching for her glasses, made her way to the small wooden desk that sat beneath the window. She retrieved a lined pad and BIC pen. Quickly, she began to write.

17

ANYA

Tired of writing, Anya put down the pen. She had been copying words from the *Daily News* at the kitchen table for the last hour and was beginning to wonder whether the effort wasn't futile, after all. Josef kept telling her how important it was for her to learn new words in English, how she couldn't remain an ignorant greenhorn for all her life, but just the same she preferred her *Jewish Daily Forward* to bring her news of the world, news of home.

Anya pushed her reading glasses to the top of her head, folded the newspaper, and stretched. As she did, she felt a spasm in her lower back, one she had gotten used to during the past year, and she hoped it would not be followed by nausea this time. These episodes made her acknowledge that she was getting older. After all, it wasn't so long ago that she had turned sixty, no spring chicken! Or maybe it was just a reaction to the distressing news she had been reading. No matter how much she searched the articles, it was always the same. Only months after US forces had returned from the long war in Vietnam, Israel was attacked, and on Yom Kippur, the holiest day of the year. It seemed that 1973 had been no better than years past, and now with the new year, the threat of nuclear holocaust was hanging over their heads. The news was always bad.

Nevertheless, it was all a necessary diversion now that her mind was preoccupied with her only child. She felt like she was perpetually on alert, not like when she was at the camps, of course, but it was still there. The sense of impending doom.

Would she ever learn? There was nothing she could do to help her daughter. Every hour it seemed, she had to suppress the feelings, the urge to pick up the phone, board a bus to the bakery and put on an apron, talk to Lena, ask her how she was doing. Was the business what she really wanted? Was her marriage? But Anya knew her concern would be useless. In fact, it would have the opposite effect, and push her daughter further away from her.

Anya tried to put her mind on other things, just as Josef advised.

"Think of the pleasant things in life, my dear," he said that morning as both sat at the table eating steaming bowls of Cream of Wheat. "Think of these white chrysanthemums I picked up for our anniversary two days ago," he added, pointing to the flowers in a green glass vase sitting atop the counter, "or the fact that tomorrow will be the first day of spring. The weathermen are predicting seventy degrees later this afternoon. Can you imagine that? It was only last week that we had a snowstorm! And now not a snowflake in sight!" He put down his spoon and reached over to pat her arm. She looked at him, the man she had known for nearly all her life. If she couldn't trust his words, then what could she trust? She turned her lips up in a smile, knowing that despite her best efforts, Josef could still see her pain.

He sat back, picked up his spoon, but didn't bring it to his mouth.

"You know, Anya, if you can't think of those happy things," he began, his eyes never leaving her face, "then think of how lucky we are. I'm not saying we should forget all the bad, no, all that is a part of us now. Forever will be. But think of our good fortune after all we have been through. The two of us sitting here now in this great country, free Jews with jobs, a successful married daughter, sitting in this apartment eating our warm bowls of Cream of Wheat, and tonight we will have our special anniversary dinner, our forty-fourth! How lucky we are, Anya! Can't you see that?"

Anya looked into her husband's eyes, trying again to find the source of strength within them. Forty-four. Not a special anniversary, but Josef liked to celebrate each one in a special way. It was one of the little things that gave him pleasure. She smiled, hoping it seemed more genuine this time. When Josef dipped his spoon back into the cereal, she did the same. The two ate the rest of their meal in silence.

As Anya rose to gather the day's newspapers and toss them into the garbage can near the sink, she felt a familiar twinge in her lower back. She tried to summon Josef's words, hoping they would lighten her spirits. How she envied him, his confidence, his ability to look into the future and find the light, even if just a glimmer, where she found only darkness. She understood each word he said, of course, understood his sometimes uncanny ability to keep the past in the past, to look forward to what was to come, and yet why was it that, despite this understanding, her heart was pulling her back, not only to the war years, the years blackened by the soot of remembrance, but to all the years that followed Lena's birth, a time that should have given her peace and contentment, but continued to trouble her even now?

What plagued her the most was the notion that she had been a terrible mother. She had convinced herself that she was. Not to Ruby, of course. She had coveted the child, the girl who seemed smarter, more lovely, skilled, than any of her friends' daughters. She had been poised to take over the bakery one day; Anya could see it even then. What did it matter that she had a clubfoot? To Anya, the affliction made her only more admirable, more endearing. And so, without reservation, she had given Ruby her heart. Only, thought Anya, her eye twitching, to have it ripped out of her. Had she any left to give Lena? And if she did, could she bear giving her heart away only to have it snatched from her by a sudden illness, an accident, an *abduction*?

Despite anything Josef said, his affirmations, consolations, Anya knew she had not been the best of mothers. Instead of praising her for a good grade at school, she would nod and smile weakly. And when Lena begged her to read stories or snuggle against her in bed when she had a nightmare, Anya turned away, not because she didn't care, but because she had begun to care too much. Worst of all were the times Lena tried to please her with her baked creations, hoping to gain favor in her mother's eyes. Anya would turn away angrily, often reprimanding her, afraid to remember the past, afraid to embrace the present.

Eventually Lena stopped begging for her mother's affections, becoming more reticent, withdrawn. She threw tantrums for no reason at all, spent hours alone in her room, ran away in a haze of anger and tears. Sometimes Anya was frustrated by these actions, but, though she hated to admit it to herself, often she felt relieved. Most times, like her daughter, she just wanted to be left alone.

No, Anya resolved as she entered the bedroom and opened the door to her closet, she mustn't let her emotions overcome her again. She would take Josef's advice. She would try to be happy.

She surveyed the dresses that hung in the small closet. She didn't have many, anyone could see that, but whatever she had was high class, of the best quality, with straight seams sewn not in China, but in the US, and of the finest fabric. Her eye went immediately to a long red dress, and, pulling it out, she placed the garment in front of her as she gazed into the full-length mirror in the corner of the room.

Anya let her hand slide down the cool silk as she assessed the dress in her reflection. It was simple, with a V-neck, a cinch at the waist, the rest of the fabric falling in folds to nearly the tip of her ankles. The rose-red shade brought a blush of color to her face, a brightness that had not been there before. It suited her skin well, she knew, but she wondered if, after all this time, the dress would fit at all. It had been quite a few years now since her menses had stopped, and with that came the extra pounds, so that now rounds of fat had begun to pad her stomach and hips. She was not the same svelte girl Josef had fallen in love with before the war. Not even the same diminished young mother he had brought to this country. But gazing at herself in the mirror now, she couldn't dismiss the pleasant feeling she had as she held the garment in front of her. And the memories.

Josef, only weeks after they had disembarked the ship, had dragged her into a dress shop as they explored the row of stores on Flatbush Avenue. It was the first he saw, sheathing a mannequin in the front window, and he insisted she try it on. Despite her protestations, Josef walked over to the shop's owner and, displaying not the least bit of discomfort at being a man in a shop that catered to women, asked her to accompany his wife to the fitting room. Except for a necessary stitch or two at the bodice, it was a perfect fit, and within minutes Josef was reaching for the wallet in his back pocket. He hadn't even bothered to inquire about the price. Learning it was on sale at one hundred dollars, still too much money considering she had no special occasion to wear the dress, Anya finally acquiesced to the purchase. After all, it was such a pretty gown.

But that day, as she stood in front of the mirror, she could still see a problem, but only a slight one. The dress, being of such a bright color and luxurious fabric, had no adornment. And Anya didn't have much jewelry to set it off, as she had purchased only a few baubles, mostly costume jewelry, in the decades since they arrived in America. The Nazis had confiscated all their valuables, along with some worthless trinkets, like a locket with a photograph of Josef, and a charm bracelet whose only worth could be counted in memories.

Now, as she laid the dress across the bed, she remembered the small gold box that sat beneath the stockings and lavender sachet in a bottom dresser drawer. She pushed aside the nylons, looking for the gift Josef had made her all those years ago. Finding it, she removed the necklace inside. The gem sparkled as it winked up at her, still as radiant as the day it was purchased. Another gift from Josef given on the day they found out that Anya was once again with child. It was a ruby, a round shape held by a circle of prongs in the center of a slender gold necklace. Seeing it again after all these years, Anya began to cry. When she had first held the necklace in her hand, she wondered whether, knowing all it stood for, she could ever bring herself to wear it. She had decided that perhaps later, when the hurt of losing her firstborn wasn't so fresh, the memories had dimmed. Now Lena was a young woman, a married woman, and Anya's thoughts drifted toward the future and what it might bring. No matter what happened, one day the stone would be hers.

It had been over twenty years since Josef had made her the gift of the stunning ruby. She hadn't worn it since, not after Lena was born, not even after she was grown and left home. And, as Anya held it against her skin now, she wondered if she ever could.

~

Despite the date on the calendar, despite the spring buds that had already begun to burst through the soil, an icy wind slapped against the tree limbs and enveloped the couple as they made their way to the subway station. The soft folds of the red dress were so wet now, the bottom half exposed beneath the gray wool coat, that the fabric clung to her knees, chilling her to the bone. Nevertheless, Anya was glad she had decided finally to wear the gown. It was, after all, Josef's favorite color, and the look on his face when she met him in the vestibule of the apartment that night confirmed that her choice was the right one.

Josef steered her down the stairs of the subway station, and as the two stood among the other travelers, those working the night shift or couples like themselves, eager for an evening out in the city, Anya clung tightly to Josef's arm.

The wait seemed interminable, but finally the D line roared to a halt in front of them, and they piled into a car with all the rest. Anya relaxed into one of a pair of seats next to a window blotted with gray soot. She felt lucky to be seated and not having to stand against a pole like some of the others, trying to balance in a pair of high heels. She removed her hood and placed a hand to her hair, which was frizzy, the tendrils going this way and that, despite the quarter can of hair spray she had doused it with before leaving the apartment. Anya was distracted and now realized that Josef was talking to her, or at least trying to, above the din of the train.

"What was that you said?"

"I asked if you were happy that we are going out?"

Anya blinked, took a moment before responding.

"Yes, Josef, I do believe I am happy! I'm sure we will have a good time with the cousins tonight."

Josef drew her closer, patted her hand, and, before she could register a protest, right in front of everyone, he pressed his lips against her cheek. Anya shook her head but smiled warmly. Their short exchange felt just like the old days, a time she could barely remember before all she knew in life had crumbled to ashes, a time when she had hope that life could be joyous. She tried to hold on to that moment as the train jostled them over the winding tracks. She tried to believe in what Josef had told her. She *would* believe, even if only for a little while.

By the time Anya and Josef arrived at Mamma Leone's on West Forty-Eighth Street, the cousins Heinek and Sarah were already seated at a table in the back of the restaurant. They both rose, and then they all kissed each other on the cheek before sitting down. An open bottle of wine had already been placed at the center of the table.

"I hope you'll forgive me for ordering the wine," Heinek said, reaching over with a flourish to fill their glasses, "but I understand this is a special occasion. Forty-four years, no?"

"That's right!" said Josef as he lifted his glass with all the rest. "Can you imagine how time flies?"

"So true, my cousin. And so we must celebrate while we can! L'chaim!" The others echoed the toast, clinking their glasses for luck.

Anya put her lips to the glass and tasted. Wine was a rare treat, saved for only the most special occasions, like this one. After one sip, she discovered she enjoyed its sweet fruity taste and nearly finished half the glass in a single gulp. She hoped the wine would make her giddy, a description no one ever used when referring to Anya.

Heinek continued talking as Josef and Anya lifted the giant-size menus and perused the long list of appetizers and entrées. The foods they planned to order were limited, though, to simple meatless pasta and fish in order to abide by kosher restrictions.

"It is an honor for Sarah and me to accompany you on this very big anniversary! And to think that it was a time not too long ago that you did not know if you would see the light of another sun," he went on, pausing only to pick up his glass and finish what was left of his wine.

Anya sat back and surveyed the couple. Heinek and Sarah, both already in their seventies, looked so alike that they could almost be mistaken for brother and sister. Both had ruddy complexions and wide mouths that filled up nearly half their faces when they smiled. And both were quite overweight, Heinek verging on obese, so that it was only through great exertion that he was able to lift himself off the seat when he toasted the pair. It was also the reason he needed to stop every so often during his monologue to draw a breath or take up the cloth napkin to wipe the sweat from his brow. Nevertheless, Anya observed, despite their weight, the cousins appeared years younger than she and Josef, their cheeks unlined, brows smooth, hardly a line appearing beneath their eyes. The cousins had arrived in the United States long before Hitler's turmoil. The years had been kind. Perhaps she and Josef did appear older than their years, and if so, that had been the smallest price they would pay, she reasoned. Her attention shifted to Josef, who, finally able to get a word in, was now speaking.

"It is Anya and me who are honored to have you with us. If not for our mutual cousin, Carl Shmuel, we would still be back in Poland, and then what kind of life would we have? We are happy to have family in this great country. For us, there is nobody else."

And to that they toasted again, after Heinek ceremoniously filled their glasses. Anya nearly completed a second glass as, relinquishing all inhibitions, she felt a blush rise to her face, making her wonder briefly if her cheeks now matched the color of her dress.

Anya found herself echoing Josef's words, thanking his cousins again in a mixture of English and the more familiar Yiddish, for what seemed like the hundredth time, for their generosity in welcoming them into the US. Josef had been correct, too, when he said that Sarah and Heinek were the only people who could be a part of such a special occasion. In fact, Anya acknowledged to herself, the cousins were the only social circle they had. Disappointments with those they considered friends back in Europe, who had either ignored them or chided them, and all because they were Jewish. The transformation of those individuals had caused the couple to be wary of anyone who was not a blood relation. Heinek and Sarah were here because they were the only ones who could be trusted.

A waiter, impeccably clad in a white shirt and red bow tie, interrupted the round of compliments to take their orders, the two ladies opting for the fish, while Josef, more daring, had a dish he had never tried before: baked eggplant parmigiana. And for Heinek, the cheese ravioli. All agreed the meal would be a break from the bland chicken or beef they usually cooked at home. Before five minutes had passed, they were all dipping their spoons into a generous goblet of fruit cocktail.

But just as Anya brought the spoon to her mouth, she felt a sharp ache in her lower back, this time more painful than she had ever felt before. Quickly, she excused herself to go to the bathroom. By the time she returned, she felt no better, and what was worse, her head began to spin. Perhaps she shouldn't have had all that wine.

She sat down shakily. Sensing her distress, Josef whispered in her ear, "Is it the same as before?" She closed her eyes, suddenly feeling nauseated, and, unable to speak, nodded. Already she could feel the blood drain from her face, where a deep blush had been only moments earlier. And although she attempted a few more spoons of the appetizer, Anya knew the effort was futile.

Josef's voice seemed distant as he made apologies to the cousins, not bothering to quarrel when Heinek insisted on covering the cost of the meal, promising to bring doggie bags to their apartment the next day.

Even though the weather had turned milder as Josef, his arm encircling her now, walked her to the subway station a block away, Anya felt a chill run through her bones.

"Feeling any better?" he asked, pressing his face close, although he could already sense her answer.

Just as they approached the stairs, she felt a churning inside her belly, knowing that if she uttered a word, the vomit would come flying out of her mouth. So, as she had done all her life, Anya silently pushed on. Before she fell asleep on Josef's arm just as the train rattled to life, she had a moment of clarity as one thought drifted across her mind. Once again she had spoiled everything. Once again, there was disappointment. And it seemed like that was all there would ever be.

18

She held the phone to her ear, waiting. But after the fifth ring, Anya reluctantly dropped the receiver back into the cradle. Why did she continue to torture herself? Why did she continue to worry about things she had no control over?

Anya took a deep breath before getting up from her chair and walking over to the stockpot, which she had filled with a sweet young pullet, chopped carrots and celery, a parsnip, and a handful of parsley. It was beginning to bubble, and she stirred it now with a long silver spoon before lowering the flame. She would have another chicken soup, along with some slices of brisket and roast potatoes ready for the Sabbath. Sometimes Anya wondered why she bothered with such an elaborate meal. After all, it was only the two of them in the apartment now. It had been over a year since Lena had stopped visiting, claiming she was always too busy running the shop she'd owned for two years, and Anya missed their weekly mother-daughter talks. And yet she tried to carry on as if nothing had changed, hoping that her daughter would show up at their door, holding one of her sweet round challahs, just before the darkness set in on a Friday evening. It had been a long time too before she had stopped waiting for the phone to ring nightly at precisely 9:00 p.m. and felt her nerves settling as she heard the light soprano tone come across the receiver. The two never spoke about anything of much consequence. *How are you? And Daddy? Yes, I'm fine. Yes, Luke too. The business, well, busy as usual. No, nothing new.* She never wanted to know more about the details of Lena's life. Anya had lived long enough not to expect more, long enough to know that "nothing new" was good enough.

But now that the frequency of the phone calls had diminished to once a week and then once or twice each month, Anya couldn't help but worry that something was wrong. Her concern grew worse when she would call the apartment and receive no answer. She had tried to call in the late afternoons when Lena might be home alone, so as to avoid a conversation with the husband, for what could she say to him anyway? But she let the phone ring three, four times, holding her breath for the pickup, which never came. She had tried calling the bakery on a couple of occasions, but only when she felt her heart beat so fast that she feared it might break on the spot. At those times, when Lena did answer, her voice was filled with angry recriminations. What was the emergency? Didn't Anya realize that this was a business? Didn't she realize that she barely had time to wash her hands, her voice nearly a shriek. Anya would apologize meekly, saying that she was just worried when she hadn't heard from her. But before she could finish her apologies, she realized that her daughter was no longer on the line. Yet, she consoled herself, at least she had heard Lena's voice. At least she knew that, for now, her child was okay.

But Anya's sense of serenity didn't last very long, for by the following week, she again found herself listening to the rings on the receiver, waiting for Lena to pick up, waiting to hear if all was fine.

Josef appealed to her to stop the nonsense. "Is not Lena a grown woman, a married woman with a life of her own? Dayenu!" he cried, using the Hebrew expression meaning "enough." Furthermore, he warned, Anya would become only more ill with whatever the problem was, and then where would they be? Nevertheless, she always imagined the worst had happened. Lena had been hit by a car or choked on a chicken bone, or maybe she had suffered a brain aneurysm, God forbid. Josef pooh-poohed it all, even though Anya always kept the worst scenarios to herself.

"Why must you be like that? Such a nervous Nelly." Anya ignored the insult, didn't even bother to lament the fact that she and Lena were most alike in these negative traits. Often, when Josef responded to her anxiety with blunt retorts, she would simply walk away, frustrated that the person she most relied on in this world did not understand. What choice had she but to think of the worst when the worst had already happened? If it happened once, couldn't it happen again?

By the time Josef walked in that evening, his jacket slung across his arm, the leather briefcase from the Old Country bulging with papers, two bowls of soup had already been placed on the kitchen table, three candles set in silver holders waiting to be lit. When she saw her husband's face brighten as he inhaled the aroma of the soup, Anya was glad she had taken the time to prepare the special meal, had earlier soaked herself in a hot bath, letting the soothing liquid wash away her worries, cleanse both her body and mind, at least for a little while.

"Mmm . . . ," he whispered, touching his lips to her neck, "you smell like lavender sachet." Whenever Josef kissed her like that, whenever he would whisper in her ear, Anya felt like the young girl who'd met Josef at her parents' door back in Lodz, a young woman waiting for her life to unfold, not a matron already in her sixties. And just as she did then, Anya took the jacket from his arm and led him inside.

"Eat before the soup gets cold," she said.

~

After a month went by and the couple still had not heard from their daughter, even Josef, who made a habit of remaining calm in the eye of the storm, had begun to exhibit signs of nervousness. On more than one evening, he had abandoned his favorite green tweed armchair, where he would relax at day's end, and instead would pace from one corner of the living room to the other, ignoring Walter Cronkite, even in his most serious newscast. Josef had also become impatient with Anya, more than usual. Finally, seeing the exasperated gaze of her eyes, the twitch in her upper lip, he relented.

"Very well, Anya, on Sunday we will go visit them in the bakery. I don't want you making yourself more sick with this worry."

Anya smiled and restrained herself from throwing her arms around Josef in an embrace. Immediately, she felt the heavy cloak of fear that she had carried the last few weeks fall from her shoulders.

"Thank you, thank you, Josef! I just need to see her, hear her voice. You know how crazy we mothers can get. But please don't worry about my health. I haven't had a pain since that time we went out with Heinek and Sarah three months ago." It was a lie, but only a small one. There was no reason Josef needed to worry about her too.

~

"It was such a sunny, beautiful day that we decided to get out, to come here for a little visit. Maybe take home some of those poppy seed muffins your daddy loves so much," said Anya, providing an explanation for their early-morning jaunt, which involved two bus rides and a three-block walk into the heart of Bensonhurst. Josef squeezed her upper arm as she spoke. Immediately Anya felt she had said too much. When had she become so afraid of her daughter? Afraid that she would scold her again for tracking her, getting into her private life, for loving her too much.

Lena shrugged and quickly reached into the showcase for four of the newly baked poppy seed muffins, their tops a warm yellow, resembling little suns. Before placing them into a white cardboard box, she handed one to Josef, who eagerly accepted, immediately biting into its soft center.

Anya wondered if she was glad to see them as Lena offered her a leftover raisin challah and one of her special fudge brownies. And, as she saw a smile drift across her daughter's face as she handed her the brownie wrapped in tissue paper, Anya decided she was. It was Josef, after brushing the crumbs from his mouth, who was blunt, blurting the real reason for their visit.

"All these days, a month already, we have not heard from you. No visits, not a phone call. Mommy and me, we did not know if you were alive or dead!"

Anya cast her eyes on the floor. She was relieved that he had included them both in their worry. Not just Mommy. Mommy and *me*.

Lena, who was tying a string around the box, now stopped and stared at Josef icily. She said nothing and resumed securing the box, but not before Anya noticed a tear slide down her left cheek. Lena shakily handed Josef the box before turning away and wiping her face with a tissue. Josef glanced at the front door to the shop and, seeing no one there, passed the box to Anya. Then, rushing behind the counter, threw both arms around his daughter as she sobbed into his chest.

Anya stood frozen in place, unable to decipher the whispered words exchanged between father and daughter. She felt helpless.

Finally, still wrapped in Josef's arms, Lena looked up, her face swollen and awash in tears.

"I'm sorry, Mommy, so sorry! I suppose I'm a terrible daughter. You must have thought I was dead! I heard the phone ring when you called, those times when I was at home. I didn't come to the phone because—I don't know!" She took a deep breath and her body shuddered. But when she opened her mouth to speak again, she appeared to choke on a sob, and the tears began anew. Finally, not bothering with a tissue, still locked in Josef's arms, she rubbed her cheeks against his white cotton shirt. When she again raised her head, Anya saw a deep sadness in her daughter's eyes, and it frightened her. "Sorry, Mommy," she repeated, letting go finally of her father. "I'm just exhausted, I guess. It's a lot of work, and it never seems to let up. Even if I'm not here physically, my mind is here. It's always here!" Lena's hands shook as she spoke.

It wasn't until she approached her mother, leaning toward her for a quick hug—not the same tight embrace she had given Josef—that Anya dared to speak.

"But it is what you wanted, Lena, is it not? This"—she let her arms sweep the expanse of the bakery—"all this is what you have always wanted." It was more statement than question, yet she watched as her daughter sighed, and, considering her words, Lena responded, "It is what *Luke* wants, Mommy. I'm not sure if all this is what I ever wanted."

Anya looked at her daughter's pale face and knew that this was not the first time she had cried that day. She had lost weight and had deep bags under her eyes. Maybe their staying away had not been such a good idea. And where was Luke?

But before she could ask the question, before she could grasp her daughter to her, offer words of comfort, they heard the jingle of the doorbell. Almost magically, Lena's expression changed back to the self-assured proprietor. As she walked over to assist the customer, Anya felt Josef at her side again, his hot breath on her neck.

"Do not bother her too much, Anya," he cautioned.

Every cell in her body wanted to respond, to tell him that she had said, had done, nothing wrong. And then she heard him add, "You know how sensitive she is." Anya bit her lip and walked away, pretending to look at the traffic out the front window. Then, remembering the brownie in the pocket of her spring coat, she removed it and sank her teeth into the fudge, momentarily relishing its sweetness before putting the rest back.

Lena wiped her hands on her apron as the customer, a young mother, head modestly wrapped in a gold paisley scarf, took the two loaves of babka, paid the bill, and slipped out the door.

Not one of them spoke, none knowing quite what to say. It was Lena who finally broke the silence.

"Look, I'm sorry about the tears. I guess I can get too emotional sometimes. I'm tired. Tired and busy. And I really have no reason to complain. The bakery is doing well. *I'm* doing well." She opened her eyes wide and looked directly at her parents as if to emphasize the veracity of her words.

"And Luke," she added, turning to Anya, "Luke has been nothing but helpful. Encouraging." She smiled. Broader this time.

Anya decided she would not ask Lena about Luke. It seemed pointless. Instead, she moved toward her child, but backed off, leaving her hands at her sides.

"Lena, please tell us. Tell us what is wrong."

Lena coughed and looked down at the floor, then up again, as if about to speak. But she only shook her head.

"She is fine, Anya," said Josef finally. "If she tells us all is good, then it must be so. Is not that right, my Lena? Just a little tired, as are we all! Right?"

Lena looked up, the same smile on her lips, but said nothing.

Josef took his wife's arm, leading her toward the door, as Anya grabbed the paper bag containing the challah. But before they knew it, Lena was next to them, hugging her father, then Anya.

"Don't worry," she whispered in her ear before releasing her.

Once outside, the couple found themselves wrapped in the warmth of a golden sun that had peeked over the rooftops. The brilliant day did nothing to soften Anya's mood, though. She thought about what she should say now to Josef, how to make him understand all her concerns for their only daughter, how to tell him all that was in her heart. But before she could speak, he had whisked her around the corner in front of an alley that was empty, save for a straggly black cat sniffing at the metal trash cans. He turned her around so that they were now standing face-to-face.

"Enough," he pleaded, his voice low, stern. "You must not bother her anymore. When she wants to tell us what is going on, she will tell us. Or she will not. This is her choice. Do you not remember what happened the last time you pushed? What she went through, what we all did? It is enough, I say."

Anya stood stiffly, trying to avoid her husband's glare. She resented his words, his demeanor, the way he talked down to her as if she were a child. And yet something inside her told her to stop the rebellion simmering within, something that told her he was right. She set her mouth in a grim line and continued walking, still holding on to Josef's hand.

Once inside the apartment, Anya shut the shades, still finding the streams of sunlight coming in contrary to her mood. She removed her coat and, hanging it up, discovered half of the brownie in a pocket, forgotten, uneaten. She wrapped it up in the tissue paper, brought it into the kitchen, and threw it into the empty garbage pail.

19

Anya had heard about people reinventing themselves—those who had become teachers, even doctors, later in life, the woman who wrote a cookbook after years of preparing meals for her family, the eighty-year-old who taught classes in accounting at the local college. Anya decided that she, too, needed to reinvent herself. Only how? What would she do? She knew only that she couldn't stay as she was, working a few hours each week in a five-and-dime, cooking chicken soup for Josef each Friday night. And the rest of the time feeling Lena sit in her brain like a bird waiting to be hatched. It was just another premonition that something terrible would befall her one remaining child. The worst had happened once before. So why wouldn't it happen again? She needed something new to occupy her mind, that was for sure.

She determined to tell Josef of her idea, some new hobby, or a job. She was already in her sixties, but it wasn't too late. Josef would have the answer. She was sure of it.

It was another beautiful Saturday morning, and for once Anya felt attuned to the weather. The two left their jackets behind and put on their sunglasses as they stepped outside to be greeted by a friendly orange sun. No sooner had they done so than they heard the gleeful shriek of a little girl.

"Mrs. Sokoloff!" The child was running so fast toward her that Anya nearly stumbled into her.

"Stacey! And where are you off today that you are in such a hurry?"

The girl responded with a giggle and wrapped her arms around Anya's waist. She placed her hand atop the three-year-old's feathery raven hair as the child hugged her tightly.

"Come now, Stacey, don't bother Mrs. Sokoloff. If you squeeze too tight, you may just break her body!" The girl gazed up at her mother, eyes wide.

"Now, now, little one, your mama is only making a joke. You can squeeze me as hard as you like!" Anya said, kneeling so that her face was on the same level as the child's. What an angelic creature, she thought. Innocence could be seen in every facet of her face—the silky white complexion, her shining blue eyes, the lips that radiated warmth whenever she laughed or smiled. How could anyone deny this face a thing?

"We are going to the park!" the child announced, finally extricating herself from Anya's body.

"Well, how exciting! And what's your favorite thing to do there, do you think? Is it the swings or the giant slide?" The girl's face turned serious as she contemplated the question.

"I think maybe the monkey bars. I am a very good climber!"

"Well, that does sound like fun!" Anya said, feeling her knees crack as she rose to full height. But then she remembered something and quickly dug her hand into her skirt pocket. Coming up with nothing, she frowned.

"Oh, sweetie, I'm so sorry. I have no lollies! They are in the pocket of my coat at home. But the next time we see one another, I promise to bring you one, a purple, your favorite!"

Before the girl could respond, the mother took up her hand. She smiled at Anya.

"Oh, Mrs. Sokoloff, there really is no need. You are much, much too kind, with your lollipops and baked cookies, and I won't soon forget that time you read to her in your apartment when I had to run out to tend to Mama when she fell," said the mother, a tall, slender woman dressed in crisp jeans and a light-blue button-down shirt. The woman brushed back some stray hairs from her hastily wound ponytail. Examining her now, Anya could see that Stacey had her mother's eyes.

"Nonsense! It is truly my pleasure," she responded. "Besides, what better things do I have to do now that my own daughter is grown up and out of the house?"

"Well, I appreciate it anyway," said the young woman as the child began tugging at her arm. "I guess we'd better be going. Stacey's been stuck at home with a bad cold and missed a whole week of nursery school at the synagogue. So she's somewhat eager to get out and play." Her last words trailed behind as, with a quick wave, the mother allowed herself to be pulled along.

The smile remained on Anya's face as she watched the mother and child walk down the block. The short conversation had made her forget her worries about Lena, her own mystery illness, the general state of the world. Children had that effect on her. Unlike older individuals, they possessed an endearing innocence, and one didn't have to worry about ulterior motives. And, lucky for her, children were naturally drawn to her, but she was never sure quite why. As a result, she had made friendships with many of the youngsters in the building, as they and their parents stood in the lobby, waiting for a rainstorm to subside, or as they strolled down the street on their way to school or the playground. Her husband, who never seemed to have time for friends of his own, seemed happy that Anya had this small diversion.

Josef, who hadn't said a word during the exchange, was waiting patiently beside her, so that Anya hardly noticed him as he took her arm once more and the two walked in the opposite direction from the park. Anya's mind had been so focused on the child that she had forgotten the thing she wanted to talk to Josef about. It was only after they had walked the rest of the block in silence that she remembered.

"Josef," she began, as the two stepped off a curb, "I have been thinking."

He turned to her curiously. "Thinking, eh? Perhaps it is a dangerous thing when a woman thinks too much." He smirked. Anya grimaced, not sure if she should laugh or be insulted by the joke.

"I am serious. I have been thinking about myself. You know, I may be past middle age, but not so old that I cannot try something new. I know I have the five-and-dime and my baking, but—well, sometimes I find myself bored, and when I'm bored, oh, I worry about everything."

She watched Josef's eyebrows rise on the last words as they kept walking.

"And I had a question for you—many questions, in fact, about what I could do, but now, well, actually, I don't have a question anymore. Now I know."

Josef waited for her to continue as they made their way beneath the rows of towering oak trees that were now crowned with emerald-hued leaves. But, for the rest of their journey, Anya remained silent, her face as enigmatic as a sphinx.

20

Anya picked up the crying child.

"Now, Ari, why so many tears?" she asked, grabbing a tissue from the cube on the teacher's desk as she rocked the child in her arms. It took a while before the little boy could finally respond through the sobs.

"Michael pushed me!" He pouted, pointing to the culprit as, still clinging to her skirt, he cast the boy an accusatory look.

Michael, a chubby child with freckles and auburn hair, gritted his teeth and gave his accuser one of those "if looks could kill" stares.

"He was in my way!" he blurted out. "I was playing with the truck, and he tried to take it from me!"

Ari lifted his head from Anya's shoulder just long enough to respond.

"Did not! I just wanted to see it!"

Holding the boy's hand, Anya walked over to the other, who still had the red toy truck tightly in his grasp. She put down the child, who had stopped crying and was now sniffling indignantly.

"You see, Michael, Ari did not want to take your toy. He just wanted to look at it, right, my love?"

The child nodded slowly as he wiped his tear-streaked face with a bare hand.

"And you, Michael, you did not really want to hurt your friend. Isn't that true?" Now Michael nodded, his lips still set in an angry line.

"Well, that's good. The two of you are friends, so why don't you shake hands like the good friends you are?"

They did as instructed as Anya moved toward a jumbo basket filled with toys and dug out a white metal dump truck.

"Here you go, Ari," she said, handing it to the aggrieved party. "Now both of you have your own truck and can play together." She stood for a few minutes longer as the boys began rolling their vehicles on the multicolored carpet, watching the smiles materialize on their faces before she walked away.

"Well, you settled that skirmish quite well," said the young teacher who had witnessed the argument a few minutes earlier. Anya turned her eyes to the teacher and smiled.

"Oh, it was not a very big problem at all. And look, now they are the best of friends!"

"Anyway, I think you are a natural!"

Anya shook her head, fixing her eyes on the nursery-school teacher, a petite woman, a girl barely older than Lena.

"I am sorry, Miss Berger, what is *natural*, please?"

The woman shook her head and laughed amiably.

"It means that taking care of children comes easy to you. You are so good with them. And, please, do call me Elise."

Anya tapped herself on the forehead.

"Oh, I'm sorry, I had forgotten," she said, knowing that no matter how many times she was reminded, she could never bring herself to call a teacher by her given name. "And thank you for the compliment. It is easy for me because I love all the children."

"I can see that you do! And we are so happy to have you here with us," the teacher added before turning away to inspect some of the children's drawings of spring.

Anya remained standing, her hands clasped in front of her. As she observed the children, she let the teacher's words of praise sink in. There was no doubt that she was good with the little ones, knowing just the right things to say when they were upset, turning their frowns into giggles with a funny face or a well-chosen word. And she wondered now why she hadn't considered this job sooner. Although she knew that working two hours a day, three times a week, could hardly be called a job. Especially since as a volunteer she wasn't getting paid to do it. In truth, though, she would have gladly paid the synagogue for the privilege of being in this classroom filled with rambunctious, curious three-year-olds. And she realized that being here as an assistant, a reader, a comforter, had been just what she needed too. Something to take her mind off her worries, both real and imagined.

She had fancied becoming a teacher once, when she was a young student admiring her sixth-grade teacher at the primary school, Mme. Muller, a kind, gentle woman who was blind in one eye and had limited sight in the other, but managed life as if she had not only perfect vision, but also eyes in the back of her head. It wasn't only her empathetic nature that Anya admired, but her confidence in all things, not just academics. Anya often thought of Mme. Muller during the early days as she raised her own child, little Ruby, teaching her that despite her disability, she could be anything, do anything, she wanted. And, indeed, Ruby did.

Ruby. Anya surveyed the nursery, the little children, those chubby and skinny, smiling and sullen, those running and those sitting quietly by themselves. So many children, and each unique, different. She examined their faces, the boys, the girls, their eyes blue and brown, and yet none seemed familiar to her now. None was her Ruby.

Had it been so long since she had last seen her, even if it was only in her mind? After all these years, had Anya already forgotten the touch of Ruby's lips on her cheek, her laughter that sounded like falling rain? She had no pictures, not one. And now she feared she had forgotten her child's face too. The thought made her shudder.

"Mrs. Sokoloff? Mrs. Sokoloff? I need to potty." A mop-headed girl with large brown eyes, already on the verge of tears, was tugging at her skirt, bringing Anya's attention back to the present.

"Okay, Rachel, let's go!" she said, grasping the child's hand and leading her to the bathroom near the entrance of the nursery. But by the time a toilet was reached, the little girl's panties were soaked. Seeing the mess, and the tears forming now in Rachel's eyes, Anya smiled, gave her a quick hug, and immediately retrieved a clean pair of underwear from the girl's backpack, resolving the situation.

"Well now, you are just fine," Anya consoled, adding in a whisper, "Everybody has accidents."

The girl nodded. "Thank you," she said meekly before going off to play with the others.

Anya drew a deep breath and looked at her watch. Nearly three o'clock, and she would be done for the day. How fast the time went when she was here with all the little ones! And to think that ever since the war, as she pondered her life in this new country, she hadn't once entertained the notion of becoming a teacher, or even a class volunteer, for that matter. In truth, she had been afraid of working with young children. Ever since she realized that the world could be a horrible place. How could she teach children to be optimistic, to look with joy to the future, when she wasn't sure they would have a future at all?

Anya knew she would forever be chained to the past, but maybe seeing all the children playing and laughing, the light shining in their eyes, perhaps—just perhaps—there was a future too.

~

Anya placed her straw purse on the floor and removed her shoes. Usually spending a few hours with the youngsters gave her more energy, to clean out a closet or prepare a Jell-O mold for dessert, but today, for some reason, she was tired and, once seated on the couch, found it difficult to get up. *When was the last time I heard from Lena?* she wondered before drifting off into a dreamless sleep.

It seemed like only a few minutes had passed when she stirred. Someone was shaking her.

"Anya, what is wrong with you? I come home over an hour, and you are sleeping here in the middle of the day. Anya," repeated the voice, more urgent this time, "what is wrong with you?"

Startled, she looked at her husband with wide eyes.

"The steak! Oh, Josef, I have not yet put the steak in the broiler. And the potatoes to fry! Why did you let me sleep so long?"

Anya moved to get up off the couch but found she couldn't. This time the pain was too great.

21

Lena

Lena hadn't realized how much she missed being a student until her first day of class. She had chosen a night class in English literature partially because of her conversation with Louise, but also because she wanted to distance herself from anything having to do with business. Of course, Luke was opposed to the idea—both of her ideas, actually. At first, when he couldn't convince her that returning to school would be a waste of her time and money, he had urged her to proceed with a major in business, which would only enhance her knowledge and, bottom line, profits. Usually, she allowed herself to be swayed by his persuasion, so she surprised herself with her response.

"That doesn't make sense to me," she told him, as the two stood in the back room of the bakery, unpacking a large crate filled with jumbo bags of flour, "since you have enough business acumen for the two of us." The flattery had worked, as when he lifted another bag to the counter, a self-satisfied smile appeared on his face.

"Besides," she added, "it doesn't really matter what subject I major in if I'm set on going to law school. As long as I get good grades and a decent score on the LSAT, I should be fine."

At this he grimaced, turning away from her to wash his hands at the sink.

Lena felt a flicker of compassion for her husband, who in that instant appeared so vulnerable and defeated. And something else too. Sexy. The softness he displayed, coupled with the alluring scent of his Canoe cologne and the sweet way the strands of his dark hair fell across his eye, was so powerful that it was difficult for her to resist running to him now, telling him that he was right, of course, and it had all been a foolish idea. Instead, Lena stiffened her back, ignored the cologne, the endearing boyish expression in his eyes, and said nothing. She began night classes at Brooklyn College two days later.

~

It was as if she had never been away. She found it hard to believe that three long years had passed. The fluorescent lights overhead as she walked in and took a seat close to the back of the room seemed to ignite something inside her, a desire to soak in all she could about the comedies of Shakespeare, a subject she had only just touched upon in a reading of *A Midsummer Night's Dream* while she was in high school. Despite her fears, she was able to keep up with her readings, only by staying up late at night while Luke slept untroubled beside her. Mornings still proved impossible, as she was occupied with preparing the day's inventory of goods even as Risa pounded the dough alongside before shoving the breads and cakes into huge ovens.

But all the pressure and exhaustion were forgotten once Lena sat in class, inching her way up each day until only two weeks later she occupied the seat directly in front of her professor, Dr. Collins, whose scholarship in the field was indeed both admirable and bottomless. She found herself settling into class comfortably amid the aroma of chalk dust and the taps as Dr. Collins wrote quickly on the blackboard. Her mind was ignited now, sparked, eager to answer each question posed. Funny, she thought, how she felt more at home in this college classroom than she had in the apartment she had shared the last few years with Luke.

She decided to take a class in anthropology that met on Mondays and Wednesdays, and began ten minutes after her English class. It was a prerequisite for graduation and not nearly as stimulating as her first class. She found some of the readings on Aztec civilization boring, but once she selected Margaret Mead for the topic of her research paper, Lena grew excited as she learned about the anthropologist's perseverance, her innovative studies, in a field largely dominated by men. And she did enjoy the class—even her professor, an elderly man with a heavy Russian accent, often difficult to understand. Lena had never anticipated that starting school again would be easy. It wasn't. What she couldn't foresee was how much she would love it. And she did—perhaps more than anything—certainly more than working at the bakery.

~

Belonging. It was a word Lena rarely thought about. It was a word that had little meaning for her in her reality. Certainly, she knew that she was an integral part of her parents' lives, a beloved daughter. But as for belonging, perhaps not, not when ghosts filled the home, leaving little room for anyone else. Her parents would deny it, would assure her that she alone took up the space in their home, that she alone occupied their thoughts and dreams. But Lena knew better. Whenever she saw Daddy return from work, remove his coat, and, still standing, stare out the kitchen window, mesmerized, as the moon rose above the courtyard, its stoic buildings looming in a circle, she knew. Whenever Mama would open her bedroom door in the morning as she wiped a last tear from her eye, she knew. She knew it was not she who held their affections or sparked their tears. Lena simply did not *belong.*

And what of Luke? There was a time when she thought she did belong to him, when she believed that he had become her true home, her future. But now it seemed that their future was uncertain. Since they'd married three years ago, it seemed like they were going in different directions. The gap widened between them as he became entrenched in the business and she pursued a degree in literature, a career in law. Lena didn't like to think about these differences, couldn't imagine a future without her husband. But there was a place where Lena had begun to feel at home, a place where she belonged. Ironically, it was also the place that brought her furthest from Luke.

She thought she would feel like a foreigner as she reentered the world of academia. But Lena soon realized that she was not much different from the other students. Most, like Lena, worked full-time jobs during the day. There was even someone who owned his own business, a pizza place that had been in the family for ten years. There was another thing she and the others had in common. Each knew where they were going, had a specific destination in mind, whether it was a career as a teacher or librarian, or as an undergrad student hoping to attend graduate or law school, like herself.

Her fears of falling behind in class were quickly allayed as she kept up with the work and received satisfactory grades at midterm. Maybe Lena was not the best student in the class, but she was far from the worst. And, if she continued her efforts, she felt confident in receiving an A in both subjects at semester's end.

Two of the students stood out. Marilyn was a quiet young woman who sat in the last row next to Lena on that first day of class. Lena had chosen the seat, sensing that the girl with long dark frizzy hair and light-green eyes had a demeanor that matched her own. She was right, as the two chatted before and after class, even as Lena, the more loquacious of the two, moved toward the front, and Marilyn, who spoke only when called upon in class, remained in the back.

There were other differences. Lena was too preoccupied with work at the bakery to attend classes full-time, while Marilyn, the eldest of four, still lived at home and worked days as a receptionist in a realty firm as she helped her widowed mother make ends meet. She had been attending night school at Brooklyn College for the past four years and expected to complete her degree by fall of the following year. Marilyn hoped to take a licensing exam soon after that and later begin a job teaching English at one of the junior high schools in Brooklyn. This was happy news for Lena in that Marilyn soon became a good source of information, not only about Shakespeare's plays, but also the classics. Secretly Lena couldn't understand why her new friend was so reticent in class, when her knowledge far exceeded that of the other students. Marilyn was also in the same anthropology class. A month after classes had begun, during one of their conversations, as they climbed a flight of stairs to their next room, Lena learned that the two even shared the same birthday, October 18, same day, same year. That made Lena like her even more.

There was someone else she grew to like as well. She had met him on the second week of English class. The young man to her right had offered her a slice of Wrigley's gum even before she had settled in her seat.

"Hope you're not a loud chewer," he joked as he watched her unwrap the strip of gum and pop it into her mouth.

"Don't think so," she said, returning his smile.

"Kenny," he introduced himself, extending his hand.

"Lena," she answered, as she relaxed in her seat as both waited for the professor to walk in. As Kenny placed a notebook and pen on the desk, she took the opportunity to assess her companion. He was pudgy and pale skinned, and his eyes, his best feature, were a brilliant blue. On second consideration, she thought it might be his smile, full lipped, open, and guileless. Even before she really came to know him, she could tell that Kenny was a nice guy, the kind of guy you would want to have as an older brother, or a friend. She felt relieved to be seated next to him on one side, Marilyn on the other. College didn't seem quite so intimidating.

Lena's first impression had proved correct, for only a month into the semester, she and Kenny did become friends, and she began to look forward to their chats in the minutes before class began, not just about Shakespeare, but about some of the details of their lives too. It turned out that he wasn't interested in English literature at all, Kenny confessed one evening while sipping a Dairy Queen freeze, but there weren't many night classes that remained open, the others filled to capacity. Besides, he needed only one more class to graduate. He was an accounting major, like Luke had been, only he planned to take the CPA exam and open his own firm after that.

"Just the same," she replied, "I wish you had decided to take anthropology with me and Marilyn. Don't you want to? It's so much fun, and I'm sure the class still has some openings!" She laughed.

"Sure, why not? I'm a glutton for punishment," he said with a grin as he pulled the straw out of the cup and flicked the chocolate off the sides. A few drops landed on the collar of his blue plaid shirt.

"Well," she sighed, "I'm going to miss you for the next five years while I'm slaving away here, still a student."

He removed the plastic lid and tilted the cup as he placed it to his lips. Draining the cup, he wiped his mouth with a napkin that he removed from his pants pocket. He ignored the stain that now materialized as a dark blotch in the shape of a claw on his collar.

"First of all, you're only going to be here for another year. But even if it's more than that, I promise to give you a discount when I do your taxes."

"You forgot; I've got Luke for that."

"Yeah," he said nonchalantly. "I don't know him, but I'm sure that I'm a better accountant."

They turned simultaneously as Dr. Collins walked in the door and opened his book at the lectern. How much she enjoyed their easy banter, how much she felt at home here in this class, Lena mused as she turned to the second act of *As You Like It*.

~

"Are you crazy?"

Lena sat stiffly on the couch, folding her arms, teeth clenched as she tried to make herself as small as possible, then somehow found the strength to get to her feet. Everything inside her told her to flee, get out, go for a walk, a run. Instead, she listened silently as Luke continued his tirade. It was best, she found at times like this, to let the anger pass like a storm cloud.

"This makes no sense. Hiring a full-time baker when it's *our* bakery, *your* bakery. Why would you want to put it in someone else's hands? Makes no sense," he repeated. He was sitting in the torn gray leather armchair, wearing gray sweats, one eye on the TV as he watched an old episode of *Perry Mason*. She realized then that even when he was angry, he gave her only half his attention.

"How much do you think a professional baker costs nowadays, Lena?"

"Not a professional. We could train someone." *Had he even heard her?*

"Besides, you've got plenty of help running the business," he went on. "There's Risa baking three days a week and the girls from the high school. And me. I handle all the finances so everything runs smoothly. Did you forget that?"

"You don't do the baking."

"What was that?"

She had his attention now.

"You don't do the baking," she repeated, her voice twice as loud.

He turned to face her, ignoring the show, as sirens blared through the screen. Luke pushed the strands of his long hair off his forehead even as his eyes sliced through her. *He needs a haircut,* she thought.

"If it wasn't for me, Lena, you wouldn't even have this bakery."

And then it occurred to her that he believed, or maybe was just past trying to believe, that the bakery really was hers. That he had done it all for her.

"It *is* mine!" she said, her voice growing louder, more defiant. Was she imposing enough? she wondered, as he got to his feet.

"Well, who else could it be? It's got the name you picked on the window: *Brooklyn Girl's Bake Shoppe.* Your title, your breads, your cookies. Lena, the whole damn thing was for you!"

Impulsively, she took a step forward. Had he really done it all for her? It was bought with the money from her parents, but perhaps she hadn't appreciated him enough. It was Luke who found the shop, planned the bakery, worked to sustain it, and now she was throwing it all away. She drew a deep breath. An urgency came over her, like a stiff cold wind. She needed to run to him, needed to rest in the safe cocoon of his arms, feel the bristly hairs on his face brush against her skin, the tender kisses planted at the base of her neck as she told him how sorry she was. Instead, for some reason, she stood rooted to the oak-planked floor.

"You didn't do this for me," she said, lowering her voice. "Luke, you did it for yourself."

She waited for his response, but this time there was none. Instead, his body remained frozen, almost as if he hadn't heard her at all, a crimson flush creeping up his face. After several minutes, he spoke, his voice measured, his words clipped.

"Sell the business."

"Luke—you don't have to—"

"I mean it. Sell the damn thing. I don't need the headaches. And if you're not happy—"

"I never said I wasn't—"

"If you're not happy," he continued, cutting her off again, "then what's the point? You're planning on becoming a lawyer anyway. Isn't that right, Lena? Isn't that your plan?"

This time she stayed quiet, letting him blow off steam. Just as his reticence a few minutes earlier had frightened her, now it was his words, a torrent of words like water shooting from a hose, that unnerved her.

"I mean it, I really do. This way you'll have more time to spend studying with your friends, that girl who still lives with her parents, and the guy, the fat one, who spills food on himself? You can have more time with them, and maybe he could even do our taxes. Hey, I like that idea! Why not? That would free me up to go back to school too. And the both of us could be home studying instead of working, using whatever profits we made at the bakery to pay tuition instead of expanding a business you have no interest in! While we're at it, I think we should drop the whole idea of starting a family. Every time I bring up the subject, you shut me down too! Who needs kids, anyway, when we can live our lives as students, reading books, going to the library? Isn't that a great idea, Lena? Just perfect." He spat out the words.

Lena felt an intense heat building within her blood as he spoke. She had seen him angry before, but never had his words been so venomous, so cruel. When the tears came without warning to her eyes, sliding down her cheeks, Lena felt ashamed. Crying was such a weak, female thing to do. And yet she couldn't help it. Just as she couldn't help going to him now, touching his cheek, cooling his face with a kiss.

Before she knew it, she was on the waterbed, lost in his arms, his tender forgiving kisses, and within minutes she was consumed once more. She had already forgotten what she'd said to him, forgotten the entire argument, because now there was nothing but his face, his soft green eyes, the youthful lock of hair falling against his brow. His voice telling her how much he desired her, how nothing would ever stop his love. And as their bodies merged, as he continued to consume her, she felt herself drowning. Drowning so that she no longer knew where she was, or who she was, anymore.

~

Lena awoke early, a full three hours before she had to go into work, as Risa was covering the first shift. Nevertheless, she threw on a pair of jeans and an olive-colored cotton T-shirt and, forgetting to take the lunch already packed in the refrigerator, or even turn on the Mr. Coffee, staggered out of the apartment. She ignored her elderly neighbor, Mrs. Minetta, who waved a greeting as she pulled her small black cocker spaniel to the curb. She disregarded the newspaper boy who called out to her before tossing the paper on the sidewalk. Lena was oblivious to it all as she moved determinedly forward. Although, on that day, she wasn't quite sure where she was going. She only knew she had to leave. Leave the apartment for now, leave him.

Lena walked into a brisk wind, replaying their conversation in her head. He told her she was wrong, selfish, unappreciative for all he had done for her. Unappreciative after he had made her cherished dream come true, to be a baker with a shop she could call her own. He reminded her how happy she was.

Lena shivered as an icy wind chilled her bones. She should have worn a jacket. She should have brought her purse. She should have . . .

A speck of dust landed in her right eye, and she blinked against its sting. The eye quickly began to water, but at least it wasn't tears this time. And again, she hated herself for her weakness, her capitulation, as she looked into Luke's sweet and confused face. She would do anything not to hurt him. But would he do the same for her? He had been wrong about her not wanting children. He had been wrong when he told her she was happy, because she *wasn't* happy. Not happy at all.

Lena walked inside a building to escape the cold. As she shielded her eyes from the sunlight flooding past a broad window, she checked her wrist. But like everything else, she had left her watch behind at the apartment. A clock on the wall told her it was already past 9:00 a.m. She had been walking for nearly two hours. Only when she saw the rows of neatly stacked books on either side of her and sensed the familiar scent of old paper did she realize that she was at the library. Not the Grand Army Plaza near Prospect Park, where she did most of studying, but the one in Flatbush, the one she had frequented as a child.

She pulled a random book from one of the shelves and ran her fingers over the plastic jacket. *Enchanting Asia*. She then scanned the library for a place to sit. It was still early, and nearly every seat, every table, was unoccupied. She chose an isolated table in a corner, under a narrow window. Lena slowly turned the pages of the giant book. Bright cherry-red pagodas, sunlit valleys, people walking leisurely across an endless bridge, wide-eyed grinning children stared back at her. If only she could escape into the pages, leave all that she knew, all that per-plexed her, if only for a little while.

But Lena knew that escape was impossible. What she really needed was to figure this all out. She knew what she had to do, of course. Confess her unhappiness to Luke, and surely he would understand, help her sort things out. But what if he didn't? She couldn't take that chance. She let her head rest on the book's glossy page. Suddenly she felt very tired.

Lena let her mind wander into a dream. She was knocking on her mother's door. She could hear her inside, humming an old Yiddish melody to herself, smell the scent of challah baking. She banged harder against the steel door, more urgently because she needed to speak with her, needed her help, but there was still no answer.

Lena couldn't tell if her mind had now wandered back to reality as she slammed her knuckles on the door, the door to her classroom. This one, though, opened easily, as she ran inside, relieved to see her friends. Kenny was seated, sharing a bag of pretzels with Marilyn, who was laughing at one of his jokes. Lena was about to ask them a ques-tion, but when she opened her mouth, nothing came out. She felt silly, useless. They were only her classmates, after all, not her friends. She felt ridiculous.

Lena dreamed of cherry-red pagodas and sunlit valleys until finally she awakened to a gentle touch on her arm. Only when she lifted her head and looked at the face of her dearest friend did she realize that she was no longer dreaming.

22

Pearl?"

The young woman searched Lena's eyes for a moment and then smiled, a smile so lovely that it filled her face with an almost ethereal glow.

"Lena! It really is you! I was coming out of the back room and saw someone seated at this corner table all alone. From the back, she resembled you, and I thought, no, it can't be her. So I walked over and then—oh, Lena, it really is you!"

Lena rubbed her eyes and opened them again, just to make sure she wasn't still dreaming. But no, the long angular face; the fair, almost white skin; the hair still the color of spring wheat held back with a large barrette; and the eyes, a light blue, intense as she stared at Lena, as she listened. The face was unmistakable. The same eyes that crinkled with laughter when the two would play hide-and-seek in the Catskill woods, the same eyes with tears that flowed freely whenever she listened to Lena confess her innermost fears, eyes that stared at her in bewilderment as she was carried off into the woods.

Lena could no longer restrain herself as she grabbed her old friend by the shoulders and enveloped her in her arms. The two held on to each other tightly, each afraid to let go. Finally, after what seemed like an eternity, as she tried to fill the vacuum of the years of confusion, not knowing what had become of her good friend, afraid to search for her, or ask if she was even alive, Lena relinquished her hold. She stared into

Pearl's face, now tear-streaked like her own, then shifted her attention to the open book, the image of a sunlit valley, moistened now with her tears. Lena closed the book, and when she looked up, Pearl was still there, sitting next to her. She was more beautiful now as a grown woman than she had been even as a child. After a few more minutes of the two staring at each other, Lena recovered her voice.

"I can't believe it's you, Pearl. I thought I saw you once, not far from the library, but then I thought it must be my imagination. And now here you are again, but—why, how?" Her words found it hard to keep up with her racing thoughts.

Pearl placed her hand on the back of Lena's and smiled reassuringly. *She still has it,* Lena thought—that calm, assuring presence that convinced her, even in the worst of times, that everything would be all right. Not her parents, not even Luke, could be capable of that.

"You probably did see me then," Pearl began, slowly opening the clasp at her hair and freeing the silky blond strands so they fell nearly to her shoulders. *Her hair is longer now,* Lena mused.

"I have been working here for a while, but just as an assistant. In a couple of years, I hope to get my certificate in library science."

"Here?" Lena gazed at her friend, wide-eyed. "You have been working here all along and I wasn't even aware?"

Pearl nodded.

"But why didn't you contact me? My parents still live in the same apartment! You could have easily let me know where you were, that you were still alive!" Lena blurted as she felt the anger simmer within her. "And you could have spared me worrying about you, and needing you, needing my best friend in the whole world!"

Pearl shrugged and then leaned closer.

"Your mother never liked me very much. Never took any concern after—well, after that day. Besides, you have been doing just fine without me."

"How do you know that? How do you know that I don't need you anymore? Do you even know anything about me?" Lena cried out, forgetting where she was, as her eyes again brimmed with tears. She wiped them away, embarrassed, as a librarian, dressed in a starched plaid jumper with a white collar, cast her a suspicious glance. But once more, the sound of Pearl's voice, which came to her like a lullaby, set her at ease.

"You're fine, Lena. You've always been fine. You're married now, and you have your own business—a bakery. Your mother used to bake the best things, and now you're a baker too!"

Now it was Lena's turn to be suspicious. How could Pearl know so many details about her life when Lena knew nearly nothing about her?

"Oh." She smiled, raising an eyebrow, suggestive of a special secret, just as when they were girls. "Don't think I haven't investigated you. I know all about your comings and goings, Lena Sokoloff. Or is it Lena Bronfeld now? It's quite easy to find out about someone if you know the right people. I've seen you when you were down on the quad carrying your books across campus."

"Wait—you've been to my night class over at Boylan Hall?"

Pearl giggled, and for a moment Lena saw the pink-lipped girl that sat on the summer grass alongside her, the two sharing a game of checkers.

"No, not now, but back when you were a freshman. I was there too."

"You saw me back then? Why didn't you approach me, say hello?"

Pearl ignored the question and instead placed her hand at the side of Lena's head, twining one of the wavy strands around her index finger, a simple move, but one that indicated the affection for her friend hadn't diminished.

"That looks like an interesting book. Is it for one of your classes?"

Lena looked down at the book on which she had been resting her head only moments earlier.

"Oh, that. No, I just grabbed it off the shelf. The pictures are pretty." Pearl removed her hand from Lena's hair, opened the book, and began turning the pages.

"Um. Hmm . . . ," she whispered, "far, far away. Lena, I never knew places like this even existed!"

"I think I'm going to leave my husband."

Pearl let the page she was holding drop. *Just like a leaf drifting from a branch,* Lena thought. Pearl's eyes focused on her so intensely that she had no choice but to meet them.

"Lena, you can't do that."

"What? Do what?" Lena realized then that, without thinking, she had given voice to her thoughts.

"Lena, why would you say such a thing?"

Lena turned away, unable to meet those eyes any longer. She found herself physically unable to speak, her tongue dried up in her mouth like ash. Silence prevailed as she searched for an answer to Pearl's question. Until the moment she had blurted the words, the thought of leaving Luke had never occurred to her.

"Lena, why do you want to leave your husband?" Pearl repeated, her voice patient, steady. Lena knew then that she could tell her friend anything, even the things she did not fully comprehend herself.

"I don't think he understands me," she answered in a barely audible tone. Almost immediately she regretted the statement. It made her sound immature, weak.

But Pearl's look of concern remained steady.

"Why, Lena? Why doesn't he understand you?"

A feeling of nausea began to overwhelm Lena, but she tamped it down. How could she even begin to tell her?

"Lena?"

She looked at Pearl again, trying to focus. It *was* her. After all these years, it was really Pearl, her best friend in all the world.

"Tell me."

Pearl's voice had a gentle tone, almost as if she were talking to a child. And before she knew it, Lena was telling her everything. Telling her about Luke and the bakery. And her parents—the parents she was never enough for. She told her about her classes, about Marilyn and Kenny, and how good it was to be back at school.

Pearl sat back and folded her arms. Lena wondered why she wasn't in a hurry to get back to her job at the library, but she let the thought go.

"So, let me get this straight. You wanted to be a baker, but now that you own your own bakery, you've changed your mind. And so now you want to be a lawyer."

Lena shook her head.

"I like baking because, well, because it's what my mother did, and I wanted to show her I could bake, too, I could be just as good as—well"—her voice dropped—"just as good." Lena drew a breath before continuing.

"Anyway, it was Luke who loved the idea of owning a bakery. It's a lot of work, but we've been successful. And yet . . ." She stopped again before going on, meeting her friend's eyes. "Oh, Pearl, I don't want any of it!"

Her friend nodded, and then a sudden flash of lightning pierced the sky and lit up the room. Strangely, neither of them moved; in fact, the event seemed to have a calming effect on them both.

A group of preschoolers and their mothers, led by a straight-backed librarian, oblivious to the sudden change in scenery outside, marched past them toward the brightly decorated children's section.

"Shouldn't you be at the bakery now?"

Lena glanced up at the round clock again. By the time she got to the bakery, she would be nearly a half hour late.

"Oh yes," she responded, getting up and, for the first time that morning, feeling fully awake.

"And you had better get back to work too," she added.

Pearl gazed up at her and smiled but remained seated.

Lena could hear the sweet, steady voice of the librarian as she read to the children a few feet away. An elderly woman bustled by, carrying a cloth bag filled with hardcover novels. The day was beginning.

Despite the flash of lightning, the clouds held their rain, and once again the sun emerged, full and brimming with hope. And yet as she stood waiting, Lena felt a shiver of cold crawl up her spine.

"When will I see you again?" she asked. Pearl's smile broadened as the sun lit up her eyes.

"I'm here Wednesday and Friday mornings," she said.

Relieved, Lena turned toward the lobby and the wide glass doors through which she had entered that morning. But before she exited, she glanced back at Pearl, who was still there, seated. Her hands were folded on the cover of *Enchanted Asia* as she flashed her one last smile.

As she rushed toward the bus stop, Lena dug her hand into the back pocket of her jeans. She was lucky—there were still some coins she could use for the bus into Bensonhurst. Once seated, a strange sense of peace overcame her, almost as intense as the feeling of desperation she had experienced earlier that day. Funny, she thought, nothing had been resolved during her short encounter with Pearl, not even after she had confessed the root of her anxiety. As she sat down, she realized how happy she was, happier perhaps than she had been in years. And calm, feeling somehow that everything would be all right. Dear Pearl.

It was only when she emerged from the bus and walked toward the shop that Lena realized that while her friend now knew everything about her, Pearl had not revealed anything about herself. Not a single thing.

23

Lena made it a point to meet with Pearl on a regular basis. Each Wednesday at precisely 9:10 a.m., minutes after the doors to the library opened, just as they had that first fortuitous day. It was easy to rearrange her schedule as Risa, a single mother with a teenage son, jumped at the chance to make some extra money. The new routine made Lena equally happy, as she was glad to confide in someone other than Luke, who had become a not-always-unwelcome distraction.

When she told him of her plan, Luke balked at first, as he did anytime he saw cash flow exiting the business, but he soon relented as he became aware that Lena's complaints had slowly dwindled and somehow she seemed more satisfied with her life. A few extra dollars each week, he reasoned, was a small price to pay not to hear her whining anymore.

Of course, he could never know the real reason for her compliance. She told him she needed time alone at the library on Wednesday mornings, which had become a serene retreat, a place to get her head together. Not a lie, really. But not the truth either. She was getting her head together, making sense of things, yet her counsel did not take the form of books, but of a person, one person in particular. She didn't dare breathe a word about Pearl. She had no reason to explain how Pearl was the most important person in her life, maybe more important than even Luke. Right now, she wanted Pearl for herself. How would he ever understand?

As they had on that first day, the two shared the same table in the corner, turning the pages of another large picture book. This time it was one Lena had found in the children's section, *Mother Goose's Nursery Rhymes*, each glossy page filled with a short rhyme and illustrations of blue-eyed toddlers with yellow hair and rosy lips, long-necked swans with snowy white feathers, and little kings with glittering crowns. And just like that first time, after losing themselves in the pages of a picture book, it was Lena who did most of the talking, and Pearl who did most of the listening.

"Last week I had a special order," Lena told her.

"Oh, what kind of order?" Pearl asked, as she sat up straight. She fixed her eyes directly on Lena, as once more she unfastened the barrette and let the curls descend, framing her delicate face luxuriously.

"It was an order for a wedding cake! Pearl, I have baked all sorts of cakes—kids' birthday cakes with cartoon characters and superheroes on top, pink layer cakes for bridal showers, graduation cakes in the shape of a diploma, but this was different. An actual wedding cake!"

"Sounds like a big deal," Pearl exclaimed, letting her fingers glide absent-mindedly over the black-ink drawing of an "itsy bitsy spider."

"It *was* a big deal," responded Lena, smiling, "and a lot of pressure. What made it even more stressful was that it was for someone related to a friend of mine. You remember Marilyn? The one who attends classes with me at the college?" Pearl nodded, now immersed in the story.

"Well, her cousin is marrying her childhood sweetheart. It's a small affair taking place in his parents' backyard in Canarsie. All the food is being catered by a kosher deli with bagels, cream cheese, whitefish, and salads. They needed a baker for the cake, so Marilyn recommended me, though I'm not sure why. All she has ever tasted were some of my chocolate chip cookies . . . oh, and the double-fudge brownies once—"

"And I'm sure they were delicious," interrupted Pearl.

"Well, they were okay, but nothing like a wedding cake—a multilayered wedding cake with vanilla and strawberry layers, a chocolate ganache, and white buttercream frosting."

"Nonetheless, I'm sure it was easy for you to put together. A piece of cake!" Pearl's eyes twinkled as she smiled at her own joke. Lena groaned.

"Not exactly. I was scared, scared as I have ever been baking something, afraid that people would react like Mama after I baked my first honey cake, when she walked in the door and gave me one of her looks. I almost asked Risa to do it, was willing to give her double what the couple was paying me, but then I couldn't very well do that. Not when Marilyn had recommended me. It wouldn't be honest. So, instead, I gave her cousin a discount and I did it all myself."

"I'm proud of you, Lena."

Lena rested her eyes on Pearl's face as a surge of tears swelled her throat. How was it that Pearl still had such a profound effect on her? Why was it that a compliment, four simple words—*I'm proud of you*—could make her feel so worthy, whole, more than Luke or her parents ever could? Maybe, unlike with the others, it was because she actually believed her. Even so, when she thought about it—which she tried not to do very often—Pearl's response was still not enough somehow, not like parents' pride in their children. A mother's pride was something not expressed in words, something not even conveyed in feelings. A mother's pride was too huge for that, so enormous that it encompassed their whole being. At least that was the way Lena imagined it. Maybe that was why she craved it so much.

"How did you make it?"

"What?"

"How did you make the cake?"

It was a funny question. Not many people were curious about the process, which was detailed, often tedious. Most just wanted to see a pretty cake and, more important, taste the final product. But as she looked at the young woman sitting next to her, patiently waiting for her answer, Lena understood that Pearl was really interested. She didn't hesitate.

Lena described the meticulous process of creating a wedding cake, from laying out the ingredients, the flour, the sugar and all the spices, the fresh strawberries, the vanilla, and the melted chocolate, the cream. She told her how each of the layers was baked separately, cooled before the cake was put together, like constructing a building in the city, but more like a skyscraper, she was quick to add. The most fun, though, was slathering on the icing and planting the strawberries between the layers and molding the buttercream that surrounds the presentation, topping it all off with hot-pink rosettes and more strawberries. And then the final flourish: "Congratulations, Shelly and Brian" written in perfect calligraphy. At the wedding, the plastic bride and groom pieces would be placed delicately atop the structure before the now-married couple, as his hand upon hers, cut their first slice of wedding cake.

"Wow! I can't believe you actually made a wedding cake!" exclaimed Pearl after listening to all the details, chin in hand.

"It was a long process, very involved. But as my mother liked to say, patience is the most important ingredient when it comes to baking."

"And I'm sure it tasted as good as it looked."

"I hope so, I think so. I made a practice layer with the buttercream and fondant before I even started on the cake. I must admit, it was delicious. And I didn't mind the work, I didn't mind it at all." Lena closed her eyes briefly as she recalled taking each fluffy layer out of the oven, stroking the icing between each level, moving the piping bag across the surface like a graceful dancer gliding across a stage. But the best part of it all, and the most intimidating, too, was knowing that this cake would be the first sweet thing the two would share as a married couple.

"Does this mean you want to be a baker, after all?" asked Pearl, interrupting her reverie.

Lena laughed. Pearl had an uncanny way of guessing her thoughts. But not this time.

"No—no, I still want to study law," she responded, "though I also enjoy baking, but only as a hobby, I think. Maybe baking the occasional wedding cake too.

"I think that Shelly and Brian are freezing one slice of the cake for their first wedding anniversary. Isn't that romantic?"

Pearl sat back, her shoulders drooping.

"If I had married, you would be the one to bake my wedding cake, Lena," she said, gazing down at the book wistfully.

Lena felt a pang. Once again she had been focusing on herself, disregarding Pearl. What kind of a friend was she? Surely Pearl had desires, maybe disappointments, just like she did. *What kind of a friend was she?*

Lena leaned over, removed Pearl's hand from the table, and placed it in her own. The hand was small, like the rest of her friend, who remained petite, with the presence of a doll, not at all like Lena, who grew only more awkward, gangly, as she got older.

"What are you talking about? Of course you're going to get married—you just have to find the one. And sure, I'll bake the wedding cake! Mocha, that's your favorite flavor, just like mine, right?"

Pearl looked away and shifted uneasily in her chair. And because she was Pearl, changed the subject. Back to Lena.

"Have you told your mother? All about the wedding cake, I mean." Lena gazed down at the open book.

Four and twenty blackbirds baked in a pie . . .

She couldn't help but smile to herself at the coincidence. No, she confessed, she hadn't told her mother about the cake. The thought hadn't even occurred to her.

Why not? Pearl pressed. As much as Lena loved her friend, she hated that aspect of her personality. Pearl had a habit of forcing her to examine just the thing she didn't want to talk about.

"Oh, I don't know," Lena said finally. "I guess I just forgot." But the fire in Pearl's blue eyes told her she wasn't buying her explanation. After a few more minutes of silence, Lena began slowly.

"I guess I was afraid to say anything about it. I guess she would think I wasn't good enough. I'm not a real baker. Not like her." Pearl looked puzzled but didn't say anything.

"Besides," Lena continued, averting her eyes as her finger tapped the glossy page of the book, "the practice slice I baked, as good as it was, is stale by now. I'm going to throw it out."

"Do you have a picture?"

Lena's eyes swept across the page.

And when the pie was opened / the birds began to sing / wasn't that a dainty dish to set before a king?

She had taken a Polaroid as a permanent record of her first effort just before sending the cake out for delivery.

"Well, yes, I do. But why should that—"

"Take it to her. Develop the photo and take it to her."

"Okay, Pearl, I guess I can show her the picture. But I'm sure she won't be too impressed."

"And that's why you're afraid to tell her," Pearl responded matter-of-factly.

Lena closed the book of nursery rhymes abruptly.

"Okay, I'll show her the picture."

"Promise?"

"I promise," she said, irritated. "Now, don't you have to be getting back to work?"

Pearl nodded but, as often was the case, didn't move. Without looking back, Lena got up, walked out the doors, and glanced up at the sky, where gray clouds now hovered over the tree branches. *Looks like rain,* she thought.

~

"It's gone," said Luke as he set a jumbo bag of granulated sugar on the counter. "Nothing but ashes."

Lena pressed the stop button on the dough mixer.

"That's awful! Does anyone know how it happened?"

Luke shrugged as he got on a step stool and agilely lifted the bag to a shelf. She watched the muscles in his arms contract under the skin. His hair was so long now that he needed to tie it back in a ponytail, nearly as long as hers.

"Well, I'm just glad no one was hurt or worse," she said, before turning the machine on again.

For the next few hours Lena found it difficult to concentrate on her work, let alone the thirty red, white, and blue frosted cupcakes she was preparing for the local Boy Scout troop's Fourth of July celebration. George LoPresti was a quiet unassuming man in his fifties who had owned the dry-cleaning establishment down the block for the past thirty years, even before she was born. Although he wasn't the sort of man to engage in useless banter with the other store owners in the neighborhood, he always seemed to have an endless supply of lollipops for the children who came in with their parents, and a few, remarking on his white mustache and short beard, had even taken to calling him Santa Claus.

"Poor George," she sighed, checking as the ingredients blended into mocha-colored waves of dough.

"Oh, he'll be all right," said Luke, who was standing by her side now with a long-handled silver spoon, hoping for a taste. "I'm sure he's got plenty of insurance. He's already put his two daughters through college, so he and his wife—what's her name, Mary?—can pretty much do what they want. Maybe they will buy a villa on the Italian coast. They don't have to be slaves to a store."

Lena glanced at her husband before taking the spoon from his hand and dipping it into the gooey mixture. The idea of being slaves to a store seemed an odd comment coming from someone who had always presented business ownership as a dream come true. She decided to let it go, though a part of her still hoped that Luke would come around to her way of thinking, that there were better things out there for the two of them. His next question, though, gave her pause, and more hope.

"Hear anything about the LSAT?"

It had been only five days since she had taken the exams in preparation for law school, the results of which would signal the caliber of school she would attend, even if she was ready for law school at all. It was just over a month since she had begun the arduous process of review, going so far as to enroll in a preparatory course, and having her baking assistants, two now, take over the work while she studied. For a while she had even stopped visiting Pearl at the library.

"Still waiting for my scores," she said, as she removed the bowl from the mixer. "I don't want to think about it."

"Oh, you'll land on top. You always do!" he said, giving her a playful slap on the derriere.

"You'll be ready, but will Harvard be ready for you?" He laughed before walking to the front of the shop.

Harvard? Even if by some wild stretch of the imagination, she did get into Harvard, there was no way the two of them could afford tuition, not even if she were to ask her parents for money, which she could never do, of course. If she were lucky, very, very lucky, she might get into a local school like Brooklyn, Fordham, or Cardozo. NYU and Columbia were out of the question, as they were just too expensive. Even so, a girl could dream.

Then there was the question of the bakery. She barely had time to think about it or even work at the business now that she was immersed in notes and textbooks at the college. Even her spare time was spent in the library or study hall with Marilyn and Kenny, who was taking his final class, poring over notebooks in preparation for a research paper or exam. Law school would be even more rigorous. But as she carefully poured the batter into paper tins and set them into the oven, Lena resolved not to think about that now. Just like her papa had always told her, she needed to take it one step at a time. After a while the sweet scents of chocolate, vanilla, and sugar enveloped the back room. Lena took a long, deep breath. How she would miss those lovely scents, she thought.

~

If Lena had any hopes of convincing Luke to pocket their profits from the Brooklyn Girl's Bake Shoppe and shut it down, they were soon squelched. It had been barely a month since their conversation at the bakery and Luke's strange observation about being a "slave" to a business. They were seated at the small kitchen table in the apartment, enjoying a simple dinner of franks and beans, since these days Lena barely had time to prepare anything more elaborate. After eating a forkful of the beans, Luke wiped his mouth with a napkin before making an announcement. What he had to say was even more startling than the news that had come just a few days earlier—Lena had done extraordinarily well on the LSAT and, along with her grades, had ensured her admission into a decent law school.

"Great news, babe. I've just gotten us another business."

Lena put down her fork and stared at him. There was so much she wanted to say, to ask, but the words were all competing in her brain, leaving her no choice but to remain silent.

"Oh, I see that look on your face. A little bit skeptical, are you? But nothing to worry about. I didn't put money down on a gas station or a Chinese restaurant. It's another bakery—in Williamsburg. Lena, we're expanding the business!" He threw the napkin on top of his plate and sat back with a self-satisfied smile. But Lena could see below the surface of that smile, could see the manipulation in his eyes, the desperation beneath the skin that somehow, some way, she would agree to this preposterous venture. He would have liked nothing better than for her to say, "Oh, Luke, what a wonderful idea! Oh, Luke, you're a genius!"

But she didn't say any of that. Instead, she simply sat immobile, still unable to summon the words that could convey her shock, her anger, her disappointment.

"Remember the old Williamsburg bakeshop that closed a long time ago when the owner passed away? Well, it's just been sitting there for the past year, growing cobwebs. No one wants it, and they just dropped the price by a bundle, so I jumped on it. It's already set up, all the equipment, counters. I mean, nothing's been touched. I used most of the profits from our business, and we don't even have to go to your parents for money. Babe, from now on, we are going to be on easy street."

Luke's words were gathering speed like a runaway locomotive, leaving no room for her to respond. Now he drew a breath, the disingenuous smile still plastered on his face. His eyes willing hers to soften, to give him the answer he was expecting. She continued to stare at him icily. If she was able to run or punch him in the same mouth that uttered the words she detested, the plans for his dream life, not hers, but *his*, she would have. Instead, she remained frozen until finally, slowly, the words came pouring out.

"Of course I would never consider asking my parents for money in the first place. My mom just left her part-time job, and I'm not sure how they are making ends meet. Besides, you've wasted enough of their gift to us—a gift for a down payment on a house, I should remind you. And now that we have this business up and running because of all the work I did to make it happen—the work *I* did, Luke—now you have the gall to inform me that you've put down money on another business that I'm supposed to run?" A sharp breath, biting her tongue to stop the tears from coming.

"And don't pretend that this is all for me, that you are fulfilling all my dreams, when it's about you. It has always been about you, Luke, and don't pretend it hasn't. Oh, Luke, I have worked hard, and I'm going to get into a good law school, whether you like it or not. Instead of using the profit for tuition, you've wasted the money on yet another silly scheme, without even consulting me." And then, remembering, she blurted, "Oh, God, how will I pay for law school now?"

She didn't watch as the realization set in, the color draining quickly from Luke's face.

"You may have to wait a year or two before starting law school," he offered meekly.

But just as Luke's confidence had begun to deflate, Lena's was strengthening.

"I don't think so, Luke. No," she said, her voice louder now. "No, I don't think that's what I'm going to do."

He didn't try to argue with her, didn't try to persuade her. Instead, he pushed his plate away, stood up, and went quietly into the bedroom. Lena washed each dish carefully, then again, and once more after that until each plate sparkled. She ran her thumb across the plate's surface as it made a small squeaking noise. The dishes were clean, but she still hadn't washed away the hurt of the conversation with Luke. Now she was the one who felt depleted. Leaving the plates and silverware on the counter, she walked into the bedroom.

He was already there, waiting for her. He was standing by the mirror, hair loosened, his green eyes bathed in tears. When he caught sight of her, he immediately, wordlessly, swept her up in his arms until her feet could no longer touch the floor. He pressed his lips, his cheeks against her face, and removed her peasant blouse, her faded jeans, as gently as if he were peeling a peach.

At first Lena stood impassive as a statue, not returning his smiles, not reciprocating his embrace. Her determination was sapped, her strength gone. She felt nothing but exhaustion. But then something extraordinary happened. He nuzzled her neck, and she could feel the moisture of his tears against her skin.

"Lena, I'm sorry," he whispered. "I shouldn't have done it without asking you first. I just wanted this for you, for us! Please, Lena, you have to forgive me. I love you more than anything, you know that.

"Please don't leave me," he implored, sobbing now into the crease of her neck.

"I'm not leaving you, Luke," she said, feeling her own tears run down her cheeks.

She hadn't even thought of leaving Luke, knew then that she never could.

Then, as he lifted her to the bed, as she gazed into the clouds in his eyes, the fearful innocence of his face, she realized that he was being sincere, that he needed her just as much as she needed him. And she fell in love with him all over again.

He made love to her, deeper than she thought possible, his skin heavy against hers, melting into her until he was a part of her, his musky cologne overwhelming her nostrils as the bed rocked slowly above the water. It was all she had dreamed of, Lena thought, as her head sank into the mattress. And yet, that night, she found herself holding back just a little, and she wasn't sure why.

~

They had been talking for nearly an hour when Lena glanced at her watch and realized the date. "It's Tuesday, Pearl, what are you doing here?"

Pearl laughed softly.

"I could say the same for you. I picked up an extra day because one of the librarians is out sick. So why did *you* decide to stop by on a Tuesday?"

Lena looked down and brushed a leaf off her jeans. When she had arrived at the library earlier, she caught sight of Pearl seated on a bench outside, wearing a black pencil skirt and white shirt with black polka dots. At the sound of Lena's voice, she had looked up casually, almost as if she had been there waiting for her all along.

It was a lovely day with cool breezes swirling between the golden branches of the trees, and since the summer heat had not set in yet, the two decided to chat outside for a while.

The minutes soon stretched into half an hour, and then an hour. And again Lena found herself doing most of the talking.

"Oh boy, I'd better get going to the bakery to relieve Risa or I'll be late again," she said, rising reluctantly.

Pearl placed a hand on her forearm.

"Remember? It's Tuesday—your day off now that you have the extra help?"

Lena sat down, embarrassed. It had already been a morning full of mix-ups, with her rising soundlessly out of bed so as not to awaken Luke.

She had been in such a hurry to leave that she had dressed quickly, fastened her watch, but forgotten to put on any makeup, not even a stroke of blush. The heat of last night's lovemaking had faded from her cheeks hours earlier, and with her hair unkempt and falling loosely around her face, she feared she looked like an unearthly creature, a ghost, next to her smartly coiffed, neatly attired friend. She looked down, noticing that Pearl's hand remained on her arm. Lena had revealed all that was said the night before between her and Luke. How he had purchased, completely on his own, another store. He had not even bothered to consult her. How smug he appeared as he assured her of its success, of *their* success. How he had the temerity to ask her to wait another year before starting law school. Had he asked? No, she was sure he had told her, now that she thought of it. How no matter how long she stood in the kitchen washing two dinner dishes again and again, her thoughts kept racing until she had begun to think she was losing her mind.

As the two sat under a flowering tree, the birds chattering overhead, listening as the library doors softly opened and closed before them, she told Pearl everything. Well, almost everything. Everything except what had happened in the bedroom. She would need time to make sense of that herself.

Lena couldn't remember what came next, what advice Pearl had given her about what her next steps should be. Maybe she told her to speak with her mother, which was unusual considering her mother never really had taken a liking to Pearl from the time the two first became friends. And yet Pearl had shown nothing but compassion for her, so that whenever Lena was troubled, she advised her to approach her mother with the problem. A lot of good that had done, she recalled now. Mama had never supported her in anything. Not when she wanted to take up baking, not when she married Luke. Come to think of it, she never liked him either. What she did remember about their conversation that morning as the two sat immersed in sunlight, Pearl's hand gentle upon her skin, was that it would be the last time they would be together. At least for a very long time.

"I'm going away, Lena," she said matter-of-factly, just as Lena rose to leave.

"What do you mean—where, how?" She slumped back on the bench as if pushed by a mighty force.

"Do you recall the program in library science at a school in the Midwest that I told you about? Well, I applied, and so today is my last day," Pearl said, her eyes wide with anticipation. "It's a master's program that begins next month, so I can be a professional librarian. It's what I've always wanted to do." Then, seeing the crestfallen look on Lena's face, she added, "Don't worry, it won't be forever. You know I'll be here when you need me. We will always be here for each other."

Her words were small consolation to Lena, who sat stunned, already feeling the pain of her friend's absence, even as the two sat close.

Pearl remained silent, allowing Lena a few more minutes to absorb this recent information. As she sat, her eyes scanned Pearl's face, her bow-like lips stained with pink; her light, almost white hair catching the sun like a beautiful halo; the warm, flawless cheeks; and her eyes in whose reflection she now saw her own face. She tried to capture the image of Pearl now in her brain, as a camera would, so that she might hold the memory forever. Would she ever have a friend like her again?

"Oh, Pearl, I lost you once. I don't think I can stand losing you again," she said under her breath, but loud enough for her friend to hear.

"Of course you can," Pearl said, leaning closer. A smile overtook her face once more, a smile as hopeful as Lena's own, which emerged through the tears. Pearl was just as sad as she was to be leaving.

"I'll always be there for you, and I'll make sure you know how to reach me this time. We will always be there for each other," she repeated, her voice softer.

As always, it would be on Pearl's own terms.

As Lena sat on the bench, feeling her spirit more alone than it was years ago at the bungalow colony, when she thought she had lost her forever, Pearl removed her hand, walked away, and pushed open the door of the library. This time it wasn't Lena, but Pearl, who was the first to leave.

24

Anya

Anya held the Polaroid snapshot in her hand and looked at it closely. The cake was baked with an expert's touch, to be sure. The hot-pink rosettes that adorned each layer were perfectly shaped and one could almost taste the sweetness in the chocolate and strawberry icing. But what most captured Anya's attention wasn't the finished product but the cake bearer, who held the platter, offering it proudly to the viewer. Lena had never looked more beautiful, more—her mind searched for the word—*contented*, not in a long time. Yet she realized that the smile that overtook her daughter's face in that moment was not intended for her, but reserved for others more fortunate.

The photograph had come in the mail only yesterday, a photograph, not a personal visit, which had become scarcer nowadays, but something hastily tossed in a mailbox. The picture was almost, almost, not quite, enough to make her forget the news she had received from her doctor earlier that morning. She placed the photo on an end table when she heard Josef's footsteps enter the room.

"How are you feeling, my dear?" he asked, lifting her hand to his lips. "Oh, I see they have finally pulled out the needles." His finger drew a circle around the spot of skin where a bluish-black mark was rising to the surface. As he sat next to her on the side of the bed, Anya noticed how gaunt his face appeared, how the skin's pink pallor had been replaced with something gray and sorrowful. Poor Josef. Hadn't the man suffered enough?

Josef stirred, sat up straighter.

"I have good news. Doctor says you can go home now. We can think about next steps in a few weeks."

"Yes, that is good news. I don't quite enjoy being pinched like one of Mama's ragged pin cushions," she answered, sitting up slowly and swinging her legs to the side of the bed. She was ready to go home. More than ready. Like most men, Josef had no idea how to bake an apple, much less an entire meal. And it had already been three days since she entered the hospital for testing, three days of cold salami sandwiches and wrinkled shirts for Josef.

"No need to rush, Anya," he said, staying her with a hand on one knee. "Dr. Fenster told me in the hall that he will come in with some instructions just after he finishes with a patient. I am eager to leave, too, you know. I do not like the smells in this place."

Anya nodded. The smells that permeated the air of the entire hospital stayed in the nose so that even after days, one was nauseated by the odor. Alcohol and death. The two did not exactly make for a pleasant combination.

"I thought we might stop at the delicatessen on our way back home. Have some good pastrami on black bread with a couple of potato knishes, the square ones that you like. We don't need to think about anything else now."

So like Josef, Anya thought as she eased her legs on top of the coverlet. Never wanting to think about the bad, never wanting to talk about it.

And what Dr. Fenster, the specialist in kidneys (the precise name of the specialty she could never remember), had told her *was* bad—certainly not good. She knew that despite Josef's intentions to meet the world with optimism, face it they must. The doctor had called it polycystic kidney disease, a sickness she had never heard of before, a term she could barely pronounce. But, nevertheless, its meaning was quite clear. Her kidneys were ruined. That was the cause of all her back pain, the high blood pressure, the exhaustion. He had asked whether anyone in the family had ever had such a thing, a mother, a father? Naturally, Anya had had no answers. When people got sick back in the Old Country, they were in bed, and if they were unlucky, they simply died. No one asked any questions.

Dr. Fenster, a man who appeared to be only a few years older than Lena, had simply nodded and pushed his wire-rimmed glasses farther up the bridge of his nose, as if he understood. But of course he couldn't. It was one thing to read about medical history in books, quite another when talking with a patient, and another thing entirely to be the person whose life hung in the balance.

After that, he had explained about another word that she was unfamiliar with: *dialysis*. Sounded like "die." The word made her heart flinch, but only a little.

∼

Anya closed her eyes and rested her head against the pillow. She recalled the young doctor's tone as he tried to explain the problem as slowly as he could so that she and Josef could understand, as gently as he could so as not to arouse panic. He needn't have bothered. When one had witnessed their world collapse on their heads, when one had experienced the loss of their only child, then any news that came after was not so bad. It did not even merit a single tear or the raising of an eyebrow. When one lost a child, anything else seemed minimal, ordinary.

Anya pretended that she was asleep even as she felt Josef's heavy presence in the bed next to her. She tried to think of the next steps, questions for the doctor. Kidneys broken. Dialysis with the needles twice a week. The medicines she would need to take daily. And then new kidneys? No, she mustn't think about that right now. But then she remembered the card, the photograph of Lena and the cake. Anya lifted the Polaroid to the sunlight streaming into the room from the locked window. She would show it to Josef. But as she turned the photo, something caught her eye, something that obliterated any thoughts of the future, any sorrows of the past. It was an inscription written in Lena's hand.

"Pearl says hello."

25

Lena

I t's just the beginning, Lena, the beginning of a big future for us!"
said Luke, rolling up his sleeves and sprinting to the counter before
removing an array of cleaning supplies from a huge cardboard box.
With his hair tied back with one of her hair bands and a wide grin
spreading across his face, he looked as gleeful as a child on his first
outing to the zoo.

Nevertheless, the minute Lena set foot in the new store, she had her
doubts. Not because it was a modern facility or it was in the middle of
a bustling neighborhood, for it was certainly neither of these things. It
was because with the mere act of stepping into the shop, as Luke quickly
swept the cobwebs off a metal chair, she knew that any resolve she had
left had now dissipated, any fire for a better future had been extin-
guished. And as she hastily tied her hair up in a bun, filled a pail with
hot water and Clorox, any thoughts of law school were also scrubbed
away. It wasn't long before her only thoughts centered on making Luke
happy, making the business a success.

And for several months afterward, it was. The Brooklyn Girl's Bake
Shoppe II, which had opened only three years after their first shop
in Bensonhurst, offered the same baked goods, and through word of
mouth, customers began coming in. At first the young mothers would

peek in the window with the bright-pink lettering written in shiny calligraphy, curious to see if the brownies and chocolate cake were as good as the Muller's brand. After a while, hard hats made their way off the beams of a high-rise to buy large black-and-white or chocolate chip cookies to go along with their paper-bag lunches. Later, as they noticed the signed kashruth certificate in the window, a few of the elderly matrons, their heads wrapped in flowered babushkas, would stop in for a honey or sponge loaf to accompany their Sabbath dinners. There were even a handful of schools nearby where children were being walked home from class and, if they had been good, were rewarded with a sugar cookie or the like, as with the shop in Bensonhurst. As a result, business remained steady, at least for a while, just like the smile on Luke's face.

But after a while things had begun to resume their old pattern, at least at home. As Lena grew busier, personally baking more of the cakes, even the intricate Italian pastries, getting up at 4:00 a.m., denying herself even one day of respite because she dared not trust anyone else, just long enough for the business to get "on its feet," Luke was pulling back. Just as with the shop in Bensonhurst, as soon as business became brisk, Luke relaxed. Only two weeks after the grand opening, after she left early on a Friday afternoon, she opened the apartment door to find him seated on the carpet in the living room, a controller in hand, avidly following the action of the ball on the screen. This time, she ignored it.

Luke ignored her, too, so focused was he on the TV that he hadn't even heard the click in the lock, the screech of the door hinge, as she walked into the room, the jangle of the hangers as she hung her sweater in the closet. She hadn't bothered to say hello. Not because she was angry—she was long past that—but because, well, she just didn't have the energy.

Lena fell, face up, onto the undulating mattress, hoping that once she closed her eyes, she wouldn't fall asleep. She knew she couldn't keep up the pace working full-time at one shop, making regular visits to the other, much longer. She would have to speak to Luke about getting more help, which meant facing a new fear. What would his reaction be? Would he tell her to wait until they had a big enough safety net for full-time employees, who surely would demand health and vacation benefits, all frightening considerations for a business just getting underway? Would he promise, as he had before, that if she just held on for a little while longer, she could devote all her time to finding that perfect law school, plunge into her studies, and finally get that degree?

But as she felt the clouds settle across her eyes, Lena admitted to herself that such a response was hardly likely. In fact, almost as soon as she had agreed to follow this latest scheme, he had stopped asking her about her plans for law school, never even mentioned it. As the business became more successful each week, Luke became more distant.

When they first opened the second shop, he had promised to put an ad in the paper, seeking an assistant baker and another counter clerk. But now, as Luke reluctantly put aside the controllers and came to the table, where she was plating slices of meat loaf and a baked potato, she felt as if she were hearing an old recording on the radio played one too many times.

"Is there enough salt?" she asked as he took the first bite and chewed slowly.

"Mmm," he responded, not bothering to look up or formulate a word. Was this how it would always be, ten, twenty years from now? she wondered. She decided to plunge in.

"Luke, about that ad in the local paper?" she asked, her eyes on her plate, which was left untouched. Now she had his attention.

"Babe, it's too soon. We need some cash in reserves before we can hire someone. A cushion before we start spending more money." He returned to his dinner.

Lena sighed and sliced the meat loaf into thin pieces that she moved around her plate, bringing none to her mouth. Why waste her breath? she thought. The more she pushed, the more he would oppose her, until after all the arguments, all the recriminations, he would look at her again in that way, tears filling his eyes, lips quivering, and tell her how sorry he was for disappointing her, how she was everything to him, how much he loved her. And it would begin all over again as, mesmerized, she would fall into his embrace, because nothing else mattered anymore—nothing but Luke.

But this time, she resolved as he placed his dish into the sink and returned to the living room, she would ignore him and think only of herself. She watched the pieces of meat loaf and potato slide off her plate and into the garbage can. This time, she vowed, things would be different.

~

Lena didn't exactly know how she was going to make things better. And it wasn't until the new shop was open for three months that she came up with an idea.

She was standing at the counter of the new shop, waiting for a rush, well, almost a rush, of customers to come in after 5:00 p.m. An elementary yeshiva for boys had just opened its doors a few blocks from the bakery, and when word got out that the Brooklyn Girl's Bake Shoppe was strictly kosher, a few of the children and their parents had begun coming in. The bell jangled as a father sporting a dark beard, a black jacket, and a hat walked into the shop. His son, no older than seven, wearing a white shirt and black trousers, skullcap askew, held tightly on to his father's hand. In the other hand was a blue balloon in the shape of a poodle, a gift from the celebration of the new school.

"Good afternoon!" said Lena, putting on a welcoming smile. "How can I help you?"

The father didn't answer but instead scanned a second kashruth certificate she had placed behind the counter, then turned to his son.

"Nu, Aron? What would you like, a black-and-white or maybe a cookie with rainbow sprinkles?"

The child didn't respond, instead turning to the array of baked goods in the showcase. His eyes, an unusual shade of turquoise, opened wide as he considered each item. Finally, without a word, he held up his finger and pointed to something at the bottom of the case.

"The brownie? Is that the one that you want, my Aron?" asked the father, who, as a pious man, never allowed his eyes to meet Lena's directly.

The boy nodded, and when Lena carefully removed the brownie and wrapped it in tissue paper, she saw the blue eyes go wider. She handed it to the child, who had removed one hand from his father's grasp.

"Thank you," he said, his voice barely above a whisper. And then his face, so serious up until then, was transformed with a full unabashed smile. Lena thought he was the most beautiful boy she had ever seen.

But as he grasped the brownie from her hand, just as suddenly as if it had a mind of its own, it slipped onto the floor, smearing the wooden planks with chocolate fudge, the cake crumbling into pieces. The boy's face, which appeared so angelic, so pure only seconds earlier, seemed to crumble as well, his eyes constricting, his cheeks flushed and puffy. He cried out, "Oh no!" Still holding on to the balloon, he shook his head in horror, the long blond sidelocks swinging from side to side.

Before the father could respond, Lena quickly reached into the showcase, but noticed that there were no brownies left. She hated to disappoint the child. She scanned the showcase display for something special as the poodle balloon dropped to the ground. Then she had an idea. A balloon was just a balloon until it was shaped into something special, so why couldn't an ordinary cookie be something special too?

Removing one of the large sugar cookies to the right of the showcase, Lena moved to a short wooden counter behind her. She grabbed two tubes of icing from a case, one brown, the other a bright orange, and set to work. She turned back briefly. "Aron is your name, right?" she said, addressing the boy. "Can you spell your name for me?" After he did, she plucked a tube of the red and, in a couple of minutes, revealed the cookie to the boy.

"Here, take this one," she said, handing it this time to the man, adding, "On the house." And before he could object: "I insist." The boy lit up at the sight of the vanilla sugar cookie painted with the face of a poodle with a bright-red tongue. Scrolled across the top, also in the striking red color, was his name.

Then she ran to the supply closet at the back of the shop and removed a bottle of Lysol cleaner and a roll of paper towels. As she wiped up the mess, she kept an eye on the child, whose tears had dried. The boy was looking at his father now, his eyes questioning. After a nod from his parent, the child took a bite. Within seconds, there it was again, the hint of a smile. Lena let out a sigh as she wiped the last crumbs away.

"I am sorry for that," said the man, pointing to the now-shiny area on the floor as the son stood quietly sinking his teeth again into the hard cookie, splitting off the "A" in his name.

"Please," Lena answered as she crunched the paper towel into a ball and threw it into the waste basket. "No harm done." The man looked down at his son and nodded.

"Well, then, I thank you," he said, still averting his eyes as he placed a hand on the boy's head.

"Shall we go, Aron?"

Lena wasn't sure if the boy heard him, as he was intent on consuming the face of the puppy. As the two exited the bakery, the boy turned his head and looked back at her, the blue poodle balloon bobbing behind.

~

That evening, minutes after Luke had gone to bed, Lena set to work. Before she left the bakery, she had stopped by the storeroom in the back and filled a bag with a variety of icing tubes. There was no need to bring anything else, as she had plenty of all-purpose flour and sugar at home. Before her, she had assembled all the ingredients on the kitchen table, the narrow counter being too small to accommodate it all. She stood, hands on her hips, surveying the packages, the bowls, and all the utensils. Lena never considered herself an artist, but since she was a child, she had enjoyed sketching simple pictures of clowns, flowers, and puppies in her notebook when she should have been listening to the teacher. Perhaps now she could make some use of her rudimentary talents. Of course, she knew the recipe for sugar cookies by heart—unsalted butter, sugar, a teaspoon of vanilla extract, an egg, flour, a pinch of baking powder and salt. First, she mixed the wet ingredients in a bowl, then stirred in the dry until it was a sticky consistency. She covered the dough with wax paper, transferred it to her refrigerator, and drew a deep breath.

As Lena waited for the refrigerator to do its work, she sat at the kitchen table, messy with flour and splotches of egg, cradling her head in her hands. She was glad she had decided to do the baking at home. Working after hours, even with the bigger counters and larger ovens at the bakery, would have felt like drudgery. And even though the apartment was not the ideal place for coming up with new ideas, her own apartment would do. Lena admitted to herself that not since she had started taking those classes at Brooklyn College nearly four years ago had she felt more exhilarated, more alive.

Lena sat quietly, considering for as long as ten minutes before heading to the living room to watch her shows. She hadn't planned on returning to the kitchen that evening, had hoped that she would have a restful sleep that night. She hadn't paid attention to the latest villain being pursued by Charlie's Angels, or considered how she could get her brown, frizzy hair to look like Farrah Fawcett's perfect locks. And she hadn't even bothered to walk into the bedroom. Instead, when just under three hours had passed, Lena went back to the refrigerator, pulled out the chilled dough, and, with a large round metal cookie cutter, shaped the cookies into fifteen perfect circles. She placed them in the oven at 350 degrees Fahrenheit, and after ten minutes, just as the edges had turned a light golden brown, she removed them. *Such a simple recipe,* thought Lena. She must have made these same cookies hundreds of times. And yet these were different. For these cookies she would be adding her own special touch.

She decided to add a layer of her own icing to create a thin white base for the drawing, so that it would stand out. As she let the cookies cool, their sugary scent wafting through the air, she worked on the icing, using powdered sugar, two tablespoons of milk, some corn syrup, and vanilla extract. Then, using a piping bag, she covered each cookie with a layer of the icing. As the icing set, she looked for the black tube of icing that she had decided on to add more definition to the drawings.

After twenty minutes, she began. As she worked, she learned to cover errant lines of the icing, turning them into hearts and stars. The first was a caricature with long lines of black icing for the hair and dots of blue for the eyes. Across the top, she scrolled his name: *Luke.* He would be the first to sample. When she was done, facing her were fifteen personalized sugar cookies with sketches of dogs and bunnies and baseballs and bows.

She heard the rush of the water sloshing as Luke shifted in the bed. He had been right about one thing. She did enjoy baking. But only when she could see the happiness her cakes and cookies brought to the faces of the children who came in.

As she tried falling asleep, she felt anything but tired. For the first time in a very long while, she couldn't wait for the sun to come up, for a new day to begin. A day that would change everything.

26

By all accounts, Lena's Creations was a great success. The baked goods were featured predominantly in the showcase and were catching on. Customers could choose one of the drawings, or, if they liked, she could create one on the spot, then, with a flourish, inscribe each with a name. Sometimes she would add sprinkles. At a dollar and fifty cents a cookie, and ten dollars for a dozen, the treats were a bargain.

Within days after their appearance, word had spread about the unique creation that tasted just as good as the traditional, plain cookies. And after some more experimentation, Lena introduced new flavors to the offerings, which were now displayed in both Brooklyn Girl's Bake Shoppe locations. Lines of customers stretched around the block at each of the bakeries, children tugging on their mothers' sleeves as they tried to decide which of the drawings, which flavor cookies, to choose. Would they have the original vanilla cookie, the chocolate, the peanut butter, the new strawberry shortcake, or the fudge? Or maybe a boxed combination of all four? And as they stood at the counter, even the parents couldn't resist sampling a cookie with a daisy design on the top.

The baking process became so overwhelming that after only two weeks, Lena was forced to bring on more bakers and assistants at the register, all at Luke's urging.

Months later, just as the weather began to change from icy torrents of snow and rain to warm skies filled with the promise of crisp green leaves and the scent of lilacs drifting in the air, so did Luke's temperament. For a change, as the business grew, so did his interest in it. He loved to sit at the kitchen table each night, counting the daily profits. No longer obsessed by video games, he turned his attention toward her, telling her often how proud he was to have a wife who was the subject of a newspaper article in the local paper, along with her picture, in which she held forth a large tray filled with beautifully designed cookies.

The attention didn't escape Lena, who appreciated the accolades but was somewhat surprised and overwhelmed by it all. As the owner of two bakeries and the creator of Lena's Creations, she tried to maintain a serious, professional demeanor with the customers and the community, graciously accepting their praise with genuine humility. In truth, she failed to understand what the ruckus was all about.

Only once did her serious facade slip. That was the day that she saw the man again, with little Aron holding tightly on to his father's hand. Now she caught the parent even glancing at her a couple of times, not quite as rigid. The boy was different, too, as his eyes shifted from the showcase of cookies to her face. This time, the smile was there from the start.

"Two baseball cookies, a plain and a chocolate, with the name Aron on each," the father said as the child pointed out his favorites.

"Yes, I remember," Lena said, smiling, as she removed the cookies, added the name, wrapped each in tissue paper, and placed them in a white paper bag. As she did, she felt a rush of joy rise through her chest. The feeling reminded her of the first time she had attended night school at the college, and while everything inside her wanted to cry out, to tell the man, "Here, take them for free! Take them all!" she knew that the offer could only be refused. Besides, she feared that if she told them the truth, that this quiet little boy had started it all, that he was the reason for her success, the tears that strained behind her eyes would be set loose. So Lena said nothing and watched as the two exited the bakery, the father taking one chocolate cookie from the bag and handing it to the child. She watched, ignoring the next customer, who was tapping on the glass, until father and son walked down the block and disappeared.

~

Lena and the new girl, Ramona, were preparing the day's inventory when she heard a sound at the front door. The steel gates had been raised for nearly an hour since the two had arrived, and streaks of sunlight were just beginning to penetrate the darkness. A light drizzle dampened the sidewalks.

Lena wiped her hands on her apron and rushed to the front of the shop. There they were, both wearing tan raincoats, standing beneath a large black umbrella.

Josef was rapping politely at the front door but raised his eyebrows when he caught sight of his daughter. Anya, holding on to her husband's elbow, bit her lip nervously.

Lena hoped her parents hadn't noticed the slight hesitation before she unlocked the door. While she sensed that this day would come, had even expected it, the sight of her parents, her father standing tall, his eyes darting anxiously, her mother stooped, her face washed of all color, sent a shiver through Lena. While she tried to telephone her parents weekly (it had been several months since she had actually visited), she knew that the publicity celebrating her recent successes in the newspaper, and even on radio, must have reached them. It was their first time visiting the new shop.

Lena swallowed the lump of saliva in her throat and embraced each of them in turn. Despite the coat, she could feel the bones protruding beneath her mother's skin. It must be another one of her fad diets, she thought.

"Why didn't you tell me you were coming?" she asked, ushering them into the shop as she silently berated herself. She should have expected this. After all, it was a Sunday. Her mother didn't answer, but Lena caught her eyes drifting up to Josef's.

"What? Do we need an invitation?" he said, striding into the shop and gazing around appraisingly.

"N-no, of course not. You know that you are both welcome anytime," she lied. In truth, she secretly hoped that her parents would be oblivious to her recent achievements or would have no interest in checking out the shop, even though they were both aware of its purchase. And now that they were here, inspecting the bakery as if they were from the Department of Health, Lena had no choice but to face her fears. As her mother stepped forward, her eyes sailing past the kashruth certificate as she placed one hand on top of the still-empty showcase, Lena knew that once again she was being judged.

"We don't open for another hour. Ramona and I were just getting things ready," Lena said, gesturing toward the back of the store. She wished her assistant would emerge, just to ease some of the tension she was feeling. She wondered if her parents were feeling it too.

"You look good. You are a famous girl now." It took Lena a few seconds to realize that her father was addressing her.

"Oh," she said, her eyes still straining toward the door in the back, "I just had an idea, that's all. An idea and a little luck, I guess."

"More than luck, I think," responded Josef, coming up to stand next to his wife. "Oh yes, more than luck. Lena, you have a talent."

Lena didn't quite know what to say to that, and just as a lull began to settle into the conversation, she heard her name again.

"Lena, I—oh, we have customers," said her assistant, who carried a basket filled with sweet rolls.

"Oh, Ramona, no—not customers. These are my parents, Josef and Anya. Mom, Dad, this is Ramona. She's my new assistant baker."

"Hello!" her father said cheerily as Anya tilted her head in greeting.

The young woman quickly placed the basket atop the showcase and, as Lena had done, wiped her hands down her apron.

She was a polite girl with long platinum hair, dark eyebrows, and an angular face. Like Lena's parents, she was from Poland. Having just arrived six months earlier, her English was far from perfect. Lights sparked in her pale-blue eyes when Lena told her about their common background, and within minutes they were all conversing in their native tongue. Lena didn't mind standing by as the three chatted away—not at all. It took the attention away from her. At least for now.

While Ramona was talking with her parents, Lena took the opportunity to retrieve more of the baked goods from the back room and checked the ovens.

She was bringing in a pan of Linzer tarts when, to her dismay, she realized the room had gone silent. *Like a locomotive that had finally run out of steam,* she thought. Ramona gave her a look of apology as she stacked the rolls at the bottom of the showcase and then returned to the back.

"When were you going to tell us?"

Lena placed the last tart carefully among the others and sighed. She knew this moment had to come eventually.

"Tell you what, Daddy?"

She gazed at him wide-eyed, feigning ignorance.

"About this!" he exclaimed, waving a hand over the rows of decorated cookies that stood atop the counter, like soldiers at the ready.

"Oh, it was just an idea I had," she said. She stopped her work, placed her hands on her hips, and faced Josef directly. If it was a confrontation they wanted, she was ready.

"No big deal," she added.

"No big deal? To be in the papers and on the radio, and our daughter says this is no big deal!" He looked at her mother for confirmation, but Anya's eyes remained downcast. Lena wondered if she was inspecting the floor for crumbs.

"Don't you think you should have made a mention about such a success?" He continued without waiting for a response, "You speak with us only one time a week and do not visit. You tell us nothing. You do not even ask how is your mama because you do not care. It is only for yourself you care about and not to tell your mama and papa a little good news, to bring them some nachas, maybe make their miserable lives a little less miserable?"

"Josef, please—" Anya placed a hand on his shoulder now, as if to stay the anger.

Lena froze in place, her tongue welded to the bottom of her mouth as she watched her papa's cheeks expand and deflate with each word. Again she was transported in time to the disappointed ten-year-old who tossed her honey cake into the garbage, after her mother's less than enthusiastic reaction. Only this time it wasn't her mother doing the scolding, but her father. She was confused by the sudden role reversal.

"I'm sorry," she finally blurted out. "I've just been so busy with both stores. I haven't even had time to apply to law school, haven't seen any of my friends in over a year. But you're right, I should have told you about the cookies. I should have—"

"Yes," said Josef, his voice at a lower register now as he touched Anya's hand, which remained on his shoulder. "Yes, you should have."

Lena swallowed hard. Her papa was right. She had become self-absorbed, even more than usual. His words only confirmed what she felt each day, stuck in the middle of her heart. She was a terrible daughter.

Josef took a deep breath, looked at his watch, his eyes shifting to the window. He glanced at Anya, who had not moved during the exchange.

"Come, my dear, I think the rain has stopped for now, and besides, Lena must open the bakery soon. She has a busy day ahead."

As he ushered Anya out, he added as an afterthought, "We are very proud of you, Lena. We are always proud."

The bell jingled as the door slammed shut, but in seconds it was opened once more. Anya rushed toward her, arms outstretched. Silently, she embraced her daughter, but more words flowed through that silence than she had said during their brief encounter. *I love you. I forgive you.* Lena did have a busy day, just as her papa predicted. A steady stream of customers came through the bakery, wanting everything from freshly baked raisin challah to sponge and marble cakes. Of course, Lena's Creations was still a favorite. Some waited in line for as long as twenty minutes, and once they arrived at the counter, they complimented Lena and her productions, expressing how happy they were to have her in the neighborhood. When the last customer finally left the shop at 6:12 p.m., minutes after the official closing, Lena was exhausted, her register brimming with bills. She could still hear the words of praise echoing in her ears. But in her heart she knew, just as she had all her life, that she was nothing but a failure.

27

Lena was still half-asleep as she stepped out of bed and plodded barefoot into the bathroom. She usually tried to avoid mirrors, but this morning she took the time to examine her face. There were lines etched under eyes that were heavy lidded, suggesting someone who was closer to fifty, rather than twenty-seven. Her cheeks were crimson colored and puffy, her coarse waves of hair soaked in perspiration and clinging against her face. She thought she detected a gray hair hiding amid the brown at her forehead but didn't bother to pull it. At what age does gray begin to outnumber the brown? Forty? Fifty? At any rate, she was still too young to be going gray.

But she still felt too young for all the events that were going on in her life, still feeling that she had not even embarked on her true purpose. Becoming a business owner of not one, but two, bakeries. Having her name in the newspapers for inventing something so silly as a personalized cookie. Being a married woman. Going to school. How many years had it been since she had sat in a classroom? How long had it been since she had last seen Marilyn and Kenny?

Lena closed her eyes and pressed her forehead against the mirror. She tried to remember. There was a dream. One of those dreams that was full of action, where she was running, not away, but toward something. And when she found it, she was so happy because things were perfect. She was soon surrounded by others, people she seemed to recognize, but now, standing at the sink, none of whom she could actually remember. It was so frustrating.

Lena dreamed every night. She was part of a world in which she was active, surrounded by those who loved her, encouraged her to go further, to reach that goal she had so long desired. And when she did finally get there, well, it was pure bliss. What was the goal? Who were those people? Each morning when she awoke, she snapped back to a reality that was worlds away from the one in her dreams. She often lay in bed, just as she stood now, head against the mirror, trying to recapture the details of that dream. Trying to remember the feeling. If only she could.

~

Lena was still trying to recall all that had taken place in her dream world when she reached the corner of the Williamsburg bakery and noticed Luke standing in front of the shop, staring at something across the street. It was only then that she realized Luke had not been fast asleep next to her, as he usually was, sleeping when she got out of bed that morning. But sometimes he liked to take walks at odd hours just to clear his head, so lately she thought nothing of it. Lena quickened her steps and within minutes was by his side.

"Luke, how come you're here so early? Is something wrong?"

He only stared at her blankly and pointed across the street. She saw the usual workers in hard hats, some she even recognized as customers, all looking up. She followed the direction of their eyes to a giant crane, where mounds of fresh dirt were being lifted and dumped into a mountain of more dirt.

"What is it, Luke?"

He cast her a bewildered look and shook his head. "They're building something here, Lena. Can't you see that?"

She turned her head back to the crane operator, who was now in the process of lifting another mound of thick black earth. As the hill grew larger, so did the massive hole, which was making way for new construction. It had been nearly half a year since the lighting warehouse in that spot had gone out of business, and since then had lain vacant except for the growing cobwebs and No Trespass signs out in front. The Williamsburg bakery had only been open barely two years now, and she worried what other surprises might lie ahead.

Lena stood next to Luke, watching the repetitive motions of the great machine, lifting the dirt, adding to the wide expanse of earth. She found herself holding her breath as she waited. She wasn't quite sure what she was waiting for, but she knew it wasn't anything good. For now, though, she was in a safe space. And so she waited for Luke to speak first.

He said, "We're doomed."

Not exactly the words she was expecting.

He sighed and looked at her, exasperated.

"Lena, can't you see what's happening? They're building something here, something that will ruin everything we've worked for."

Lena shook her head and looked up at the crane operator blithely doing his job. Ignoring the comment about them both working hard, she instead searched her mind for what type of menace could be going up that would threaten everything that they—no, *she*—had worked for.

"It's a supermarket," he said, as if reading her thoughts. "It's called Grand's, and they carry everything a family could possibly want on their kitchen table."

Lena shook her head again, trying to string his words together, trying to envision the monolith that within a few short months would materialize across the street.

"But, Luke, I don't see why that would be such a threat to us. We're a little shop, selling our own specialty baked goods. Surely this will be no competition."

He turned to face her now, silently forcing her to turn as well. Lena looked directly into his eyes, and what she saw made her shiver. The eyes, the dark-green eyes that she loved so much, spat fire. And for the second time since she had known him, Lena was afraid.

"Are you an idiot?" he said, a little too loudly. "Everything is going to change in a year. Grand's is a massive conglomerate with its own baking department," he continued, stressing the last words. "They employ hundreds, and they bake all their products daily on premises. We can't possibly keep up—not with our breads, our honey loaves, not even with your special cookies," he added sarcastically, as if something bitter had just landed on his tongue.

Again, she ignored the insults as she tried to make sense of Luke's words. Was it really all that bad? Even if a Grand's supermarket was built within the year, she doubted that their bakery department, if they had one, would carry the number of items, the quality, that was offered at Brooklyn Girl's. And even if they did, would they be kosher, would they take custom orders for birthdays, graduations, wedding cakes? And have those orders ready within a day, sometimes within hours? Even if the new supermarket met all those contingencies, surely Lena's customers were not so fickle as to turn away so easily, even if her prices remained just a little bit higher. No, she reasoned, they were loyal to the bakery that had been a part of their neighborhood for two years now. They were loyal to her.

Lena watched the rhythmic motion of the crane, which had not stopped its repetitive work of scooping and piling. Was it twenty minutes, a half hour, since the two remained mesmerized on the corner? She was already behind in her preparations at the bakery, hadn't even opened the doors for the customers who would be eager for a roll with a pat of butter or a chocolate croissant on their way to work that morning. Or a black-and-white treat to add to their child's lunch box. She vaguely hoped Ramona was there already. But in truth she didn't care.

The grinding sounds of the machine provided a musical though sinister background as her mind raced, as she recalled Luke's ominous words: *We're doomed.* Were they ruined? And what of their other shop, the one in Bensonhurst? Despite an early surge on the decorated cookies this year, business had gone down as a new population moved into the area, not so interested in kosher products, many unable to afford the quality of her goods. And if they lost both shops, what would happen then?

Lena turned away from the lot, the machine, the working men. She and Luke would have to figure something out.

But when she opened her mouth to tell him that yes, she understood, that somehow they would get through this together, Luke was no longer beside her. He was already on his way home.

~

Lena was not surprised when Luke's words, as usual, proved to be prophetic. He had been wrong about only one thing. It hadn't taken a year. From the moment the two had stood dumbfounded, watching the hole in the ground grow wider and deeper, to the day ANOTHER GRAND'S GRAND OPENING sign replaced the No TRESPASSING warnings and an array of sourdough breads and marble ryes magically appeared on shelves behind the large front windows was less than four months. Fifteen weeks, to be exact.

But the consequences of all that construction weren't felt by their small bakery at first. Each shovel that sliced into the ground, each beam that was securely fitted during those hectic months, seemed to spur Lena on so that she barely took the time to brush her hair in the morning. As sunlight faded each day and the construction workers put down their hammers and stacked the remaining bricks neatly to the side, Lena would wipe her brow with the back of her hand, smack her fist into a third round of dough, as an extra pan of round challahs morphed into golden-brown suns in the oven. She added more flavors to her famous cookies, including now a cherry, blueberry, and specialty mocha nut to the mix. As products increased, the couple made the risky decision to lower prices on their breads and decreased the prices of Lena's Creations to a scary dollar apiece. Nothing was wasted, either, as Lena scraped the leftover dough she used for the bagels and hard breads, turning them into chips that were offered, practically given away, for fifty cents a bag.

At first, all these measures worked and, even as the new supermarket lured people in, curious to try their sliced cold cuts and specialty cream cheeses, the Brooklyn Girl's Bake Shoppe thrived. Still, Lena felt the tenseness in her shoulders loosen each morning as she prepared for another busy day. Even Luke, though he said nothing, would occasionally glance over and wink as she set another tray of black-and-whites in the showcase. And although, at times, a customer would walk in, point to the new supermarket across the street, and ask what she thought, Lena would merely shrug her shoulders. *It is what it is,* she would say, adding that she hoped his family would enjoy the challah with their Sabbath dinner that night, or that the children liked the chocolate chip cookies she had prepared. Often she would throw an extra sugar cookie or sometimes a loaf of day-old rye into the bag for good business. The customer would then smile and some even pat her hand reassuringly before they left. She was confident that Brooklyn Girl's Bake Shoppe had nothing to worry about. But after only two months, as more people discovered Grand's and its array of tasty baked goods, where they could buy doughnuts and white bread and milk in one shopping excursion, and all at lower prices, well, that was when the couple's fortunes began to turn.

~

"You can't trust anybody," Luke fumed as he slammed the ledger shut on the coffee table. He had spent the last hour sitting on the sofa, leaned over, pushing the pencil against each page as if magically it could transform the numbers into other, friendlier shapes. Once again he was unsuccessful.

Lena stood silently in the kitchen, watching her husband. She wanted to go to him, wrap her arms around his skinny torso, kiss the top of his head as if she were coddling a child, but something prevented her, held her in place. Such an act of compassion might calm him, spark a warmth that she had not witnessed in a long time so that he would

28

It was a good day to be alive. These were Lena's thoughts as she stepped outside on a perfect spring day when the sky shimmered a silvery pink dotted with round white clouds that resembled vanilla frosted cupcakes. She scolded herself as she brought the metaphor to mind. She would have to stop thinking about baked goods all the time. She would have to stop because soon that part of her life would be over.

It had been a year now since the opening of Grand's, and, as feared, the grand opening, which was heralded with whoop and holler throughout Williamsburg, proved to be the death knell for their beloved shop. Luke—too soon, she thought—had decided to take matters in hand, so when he received an offer for their bakery in Bensonhurst, run largely by employees, from a wealthy businessman who was opening a string of dry cleaners throughout the Northeast, he grabbed the opportunity. And even though the offer wasn't nearly as much as the couple had paid for the property almost four years earlier, after only a little fruitless negotiating, Luke was compelled to take it. What with the change in population and the increasing competition in baked items, the store was, he reasoned, leaking like a sieve. Better to get out while they could.

Lena surprised herself with the tears that flowed freely down her cheeks the day they signed away the shop. Even though she had hated almost everything about the bakery—the countless hours she spent at the ovens, the labor, the constant worry that all entrepreneurs carry—still, it was hers. The Brooklyn Girl's Bake Shoppe, in a weird way she couldn't quite understand, had been a source of pride.

Nevertheless, at that moment, Lena was happy. It was time, finally time, for that chapter of her life to end, and another (maybe less stressful) to begin. What was that saying about one door opening just as another was closing? Another damn metaphor. Lena shook her head and laughed out loud. She lifted her chin and inhaled, drinking in all the flavors of the sky—pink, lilac, rose, and jasmine. Then she stepped off the patio and began the long walk to the bus stop and another day of work.

Lena was extra nice to the customers throughout the day—not that she usually wasn't cordial—but there was something inside her, a thing of joy that was jumping excitedly like a kid at a birthday party, and she wanted to share it with everyone. She couldn't exactly account for her feelings, so she couldn't explain it to them, not even to herself. Nevertheless, her exuberance spilled over so that she engaged in prolonged conversation with each customer throughout the day, inquiring as to the health of a sick uncle, doling out profuse congratulations on the birth of twins. Lena was extra generous to all the customers, offering two pounds of assorted cookies if the order called for one, and one of her special cookies, no charge, even if the buyer had just come in for a loaf of rye.

She was even pleasant to Mrs. Irving, a stodgy matron who came in each Friday afternoon, surveying each of the items in the showcase with a cynical eye and never speaking, but merely pointing at the desired product, snorting a quick thank-you as Lena wrapped the challah or honey cake and placed it in her hand. "Hmph," she said as Lena threw two of the vanilla cookies with bears on them into the bag. As the woman left, taking a second look inside the bag, she glanced back at Lena, the shadow of a smile on her broad face.

Lena kept these freebies to herself, knowing that Luke would frown on her magnanimity, calling it frivolous at best, at worst, foolish, maybe even stupid. And he would be right. They were in no position to be giving away the merchandise, not with the losses they had endured in the Bensonhurst store, not with Grand's attracting more crowds each day. But somehow, as the weeks and months had passed, Lena grew more comfortable in her role as a baker and merchant. Maybe because she knew with only one store to maintain now, it would soon all be coming to an end.

Lena handed the last customer of the day a honey cake, along with one leftover chocolate chip cookie, then followed her out.

"Have a good evening, Mrs. Mayer," she said as she shut the glass doors and turned the lock. She proceeded to remove the extra goods to the room in the back, then returned to wipe down the shelves. It occurred to her that she hadn't telephoned her parents for the last two weeks. This wasn't so unusual, as there were numerous times that she was just too busy to remember. Besides, if there were any problems at home, she was sure she would have heard from them.

Her father used to have a habit of calling Lena whenever they hadn't heard from her in more than five days. Lately, though, it seemed like he was forgetting too. Perhaps that was a good thing, she reasoned now; perhaps finally her parents were getting a life of their own, not so dependent on their only daughter.

Nevertheless, Lena was in such a good mood that she decided to call them immediately. She knew that hearing the upbeat sound of her voice would make them happy. Perhaps her newfound enthusiasm would even brush off on them.

"Lena? It is you?"

"Yes, Daddy. It's me. How are you and Mommy doing? I guess it's been a while since we spoke."

"What is wrong?"

"Wrong? Why, nothing. Everything is right, as a matter of fact. I just wanted to say hello."

There was a long pause at the other end of the line.

"Daddy? Are you okay? Is Mommy—"

"Mommy is fine. We both are good."

Now it was Lena's turn to be quiet as she took her father's words in. "Daddy? Please tell me. I don't like the sound of your voice."

"My voice? I have the same voice. I don't know what you mean."

"Please, Daddy. If Mommy is sick, or you, or something happened"— she found herself pleading—"just please tell me." She sounded like a three-year-old trying to cajole her parents into buying her an ice-cream cone. But instead of giving in to her demands, her father became irritated, more abrupt.

"Look, Lena, I do not have time for such games. I am telling you we are fine, nothing to worry about. Thank you for your call."

The phone quickly clicked off. Lena stood staring at the receiver for another minute, feeling its cool plastic against the palm of her hand, as if by waiting, somehow she could glean an answer in the silence. But none came. As she put away the last of the baked products and pulled the metal screen down over the front doors, she knew only one thing for certain. Her parents were far from fine.

~

If Lena thought she might find solace back at home, she soon learned that hope quickly faded as she walked into the apartment. Luke was seated in his customary position on the couch, going over the numbers in the ledger.

"How was your day?" she offered, placing her purse on the small table in the hall and hoping that somehow the animated tone of her words would brighten his response. She'd had the same hope earlier when she called her parents. But once again she was disappointed.

Luke didn't so much answer her as grumble. She could see the tightness in his shoulders, the stiff set of his jaw as, with the stub of a pencil, he angrily slashed at the numbers on the page. His hair, dark and nearly to his chin, now fell in front of his eyes, and he pushed the strands hastily away with his fingers. The hair looked like it hadn't been washed for days. For that matter, judging from the gray streaks along his arm and the body odor emanating across the room, neither had he.

Lena refrained from inquiring about the two interviews he had scheduled for accounting positions, as it became clear from both his appearance and demeanor that he'd failed to show up for either one. And although she had encouraged him to take a job as a payroll supervisor at the local printshop, which had been advertising for the past week, she knew her attempts were futile. Without a college degree, it was unlikely that he could secure a job as an accountant, and he was adamant that the payroll position and the meager salary that came with it were far beneath him.

Lena was about to tell him about the conversation with her father, hoping for a touch of empathy or even a suggestion on how to best deal with the situation, but she thought it advisable not to say anything. The look in his eyes as he glanced in her direction confirmed that this was not the time. Lena had a sudden craving for a cup of black coffee. She had just turned into the kitchen when he pounced on her.

She didn't remember much after that. A ringing in her ears, and when she tried to stand up, a soreness at the waist and the side of her head. She touched her eyebrow, which had begun to sting, and looked at her finger. The blood in the crease of skin was thick and black.

Lena didn't know how long it took her to get up off the floor, but when she did, it was like a toddler taking its first steps. Knees first to a standing position, arms stretched out as she tottered across the floor and into the bedroom. Her head was still throbbing from the smack against the hard linoleum, but she ignored it as she let her face sink into the undulating waves of the mattress. Lena opened her eyes once, to a world in shades of gray, before finally succumbing to the blissful blackness of sleep.

That evening and throughout the night, she dreamed. It was the same dream she'd had over the last few years. She was running, running toward something that she had yearned for all her life. Moving quickly, her legs as light as a breeze on the wind, her eyes bright, free of the clouds that had plagued her. As she grew nearer to her goal, a sense of peace enveloped her, such as she had never felt before. The red flannel blanket embraced her as her mama secured the corners. She was home.

The dream no longer frightened Lena. For the first time, she could reach the person, discern a face. She tried stretching her mouth into a smile, but it hurt too much. And yet she did smile, because she recognized the face, open and warm. And she knew that finally, after all the years, she had found herself.

29

A buzzing circled in her head. She wanted to go back to the euphoria of the dream, where she felt safe, untouchable. A thought came to her, drifting like a feather, that perhaps all that had occurred the day before was a dream, too, and, along with it, the wish that the past seven years, with their brief moments of happiness, always with an undercurrent of anxiety, had been a long nightmare that she would blissfully awaken from.

Lena felt a warmth seep through her body, as if it held a multitude of suns. She had stepped off the bus that day, had barely spoken to the handsome stranger with green eyes and too-long hair, had never even given him her phone number. If only she had not! The marriage beneath the chuppah, the opening of a bakery, *their* bakery, with the sunlight flooding the shop as they parted the doors. The customers, their children, all eager to taste the source of the rich scents of chocolate and cinnamon and sugar that permeated the air. The second shop, and her name in the paper for an invention, an honor she never really wanted. The numbers in the ledger, blurry now, as he pored over them, trying to make them something they were not, a work of fiction, no longer based in reality. The years of anger, the pound of her head as it smacked against the floor. The taste of blood on her tongue as she wondered how something so sweet could taste so bitter. But the worst of it was the feeling that accompanied her, like a shadow each day, knowing that she had become too much of a thing she never wanted to be, and yet, when she thought of her childhood, somehow never enough.

The buzzing was persistent. Finally, painfully, she moved her legs from the bed. Her eyes were fully open now, and she realized she was no longer asleep, no longer part of the elegant dream that had caressed her like a mother's arms throughout the night.

As Lena made her way to the front door, hand against the wall for support, she had the vague hope that she would once again see the face of that friend who, four years earlier, had promised to return to listen to her sorrows, to provide the guidance that she seemed to need now as the pieces of her life had crumbled like stale cupcakes beneath her.

Her eyes were bright with expectation as she opened the front door, hoping to see the calm smile, the sun glinting off the pale-blond hair of her dearest friend. Instead, she found herself staring into the blue eyes of another, someone she knew quite well yet in that moment couldn't fully recognize.

"Kenny? Kenny is that you?"

A smile swept across the young man's face as he took in the sight of his old classmate and, with no hesitation, threw his arms around her, hugging her body against his. The sudden movement made Lena somewhat dizzy, but she held her head high, nonetheless, hoping he wouldn't sense anything wrong. He seemed not to notice her injury and instead, without being asked, strode into the apartment and the welcoming kitchen, where sheets of sunlight cast a warm glow across the Formica table.

She followed him meekly, her hand still against the white wall, as if she were a guest and he the host. As she sat down opposite him, she became aware of why he looked so unrecognizable at first. While the face was much the same, except for the ruddiness now replaced by a more natural color, the body that was dressed in a pale-blue T-shirt that reflected the color of his eyes, and dark-blue jeans, seemed no longer Kenny's. Instead of a rotund belly that strained at the buttons of his plaid shirts, there was a flatness resembling a wooden washboard, and a muscularity that took the place of the flabbiness in his arms. There was something else. After only a minute, Lena realized what it was. The bag of chips or pretzels that had dangled from his hand for so long that it almost seemed a part of him was absent too.

"Kenny! I can't believe it. Why, I hardly recognized you. You—you've lost weight."

This new, healthier stranger shifted in his seat uneasily and blushed at the compliment, then glanced down at his stomach, only the slightest of bulges beneath the cargo pants, as if he, too, had noticed the change for the first time. But after the two began to exchange words, she could see that no matter what he looked like, he was still the same lovable guy.

"Fifty pounds, Lena. After I left school and was done with all that cramming for the CPA exam—I think the nerves over exams, starting a new job, got me eating so much—I decided to focus on me for a change, not my mind, but for the first time, the way I looked. So I went on that diet, you know, the Atkins plan, where you pretty much consume only protein. My cousin Randy, who was skinny to begin with, lost ten pounds after only a month, so I thought I'd give it a try. And, well, here I am." He patted the almost-flat tummy and smiled proudly. Lena was certain now that Kenny's unaffected smile was even more attractive than his blue eyes.

"Well," she said as she placed two fingers over her eye, which had once again begun to sting, "you certainly do look good! Almost like a different person." Then she added, on second thought: "Not that you were so bad to begin with."

Kenny shrugged off the compliment. He settled back into the metal chair and in the minute's silence stared earnestly at her before lowering his voice.

"Lena, what's happened to you? Were you in some sort of accident?"

She ignored the question, got up, and began preparing coffee. She appreciated the gift of Kenny's silence as he waited for her answer, an answer she knew she was unprepared to give. She wondered if she ever could. Instead, as she poured two cups from the Mr. Coffee carafe, she sensed something gnawing at her brain. It was something Kenny had said earlier. He had passed the CPA exams. He had a job. Lena felt a pang in her heart then, sharper than any of the pains she had experienced throughout the night. Luke had wanted the same career once. Yet for him the desire had never transformed to action. Luke had gotten derailed, and so had she.

Kenny accepted the cup and, like her, declined the milk and sugar. Lena took one long gulp from her mug with the logo Brooklyn College written in bright red. The hot liquid burned her tongue. She swallowed the coffee and, along with it, momentarily, the pain.

"Kenny, how were you able to find me? I mean, we haven't really spoken in two years," she said, hoping to divert his attention from her appearance, but also because she was curious.

It worked, as Kenny looked down at his fingernails, immaculately clipped with a hint of clear polish. He curved his lips into that beautiful smile.

"Haven't you heard of a phone directory, Lena? Nowadays it's quite easy to locate just about anyone. I remembered your last name and just looked you up. You never told me your address or had us over here— mostly we were at Marilyn's place—but then I recognized you from that article in the newspaper. The *Daily News*! That was quite impressive."

"The personalized cookies," she whispered to herself, embarrassed.

"Hey!" he said, reaching over casually as he placed his hand on her shoulder. "You should be proud. I guess you decided to stay with baking, after all. We always enjoyed those chocolate chip cookies you baked for our study sessions." He lifted his hand from her shoulder and continued, "Anyway, I was staying with my uncle down in Jersey for a while, helping him out with his chicken farm while I studied for the last two parts of my exam. It turns out it's really easy to stay on a diet when you're looking at nothing but eggs all day. Anyway"—he shifted again—"a month ago I rented an apartment on the Lower East Side close to where I work and decided to visit my famous friend!" He cackled softly. An empty laugh.

"Why didn't you just come to the bakery?" she asked. The meeting would have been safer there. He shrugged.

"Didn't want to bother you at work. And besides, today is Saturday. Your bakery is kosher, right?"

Lena nodded, a defeated look in her eyes. She felt the fingers of his hand upon her again, lightly pressing against the skin.

"Lena," he said, his voice tender, "what the hell happened to you?"

And then, without warning, the tears were released, pouring from her eyes so that she could no longer see. Her mind became muddled, making hearing, even speech, impossible too. Kenny waited patiently for the trauma inside her to subside. The two sat in a calming silence, only interrupted by the steady ticking of the clock on the wall, until finally her brain could form words. And when she did, much to Lena's shock, she told him everything. How from the beginning her marriage to Luke had been filled with so much promise, how they had vowed to support each other in their goals until one day Luke had a dream that would send them on a journey of peaks and valleys neither could have ever imagined. And when that dream had come crashing down, just as she had feared, so had her marriage, crushing any hope of attaining the bright future both had longed for.

"He was so upset, so hurt that he didn't realize what he was doing!" she cried. Even as she defended Luke, she realized that her words had become hollow, meaningless.

Kenny took a long sip of the now-cool coffee, tasting its bitterness before rubbing his eyes, considering his response to all he had heard.

"I don't know much about this, Lena. I've never been married, never owned my own business. But I do know one thing. This guy—Luke—is not a good guy. Not if he could put his hands on a woman. Not if he could put his hands on you." He turned his head to the wall, choking on the last words.

"You don't know him, Kenny, not the real person he is. He was the one with all the great ideas, the one who made it all happen. Everything he did, he did for us. He just gets a little too passionate, but—but he's kind." Her voice was deflating, like a balloon that had been blown up too quickly. Kenny leaned forward, and for the first time she saw something new in his eyes. They were ablaze, like blue fire.

"Lena, he hurt you."

She lowered her chin as she peered into the swirl of liquid in his eyes, now a black ink. Still, unable to look at him too long, she somehow squeezed out the words.

"Kenny, you'd better leave." He sat motionless, waiting. She knew she would have to make the first move, knew she would have to do something.

She pressed the palms of her hands against the surface of the table, rising painstakingly to full height. She wondered whether this was how it felt to be seventy, eighty, or even ninety years old, knowing even then that she would never live that long. A sound floated overhead, like a gentle breeze, again and again, until the sound became words and the words had meaning.

"Come back home with me, Lena, just for a few days. Come to the apartment with me."

She looked at him then, ready to lash out with all the anger, the contempt, she could muster. But when she did, Lena saw, instead of fire in his eyes, something soft, gentle. She went into the bedroom, packed a bag. Ten minutes later he was guiding her out, his arm secure around her shoulders as she shut the front door behind them.

~

She was kneading dough early the next morning at the wooden bakery counter when he walked in. Luke looked almost as bad as she did, his long hair greasy and disheveled. His face, an ashen color, was drawn, making him appear to be a man in his fifties rather than at the precipice of thirty. He faced her for a few tense minutes, which spoke louder than perhaps all the years they had spent together. He waited for her to speak, and when she did not, he grabbed a broom from the corner of the room and began sweeping the trail of flour, which flew in different directions, scattering starlike patterns throughout the room.

"I have a plan for us," he said, looking down as he swept, "and this time I think it's a good one." The flat of her palm smacked hard against the dough. A thin breeze created by his sweeping made her shiver. More to the point than Luke's comment were the words he had not said: *How are you feeling? Where did you go last night? I'm sorry.*

"I bought nearly every newspaper at the newsstand and was up all last night looking through the classifieds in each one. Until I saw it. And, Lena, I think this could be the answer to our dreams."

Lena let his words float over her like a summer rainstorm. She hadn't absorbed anything he'd said, and it occurred to her to ask where he had spent the night. But on second thought, she mused as her hand slapped hard against the dough, she didn't really care.

"Lena, it's a sweet little shop, not as big as this one, not even the store we had in Bensonhurst, but there's potential there in Sheepshead Bay for a bakery, Brooklyn Girl's Bake Shoppe III, and I think it might work. It was a small grocery, so the space already has a giant fridge, but we'll have to get another stove."

She punched harder into the dough as she felt a throbbing in her right hand. In empathy, the pain had begun to flash through her arm, her shoulder. Her head was beginning to hurt again. Lena plunged her fingers deep into the soft pillow of dough, hating it more than she hated anything in her life. What was it, after all? Flour and water and eggs. By the time she stopped, her energy was sapped. Lena feared she was losing her mind.

"Lena? Did you hear me? It's only been on the market for less than a week, and if we don't jump on it—"

"What?" She stared at the sad lump of dough as she tried to remember whether it was to be a sponge or a pound cake. She stared at the dough, waiting as if magically somehow it would speak.

"Lena? What do you think? Should we go ahead and put in a bid? Lena?"

Her hand was still throbbing as she clasped the wedge of dough and tossed it into the large metal garbage can in the corner of the room.

~

She was getting used to her new bed, which wasn't a bed, really, but a wide sofa, upholstered in a charcoal velvet suede with three boxy pillows in the same fabric. Although that first evening Kenny had insisted she take his bed, even in her fragile state, Lena would not be budged. She pulled Kenny's old navy-blue woolen blanket gingerly up past her jeans, her white cotton T-shirt and the bruises hidden beneath, and tucked the scratchy wool up past her chin. As she sank into the sofa, it felt uncomfortable, a foreign thing. She missed the liquid undulations of the old waterbed. And yet, the next morning, Lena awoke clear-eyed, refreshed. The bruises, the aches, the invisible scars that rested in her soul, they were all still there, but the restful night helped. She no longer missed the waves that surged each time she moved; she didn't miss the unsteadiness, bobbing on the water, sailing to a place that was strange, and a future just as uncertain. As Lena stood up, her legs still unsteady, it occurred to her that maybe—just maybe—she had begun to crawl out of the abyss.

The morning after Kenny had rescued her—that was the way she liked to think about it now—she watched as he got up early so that he could check on her before she left for the bakery in Williamsburg. Before the sun had cast its first shivering rays of light against the windows, he got ready for work. He had to look the part for his job at an international CPA firm on Wall Street. As he stood inside the kitchen, scooping spoonfuls of Sanka into two mugs, Lena, still curled up in the woolen blanket with her back against the large gray pillow, watched, admiring her friend. In a navy pin-striped suit, an aquamarine shirt that nearly matched the color of his eyes, and a navy-and-red-striped tie, Kenny was the model of an up-and-coming executive. Again, Lena marveled at the transformation from the happy-go-lucky, chubby young student to the confident young man who stood before her, handing her the mug of steaming instant coffee.

"Black, right?" he asked before returning to his own cup of the same. Ironically, each of the mugs had the BROOKLYN COLLEGE logo written across the front, just like Lena's back at home.

She declined his offer of a toasted rye with butter, assuring him that once at the bakery, she would have plenty to eat. Instead, she watched as he sat at the counter in his kitchen, even tinier than Lena's, and took a few bites of the toast as he calmly reviewed some papers from his expensive-looking black leather briefcase. She appreciated his reticence. She had no desire to be the victim of endless questions, prying further into her life. Earlier, he had asked only how she was feeling, if she needed a baby aspirin or some salve for the bruises. And now, as Lena watched this boy, this *man*, she admired him. Not exactly handsome, even with the weight loss and those striking blue eyes, there was a charm about Kenny, a certain charisma. What was most attractive, in a platonic way, of course, was the confidence he possessed. Kenny Tannenbaum was a man who was going places, a man with a bright future ahead.

Funny, she thought, watching as he placed the papers neatly back into his briefcase, she never had the same thoughts about Luke. Sure, she had loved him, loved him still, but in all the years she could never start planning a future together, a family, even when things were at their best. With Luke, she often felt the same way she did just before she fell asleep on the round waterbed each night, directionless and unsteady.

~

Luke, sensing that Lena would probably never respond to his latest proposal, went ahead with the preparations for purchasing the former grocery in Sheepshead Bay. By then she had informed him that she was staying with an old friend from college in the city. And even though he knew this friend was a male, someone with a full-time job, a career, Luke was not the least bit jealous. In fact, Lena guessed he must have felt relieved not to have her watchful eye at his back every minute, no longer having to endure her silence.

Lena knew she had to formulate a plan for her life. After all, she couldn't stay with Kenny, as accommodating as he was, forever. Nor could she return to the apartment—at least not yet. She would have to decide soon, but before she could, she needed to wait until the throbbing in her head subsided.

She was still waiting when two weeks after her fateful escape, she received a phone call at the bakery.

"Babe, I've got good news! Do you remember that young couple that came to check out our shop? The one who wanted to open a Greek taverna? Well, the fridge is in good shape, and they are very interested in keeping the oven even with the glitch with the starter, so we don't have to worry about that. I contacted our lawyer, Feingold, already, and he's drawing up some papers. Lena, this couple reminds me of us, you know, when we were starting out. I mean, he's bigger than me, a moose of a guy. His wife is tall, quiet, like you, only you're much prettier. Anyway, I think it's kind of like fate, Lena, this couple willing to take the shop off our hands so we can buy the place in Sheepshead Bay for Brooklyn Girl's Bake Shoppe III. They know all about Grand's across the street, and it doesn't even bother them. The guy told me her parents are helping them out just like yours did. Kind of ironic, right? Lena, are you listening?"

"Yes, it's great," she said, the words coming out mechanically. "It's all great."

"And one more thing." He paused, drew in air. "Once we sign that contract, you'll come home? There's no reason why you can't come home?"

After their conversation ended, it was nearly 9:00 a.m. She greeted customers, making sure to throw a personalized cookie into each bag before they left. She decided to take an early lunch, and so removed a chicken leg, left over from last night's meal she had cooked for her and Kenny, along with some tomato and lettuce she had sealed in a

Tupperware container. As she sat nibbling on the cold chicken leg and sipping a can of Tab, a well of emotion began to stir inside her. She waited for the familiar jingle of the bell, not knowing whether she was about to laugh or cry.

~

Lena pulled a carnation-pink tweed suit, the only suit she owned, out of the closet and laid it on the bed. They had a 10:00 a.m. appointment for the closing at the lawyer's.

The deal for the shop in Williamsburg had gone faster than expected, with Luke agreeing to the young couple's proposal, even if it was for considerably less money than they expected. For her part, Lena stayed out of the financial discussions. All the money talk made her too nervous, and besides, with the Passover holidays coming, she was just too busy.

She had been back at the apartment with Luke for the past two months. Unlike their contract with the young couple buying the shop, their agreement to come together again had been a tacit one. While she admitted to herself that she had become a bit frightened of him, what alternative did she have? She couldn't live off Kenny's generosity much longer, and returning to her parents' apartment on Ocean Avenue was out of the question. She couldn't bear to see the look in their eyes when she admitted that the marriage had been a mistake. Instead, she chalked up his brutality to a momentary lapse, an impulsive act that would, she hoped, never occur again. She told herself that he loved her, perhaps more than anyone, and began to regard him with compassion, as one would for a frustrated child. He was just a man who had lost his way. And so they resumed life together, eating their meals, watching *Happy Days*, and even their lovemaking continued its usual pace. Perhaps if she pretended that everything was okay, then it would be. Yet Lena knew that even as the throbbing in her head had stopped, the bruises faded, there was still an ache. It was right in the center of her chest.

She pulled at the hem of her pink skirt, then crossed her legs. Lena was too nervous to take even one sip from the coffee cup placed on the long mahogany table, and so she let the cup remain cooling as they waited for the young couple, already ten minutes late. Luke was animatedly chatting with the lawyer, something about the current state of the economy, as he fiddled nervously with a ballpoint, the same one placed in front of each seat, imprinted with their lawyer's name.

A cardinal alighted on the huge picture window behind where Feingold sat. Feathers trembling in the breeze, it perched on the sill between the clouds, chirping at a muted sun overhead. A good sign, Lena thought, before she watched it fly off between the trees. But when she looked at the lawyer, a balding man in his sixties, his neck constrained in a gold-and-brown-striped tie that was knotted too high, she noticed small beads of sweat gathering on his forehead. She glanced down at the silver Seiko watch, not the gold one she wanted, but a cheaper version. Ten thirty. They were now half an hour late.

There was a soft knock on the door. Lena jumped as her heart quickened. A middle-aged, frumpy woman with a notepad in hand, a BIC pen secured behind her ear, entered and whispered something into Feingold's ear. He excused himself and followed her out of the room. Lena and Luke exchanged worried looks.

"Do you think something happened to them?" she asked, lowering her voice even though she didn't need to. He gazed at her, ashen faced, but gave no response. Her eyes stayed riveted on her husband as he gulped, still unable to speak. His hand moved toward the coffee cup, also branded with the lawyer's name, but he couldn't pick it up. She placed her hand over his.

"I'm sorry, folks, but we're going to have to cancel for today." Feingold walked in briskly and stood by his seat, now swiveled to face the window, at the head of the table where only minutes ago she had seen the bright-red cardinal.

"It seems there's been some sort of health problem," he added, pursing his lips as he lifted a folder from the table.

"We'll have to reschedule. I'll have Edna get back to you," he said, directing his attention to Luke before leaving the room as suddenly as he had entered it.

Neither moved from their seats, instead stared at the lawyer's empty leather chair, the long surface of the shiny mahogany table. Finally, Luke arose and, not bothering to wait or even signal to her, left the lawyer's office. Lena remained, smoothing the folds of her carnation-pink pleated skirt. She was enveloped by a great hurt. She felt the aura of pain encircle her, then close in until she became the wound itself. She sat fixed to her seat, waiting for the cardinal's return, until she, too, left the room.

~

Luke could not be consoled. She had never seen him sob so loudly before, so passionately, as he did when he heard that the young Greek's mother-in-law, or was it his mother, had suffered a massive stroke. Now there would be a delay in the closing, maybe even putting an end to the sale altogether. Luke could no longer hide his pain.

"It's off! The whole thing is off!" he cried, pacing the living room from one corner to the next. Lena followed at his heels, like a small puppy, imploring him.

"We don't know that, Luke. After all, they've signed a contract, didn't they? It won't be that easy to get out of it! Besides, it's a tragedy what happened to the family, something nobody planned. I feel kind of sorry for them."

At those last words, Luke turned sharply around, fists clenched at his sides, his eyes masked by tears.

"You feel sorry for them?" he bellowed. "What about us, Lena? Don't you feel the least bit sorry for us?" He drew a breath, let his hands go limp. "Maybe what you feel is happy. Happy the deal went south, happy the owner of that grocery in Sheepshead Bay is now considering another offer. Happy never to be part of a bakeshop again, even if it was all for you."

Lena let the last comment wash over her like a spring rain. She couldn't deny it. Owning a bakeshop had never been something she wanted, but she had become resigned to her job, caught up in the whirl-wind of Luke's dreams. Yet now, seeing him so hopeless, defeated, she found herself wishing fervently for the deal to take place. She wanted it for Luke, even if it meant her own dreams were slipping away—maybe forever.

~

The Greek couple's maternal figure had not succumbed to her illness, at least not yet. Nevertheless, the tragic circumstances changed everything for the young Greek couple and, as a result, for Luke and Lena too. How could the purchase be concluded with a family member in such dire straits? How could anyone focus on plans, a move to a new home, the purchase of an automobile or a business, when one's heart was filled with worry? Lena understood this, yet whenever she looked at Luke, drawing more and more into himself each day, she thought a little less about the poor Greek couple, and more of her own troubles.

"It's time," she said one morning, only two weeks after they had learned that the sale had fallen apart, and along with it, Luke's hopes of purchasing a new shop. His mouth still full of scrambled eggs, he put down the fork and merely nodded. Lena wondered at this new husband sitting before her, passive, dejected. Gone were the long hours past midnight when he would scribble hurriedly into his ledger, and the phone calls to the bakery in the middle of the day when he would tell her of another wild scheme, sure that this time success was knocking at their door. Now, as she remained home, polishing the furniture and vacuuming the rugs, just as she had done the day before and the day before that, he would leave the apartment early and walk the streets—where, she did not know; nor did she ask. She had baked through her supplies, laid off her staff, and sold off fixtures that she knew the Greek restaurant wouldn't need. The bakery had been closed in preparation for the sale of the building, leaving them both aimless. Sometimes she would go to the nearby newsstand and buy a *New York Times*, riffle through pages of the classifieds for a possible site for a bakery, but only half-heartedly. She had never had much of a head for finances. But now, as Luke sat opposite her at the breakfast table, slowly finishing the last curls of scrambled egg, his buttered toast left drying, untouched, Lena knew she would have to be the one to take the lead.

All that remained in the former Brooklyn Girl's Bake Shoppe were a few bags of flour, the appliances, the counter and display case, and odds and ends of baking sheets and cooling racks left in the storage room. Now they would have to begin all over again. After Luke left on his daily excursion to who knows where, Lena sat down to make a list to restock the shop, maybe add ingredients. A few new items, some apple turnovers, or a cinnamon twist. They would put a new sign in the window heralding a GRAND REOPENING, just like Grand's had done.

She would do it all herself, without Luke's help, try to show him that she was more than just a baker, but a good businesswoman too. She sat on the couch and made a few phone calls to suppliers, but as she did, even in midconversation, she couldn't quite concentrate. After a morning when gray clouds had consumed the sun, which finally emerged, turning the sky a bright cerulean blue, the light coming through the front windows reminded her of Kenny's eyes and the last time she had seen him. The morning she had told him she was going back to Luke, he hadn't said a word as he had left for work, dressed in a charcoal suit and pink paisley tie. He hadn't said a word weeks ago when she told him of the new store they were planning to buy and how she had finally given up her dream of becoming a lawyer. Instead, he just stared at her silently, his sparkling blue eyes disappointed, veiled. She wouldn't tell him about reopening the old bakery. It was all for the best, she convinced herself, and tried instead to think of Luke, his green eyes awash in tears each time she looked at him.

She went to bed early that evening, even before Luke had returned home. This was nothing unusual, for he often spent evenings out now as well as mornings, sometimes missing breakfast, coming home just as darkness seeped into the earth as a pale sun emerged from behind a veil of clouds. She didn't mind it, not really, not if being outside for all those hours helped clear his mind.

As her head touched the pillow and her body fell into the familiar undulations of the bed, Lena's mind was filled with plans for the next morning. She would return to the Williamsburg shop, bringing a full bottle of Lysol for the floors, a box of steel wool, and some rags to take care of any stains.

She needn't have worried, because by the time she woke up that morning, the stains were gone. And so was everything else.

PART III

INTO THE FIRE

30

Lena

Outside the shop she held a handkerchief to her nose and eyes. The heat from the fire had not fully dissipated, and she had begun to feel a sting singeing her eyebrows, as she stood close. Yet even with her eyes closed, she could see nothing but gray. The grayness of the ashes still smoldering across the floor she had swept only two weeks earlier and that was now covered with dirt and despair, an unfulfilled promise.

Lena removed the handkerchief from her face and looked up at the sky, hoping it would obliterate the grayness. It didn't.

Somewhere far away, she heard a sigh, then soon realized that it wasn't in the distance at all, but next to her. She felt Luke's arm tighten around her shoulders.

"It's a shame," he was saying, not for the first time that morning, "just a damn shame." Lena, as before, did not respond, but stood watching as one of the two remaining men from the fire station, still hampered by his sturdy uniform, extinguisher on his back, walked across the rubble, making notes on a clipboard.

Eight minutes. After receiving the call, eight minutes was all it took for her to rub the sleep from her eyes, pull on a pair of sweatpants and a T-shirt. She knew the buses did not run so frequently at that early hour, and so, her fingers still twitching, she dialed for a cab, which sped her through the still-vacant streets. Fifteen minutes later, she was there.

She didn't recognize it at first, thinking the cab driver had not heard her correctly, had taken a wrong turn. But then, as she slammed the car door shut and stepped out, she realized that no, no mistake had been made. She stood across the street from the site, fully awake, gazing at Brooklyn Girl's Bake Shoppe II, now reduced to a mountain of rubble, ashes covering the sidewalks, drifting up into the air like paper dreams. Within the rubble she recognized the metal chairs from the back room now reduced to twisted pipe cleaners, lying tired against the earth like defeated soldiers. The long silver handles of the giant refrigerator lay off to the side like sticks of black licorice. The oven, the culprit behind the inferno, was nowhere to be seen, as knobs, doors, trays, and all were incinerated, its black heart smoldering, oozing among the rubble.

Luke was already there, frozen—his clothing, his cheeks, dusted with soot as he turned to face her. How long had he been there? she wondered. A few minutes, an hour? As usual for mornings these days, he had not been lying next to her in bed when she received the call. No, she remembered now, he was the one who had called her, told her about the fire, the damaged starter on the ovens that had ignited it all, setting their shop and their dreams for the future ablaze. *A damn shame.* Where had he been that night? How had he heard the news? Had he been alone? It would have been better if she had been with him.

As she stood next to him, another thought came to mind. A day long ago when she was just a child. Lying next to her best friend, laughing, and telling stories; the lights of the bungalows twinkling at their backs; the full moon shining ahead in all its splendor. And then her friend was gone, gone in the clutches of a great bear who carried her off into the darkness. And now beside her husband, as he grasped her hand in the same way the bear had tightened its hold on her friend, as he lifted that hand to his lips, imprinting black kisses upon the skin, all those feelings came back to her. Lena's heart quickened as she stared into the silent darkness left by the cooling embers, just as she had gazed ahead deep into the forest all those years ago. And again she was afraid.

~

Lena recalled a saying: "Time marches on." In the days and months that followed the tragedy, no one felt those words more keenly than Lena. She could see no further than the next day, or often, the next hour or minute. There were questions to be answered, forms and affidavits to be signed and filed, and yes, there were tears, many tears yet to be shed. Even as she did these things, even as Luke's sturdy shoulder pressed against hers, she did them mechanically, never daring to consider her future, which now seemed murkier than ever. And although during those long gray days when she desperately yearned to recapture the past, hit the replay button, hoping like an irredeemable Pollyanna that this time things would be different, there was only one thing she knew for a certainty. Time marched on.

"You know, Lena, this could be a good thing."

At first she wasn't sure that she had heard him correctly. It was just before darkness had captured the sun, just before summer's onset, when she placed the customary dinner of roast chicken, mashed potatoes, and carrots in front of Luke. The calming voice of Walter Cronkite droned softly on the TV.

Lena had heard the words clearly, but still couldn't quite comprehend them. She tried making sense of them, to no avail. How in heaven's name could the massive conflagration, whose cinders she felt burning in her nostrils even now, ever be seen as a good thing? She kept her mouth tightly shut for fear he might call her ignorant, or worse. She would let him explain. If he could.

"Feingold explained it all to me. We were insured for that bakery, paying a hefty installment each month. There's a reason for that. The insurance, the money, comes back to us in case we lose our livelihood, in case of earthquake, a hurricane, a *fire*." He stressed the last word.

"What I'm saying, Lena, is that we stand to recoup quite a lot of money. We might even be able to sue, and in a few months or maybe a couple of years—who knows how long these things take?—why, we'll have more than enough for another bakery. Maybe two."

"Sue?" The word emerged somehow from her muddled brain.

"Yes, Lena, sue the company that made the oven, the faulty starter. When this is over, who knows, we'll be happy the deal with the Greek couple never went through."

He picked up his fork and stabbed the chicken breast, a smug look on his face. Lena sat staring at him, her fingers curled around her water glass, unable to bring it to her lips. Who was the man in front of her? Surely he bore no resemblance to the young, handsome boy with the long hair, the winning smile, whom she had met on the bus and married, much to her parents' dismay, under the chuppah. The man seated in front of her now, eating quickly as if he had not a care in the world, was nothing more than a stranger.

~

As Lena thrust her hand into the hot, soapy water, she was immune to the burn as she tried to sort out the puzzle in her head. Luke was already settled on the sofa, watching *Jeopardy!* as he nibbled on a Hershey's bar. She washed both their dishes thoroughly, not a morsel left on his plate, while she had tossed what was left of her dinner in the garbage. Had he even noticed?

Luke had talked about their prospects once again, a bright future filled with riches. Pointedly, he had not mentioned her returning to law school. That idea had been buried long ago, destroyed just as the fire had destroyed their store. Nothing but ashes. He also had failed to mention the investigation into the blaze, something that was not out of the ordinary, and yet was ongoing. He had talked about only the money. Lots of it. And how soon they would have enough, more than was needed, to fulfill all their dreams. He seemed so sure.

Lena puzzled over his words as she laid the dish towel aside and sat next to him on the couch. And while Luke was taking great pleasure calling out answers to the quiz show, Lena could hear none of it, felt nothing. Nothing except fear.

~

He went out early that night, but this time it was different. He didn't need to clear his head, figure a way out of their predicament when no solution was apparent. This time he was going out for a quart of Breyers ice cream, mint chocolate chip, his favorite. He planned on celebrating their good fortune, all that cash that was not yet in his hand. She stared for a while at the closed front door, listening to the echo in the back of her mind. It was telling her something. *Get off the bus.* But was it too late?

She picked up the sofa pillows he had left tossed on the floor, then retrieved the vacuum from the hall closet, turned it on, and listened to its steady hum as she went over the rug. Whether it was vacuuming, polishing the dresser, or kneading a lump of dough, being busy helped her think. She certainly didn't want to think about what had occurred subsequent to the fire—the ride in the back of a police car to the station; the interrogations of them both, separately; the detectives asking them to account for their whereabouts before the big blaze that had consumed their shop. She was so emotional then, so heartbroken, that her interview had lasted mere minutes, whereas Luke's took nearly an hour. She wasn't sure why, and, in truth, she was afraid to ask too many questions.

As the vacuum cut a clean swath along the rug, Lena tried again to make sense of her thoughts. Her mind was all a jumble. Too many thoughts competing in her head, until finally one emerged. Luke was happy. It had all happened so suddenly, like a light that had been switched on. And she wondered if he had ever been sad at all. Maybe once when the deal with the young Greek couple had gone sour. Then there was nothing but silence as he walked the streets at night, mute, in an almost catatonic state. Until. Until the fire, when it seemed a spark had been lit inside Luke, too, giving him hope, something he had not had in a long while. He was happy. Maybe *too* happy. How could he be so sure that things would get better? So confident that they would soon have the money for yet another bakery—one she didn't want—maybe two? And that was when she realized why she was so afraid.

Lena moved the vacuum back into place in the closet. She was about to shut the kitchen light when something caught her eye. It was the calendar on the wall, one she had picked up for free at the market, featuring a photo of a cute puppy on each page. It wasn't the month or the picture of a small beagle lying in a basket that had caught her attention, but the day of the week. It was Friday. Friday night, the night when her mother would light the Sabbath candles each week. Instinctively, Lena reached up for the sterling silver candelabra that sat at the top of a shelf. It had been a gift from her parents on their first anniversary. She removed two slender white candles from a box, along with a matchbook.

For the first time since she'd become a married woman, Lena lit each candle, representing the two of them, husband and wife. She whispered the prayer. When she was finished, she felt a wave of exhaustion sweep over her. A yellow mist of moonlight seeped through the blinds as she sat down at the table, cupped her head in her hands, and watched the quivering flames from the candles become dancing shadows against the wall. Minutes before she was about to get up, before she would hear the key in the door and Luke's familiar whistle as he walked in, Lena remembered something. A name, one that she had heard long ago, one that would stay with her throughout that night and for many nights afterward. George LoPresti.

31

Anya

M

y dear, you must not be so stubborn. If the doctors say that you
need this, then what else is there to do? There is nothing to be
afraid of."

Anya looked up at her husband, hoping he would not see the gathering tears in her eyes.

"I am afraid? Is that what you think? To have the doctors remove
what is sick in my body and replace it with something good, something
healthy? Something that will keep me . . ." She let her voice drop, leaving out the last word. Something that would keep her *alive*.

"Pain is not what I fear, Josef," she continued. "It is only that, well,
there must be another way." Again, she looked at Josef's face for some
sign. He was sitting close to her as she lay wrapped in a muslin blanket. Anya watched as the stern line of his lips relaxed, his brown eyes
softened. Before they knew it, they would be married fifty years, a long
time to be married, long enough so that she could recognize each mood,
each meaning, even though he had not said a word. He understood.

"Josef," she tried again, her voice taking on a more tender tone,
"you must know that my worry is not for me. God knows, this is not
a good thing, and sometimes the days are not as I would like. But not

the worst. We have been through much more than this. All those years ago—"

"You needn't remind me!" he interrupted, his eyes resuming their insistent glare. "Do you not think I am remembering every day of my life? Every day since we got off the boat, I am remembering her?"

Anya felt her body stiffen, felt the lump form again in her throat, preventing her from responding as she confronted her husband's eyes. What more was there to say?

His voice mellowed as he began again.

"This is different, Anya. This is not the war or the gas chambers, but only you and me. I know you are afraid of asking her, but you cannot be more afraid than me. Anya, if anything happened, if I lose you, too, I don't think I could bear life anymore." Josef sighed and turned away, reluctant to let her see the tears that had begun to stream down his cheeks. On the pretense of getting a glass of water, he left Anya to herself and her own thoughts.

Josef was right, of course. They would have to go to her, ask her this one favor, a big favor, but simple for a daughter who truly loved her mother. And Anya was sure Lena loved her; at least she hoped she did. The doctor had explained it all to them. Anya's kidneys, left unattended, were now only working at not even a quarter of their capacity. If they went through with this, there would be no pain to their only child. And Lena could live a full, long life with one kidney. Plenty of people did. As for Anya, she would return to good health. She would live.

But there were things the doctor did not know. Lena was a sensitive child, prone to outbursts even as an adult. He did not know of the sullen moments their daughter spent as a child, brooding over an imagined slight, rocking on the floor of her room hours into the night or, worse, running off as she had done on more than one occasion, mumbling to herself, forgetting the next day where she had been. Therapists, when she agreed to see them, had provided only temporary Band-Aids to the problem. Only in school was her child most at ease. The other times, she accused them, Anya mostly, blaming her for her ignorance with the language; for going back to work; for her overprotective nature, which kept Lena from the things she loved; for blaming her for not being the firstborn.

Anya had hoped that her daughter's marriage, even if it was to someone they did not completely approve of, would make her somewhat more mature, provide an emotional stability she had not had before, but it was not to be. While physical separation had eased some of the tension between mother and daughter, Anya could see the anxiety in Lena's eyes each time her daughter visited. And who could predict this latest tragedy, the loss of their shop to fire? Anya and Josef, hearing the news, had mostly stayed away, not wanting to interfere. Afraid of what they might see.

~

She had never lied to Josef. But she wasn't exactly truthful either. All her life, Anya's father had told her how strong she was, how like iron. And she carried that memory with her through the years, like armor, protecting her from whatever adversity should befall them. She had carried it even at age ten as she learned the workings of her parents' bakery, not only the things that go inside the ovens but what was taken in at the cash register too. She carried it under the Nazi terror, which robbed them not only of their livelihood, but of their one child, their future. And yet, here in this new land, Anya had recovered. An apartment, a job, a little girl who had restitched Anya's heart when she thought it was lost forever. But now, even as she turned sixty-seven, when she should be reaping the rewards of a tumultuous life, with trips to Miami, treatments at the mud baths in Italy, just as Josef's old cousins had done, maybe even grandchildren, now for the first time, chinks had begun to show in the armor. She was afraid to let Josef know how bad it really was. Who would think, after all she endured, that it would be her own body that would vanquish her?

Anya had worked at the nursery school longer than she should have. It was already 1979, two years since she had begun her volunteer work. But she had hoped that seeing the innocent smiles of the children, their intuitive hugs when Anya looked like she was having a bad day, would restore her spirit, fix the things that were failing inside her. Instead, she concluded unhappily, school was having the opposite effect. She would arrive late to the synagogue, having slept well into the afternoon, and, once there, she would be compelled to sit on one of the small chairs as another wave of exhaustion swept over her. Once, Mrs. Feldman, the head teacher, had seen Anya wince as she had picked up one of the children, a chubby little boy with golden curls and doll-like features. Seeing the look of pain on her face, Mrs. Feldman had rushed over from behind her desk and tenderly lifted the boy from her arms.

"Let me help you, Mrs. Sokoloff. Come, Scotty, there are more toys to play with over here." Then, turning her head toward Anya, whose arms remained wide open: "Why don't you take a seat at my desk and relax?"

Anya, feeling the blood rise to her face, had been mortified. She hadn't gone to the desk but had instead walked out the door and into one of the stalls in the teachers' restroom. There, minutes later, as she let the cool water stream from the faucet onto her hands, she gazed at her reflection in the streaked mirror. And, for the first time, she saw what others saw when they looked at her. A tired old woman.

Anya would have to come to terms with the weakness, and now with only 18 percent of her kidneys functioning, she had no more choices, admonished her doctor. Josef, too, was full of "I told you so's." But could Anya tell them that she had hoped her armor was still intact, could protect her, just as her father had predicted all those years ago? Even as extreme exhaustion sapped her energy, the pain in her lower back grew worse, the nausea more demanding, she tried to hide the truth, hoping that she could overcome this problem. It was, after all, only a setback. Though she tried to cover the symptoms as the illness ravaged her body, if not her spirit, Anya could tell by the look in her doctor's eyes, in Josef's, that they knew the truth. She began dialysis the following week.

Three times each week, Josef would accompany her to the hospital, where they would hook her up to a machine that, as the doctors explained, would take all the garbage from her blood, do the things her kidneys could no longer do. She needed hemodialysis to stay alive.

Anya had undergone an operation, a "surgical procedure" was what they called it, so that her blood could flow more easily in and out of her body during the dialysis. Even though Josef patted her hand afterward and asked her how she was feeling dozens of times, the operation didn't bother her. Even when the nurses stuck the needles in her arms to clean the blood before it went back into her body, none of it troubled her. The thing that most bothered Anya was the four hours she was forced to lie down with the needles as the dialysis machine did its work. She had no patience for reading the *Forward* or practicing her English with one of Lena's old books, like *Robinson Crusoe* or *The Three Musketeers*, classics that her daughter loved to read as a schoolgirl. All she could do was lie there and stare at a painting of a beach somewhere in Nice, a place where she had never been, tacked up on a faded blue wall. If it was cloudy outside, the swirls of gray that drifted into the room through the shutters reflected the despair Anya was feeling. But if it was brilliant outdoors, it was worse, for the sunlight would pierce into the air-conditioned room like arrows, taunting her, reminding her of the life she no longer had.

Anya's father had another expression to describe his only daughter. Whenever she would tap her fork against the plate impatiently, as he removed golden raisin rolls from the oven, or when on Rosh Hashanah she would be the first one dressed, already pacing by the front door, ready to leave for shul, her papa would shake his head and chuckle softly.

"You have shpilkes, my child," he would say as Anya frowned in response. She understood the expression was far from a compliment. *Shpilkes*, the Yiddish word for "needles," were the things that drove

Anya's impatience. Never one to wait for life to resume, whether it was standing by for a treat to come out of the oven, or nervously pacing before the short walk to shul, she could not abide wasting her time doing nothing. Here, in the United States, she would be labeled as having a "type A" personality. During the long mornings, three long mornings a week, as she lay there with "shpilkes," this time, real needles beneath the skin, she felt each one, urging her to get up. Get up and *do something*.

For the first year, she tried. She would jump off the bed—well, maybe not jump—*go*—to the supermarket, check in with some of the neighbors, prepare a brisket, just the way Josef liked it; sometimes she even baked a challah or two for the Sabbath. And then, the next day, a day off from the dreaded dialysis treatment, she would get up early, prepare for work, where she would spend the afternoon reading to the little ones, wiping the floor should someone have an accident, placing a Mickey Mouse Band-Aid oh so delicately over a paper cut. All this she had planned on doing, but there were ways in which her body continued to rebel against her that she hadn't counted on. She hadn't counted on feeling a cramp lock the muscle in her leg so badly as she stirred a stockpot that she had no choice but to lie down. She hadn't anticipated the nausea that came on so suddenly that once, as she stood on the corner listening to old Mrs. Emery complain about her sciatica, she had to turn away as a stream of vomit spilled from her mouth and into the gutter. And nothing could have prepared her for the spinning in her head as she had bent down to help little Mindy with a block on the castle she was building, a dizziness so bad that it had taken her more than a few minutes to steady herself, to realize that no, she was no longer ensconced in the comfort of her bedsheets, but here at the synagogue in a classroom.

Now, as she rotated her legs off the sofa and slid her stockinged feet into brown loafers, she tried to forget all that. Anya had but one thought in mind. She had to get out.

"Josef," she called into the kitchen as she stood finally at full height, "I'm taking a little walk."

"What did you say?" The voice drifted in from the kitchen.

"I said I'm going out for a little while." This time louder.

Even though it was still fall, Anya was already dressed in her gray woolen coat and matching fur hat tied securely at her chin. For her, even a slight chill might spell trouble.

Josef came running from the kitchen. Though, these days, Anya did not have much of an appetite, he had decided to prepare a late lunch and was holding half of a tuna sandwich.

"Wait, Anya, I will come with you. I'm just going to finish this and clean some crumbs off the counter."

Anya sighed as her hand tightened on the doorknob. He was such a sweet man, she thought, a man who did not deserve any of this. No, she needed this time by herself, she reasoned, and probably so did he.

"I won't be long," she said, and quickly closed the door behind her.

Once outside she marveled at how different everything looked— the red and black awnings of the old shop buildings seemed sharper, the golden hue of the sky more vibrant, even the tufts of gray as squirrels scampered up the trees took on a brilliance as if only now was the world coming into focus. The city sounds, once nothing more than an annoyance, now seemed magnified, even musical, the laughter of the children on the street spilling like rushing water into the air as the rumbling of the giant wheels on the bus harmonized in tune. Why had she not noticed it all until now? Had she been so self-absorbed in her own worries that she had become unaware of the beauty of each new day?

Anya was so immersed in her surroundings that she barely took note of the woman standing at the corner, trying to get her attention.

"Mrs. Sokoloff, Mrs. Sokoloff! How are you feeling? We've missed you at the school." It took but a moment for Anya's mind to register who the woman was. It was the young mother, wheeling a stroller, the neighbor with the little girl who had given Anya the idea of becoming a teaching assistant at the school. She vaguely recalled that there was a son now, too, though not yet of school age. It was almost one o'clock, and she was probably on her way to the elementary school to pick up her daughter—Anya couldn't quite remember her name—from kindergarten.

"Fine, I'm just fine." Anya waved back, not stopping to inquire about the woman as she hurried across the street. She reached into her pocket, found the coins she needed, and, as the metro bus screeched to a halt, climbed in.

Only when she sat down directly behind the bus driver, tired and breathless, did it occur to her where she was headed.

It was ten minutes later, after the bus had discharged her along with a handful of passengers, when she found herself standing in front of the small cobblestone building. She took a few deep breaths as the cramp in her lower back grew more persistent, as she tried to summon the courage.

She was still standing there minutes later, before slowly, laboriously, she retraced her steps to the bus stop down the block. She realized then that she no longer had any choices. She would have to ask her daughter this one favor. But not today.

32

Lena

Lena stood at the living room window and stared down at the streets just awakening with gangly teenage boys, their backpacks slung over their shoulders as they tossed an orange football to one another, and tired mothers pulled along by their young children, who were eager to get home for a glass of milk and cookies after a day glued in their seats, turning the pages of workbooks and figuring out fractions. Everyone, it appeared, was in constant motion, all except for the solitary figure who stood rooted in front of her building, just like the slender maple tree shivering on the curb. She thought she recognized the person with her gray coat and matching fur hat, and, at first, Lena was inclined to grab her jacket and rush outside. But after another minute of staring at her, logic took over. Anya would never have reason to come to an apartment she hadn't entered for the past seven years, and certainly not by herself. Surely Lena's eyes were playing tricks on her.

She had been returning to that window every few minutes as she waited yet again for Luke. Finally, Lena turned away and sank into the sofa. He had been gone for nearly five hours now, but unlike the other times when he had fled the apartment out of frustration and anger, this felt different. It *was* different. And she had an ominous feeling that the cause was the phone call he had received only minutes before he left.

She had been in the bedroom, folding the laundry, when the phone rang. By Luke's somber tone, she had guessed he was talking to someone important about a serious matter. Maybe it was their lawyer, but since she couldn't make out the words, she wasn't sure. Maybe, finally, they would receive the windfall Luke was always talking about. But when she heard the slam of the receiver, followed by the door, Lena was pretty sure that was not the nature of the call. And because he left so abruptly, she didn't even have time to ask. She had lifted a pair of Luke's faded jeans from the basket and folded it with trembling hands.

By the time the sun began to fade, there was still no sign of Luke. She had already vacuumed all the rooms, cooked a pot of ravioli, prepared a salad, baked a batch of dinner rolls, and even completed another application for law school. But the frenetic activity granted her no relief as her heart began to beat wildly, her nerves dancing beneath the skin. She promised herself that as long as there was a flicker of sunlight in the sky, she would return to the window, hoping to catch a glimpse of Luke coming down the street.

By ten o'clock she thought of calling the lawyer, hoping his after-hours answering service could help. But she thought better of it. Luke would be embarrassed, or worse, angry when he found out. And, even if he wasn't, she feared what the lawyer might tell her. She took one last look out the window. The night sky was ink black, moonless, as she strained to catch sight of a shadow beneath the streetlamps.

Lena transferred the cold ravioli into a Tupperware container and placed it in the refrigerator, then picked out a slice of cucumber, her only supper, and popped it into her mouth before also placing the salad bowl into the fridge. She transferred the clean silverware into the drawers and put the red-stained pot into the sink, where it would wait until the next morning. Then she shut the kitchen light. She was about to go into the bedroom to change into her nightdress when she heard a loud knock at the door. Luke had left so quickly that he had probably forgotten his key. Lena put aside all her reservations about her husband; whether he would yell or cry, she didn't care as long as he was home.

But when she flung open the door, her anticipation was quickly replaced by terror. Standing at the door were two grim-faced, larger-than-life men, shiny badges on their chests. Only then did she realize that her worst unspoken fears had been confirmed.

33

Even before he spoke, she knew the words were a lie. Luke, desperate to find a way out, to redeem himself from his failings as a businessman, had deliberately set fire to the bakery, hoping to cash in on nearly a million dollars in insurance. It would mean another shop for the two of them, a new beginning. And it made no difference that she didn't want any of it.

Shortly after the marshals arrived, she received a phone call from Luke. At any other time, hearing his voice after such a long and torturous wait would have made her heart leap with joy. Now, though, as the two marshals stood stiffly in the foyer, Lena's voice went flat. She told Luke they were already in the apartment, with a warrant for his arrest. He didn't sound surprised at the revelation. He knew it was coming. He said that he and his lawyer were already on their way to the station house.

She would not hear from Luke for two days, when he called again to tell her that his bail had been posted, and as soon as he was processed, he would be returning home. Lena passed the next few hours mechanically, just as she had done yesterday and the day before that, shopping for milk and eggs at the grocery, exchanging her tank tops and shorts in a chest of drawers for heavy sweaters and woolen pants she would need as the cold weather set in. She scrubbed the pink cream off her hands after polishing the meat and dairy silverware over the kitchen sink. By the time she heard the turn of Luke's key in the front door, the house was filled with the scent of baked lemon. Although she hadn't baked for months, she gave in to the desire for lemon drop cookies. They were her favorites.

Luke walked in stoop-shouldered, his lean face streaked with bristly stubble. Barely catching her eye, he removed his jacket and fell into the sofa like a man who knew his life was already over.

"Dinner will be ready soon," she said with the same tone she had used over the phone. She watched as he nodded, closed his eyes, and let his head fall back into the pillow. Later, as the two sat facing each other at the kitchen table, she watched him bring the warmed-over ravioli to his mouth and chew each piece slowly, without his usual gusto. Leaving her own plate untouched, she stared at her husband, taking note of his colorless eyes as they rested on the dinner plate, the movements of his hands, still unwrinkled, yet like those of an old man, one who had lived and known life far too long. Lena had no more questions, no expectations, all desire having seeped from her spirit the moment she had opened the door two days ago. As she looked at him now, her eyes became a barrier preventing any more questions, explanations, or pleas. If she did feel any emotion, it was only pity. The kind of pity one might have for a homeless addict on the street, one who was beyond reform, beyond help.

Hearing the ding of the oven, Lena got up, removed the pan of lemon drop cookies, still hot and seething juices, and, without offering him any, placed one in her mouth. She let it linger on her tongue, breathing in its warmth, its sour taste.

~

After speaking with Feingold—Lena didn't yet trust Luke to give her the facts—she became an expert on arson and its penalties in New York. Although she wasn't sure how Luke had tampered with the burners or where exactly he had used the BIC lighter to make sure the whole establishment would go up in flames, his intent was indisputable. Luke had deliberately set fire to the bakery, with disregard for people or property, in an attempt to deceive the insurance company so he could collect the benefits. From the beginning, it became apparent that Lena was not an accomplice. He had acted on his own. Committing arson in New York State, for financial gain, was considered a class A-1 felony. Luke was looking at a minimum of twenty years in prison. But since he had committed no other crimes, not even received a ticket for speeding or driving under the influence, perhaps the judge would be lenient.

Lena absorbed all the information like a sponge and sat with it for a while. Silence dominated the apartment for two days. There was only one question left unanswered: If she hadn't posted bail, and it certainly wasn't her parents, who still had no knowledge of the crime, then who had?

~

A shaft of misty sunlight accompanied Kenny as he walked into the coffee shop situated on a corner near Trinity Church. Lena was already seated in the back, nursing a black coffee and a cruller. Kenny's blue eyes glittered when he caught sight of her. He looked so slim in a gray tweed suit and light-blue tie that she had almost forgotten his boyishness of a few years ago. When he caught sight of her, he signaled a thumbs-up before going to the counter and ordering a coffee black, then sat down to join her.

"How about this crazy weather?" he said, smiling. "It's almost winter and sixty degrees!"

Lena nodded. It was the first time she had felt a smile lighten her face since Luke had rushed out of the apartment two weeks earlier. She hadn't told Kenny the whole story, only that she had finally had enough. But she didn't have to. He had already read about it all in the paper. Lena's cheeks blushed pink.

"I'm so sorry for bringing you into the middle of this mess."

Kenny placed his hand on hers, which was already encircling the cup, adding another layer of warmth inside her.

"What are friends for, anyway? Besides, I'm not in the middle of anything. I just want to help."

Lena settled back against the paneled wall as Kenny, hearing his name called, got up to retrieve his coffee. He had nothing to gain by taking time off his lunch hour to meet with her a few blocks from his office. And yet, here he was again, picking up the pieces after she had stumbled. A regular knight in shining armor. When he came back, flashing that smile again, Lena felt ready to talk.

"It's terrible what Luke did, I know, and I can't help thinking about the possibility that someone, a person or a stray cat, could have been burned or even killed in that fire. I don't think I could ever live with myself if that happened."

"Lena, this isn't your fault," he said, taking a slow, thoughtful sip of the coffee. "None of it is. I wish I could make you believe that."

Lena sighed. Of course Kenny was right. She needed to release herself from the past just as she was learning that Luke was not the person she thought he was. If she didn't, he would take her down with him. And, she shuddered to think, maybe her parents too. Finally, she summoned the courage to look into Kenny's eyes, now a steely blue, and to ask the question that had been playing at her lips.

"Kenny, when Luke spent that night in jail, someone posted bail. That someone wasn't me, and it certainly wasn't my parents. He has no one else. Or maybe he does. I've found out so much about him, his character, in these last few weeks, that it makes me wonder if I ever knew him at all. So I guess anything is possible. But I don't dare ask him about it. To be honest, I don't think I want to know the answer. Besides, we've barely spoken to each other since he's been home. And now, with a court date coming up soon, it's just that, you know so many people, and didn't you once tell me that you handle the accounts for a detective agency? It's a long shot, but—"

Kenny leaned into her, his eyes never leaving hers as tears, seemingly of their own will, streamed down her face.

"And you want to know the answer." She didn't trust herself to speak, not sure if she could stem the rush of emotion that would follow. She nodded.

"Don't worry," he said, sitting back before taking another quick sip of the coffee. "I'll take care of it."

~

She couldn't take her eyes off Luke's face. Only it wasn't Luke she was looking at. It was his brother. His hair, sandy with premature strands of gray, was cut close to the head, but if you darkened it, added a few inches, thickened the eyelids, and softened the curve of the lips, he was the mirror image of Luke.

When they appeared at his door in Woodmere, only an hour's drive from the apartment, Roger didn't seem in the least bit surprised to see them. It was almost as if he had been expecting them to show up. He ushered them into the dining room, where Lena and Kenny took seats on gold velvet high-backed chairs at a round oak table, the only furniture in the room save for a low wooden console on which rested some black-and-white photos in gilded frames, a tall glass vase filled with artificial baby-pink tulips, and an ornate, but empty, Limoges candy dish. He didn't offer them a drink or anything, and Lena thought that was because there was no woman in the household to do so.

"I appreciate your seeing us," she said, glancing at Kenny, who seemed as confident as ever.

Roger, wearing a light-blue work shirt and wrinkled jeans, made a huffing noise as he sat down. He was at least twenty pounds heavier than Luke. He was around her age, Lena guessed, but looked a few years older.

"Well, I figured you were bound to find out sooner or later," he said. His green-eyed gaze was so intense that neither could look away. "Does he know you're here?"

Lena shook her head.

"No, he doesn't. And we'd like to keep it that way." A short, awkward silence ensued, alleviated only by the chime of the grandfather clock in the hall.

Lena's mind was filled with a jumble of questions, yet she didn't quite know how to begin. She was glad when Kenny broke the silence.

"So you paid Luke's bail. That was—that was very nice."

"Yes, I told you that on the phone," he began gruffly. "Both me and my younger brother, Keith. He's in the army, stationed in Germany now. He doesn't know too many of the details but told me if Luke needed the money, well, we had to let him have it." Then adding under his breath: "Not that he ever deserved it."

Lena rubbed her eyes with both hands, hoping that when she opened them, she would have clarity. When she didn't, she couldn't help but blurt out the words.

"I didn't even know you were still in touch!" She continued, "I mean, Luke never wanted to talk about you, barely mentioned his family. He didn't even invite you to our wedding." She gulped. "And I could never understand why."

Roger shifted in his seat and threw an arm over the high-backed chair.

"Doesn't really surprise me. He wanted nothing to do with me and Keith. In fact, we hadn't heard from him in about ten years. And that included our dad. He died about five years ago."

Lena stared at Luke's younger brother, unbelieving. Five years. She and Luke were married by then. And not a word.

Roger ignored her, continuing, "No. He knew where we lived, that we were living here in the place Dad bought, new furniture and all, since our mom passed away. Guess he didn't tell you about her either?"

Lena sat dumbfounded as she felt Kenny's soothing eyes upon her.

"No, I'm sure he wouldn't tell you about Mom. That's what caused the whole rift in the family. But now that I think about it, the argument began long before that." Roger turned then, eyeing the kitchen, which faced the dining room.

"I think I could use a drink about now. Would you like a glass of water?" The two said nothing. Water was the last thing she needed, Lena mused, but maybe if it lubricated his throat, caused Luke's brother to open up some more, then water would help. She didn't want to hear the story, but now, sitting here at the sterile dining room table, glancing at the dust on the plastic flowers, she knew she no longer had any choice.

Roger returned, holding a tall, bubbled glass of water, sat down, and took a long sip, drinking half of it in one gulp. After that his demeanor appeared to change. He pushed his chair forward, placed his elbows on the table, and looked at his guests earnestly, almost as if they were the best of friends and had known each other for many years. The water seemed to have unlocked his voice, so that once he spoke, the words unfolded, and so did the secrets.

"Luke wasn't treated fairly. Not ever. Maybe it started from birth, since we all kind of knew he came along two months into the marriage. Or maybe it's because our parents were kids themselves when they were raising him. A few years later, my parents had me and then Keith. Luke was a spoiled brat by then, and a jealous one too. Maybe it was because he'd been spoiled or maybe because he found out he'd never been wanted to begin with. Who knows why people turn out that way? It doesn't matter now anyway, right?"

He glanced at them for affirmation but kept on.

"My father was hard on him, I think, because he was the eldest and cut school, then would lie about it. Luke rebelled. He mouthed off to the teachers, stole candies and Spaldings from the five-and-dime in town, and even when he'd get caught, he would do it all over again the next day. The thing about Luke is he just didn't care. I mean he didn't care about anything. Scoldings, detention, not even my father's strap, which he used more than a few times, none of it ever made a difference.

Luke always came back and did something worse the next day. I remember once when I took a ride around the block on the new bike Luke got for his birthday. Man, was he mad! But I was just a kid, you know? I mean my feet barely reached the pedals! But when Luke found out, well, there was no way he'd let me get away with that. So one day he cut out of class early and, with me and Keith still in school, our parents at work, he came home, found my collection of baseball cards underneath the bed, brought them into the backyard, set fire to the whole thing, all those cards! He didn't even bother to take them out of the albums. We laugh about it now, though I still miss that rookie, Mickey Mantle." Roger chuckled dryly, unaware of the shock that flickered like a slash of lightning across their faces.

"Dad beat him hard for that one too. So, you can see, I guess, why our brother is the way he is. Just Luke. And the worse he behaved, the madder and meaner our dad would get. Like a never-ending cycle. Me and Keith kind of ignored him, even though now that I remember, we were also proud of him in a weird way. The way he stood up to Dad, I mean, not crying even once. The way he always did his own thing, fearless. But, of course, we never would admit that. We were jealous of him too. He had something with our mother that we never had, something we could never touch." Roger paused, finished the glass of water, and licked his lips. When he continued, he seemed to be talking to himself as he recalled his childhood, almost as if Lena and Kenny, transfixed in their seats, had disappeared.

"She had a special name for him. Lucky Lukey. Though I could never figure out why since he always seemed pretty unlucky to me. But Mom, she saw great things in him, I guess. My dad was a plumber, so he was out more than in, and Mom had a part-time job doing the books for the grocery a few blocks down. Luke took an interest in that, was always good with numbers, and would sit by her side and watch. She encouraged him to keep up with school, become an accountant or better. She promised him he would be something in this life, and it was only a matter of time."

Lena listened quietly to the story, but something troubled her. The pieces seemed to fit, creating a picture of the person who had become her husband. And yet there was something missing.

"I understand why Luke is the way he is," she interjected, "but why would he walk away from his family? Why didn't he mention any of this?" Now that he had begun, she needed to hear it all.

Roger nodded, bit his lip, and drained the last of the water clinging to the bottom of the glass.

"My brother's a strange bird, I'll give you that. But all the anger, the fighting, was nothing compared to what happened when he got called up. Lucky Lukey turned out not to be so lucky, after all. The draft had him at a low number. Keith and I were too young to be drafted, too young to understand any of it. All we know is that once he got that letter, nothing was the same. Dad yelled a lot, Mom cried a lot, and Luke, well, he was kind of quiet, made up his mind that he was going to Canada, and the sooner the better. But my dad had other ideas. He'd served in the infantry himself, and was damn proud of it, which I can see. He saved some Jews from Auschwitz, Jews like himself, like us. And it didn't matter that saving Jews in World War II was a righteous cause and that Vietnam was nothing but a sinkhole where young men went to die. No, for him, it was the patriotic thing to do. One and the same. Luke had no money and not many friends, so he took the draft and spent three years out in the jungles. We were surprised he made it out alive, with nothing but a shrapnel wound in the shoulder. I guess he really is Lucky Lukey, after all."

Lena swallowed as she remembered the pink scar on Luke's shoulder, the scar she had let her hand run over each time they made love.

"Hey, are you sure you wouldn't like a glass of water?" Roger asked, suddenly noticing Lena. "You're looking kind of green."

Lena felt her insides tumble as Kenny placed an affirmative hand on her shoulder. It was all she could do to stay seated. Another lie. She shook her head as Roger took up his glass again and, seeing that it was empty, resumed the story.

"By the time Luke returned home, things had gotten worse. Mom spent most of the first year crying while Luke was away. When you looked at her, she was all red-rimmed eyes and sunken cheeks. She got so thin it looked like all the womanliness was sucked out of her. And we realized it was all because of Luke. He was always her favorite. The worry ate away at her so much that she became sick. None of us was surprised when they diagnosed her with stomach cancer, and, after that, well, it was in and out of hospitals, waiting. As usual, Dad didn't show any feeling. I guess if it was something he couldn't fix, then he just kept to himself, locking it all inside, you know? Me and Keith didn't know how to fix it either, so we just kept our heads in school. That didn't stop us from thinking about her all the time, though. She died three months before Luke came home."

Roger sighed and looked up at the strands of light beaming from the chandelier, his eyes reliving it all.

"Luke didn't stay home long, though. When he heard about Mom, he blamed all of us, especially Dad. He even threw a few wild punches at him. And that was pretty much it. We didn't hear from him for years. Not a word. Not until he called our dad a few years ago, asking for money. He mentioned that he had met someone, was getting married and thinking about setting up a business. But by that time Dad's anger had become rooted in him like a tree that keeps on growing. He wanted no part of him and hung up the phone. And that was it. Dad got us out of the apartment on Albemarle Road and bought this place on the Island. Keith enlisted in the army a year earlier—I guess he was the patriotic one in the family—and I set up a glass-and-mirror repair shop in Forest Hills with the money Dad left for the two of us after he died. And that's where we are today."

An eerie silence fell over the room, suspending time. Kenny glanced at the watch on his wrist, then at Lena. It would be three o'clock soon, nearly an hour since they had knocked on the door of the home in Woodmere. Lena braced for the hollow sound of the grandfather clock.

But it didn't chime. Not yet. There was only one question that remained unanswered.

"You paid his bail, but why? After all that happened between you."

"Why?" Roger shrugged with a half-hearted smile. "We're brothers."

34

Lena

The smooth forward motion of the bus, the low and steady moan of the giant rubber wheels, forced Lena's eyelids shut. In her dreams, she had forgotten the nervousness she felt that morning, the almost ritualistic fear she felt at the start of each school year. Would she be able to locate her classroom on the north side, the farthest end, of campus? Had she lost her schedule, dropped it on the road as, in her hurry, she stepped off the curb? Or, worst of all, would she oversleep after hours when sleep eluded? Would she miss that first day?

It was not a sound, but a scent, that caused Lena's eyelids to flutter awake. Peppermint on the breath of the person next to her as he sneezed softly. When he moved his body slightly toward her, she noticed that, like her, he was a student, only instead of holding a bag filled with newly minted textbooks, BIC pens, and sharpened pencils, there were only two slender composition notebooks resting on his lap. When he turned toward her, she noticed the stranger, whose long strands of black hair glistened past his chin while thick eyebrows over green cat eyes gave him a roguish look. When he spoke, she felt a shiver rush up her spine.

"Early class?" he asked.

Afraid that her tongue had frozen permanently in her mouth, she could manage only a nod. A secretive smile rested on his lips, as if he were trying to suppress a laugh. Besides the peppermint, she now detected the distinct scent of Canoe, a cologne her father wore.

As Lena's lips loosened, the two chatted for a while, although later she would be remiss not to remember any of the details. When he asked for her number as they descended the steep steps of the bus, she hesitated. Luke wasn't the kind of boy she usually dated, the kind she met at dances at the Jewish Community Center or on blind dates, nor was he the cousin of a close friend. There was something different, maybe dangerous, about this hippie boy who seemed older and, she guessed, knew much more about life than she did. Yet she couldn't help feeling drawn to him. She set her bag on the sidewalk, removed a small spiral memo pad, but before she could tear out a page, the boy thrust the palm of his hand in front of her. No, she thought, this character was nothing like anyone she had ever been interested in. She hesitated for only a second before scrawling her name and a phone number, a phony one, onto his skin. Later, seated in an American history class, she was still thinking of the good-looking stranger. And she wondered if she hadn't made a mistake.

~

Lena got off the bus and walked briskly down the avenue. She hadn't considered where she was going that morning, but now that she was almost there, it seemed a reasonable choice. The dream she had on the bus had almost vanished, but the uneasy feeling remained.

She pulled open the double glass doors. As soon as she did, she walked to the back of the library, and, even though the woman stood with her back toward Lena, she could tell it was her.

"Hi, Pearl."

The young woman turned around and, recognizing her old friend, flashed a bright smile. Lena could see her own reflection in the pale-blue eyes.

Lena sat down opposite her, in front of the wide multipaneled window. It was the same window, the same wooden table, they had occupied the many times the two had met. Even the book, *Enchanted Asia*, was the same, its glossy pages spread open to a purple and orange sunset, forming a majestic canopy over the scene. Neither remarked on the irony of the situation, nor did Lena wonder why she had decided to come to the library on that day. They just resumed the conversation as if no time had passed at all. It seemed the most natural thing to do.

"Did you ever see such beauty?" Lena asked, her hand stroking the page, but her eye was on the barrette holding Pearl's tendrils tightly in place, the tiny rhinestones set in silver, catching the sun, reflecting the light in a rainbow of colors.

"Lena, what's wrong?"

She removed her hand from the picture book and looked down, no longer distracted by the display of light. Pearl was funny that way, Lena thought, could always tell when she seemed troubled. This time, as usual, she was right.

"Oh, Pearl," she said, now averting her eyes as she looked down at the dingy black-tiled floor. The library was more silent than usual that afternoon—no shuffling of feet, no hushed snippets of conversation. Almost as if the world had suspended all momentum, waiting.

"Just tell me." Pearl's voice floated into the air, like a breeze on the ocean. The wings of an angel.

Lena took a deep breath before meeting her friend's eyes again, but this time it wasn't the eyes, but her face, that caught her attention. Pearl's skin was so smooth, like a bowl of cat's milk, pale and white. Lena's voice cracked when she began, but as she continued, it became more agile, assured. Even when she got to the part about the fire, how she and Kenny had found out about Luke, the man he really was, and the decision, the only decision, she would have to make, her voice grew in strength.

Pearl listened calmly as Lena related the story, her face expression-less. Her pupils, like a silver mirror, continued to hold and reflect Lena's face. As Lena reached the end of the story, just at the point when she felt she would break, a miraculous thing occurred. She didn't fall apart because, finally, as Lena sat in the silence of the library surrounded by volumes spanning the history of the ages, as Pearl, her friend, her very best friend, sat listening, uttering not a word, Lena had all the answers she needed. She knew what she had to do.

"I'm leaving him, Pearl. This time I'm really going to leave."

Pearl smiled and folded her hands in front of her.

"Of course you are," she said. Lena looked at her friend, perplexed, and before she could think about what to say next, she felt an urge, a tickle in her throat, and then, much to her surprise, a laugh. She pushed her chair back, forgetting the picture book, still open to the splendid sunset, forgetting that, minutes earlier, she had been on the verge of tears, and stood up, laughing uncontrollably, like a hiccup that couldn't stop. The response proved infectious, as Pearl left her seat, meeting her friend, arms outstretched, the two giggling uncontrollably like school-girls sitting in a sleeping bag outdoors in the country, waiting for their lives to begin.

"Oh, Pearl, I've missed you so!" Lena cried, restraining herself to wipe the tears, generated by joy this time, afraid to let go.

"I've missed you too," whispered Pearl, her lips now close to Lena's ear. Lena softened her voice.

"Pearl, you can't leave me again," she said. "You're my good friend. My very best friend!" One of the librarians walked past the alcove, casting them a strange look, which they both ignored.

The two stood embracing each other for a few minutes, their laughter spent, their tears leaving dark shadows against the skin. And then the library appeared to awaken, with toddlers running this way and that, their mothers chasing behind, people passing by, chatting in hushed tones between the aisles as they wrapped their arms around treasured books.

"I've got to get back to work," said Pearl, the first to relinquish their embrace. Lena looked at her quizzically.

"So you've come back then? You're here to stay?" She stood in place, her arms still stretched in front, not yet ready to let go.

"No," said Pearl with a quick smile, but her eyes, still tinged with tears, remained sad.

"I have to return, you know, I have my studies. I only came back here for the holidays."

Lena, still standing, opened her mouth as if to speak. There was so much she wanted to say to this friend of hers who had returned only to leave again. So much she wanted to ask. Too many words to be spoken, and so she said nothing.

"How are your parents? Your mother?"

Such a strange thing to ask, thought Lena. Her troubles seemed so much greater than a polite, but meaningless, question.

"Fine, I guess," she responded, sitting back down. "I don't speak with them very often these days."

Pearl nodded, then placed her hand to her forehead as if she had a headache. She unclasped the barrette at the top of her hair, placed it on the table, freeing the mass of yellow-white curls that formed a halo about her head.

"They're fine people, your parents, especially your mom. You should call them more often."

Another strange thing to say, mused Lena, considering her parents never seemed to have anything nice to say about Pearl when the girls were growing up.

"You've got to help her out, you know. She hasn't had an easy life."

Lena ignored the statement.

"What the hell am I supposed to do now, Pearl? I've lost my husband; I've lost the stores. I'm a total failure." She slunk deeper into the seat.

Pearl ran a hand through her wavy locks.

"Oh, Lena, you're being so silly. You're going to do what you need to do, what you must do. You're going to be a success."

Lena didn't know how to respond, but she didn't have much time to think about it, as Pearl looked behind her. The library was getting busy.

"I've got to get back to work," she said, abruptly turning around and into a corridor.

Lena watched as her friend disappeared into the recesses of the building. She reflected on their meetings through the years, their heartfelt talks that she would later pluck from her memory, like gems, each time she needed to lift her spirits. The many days spent as the void in her soul widened, as she tried to remember. What would Pearl say now? What advice would she give? And though Lena never doubted that Pearl held a special place in her heart that none could touch, not even her parents, she knew that within that place, she despised her too. Pearl was a puzzle, appearing like a ghost when she most needed her, only to leave just as quickly.

A ray of light illuminated the silver barrette left behind on the table's surface. Feeling no remorse, Lena quickly scooped it up and placed it into her bag.

35

Lena

When the doorbell rang just after dawn on Sunday morning, Lena wasn't sure who it might be. Perhaps it was Kenny with a coffee in hand, asking her to go on an early-morning run, or Luke, living with his brother in Long Island after she insisted he move out, coming to check on her. Maybe even Pearl. But when Lena, clutching her bathrobe around her, opened the door, she felt the color drain from her face, and her body went numb.

"Hi, Daddy."

Josef, holding his hat in hand, stepped into the apartment, uninvited. As he gazed around the living room and into the kitchen, he seemed to be looking for something or someone, more than just a place to sit. In the seven years that Lena had occupied the apartment, he had been there only once.

"Daddy, is something wrong?"

He looked at her then, as if only just now she had appeared, but said nothing.

"Daddy?"

Still, hat in hand, he shivered as if he had just emerged from a frost, yet the day was warm and balmy. Without prompting, he walked over to the couch, laid the charcoal bowler aside, and ran fingers through his sparse gray hair.

"And you are well?" he asked, still looking distracted. It was the first time in nearly her thirty years of knowing her father that the parental glow in his eye, the compassionate smile, was missing. In its place was a void that masked some unreachable sadness. He did not wait for her to answer but continued.

"Your mama, she is sick," he said, the words coming with great effort. "She has been sick for a very long time. Too long."

The information shocked Lena but, more than that, placed a fear in her heart unlike any she had ever known.

"Daddy, I—"

"No, no, Lena, let me finish!" he went on brusquely. "It is not so good with her. Something is wrong with the kidneys. I am not sure what it is. The doctors speak in riddles. But it is not good, as I say, for a long time. She is weak, she hurts, she throws up the food, and even she can work no more. This is for a long time," he repeated, drawing a deep breath as he stared at the floor.

Lena sat silently, afraid to speak, afraid to ask too many questions, fearing the answers she might hear.

"So she goes for the needles, you know, with the tubes coming into her body, coming out of her body, like caterpillars. It is not a good thing to see, but she needs it."

"Daddy," Lena began, finally finding the words, "are you talking about dialysis?"

"Yes, yes," he said, nodding, as he lifted his eyes to meet hers, "the dialysis she goes for three times a week. For two years she goes."

"Oh my God! Mommy's been on dialysis all this time and you didn't even say a word!"

As her anxiety grew, Josef slumped in his seat, became more calm, more sedate. This lack of emotion infuriated her, but gazing at him again, she could see how much he had changed, no longer the gentle, reassuring father she knew, but a man whose tears had drained him of life, an empty vessel.

"Do not be mad, Lena," he said, his voice flat. "So many times I had told your mama, begged her, even, to come here, to tell you. But each time she refused, insisting she was made of iron, reminding me of how much we had lived through already. Besides, she would say, she did not want to bother you with this now when you have your own troubles."

Troubles, thought Lena, forgetting momentarily. What troubles did she have? What troubles could compare to this?

"You should have told me," she said, tamping down a flash of anger. She could feel the adrenaline surging through her veins even as her father became more deflated, his face a mask of despair.

"I wish you had told me," she said again, tempering her voice, softer, gentler.

One tear, perhaps his last, slid down Josef's cheek.

"Ah," he said, his voice low, spent, "your mother is a stubborn woman. You take after her in that. We know of your suffering, even though we have been seeing you not so much. Maybe you are too busy or maybe you do not want us to know what is going on with the store, the fire, and your husband in the jail for such a crime!"

Lena listened to Josef's words, which scattered like grains of sand into the wind, yet one boldly stuck in her brain. *Suffering.* Had she really suffered? Mommy and Daddy had suffered, had known what real suffering was. But had she?

Josef sensed her confusion.

"I know it has not been so easy for you, Lena. I understand this. No one escapes misery from this life, but, oh, I wish your mommy had told you this one thing. She told me just yesterday that she was here a few months ago but changed her mind. I wish she had not."

A vague memory of her mother skirted over Lena's mind and was quickly forgotten.

"Daddy, I will see her, I promise. I will go home with you now, if you like."

"Oh, no . . . ," Josef sighed aloud, more like a moan, as if he had received a stab directly to the heart.

"Daddy, what's wrong? Are you okay?"

"Lena, we do not need you to come. That is not why I am here. We need you to *help*."

Lena waited as he took another breath to clear whatever was plaguing his soul. Outside, a gentle wind whistled through the trees. She felt then as if she had waited all her life for this one chance. A chance to help.

"Your mommy cannot go on like this. The doctors say she is a fighter. But even she cannot stand much longer under God's sword. Lena, she needs a kidney. I wanted to do it for her—you know I would give Anya my life, if I could, but they say I am not a match. But maybe—"

"Maybe *I* am," Lena whispered.

Now it was Lena's turn to sit. She placed herself on the couch a good distance from her father. The information was almost too much for her to take in as again, in a matter of minutes, her entire life had been upended. She tightened the rope around her bathrobe and squeezed her eyes shut, hoping that when she opened them again, she would wake to the end of another one of her dreams. But, sadly, looking at her father's distraught face, whose misery now matched her own, she let his words sink in. Her mother needed her. For the first time in her life, her mother needed her.

"Pearl knew this would happen." The words came unbidden under her breath.

"What did you say?" When Josef raised his head, she noticed his eyes were now two limitless orbs.

"Pearl. She told me that Mommy needed me."

"Pearl?"

"Yes, just last week when I saw her at the library."

"No, Lena! No, no, no!" Josef bellowed, standing at full height, cheeks puffed out, eyes ablaze, no longer resembling the weakened old man who had come through her door that morning. Lena glanced up at him, afraid. Afraid of her own father.

"No, Lena." He spat out the words, his voice losing none of its vehemence. "Not Pearl. Do not ever speak of this—this *person* again!"

Lena knew that her parents had not approved of her friend, but she never realized the intensity of their venom. Not until now.

"Oh, I don't understand what you mean," Lena mumbled, forgetting momentarily about the all-encompassing fear she had mere moments ago, wondering what would prompt her father to react in such a strange manner. She tried to modulate her words, but looking at Josef's face, which had transformed so rapidly from a sagging lump of clay to stone, impenetrable, she realized that any words she would say could never pierce whatever it was that was making him so angry.

"I want only to know one thing. Will you help your mommy? That is all."

But as Lena continued to stare at the man now seated next to her, her mind became only more muddled. What monster had come between them to transform him from the sweet papa who would hand her all the stars in the sky if she asked, to this icy figure who looked at her with vicious flames in his eyes? And what venom was this that caused such hatred for Lena's one true friend?

"But Pearl loves you both," she began meekly.

Josef sprang from the couch, fists at his side. If Lena didn't know him to be her father, she would have sworn that in mere seconds she would soon become the object of his wrath.

But just as quickly as his ire began, it deflated. Once again he sank down on the couch, almost as a child who had exhausted his tantrum.

"Oh, Lena," he said, his voice barely audible, "I am asking you, no, *begging* you never to speak of that—that person again."

Now that they were face-to-face, that she could see the hopelessness again in his eyes, Lena answered him in another voice, the voice of a child imploring her father. Begging for just one more treat.

"But, Daddy, why? Why do you hate her so much? Why do you hate her when she has only spoken of you and Mommy with kindness?"

Josef lowered his eyes, and when he looked up at her again, they were filled with tears.

"Ah, Lena," he said, his voice still low, "I do not hate her. How could I hate anyone who doesn't even exist?"

A siren blew loudly through her brain, its echo shattering her past, her present, anything she knew to be true in her life. She began to question her papa's sanity. She had to question it, because not to do so meant she would have to question her own. She was grateful when Josef spoke, filling the void between them.

"Lena, you may not understand now, but you will in time." He sank farther into the sofa, but now his eyes never left her. And when he spoke, he said more to her than he had ever said in her entire life.

"Do you remember those stories your mommy and I would tell you when you were barely old enough to walk? The stories of our lives back home, in the Old Country? The stories of our firstborn, your darling sister, who was born with a clubfoot, yet never complained? How she would help us in our little bakery until she could bake the raisin kuchen and egg challah better than any of the grandmas in the whole neighborhood? How she had a head for counting and business and selling, better than any of the merchants three times her age? How everyone who came into our shop would marvel at our little blond-haired beauty?" He paused and drew a shallow breath, not waiting for Lena's response. Yet if he had, he would not have received one. Instead, she sat, biting her lip, afraid to meet the intensity of Josef's eyes.

"She went off to school one day just like children do thousands of times. But that day she didn't come back." His voice dropped an octave. "We never saw our dear Ruby again."

Lena shifted uncomfortably in her seat. She wished she were anywhere but here, listening to her father, who had been so reticent throughout the years but now was making all her memories, memories she never hoped to revisit, rise to the surface.

The Baker of Lost Memories

"Sometimes I ask myself why we, your mama and I, survived and Ruby did not. She had so much of a future in front of her, could be whatever she wished. Why, she would have owned the world, if not for—ah, that is past already. It is not good to think of the past too much, Lena," he mused, for the first time acknowledging her presence.

"But after you were born, here in Brooklyn, a true American, Mommy and I could finally breathe, and maybe hope a little too. Here we had a new chance; we could work, send our daughter to school where someday she could be somebody. Maybe even president, who knows?" A twinkle appeared in Josef's eye, but quickly faded.

"From the time you could understand words, we told you stories. How Mommy worked next to the hot ovens, cooking breads for those swine, how I hauled rocks more than twice my weight! We did not only tell you the sad stories, but the good ones, too, of Ruby, the sister you never knew, how good she was, so kind and good. How she was as sweet as the sugar cookies she baked. We knew you would be our last child, our only child, so we told these stories so you would know and love the sister who was no longer here. But maybe, I am afraid, we told too many stories. Maybe it would have been better that you did not know."

Lena's throat felt parched as her eyes, never leaving her father, stung. She wanted desperately to leave, to be any place but here.

"We knew our mistake when you were only five, and you began speaking of a girl you met in the park on the jungle gym. We asked to meet her, but you said we were too late, she had run back to her mother. When you got a little older, you would see her, usually at the library, your little friend, Pearl, who always seemed to lead you down the wrong path, playing hide-and-seek between the rows of books or racing outside in the gutter without your coats. We knew soon that something was wrong. Pearl's parents were working always, so we could never meet them, and never did you bring her to the apartment like your other friends. Even in the country, where we spent the whole summer, you insisted that Pearl and her parents had a bungalow too. And, oh, the tantrums you threw when we said Pearl was not real, that it was only a child's imagination! And so, your mommy and me, we said nothing. Always when you are angry or unhappy about something, how you got only an eighty-eight on a spelling test, or couldn't bake cupcakes with your mommy, something she could never permit, something that brought up the old memories, you would go back to your Pearl. You would read to each other, play games, collect rocks, and look for fireflies in the night. Pearl was the only one who could make you calm, could bring our child back to us. So we let it be, even though we knew, we knew there was no Pearl, that there never was." Josef bit his lip.

"Ah, Lena, if only you knew how much we worried about you. The phantasms you had, that no one spoke of. Even once we asked a doctor, that day when you went into the woods, spending the night with your Pearl. Oy vey, and the story about the bear—the tears, the tantrums. It was your bubbe all over again!"

"Bubbe?"

Josef hung his head.

"I did not know her very well. I married your mama just a few months before her mama passed away. But from what your mommy told me, it was a blessing. She saw phantasms, ghosts of cousins and aunts, an old shoemaker, a trashman long dead, frozen in the ground before the century. And she talked to herself always, Mama would tell me, sometimes even yelling so the whole neighborhood would peek out from their doors late at night. There was no medicine for it, no medicine at all. Ah, what a crazy woman."

Josef's head snapped up, and he stared at Lena, still quietly listening. She had shriveled in her seat, a flower folding into itself.

"Oh, Lena, I am sorry! We never thought it was you. You are nothing like your bubbe, no! Just a girl with an imaginary friend." He stopped, waited to see a change, a rebuke, and, seeing none, went on.

"That night, the night you ran from the back of the bungalow, tearing at your clothes, the tears flooding in your face, you were screaming, begging us to find Pearl. So we made believe for a little while. I pretended to go out and look for her, even though I knew her ghost I could never find. We did not tell anyone, of course. No one in the bungalow colony must know about what happened. What would they think? And when you said the next day that Pearl had gone back to Brooklyn with her mama and papa, well, we were happy. And we thought that maybe this time everything would be good. We came back to the apartment, and you went back to school and got good grades, the best! You had new friends, too, nice girls who you would visit in their apartments to study, play Monopoly. Do you remember how you loved to do shows with your friends, how you would sing in the streets! What was that movie you played at?"

"*West Side Story*," Lena murmured under her breath.

"Yes, yes! The Bernstein one. Oh, how Mommy and I loved to hear you singing the songs, dancing on the sidewalk. You were going to study in that Brooklyn College, our child, a college student! How proud we were!"

Josef stopped as a gentle smile came to his face, the first smile since he had entered her door that morning. How she longed to see that smile, how as a young girl she had waited for it as he came home from work each evening.

"For the first time, we thought our lives were good," he continued, "that we could be happy. But we did not know the earthquake that was coming under our feet. Because one night you came home crying. Maybe because of another fight you had the day before with Mommy or the boyfriend, I don't know. And you told us about Pearl. You saw Pearl by the library, and you stayed out late that night, and again we worried, but we could not question it. You were a big girl now, almost a woman. Like always, we hoped for the best and kept quiet.

"Ah, Lena, why does God always give us only a taste of happiness? Why is it every time we put our lips to the honeycomb, it is snatched away? Mommy got sick then, oh yes, very sick!" Seeing the stricken look in his daughter's eyes, Josef shook his head again.

"You are surprised? No, you didn't know. We did not speak of it. After all, you were a married lady with one, then two, businesses!

You did not need more trouble on your head. But Anya is so sick, so sick, Lena! Why do we have so many troubles in this life? Many times, Mommy and me, we ask ourselves, for what did we survive?" He gazed at her fully now, taking in all of her, as the tears glistened in his eyes.

"But then I think we did survive, Lena. We survived to have you." Josef's voice dropped, his energy spent. She wanted to run to him then, feel his arms around her as she had when she was a child, but she could not. It was as if something was holding her down, keeping her frozen in place.

Josef was the first to break the meeting of their eyes. He glanced at the old Bulova on his wrist and sprang out of his seat.

"I told her I was going to the bank, and it is late now. Mommy will worry." He walked toward the door, forgetting the customary kiss goodbye, and left as preoccupied as when he had entered.

~

Lena remained on the sofa, her body assailed by the chill in the air as she craved the blue woolen blanket still on the bed in the other room. Yet movement was impossible. So much to think about, so much to question. Then she saw Pearl dancing, her movements slow and graceful, like a ballerina. Her eyes, the palest of blues, her delicate blond curls glimmering in the early-morning light that streamed through the expansive picture window. Her Pearl. Was she just a figment of her imagination? Something contrived when life got too tough? If so, how could she trust herself anymore? Was the brown tweed pillow against her head real? Was the wooden coffee table? The mute TV staring at her with no answers? Pearl was just as real as any of these things. Or perhaps Daddy had been right: maybe it was all a dream. Something sparked in Lena's heart. Yes, maybe she had dreamed the whole thing. Daddy standing at her door, bowler in hand, telling her a ridiculous tale of Mommy being sick, of an imaginary friend. Yes, another dream like the ones she had about meeting Luke on the bus, giving him a phony number, and walking away. She laughed out loud, shocking the silence in the empty apartment. If only all this were just another dream . . .

Lena decided she was tired. She had been awakened too early that morning. Perhaps another hour of sleep might do her some good. She went into the bedroom, removed the terry cloth robe, and lay down. The movement of the waterbed rocked her gently to sleep. Just before she drifted off, Lena relinquished her dreams, leaving but one thought in her mind. She had to help Mommy.

PART IV

HONEY CAKE

36

Anya

"You brought honey cake!" exclaimed Anya, throwing open the door as she removed the loaf from her daughter's outstretched hands. Cradling her gift as if it were a newborn, she moved into the small kitchen, savoring the familiar scents of warm cinnamon and honey, which reminded her of home.

"Did you know that honey cake is my favorite cake?"

"Yes, Mommy, we know. You've only mentioned it about five hundred times." Lena laughed, exchanging conspiratorial glances with her friend Kenny. He had taken the subway directly from work and removed his navy-blue blazer, draping it across the back of the kitchen chair before sitting down.

Already he knows all the family secrets, Anya chuckled to herself, before taking a seat across from the two young people. She would have preferred to busy herself tending to the roast chicken in the oven and her special chicken noodle soup heating on the stove, but ever since her kidney surgery two months earlier, Josef was adamant about not letting her do too much. So now she had to remain content folding the white silk napkins and handing them to her daughter, who placed each one next to the gold-trimmed china plates on the table. No matter if they regarded her as nothing but a fragile egg while she recuperated, Anya insisted that traditions be maintained. For now, she had to remain content sitting with the most menial tasks only to appease her family. No matter. She was determined that in a few short weeks she would resume her normal activities, maybe even pay a visit to the nursery school at the synagogue once more, and she wouldn't take no for an answer. Besides, Anya was much more worried about Lena's condition than she was for herself. But now that she watched her daughter animatedly relating one of her stories about an eccentric professor at Cardozo Law School, Anya's heart lightened. Lena's cheeks were tinged crimson, her hazel eyes bright, and overall she exuded serene confidence. Anya needn't have worried. Lena looked healthy now, just as before. She looked happy too.

"Mommy, did you hear anything I just said?"

Anya startled as she opened her folded napkin and placed it on her lap.

"Of course I did," she lied. "You talked about that Professor Cooperman, is that not so?"

Lena shook her head and answered good-naturedly, "It's Professor *Copperfield*, Ma, like in the Dickens novel."

Although Anya was never one to appreciate criticism, she found herself laughing along with the others at her error before asking Lena to repeat the tale. Something about the law professor calling on each of the students to answer a question in torts, only to provide the answer himself as they were speaking. Anya realized that the story itself didn't matter, but rather the nature of the person telling it. She was enjoying this new version of her child, this daughter who shared stories, looked to her for approval, openly delighted in their company. Lena was no longer the daughter who seemed perpetually holding back, her demeanor shrouded by some inexplicable bitterness.

But what accounted for this change? It wasn't only that she had given Anya the gift, a kidney that had restored her life and the realization that now a part of her resided within her mother, just as her mother was always a part of Lena. No, it was more than that. Perhaps it was what Josef said to her that day he traveled to Lena's apartment on Avenue M, to appeal to her, to give the mother she resented all her life this one gift. Although Anya was angered when she lay doubled over in pain one gray November day, when Josef confessed the visit, she was grateful now that he had. Miraculously, Lena had responded immediately. Her child had given her back her health, and wasn't that the greatest gift anyone could receive? Even if it was from a child who had spent her years being distant, indifferent, whose very aura each time she walked in the door exuded an incomprehensible resentment. Nothing either she or Josef could do seemed to please her. But now, well, things *were* different. If it was something Josef had said that day or a sudden awakening, Anya no longer cared. She vowed to ponder the question no longer, but instead to enjoy this new life, this family all together for another Sabbath.

After Josef said a prayer over the challah and each had savored a piece, Kenny looked quizzically at the small plate that was placed in front of him. The appetizer was one of Anya's grandmother's recipes, a thick slice of yellow gelatin with a piece of hard-boiled egg at its center.

"Go ahead," nudged Lena, taking the seat next to him. "It's one of Mama's old Ashkenazi recipes. It's called p'tcha, an aspic made from calves' feet. It's a little weird, but I like it."

"Calves' feet," he repeated, raising his eyebrows, but then gingerly lifted his fork and took a bite.

"Not bad," he pronounced. "Has a lemony taste." After only a few more forkfuls, he pushed the plate to the side. But instead of feeling insulted, as was usually her way when guests didn't finish her food, Anya felt the opposite. At least Kenny had tried it, and Anya had a feeling that this boy, a study friend Lena had met at Brooklyn College, who had accompanied her during the surgery and afterward, trips to the hospital, would do just about anything her daughter asked of him. Anya hoped, as she watched Lena blowing on her bowl of steaming chicken soup, that maybe they were more than just study friends.

"Ma, eat your soup," Lena admonished. Then, turning to Kenny, she said, "She feeds everyone, but when it comes to herself, she waits until everyone has eaten and then has the scraps!"

"Not true," protested Anya, stirring her soup, "and besides, don't you know that the chef always tastes everything while they are cooking?"

Lena blew on her spoon before savoring the taste of the soup and, turning to Kenny again, added, "Don't listen to her. When we're putting the dishes in the sink, she is sitting there sucking the juices from the chicken bones."

"That's the best part," Anya laughed, marveling at how well her daughter knew her. Meanwhile, Kenny was not distracted by the banter between mother and daughter as he scooped up the last of the noodles in the bowl.

"Do you know what I think?" he asked, scanning for remnants of vegetables at the bottom. "I think this is just about the best chicken noodle soup I've ever tasted."

"You are right," chimed in Josef at the sink. "Everyone says Anya makes the best soup, like nobody else." He removed the golden roast chicken from the pan and began cutting it into thick pieces.

"I don't know about the best," Anya said, blushing, as she stared into her half-eaten bowl, then turned to Kenny, who was sitting back now, a placid expression on his face.

"Your mother, I am sure, makes one just as good as me."

Kenny scratched his curly light-brown hair, his smile broadening.

"Well, if you consider the grocery-store brand good, then maybe. My mother was born and raised in this country, not like you, Mrs. Sokoloff. She never developed a knack for cooking or baking, either, for that matter. My brother and I ate well, but if we wanted Jewish home cooking, we'd walk to the deli a few blocks from home."

Anya nodded but wondered at Kenny's confession. These modern American women surely were not like those who came from Europe, like herself. They didn't make sure that the oven was just at the right temperature, that there were no gaps left on the top of the cake when frosting it. They didn't work nearly as hard. Maybe that *did* make the Americans smarter.

"Anyway, I stand by my argument that your soup is outstanding," continued Kenny. "After all, Lena can tell you that I'm somewhat of an expert on food."

"Very well, then, I thank you for the compliment."

Anya sat back, smiling, and lifted her bowl, but before she could get up, Josef slipped it from her hand and placed it in the sink. Within minutes he returned with a platter of neatly sliced roast chicken, a mound of fried potatoes, and a helping of peas and carrots all on an elegant china plate. Kenny declined the potatoes, which he scooped up and placed on Lena's already overloaded dish and, without prompting, began to eat. Anya remembered a conversation she'd had with Lena about Kenny's diet, which was very strict: he limited himself almost completely to proteins. A few years earlier, he had lost over fifty pounds. Fifty pounds! What Anya found more unimaginable, though, was his desire to lose weight when so many were starving, still starving, in this uncertain world. Why, Josef had lost nearly as much in the war. Anya decided to keep quiet.

"Again, quite wonderful," Kenny was saying between bites. "The chicken is so juicy, and I love all the garlic."

"Almost as good as Anya's chicken soup," added Josef, kissing the tips of his fingers in approval before sitting down.

Anya made sure everyone had begun before she lifted a fork to her own plate. She would eat slowly, one or two slices followed by the vegetables. Even though months had passed since the surgery, she remained cautious, expecting a sudden cramp in her back or a lurch in her stomach as she felt the food come up. Though the doctors reassured her, after so many years of being sick, she had grown to expect the worst. While everyone, even Josef, claimed that she was healthy, *feeling* healthy would take some time to accept.

She pushed away her plate finally, acknowledging that tomorrow's dinner would most certainly be leftovers. In truth, she thought, eyeing

Lena cautiously, she *was* looking forward to sucking on the bones later that evening.

The conversation turned now to sports, a subject Anya knew very little about. She was content to sit back, hands folded in front of her, and observe the family. And they *were* a family now. How good it was to have a family again!

"What do you think of the Mets being sold to Doubleday and Wilpon?" asked Kenny, turning to Josef, who was already out of his chair and had begun to collect their plates.

"I hear it's the biggest amount paid for any baseball team! Is that so?" Josef asked, standing at the sink.

"Yup, $21.1 million."

"Well, maybe they can get some good players this year. Are you a Mets fan?"

"Ever since '69. It's always fun to root for the underdog."

"I like the Yankees. But at least the Mets are for New York also—"

"Daddy," interrupted Lena, "I think you took me to Yankee Stadium only once in my whole life!"

"So? Can I not be a big fan just the same? I listen on the radio!" he protested, feigning indignation as he began rinsing the dishes.

Josef a sports fan? Anya stared at her husband. For fifty years, the two had been together, and still she was learning something new about him every day. Lena reached up to a top shelf and retrieved four tulip-shaped glass teacups. She picked up the metal kettle, which was whistling on the stove, and carefully poured the steaming liquid into each cup. The vapors escaped into the air and enveloped the kitchen with tranquil heat. Anya closed her eyes, wishing she could capture the moment, afraid of what the future might bring. But then she remembered something, something only *she* needed to do.

Anya hoisted herself slowly off the chair and moved to the window shielded by white Dacron curtains. Reaching behind, her fingers touched the cool metal candelabra she and Josef had meticulously packed into their suitcase before embarking on the ship to America.

She set the ornate silver on a matching tray set and placed three slim white candles into the openings. Lena, as was their tradition, handed her mother a simple white doily and, placing a similar one on her own head, waited for Anya to begin.

Just as the tip of an orange sun slowly descended in the shadowy sky, and as voices quieted until the room held an anticipatory silence, she raised the palms of her hands to her eyes and began to pray.

"Baruch atah Adonai Eloheinu melekh ha'olam . . ."

When Anya had finished, as usual, she added something.

"Dear Lord, thank you, for your multitude of blessings, for keeping us safe from fear, for providing sustenance, for granting us prosperity, but mostly, Lord, for our health. Watch over our cherished daughter, and also her friend. Take care of Josef, too, who is my rock. And if you have more blessings left to give, I ask that you watch over me. We pray for peace. Amen."

Anya did not say any of those last words aloud, of course, but held them in her heart. And though the others could not hear her final prayer, when Anya dropped her hands from her eyes and gazed into her daughter's face, she knew that Lena had understood each word.

No one embraced after the Sabbath had officially begun; they didn't have to. Instead, Lena cut each person a thick slice of honey cake, placing small plates before them as they dipped tea bags into their cups. When she tasted the cake, Anya knew that it was just as good as the ones she had baked in the shop with Ruby, even better. She told them that, too, adding that even though Lena had given up the baking business, nonetheless, she was glad she had kept it as a hobby. Lena seemed pleased with the compliment, and even more pleased when Anya requested an extra slice.

After all the crumbs had been swept from the table, Anya stood up and went to the kitchen window. The sky had transformed from a violet dusk to an inky blackness, a white moon shimmering at its center. She reached up and closed the shade.

It was time for the couple to leave. After putting on his jacket, Kenny extended his hand to Josef, then Anya, who instead wrapped her arms around the broad-shouldered young man. She saved the warmest hug for Lena, though, giving her an extra squeeze before releasing her.

Fixing the tan collar of Lena's coat, Anya noticed an object glistening within the wavy brown hair. A silver barrette with rhinestones throwing off a rainbow of colors at the center. *Such a pretty thing,* Anya thought, as she patted down the collar. She had a strange feeling that she had seen it before, but she couldn't think where. Perhaps it was in one of the fashion magazines she browsed through at the beauty parlor. She stood watching as the couple went down the hall and into the elevator. Then she shut the apartment door and went back into the kitchen to join Josef.

37

Pearl

No one noticed her. She had been walking for most of the day, and judging by the gray lines that stretched across the sun, she knew that it wouldn't be much longer before night fell.

The young woman whose pale-yellow hair floated behind her in waves as she moved forward in a liquid motion didn't think it unusual to stride unmolested past the truck drivers whose massive arms stretched against polo shirts, the construction workers whose ruddy cheeks billowed with each bite of their packed lunches, their legs swinging from the beams of skyscrapers. Perhaps it was because they were too occupied to take notice or had intuited the determination they saw in the sapphire-blue eyes. Or maybe they realized what she had come to know on this day in late autumn when the sidewalks were adorned in patches of crimson and gold: that the pretty woman with the fair skin and pink bow-like lips was little more than an apparition. In any event, she knew she had nothing to fear from them or anyone. Not anymore. It occurred to her that if they saw her at all, perhaps *they* were the ones who now held fear in their hearts.

The wind picked up as she stepped lightly off the sidewalk, the soles of her shoes hitting gravel. Although she wore only a light beige cotton sweater jacket, white linen shirt, cotton twill pants, and flats, she wasn't chilled. She recalled being far colder in her lifetime. Her steps quickened with anticipation as she saw the outline of trees waving their hoary branches in the distance. It wouldn't be long now.

A peaceful feeling came over her as she made her way past the sharp pebbles that prodded the bottoms of her feet with each step. A smile, ever so slight, settled on her pink lips when she fully realized that she no longer had anything to fear. The large steel-jawed men with their truncheons now toiled eternally within the fires of hell, and even the bears were in hibernation. Although she had once been plagued by the memory of her dear mama and papa, she knew that their souls, which never earned their place beneath the thick soil of a burial ground, were finally circling tranquilly in the atoms of the still air. And, at long last, there was another, one lost too soon, who could sleep undisturbed.

Although a heavy silence surrounded her as she walked, interrupted only by the stir of an icy breeze wafting through the trees, she could still hear the echo of the foot dragging across the wooden classroom floor. She could see the small hands stretched trembling as the girl placed a bowl of cold soup before her. The body, no sturdier than her own, that stepped in front, shielding her from a dismal death. Looking up at a sliver of gold in the sky, the young woman also recalled the mother who protected an orphan child, not yet knowing that she was destined to soon lose her own. And although her heart told her it was small recompense to replace one daughter with another, born scant years later, she felt glad that her debt had been paid. Glad, too, that peace had come to the dearest of friends and now, finally, to herself as well.

She ambled determinedly on, letting her feet sink into the blackened loam of the woods, and inhaled the wet fragrance of its last leaves. Soon, she, like the others, would be hidden, and as generations passed, all but forgotten, except maybe for her name. She set her eyes, her lashes coated in joyful tears, on the mist hovering above where the shadows of ghosts stretched ahead before heading deep into the heart of the forest.

ACKNOWLEDGMENTS

There is a cup that sits on my desk inscribed with the words "my cup runneth over," a quotation from the Hebrew Bible (Psalm 23:5). I realize now how appropriate the message is whenever I think about how grateful I am to have such loving, encouraging family members and friends.

Last year, when my first novel, *A Castle in Brooklyn*, was published, I was ecstatic to finally have achieved a long-awaited dream. The novel has been well received, and I am still pinching myself over all the accolades. Now that this second novel embarks upon publication, I am still overwhelmed with gratitude for all who have helped me achieve a true career as an author. They have given me the confidence to leave a profession as a college English professor, a job that I have cherished, and devote myself to writing full-time.

I have many people to thank for seeing my debut novel and this one to publication. First and foremost is my literary agent at William Morris, Eve Attermann. From day one she has championed my work; and it is her patience, encouragement, and commitment that have made my dream possible. I remain in awe at my fortune in having Carmen Johnson, senior editorial director at Little A, as my editor. She has embraced my manuscripts with encouragement, vigor, and fresh ideas. Any success the novel attains, I share with her. This book would not be what it is without the assistance of Tegan Tigani, who came on board for this novel. Her hours spent rereading, her meticulous editing, and suggestions have made all the difference. Likewise, I thank the entire team at Little A—all the editors, illustrators, and facilitators who have helped bring this book to fruition. As novels do not exist in a vacuum, a special thanks goes to Paige Hazzan at Amazon and publicist extraordinaire, Rachel Gul of Over the River Public Relations, for her tenacity in spreading the word about my first novel. I hope we can continue working together.

Where would I be without the friends who have read, criticized, and praised this novel and so many other works that I have placed in their hands? Marcie Ruderman, my lifelong friend, has spent countless hours offering honest advice; Donna Danzig, a dear friend, has never failed to read, listen, and encourage; and Helena Swanicke, a colleague who has become a friend and confidante, is quick to dig into a manuscript, making inspiring suggestions. My thanks go to my sister-in-law/ sister, Emily Russak, an avid reader, for her frank and insightful comments; and Flo Teitelman, who proclaimed this manuscript my best yet (wait for the next one!). My gratitude spills over to Linda Herschfeld, Harriet Brown, and Sue Saad for taking the time to read and for their uplifting remarks, and to Renee Price for giving me the courage to pursue my dream. I am deeply indebted to my wonderful friend Susan Strumwasser for reading, commenting, and advising me on all the ways to get around Brooklyn. Many thanks to Alan Bernstein, a kidney recipient, who shared his story with me.

The stories I write are about families. When I wrote *A Castle in Brooklyn*, I wanted to explore the traumatic effects of the Holocaust on survivors trying to build a new life in the United States. With *The Baker of Lost Memories*, I focus on the quiet reverberations of loss in the second generation. Family is the nucleus of life's experiences.

My family means the world to me, and none of this would be possible without them. Arthur has been by my side through the hills and valleys, and I am grateful and proud to be his wife. My wonderful sons, Howie, Brad, and Charlie, each own a piece of my heart and are the reason I write. I am blessed to be their mother. Thank you, too, to my dear brother, Jack, who exemplifies the meaning of family; and Jaime and Elisha, who came into our family and whom I have grown to love more each day. My cherished granddaughters, Zoey, Emmy, and Stella, remain my inspiration, and it is my hope that the stories I tell will influence their lives in years to come.

Last, once again, I am grateful to my parents, Charles and Betty Russak, for their sacrifices, dedication, and love. It is to them that I dedicate this book.

ABOUT THE AUTHOR

Shirley Russak Wachtel is the author of *A Castle in Brooklyn*. She is the daughter of Holocaust survivors and was born and raised in Brooklyn, New York. Shirley holds a doctor of letters degree from Drew University and for the past thirty-five years has taught English literature at Middlesex College in Edison, New Jersey. Her podcast, *EXTRAordinary People*, features inspiring individuals who have overcome obstacles to make a difference. The mother of three grown sons and grandmother to three precocious granddaughters, she currently resides in East Brunswick, New Jersey, with her husband, Arthur. For more information, visit www.shirleywachtel.com.